MORE HIGH PRAISE FOR COLLEEN THOMPSON!

Fatal Error

"Fast-paced, chilling, and sexy...[with] chemistry that shimmers."

— *Library Journal*

"Thompson has written a first-class work of romantic suspense."

— *Booklist*

"Excellent characters, a tightly woven, intriguing plot, and superb narrative make [*Fatal Error*] hard to put down."

— *Affaire de Coeur*

"Ms. Thompson has created a romantic suspense that's sure to entertain you with its fast pace and intricate details."

—The Best Reviews

"*Fatal Error* is a brilliantly told story of murder, obsession, and love that will set your heart to pounding and your toes to tingling...a full-bodied tale that takes you deep into the plots, deceit, and the danger spurred by hatred, greed, vengeance, and twisted desire."

—Romance at Heart

A HIGHER CALIBER

She had only a split second to take in the intensity of his expression, the conflict building like thunderheads in the clouded field of his gray eyes. And then his mouth was on hers, his kiss fierce and possessive, his hands pulling her close enough to feel his impossible hardness against her—unless he was wearing a gun she hadn't spotted.

Whatever it was, it felt like just the right caliber.

Greedily, she kissed him back, her every nerve firing with the touch of tongue to tongue...sending the word *yes* blazing like a meteor across her consciousness.

But with consciousness came conscience, and hers roared back with a vengeance, screaming that she had no business enjoying this man—enjoying *anything*—while her friend lay in a morgue somewhere and her own family and coworkers worried themselves sick about her well-being.

HEAT LIGHTNING

COLLEEN THOMPSON

LOVE SPELL NEW YORK CITY

LOVE SPELL®

November 2006

Published by

Dorchester Publishing Co., Inc.
200 Madison Avenue
New York, NY 10016

ISBN 0-505-52671-9

Printed in the United States of America.

Visit us on the web at www.dorchesterpub.com.

In loving memory of Betty Joffrion.
Your laughter, your insights, and most of all,
your friendship will be sorely missed.

ACKNOWLEDGMENTS

I would like to thank several people who have helped make *Heat Lightning* possible. To first readers Patricia Kay, Jo Anne Banker, and Barbara Sissel, I appreciate your sharp eyes and insightful suggestions more than I can say. Thanks as well to Wanda Dionne, Linda Helman, Betty Joffrion and my fellow members of the Northwest Houston and West Houston chapters of the Romance Writers of America. Your unwavering support means the world to me.

Thanks to my family, especially my husband, Mike, and son, Andrew, for their patience—and for at least trying to resist the urge to interrupt me when the office door is closed. I'd like to thank Mike, too, for sharing his expertise on details relating to the Houston Fire Department.

I am also grateful to agents Meredith Bernstein, Helen Breitwieser, and all the wonderful people at Dorchester Publishing, especially editor Alicia Condon, publicist Brianna Yamashita, and Brooke Borneman, director of sales.

For providing me with background on the workings of the Houston Police Department, I owe a debt of gratitude to Lieutenant Gary Schiebe. Thanks also to William Simon of Abberline Investigations for sharing his knowledge of FBI matters and electronic surveillance. And finally, a warm thanks to Leticia Gomez-Almughrabi of Spanish Language Solutions for her assistance.

HEAT
LIGHTNING

CHAPTER ONE

Beneath the vapor lights past moonrise, all color is corrupted. From the humid summer night sky to the paint of cars in a parking lot to the ski mask worn by the single sweating man there, nothing appears natural. Nothing appears real.

But the man inside the ski mask doesn't notice, absorbed as he is by the small, square SUV whose lights have just winked out. His full attention is commanded by the slender figure emerging from the vehicle and by his own vise-like grip on the steel shopping cart he has maneuvered into prime position.

That focus is his gift, the blessing left to him in place of the fool's burden of a conscience. Tonight it serves him well—or would, except he fails to note the other vehicle that slips into the lot, its headlights dark despite the dim illumination. The movement is peripheral, no more important than the stirring of hot breezes or the first pulse of distant thunder. . . .

Or the question of what color blood will gleam beneath these eerie lights.

* * *

If anyone in Houston should avoid a poorly lit grocery store parking lot after sunset, it was Luz Maria Montoya, who had spent the past three years pissing off people for a living. Not that she lost much sleep worrying about it. Her job as spokesperson for the Voice of Poverty charged her with speaking out for those who couldn't afford the fancy lawyers of the select citizens she offended during her frequent appearances on the evening news.

The trouble was that the business leaders, politicians, and prominent sports figures she went after could afford more than just attorneys. And some of the "help" they hired didn't hesitate to color outside the lines. Besides that, a number of public figures, especially the sports icons, had unbalanced fans, who wrote her equally unbalanced letters. And then there were Luz Maria's own "admirers," men—and the occasional woman—caught up in the drama of a fresh-faced twenty-six-year-old battling the system. With her wavy, waist-length hair, her flowing skirts and tinkling bracelets, Luz Maria had apparently become a gypsy warrior goddess in the pantheon of the slightly off. So far this summer, along with the usual hate mail, she had received twenty-seven letters of admiration, eight marriage proposals, and a good many more less traditional invitations—the kind that would have her mama insisting she give up tilting at windmills, or at least cut her black hair short and dress *en ropa profesional.* Luz Maria sighed, thinking how Mama's version of business attire would likely involve a suit of armor bristling with padlocks.

But as she hustled through the scattered parked cars at 10:37 on a suffocatingly humid August night, Luz Maria Montoya wasn't thinking of the nasty phone messages or the even uglier e-mails and letters she had received in recent days. Her work attracted such things as naturally as her exhalations drew mosquitoes angling for a late-night snack.

She swatted at a small cloud of the insects as thunder murmured in the distance, then teased her with a half-hearted breeze that stirred the heavy air. Heat lightning licked at the horizon, and Luz Maria thought of turning back for her umbrella. Instead, she flipped her single braid over her shoulder and picked up her pace, eager to escape to the air-conditioned store and grab the only necessities she would be desperate enough to stop for on her way home from a late meeting: Chicken Nibblets canned cat food and a box of tampons.

The Nibblets were for Borracho, the battle-scarred old tomcat who had wandered into her life—and the open window of her apartment—about six months earlier. The yellow-eyed tabby, with his torn ears, scruffy black and silver fur, and broken-off fang, had been so put out after she had had him neutered that ever afterward, he yowled with outrage if she dared present His Majesty with anything less than the most expensive cat food known to man.

Neutered or not, Borracho—Spanish for "drunkard"—had no use for the tampons. But as crampy as she felt, Luz Maria figured she would need them any time now. And a pint of vanilla Blue Bell ice cream, too, since Borracho wasn't the only one known to compensate with a little pampering.

Heaven only knew that she could use some TLC after this evening's meeting with the board of Tex-Rid, a company planning to build an industrial incinerator a couple hundred yards upwind from the only low-income day care center in a rural corner of the county. She'd even put on *pantyhose*—in this heat—for those *idiotas*, yet neither her sacrifice nor the half-dozen adorable toddlers she'd rounded up had dented their resistance.

"Certainly, we would have considered other locations"—not bothering to hide his sneer, their pompous *piojo* of an attorney paused to clean his half-moon glasses with a linen handkerchief—*"had there been any licensed child care facilities in the vicinity."*

She would see how smug the louse was when she took reporters to film the sweet-faced grandmother hugging her little charges and serving homemade soups and *tortas*—irresistible Mexican sandwiches. That, in addition to the air quality reports her assistant had unearthed from other areas where Tex-Rid ran incinerators, ought to poke some anthills.

With her thoughts wandering toward a petition demanding a public hearing, Luz Maria was slow to see the movement out of the corner of her eye. Slow to recognize—was that a shopping cart pushed forward by the breeze? Reflexively pulling her shoulder bag beneath her elbow, she jerked her head toward the dull gleam—and cried out at the sight of the steel cart rushing toward her, or more accurately, of the man running behind it, his face obscured by a ski mask.

With a grace borne of years of Latin dancing, Luz Maria whirled out of the cart's path. Letting go of the handle, the man leapt at her.

Their collision abruptly cut off Luz Maria's scream. She found herself pitching forward, her body twisting in mid-fall to land hard on her side.

A fraction of a second later, her attacker hurled himself onto her, slamming her rib cage against the asphalt and bumping her head painfully. There was a metallic clang—the cart striking a parked car. The shrill blast from the car alarm cut through the buzzing in Luz Maria's ears and the terror ripping through her.

Now straddling her, her attacker had his hands around her throat, the fingers digging painfully into the soft tissue. She struggled to scream again, but her lungs refused to fill. Fighting to pull his hands away, she ripped her nails digging into what felt like gloves. Too late, she remembered the self-defense lessons her sister-in-law had taught her and slashed at her attacker's face in a desperate struggle to reach the dark mask's eyeholes.

Luz Maria's world exploded into shards of sound: the buzzing in her skull, the wailing of the car alarm, an angry snarl of thunder, and a distant voice—all overlaid with a torrent of profanity as her assailant shook her by the throat like a pit bull throttling a stray cat.

Behind her eyelids, heat lightning strobed, and there were a series of pops a moment before the cacophony inside her head rose to a crescendo. . . .

But in the end, a deathly silence reigned.

"The way I see it," Grant Holcomb's newly promoted partner, Billy Devlin, went on, "there's not an honest man within a hundred mile radius who's got a ski mask in his closet. If we could get Wal-Mart and the like to track sales, we could just go ahead and bust the guys before they did any harm."

Grant knew his young partner was deadly earnest, but if Grant laughed at him, the redheaded rookie investigator would simply stare back in confusion. Sucked the joy right out of teasing Howdy Doody.

"Interesting concept, Billy." As Grant turned the corner, the unmarked Crown Victoria's balding tires squealed and it rent the thick night air with a greasy-sounding backfire. Unlike the "real" investigators in Homicide, those assigned to the Major Assaults Unit's night shift always drew the shittiest heaps. "But what about all those guys preparing for their ski trips?"

"In August?"

Grant shrugged, then decided to screw with the kid despite his cluelessness. Grant told himself he was doing it to keep his skills sharp for the day he'd finally be assigned another partner evolved enough to appreciate his sense of humor, another partner who would get him the way John Zeman had. Besides, jerking chains was just as good as a fresh jolt of caffeine when it came to revving Grant up—or getting him through what promised to be one of the toughest victim interviews he'd ever conducted.

"Oh, yeah," he said with a mock seriousness that would put the veterans in his unit on alert, "most of 'em are headed somewhere south of the equator. Probably the Andes Mountains, down in Chile."

"Don't tell me they got skiing down there, too." Billy's blue eyes widened, looking lonesome in their nakedness, since his pale blond brows and lashes were almost invisible. The effect was to make him look younger than his twenty-eight years and somewhat dim, too, which Grant figured could come in handy in their line of work.

Provided that Billy turned out to be smarter than he seemed. After just a week together, he was undecided on that question. If it proved to be the case, though, Grant thought they could get a lot of mileage out of the good cop/dumb cop routine.

"Oh, yeah. It's a well-known defense among criminals in this part of the city," Grant said as they rolled up to a red light on Fannin. "Just before popping on their ski masks to commit a violent crime, they book Chilean ski trip packages on the Internet. Then if they don't get caught, they cancel."

During the pause that followed, Grant could've sworn he actually heard gears grinding inside his partner's head. As Grant wondered who the hell had given the kid the answers to the investigators test, Billy burst out with, "I've been warned about you, Holcomb. By more than one of your ex-partners. You like to fuck with people. Well, I'm here to tell you to save it for the suspects."

Billy shot him an intense stare and Grant flipped on the dome light. Amazing. Though he was clearly pissed, without visible eyebrows, the kid couldn't muster a facial expression if his very life depended on it.

"What the hell are you looking at?" asked Billy as he switched off the light.

"An edge," Grant told him seriously. "And I can damned well guarantee we're going to need one to get through an investigation involving this particular victim."

"Luz Maria Montoya? I saw her on the news last week, demanding that somebody tear down those crack houses off of Navigation. Sure, she stirs up her fair share of shit now and then, but what's the big deal? It's the city she goes after, and rich jerkoffs who can't think past their wallets. Not regular guys like us."

After crossing the light rail tracks, Grant pulled into the hospital parking lot, swung into a space reserved for a day shift administrator, and jammed the brakes on hard. His gaze locked front and center, he said, "The Z-man was a guy like us. A guy *better* than us—or me at any rate."

Billy gripped the door handle, then hesitated before saying, "Aw, hell. I forgot about that. I—uh—I'm sorry, Grant. I heard he was your partner, but I completely forgot *she* was involved. I was still with the Northwest Patrol then, and I'd only been with the department for a few . . . Listen, you think you can handle this tonight? You don't want any trouble your last shift before vacation. Let's call the lieutenant to see if somebody else can take this—"

Grant popped the steering wheel with the heel of his hand, then ripped his shaking fingers through his short-cropped, wavy hair. "Lieutenant Mouton's out on leave—and I can do my job. I just have to remember that *this* time, it's Luz Maria Montoya who's the victim, and looking into it is my duty."

If he were going to get through this investigation, he needed to keep focused on those two facts, instead of his regret.

The regret that Montoya's assailant had fallen short in his attempt to kill her.

The ER doctor who had treated Luz Maria was busy in a trauma room, but Grant and Billy found her brother pacing around the surprisingly crowded waiting area. The harried clerk they interrupted looked up from her keyboard and pointed out a tall Hispanic man who appeared to be in his mid-thirties.

"That's Jack Montoya. He can fill you in on his sister's condition." The round-faced Asian woman added quickly, "He's an MD."

But Grant already knew it, for Jack Montoya had been at the center of a high-profile, multi-agency investigation several years earlier. Though the task force had eventually determined him innocent of the charges that concerned them, Grant had heard the man went out of his way to avoid the media—the same media his younger sister had embraced.

Tonight, he wore a pair of khakis, a dark T-shirt, and the look of a man who had rushed to the scene after an upsetting late-night phone call.

"Dr. Montoya," Grant said as he offered his hand. "I'm Investigator Holcomb. Investigator Devlin and I would like to have a word with you if we might." Plastering on a less-sincere-than-usual expression of professional concern, he led the group to a more private set of chairs, which were clustered beneath a muted television. The TV screen showed the weather forecast, which predicted the same high of ninety-three with a twenty percent chance of showers that it had for the past few weeks. Freaking never-ending August . . .

"I'm very sorry about what happened to your sister." This was more or less true, since Grant would rather continue to hate her from a distance than deal with her face-to-face. "How's Ms. Montoya doing?"

Jack Montoya grimaced, his dark eyes radiating pain and anger, sharp and hot. "I've told her a hundred times, a woman in her position has to be incredibly careful. I know her work's important—God knows, I understand that. But with the hornets' nests she stirs up, the people she takes on . . . for her to be out in a parking lot alone, at night . . ." He shook his head, then brushed his dark hair out of his eyes. "I'm really sorry. You must think I'm a terrible brother, getting mad at Luz Maria."

Grant excused the outburst with a shrug. "It happens. When people are scared something's happened to a loved one, their first reaction is to get pissed at the relative in question. Didn't your mother ever shake you when you went off on your bike and forgot to check in?"

Beside him, Billy nodded, chuffing a short laugh. "Mine would say, 'Thank God you're alive,' then blister my ass but good. How 'bout yours, Doc?"

Grant gave Billy props for that one, because Montoya nodded gratefully and audibly released the breath he had been holding. When Grant gestured toward the chairs, each man claimed one, though the doctor was perched on the edge of his seat, one foot tapping out thinly veiled anxiety.

"The name's Jack," he said, "and this isn't the first time Luz Maria's given me a bad scare. But somehow it's the worst . . . hearing how that security guard saw some bastard in a ski mask on her, grabbing her by the neck and . . ." Again, he shook his head, obviously struggling to get himself back on track. "I'm sorry. You asked about my sister."

Grant nodded. He and Billy had just come from

speaking to the witness, an out of shape rent-a-cop whose shouts had supposedly frightened off the attacker. The guard hadn't seen much, seeing as how he hadn't bothered to give chase. "I couldn't just leave the poor girl lying there," he'd said to excuse his inaction, even though by the time he'd reached Luz Maria, a couple of store employees had rushed outside to help.

None of them had felt especially inclined to chase a clearly dangerous man in a ski mask into the darkness. Which went to show that, news reports to the contrary, the average Houstonian *did* have more sense than a thimbleful of warm spit.

"I'm told Luz Maria regained consciousness quickly," Grant said.

Dr. Montoya nodded.

"She was pretty damned shaken up, but she remained alert and responsive throughout transport and arrival. She has a number of abrasions from the struggle, claw marks around her neck—probably from her own nails, from trying to pry that son-of-a-bitch's grip off her throat." The doctor's voice dropped to a low growl as he added, "I'd like to get my hands on that piece of filth."

The hands in question were shaking, but Grant wasn't surprised. After a violent attack, male relatives—and a good percentage of the women— always had to get this sort of statement out of the way. One thing was for certain: Jack Montoya was genuinely upset.

Was he upset enough to gloss over his sister's injuries? Grant thought about the scene, about the blood the ambulance crew had reported seeing on Luz Maria and the trail of wet splotches he had spotted on the still warm pavement. Way too much blood to be consistent with "abrasions." The techs would work their magic in the lab by feeding their measurements into a computer, but to Grant's eyes, the pattern of spatter had looked like a nicked artery.

Yet the paramedics hadn't mentioned a cut or gunshot wound on the victim, either. So whose blood was it at the scene?

Once more, Jack Montoya looked apologetic. "Sorry. When it comes to my little sister . . . Our father was killed when we were kids, so I'm afraid I've always taken the big brother role a little more seriously than I should. At least, that's what Luz Maria always tells me."

At the staccato beat of footsteps, Jack glanced up, then rose as an attractive blond woman in a blue firefighter's uniform rushed toward them. The investigators stood, and Grant had only time to catch a glimpse of her paramedic's patch before she launched herself into Montoya's arms.

"I got your message from the captain. What's happening?" The woman was breathing hard, and perspiration dampened hair that brushed her shoulders. "Is it Adam?"

There was a rawness to her fear that had Grant guessing she was speaking of a child—her and Montoya's child.

The doctor shook his head. "Adam's with my mother. He's fine—didn't even wake up. It's my sister. Someone jumped her in a grocery parking lot near Fannin."

The blonde pulled back to look into his face, her blue eyes full of concern. "Oh, no. Is Luz Maria—"

"She's being transferred to a room now. She's going to be fine," Jack said. Judging from his voice, his woman's presence seemed to have a calming influence on him. "She's scraped up, and I expect there'll be a lot of stiffness and bruising, but the doctors don't think there are any fractures."

"She must be terrified," the woman said. "Shouldn't we go sit with her?"

"She'd just fallen asleep when I arrived, so I came down to wait for you. They couldn't give her narcotics, in case of a concussion, but she was totally exhausted. Tears can do that to a person—not to mention all that adrenalin."

Finally, Grant had a straight answer as to Luz Maria Montoya's condition. One that seemed to confirm the suspicion in his mind. They should be checking ER's citywide, looking for a wounded suspect.

Jack glanced his way, then told the woman, "These are Detectives—I mean Investigators—Holcomb and, uh, Devlin, is it? This is my wife, Reagan Hurley."

"Why not Montoya?" Billy broke in, causing Grant to put another tally in the Dumb-As-He-Looks column.

In lieu of an answer, Reagan simply raised an eyebrow and returned her attention to her husband. "You didn't tell your mother?"

Dr. Montoya shook his head. "When I dropped off Adam, I told her I'd been paged to deal with an emergency for one of my patients."

"That was probably a good idea." Glancing toward the investigators, Reagan explained, "If she were here, we'd end up having her sedated instead of Luz Maria. Although when his mama finds out Jack here wasn't straight with her, there'll be hell to pay."

Jack sighed. "It's still worth it."

"Sorry to interrupt," Grant said, "but we'd really like to speak with Ms. Montoya. Get her take on what happened, find out if she has any idea who might want to hurt her."

Besides me. The words echoed uncomfortably in Grant's mind. Perhaps the family's fresh concern was bleeding past his own two-year-old anger.

At the thought, his pain redoubled like an abscessed tooth that flared into agony at the slightest touch. He reminded himself, *John Zeman's dead, and that sanctimonious bitch is still living*.

"We're trying to cover all the angles," Billy said, now sounding like a real investigator, "in the event this wasn't a random act. Especially since her purse was recovered, with cash and credit cards intact."

Montoya was shaking his head. "Maybe after she rests for a bit."

Grant thought of telling him it was his sister's doctor's call whether or not they could interview Ms. Montoya.

Before he could say it, Reagan Hurley put in, "We might be able to help you a little, as far as enemies."

"My sister doesn't have enemies," Jack said defensively. "It's not like she sets out to hurt anyone. She only means to help the most vulnerable of—"

"Oh, come off it," Reagan countered. "You know as well as I do, Luz Maria ruffles feathers. She has to, to do her job. She's gotten people fired, changed the course of at least one election, cost companies hundreds of thousands of dollars, maybe more."

And she's cost one good cop his life, Grant thought, but he couldn't say it, not with the memory shuddering through him of the day he'd scrubbed his best friend's blood and brains off a wall. Nausea followed, and for a moment, he had to turn away.

Reagan Hurley added, "Jack's right when he says Luz Maria doesn't set out to make enemies, but I'm absolutely certain she has plenty. For one thing, I've seen some of her 'love notes.'"

"Hate mail?" Billy asked.

At the same time, Jack demanded, "What?"

Reagan looked at her husband. "When she went to that symposium in Austin a couple of months back, I was picking up her mail and feeding that moth-eaten, walking allergen she calls a house cat. Remember? Anyway, I saw someone had sent what really amounted to a sheet of copier paper folded into thirds, with her address scrawled on the back. The tape had broken loose, and something about the print grabbed my attention."

She gave a shudder that had little to do with the overly air-conditioned waiting room. "It was nasty stuff. You know, the usual ugly names people call women when we get under their skin. No particular threats, but plenty of underlines and exclamation points."

"Signature? Return address?" asked Billy, who had whipped out his notepad.

She shot him another incredulous look before saying, "Are you kidding?"

"So, was Ms. Montoya upset about this letter?" Grant asked.

Reagan flashed a smile, and he thought again that she was a damned good-looking woman. Not his type, but still . . . if he'd met her under different circumstances and didn't know she was married, he might take a run at her.

The thought surprised him. For the past couple of years—since Zeman—Grant's libido had gone fugitive, outside of a couple of ill-advised one-nighters.

Shaking her head, Reagan said, "She seemed awfully blasé about it to me. Said there's a folder full of similar messages back at the foundation, with one of their staff guys. She told me he has a security background, and a big part of his job is assessing letters, e-mails, and phone threats and referring the ones that look serious to the police. I gather she doesn't even bother reading most of them."

"And you didn't see fit to tell me about these letters?" Jack Montoya looked annoyed.

Reagan shrugged. "She asked me not to worry you or your mother. And it seemed she was taking reasonable precautions—a gated apartment complex, really good alarms on both her unit and her car."

"How about a pistol in her purse? She consider that a reasonable precaution, too?" asked Billy, surprising Grant once more.

He was never going to get a handle on this kid.

"No way," Reagan answered quickly.

Jack, too, shook his head. "Luz Maria hates handguns. We've heard her quote statistics half a dozen times about how when people buy guns for security, they're more likely to end up shooting a loved one."

"So we can mark down the NRA on her list of enemies." Grant mustered an approximation of a smile to show he was joking.

But Jack Montoya frowned. "Why'd you ask about a gun? You didn't find one, did you?"

Grant shook his head. "No, and no spent bullets, either, but there was plenty of blood at the scene. And plenty of blood on your sister when the first responders found her. We'll type and cross-match it against hers, but I'm guessing someone else was hurt tonight."

"So you think my sister might have wounded her attacker? My sister, who's five-two and maybe one-oh-five?"

Grant said, "Stranger things have happened, especially when you throw adrenalin into the mix. Could be her assailant had the weapon, but she got it away and turned it on him before he—"

Reagan's blue eyes widened. "You know, I was finishing some paperwork over at Ben Taub's ER when I got my husband's message. But right before I left, some of the guys were talking about the patient they'd just brought in. He'd wrapped his pickup around a pole near Congress at Crawford. Only, when the firefighters used the Jaws of Life to cut him free, they found he had a gunshot wound to the chest."

"Congress Street at Crawford?" Grant repeated. "That's not far from the place Ms. Montoya was attacked."

Billy once more hopefully whipped out his pad and pen. "Did you catch this man's name or his condition?"

"Sorry," she answered, her head shaking, "but if you call over to Ben Taub, I'm sure they can put you in touch with whoever's investigating that case."

"We'll do that, thanks," Grant said before the pocket of his sports jacket vibrated insistently. "Let me shut this damned thing off." He pulled out the cell phone, his thumb moving toward the power switch before he caught sight of the number and ID on its lit screen. "Sorry. I'd better check this out."

As he walked outside in the still hellish humidity to return the call, Grant heard Billy launch into a standard question about Luz Maria's current or past boyfriends.

"She goes out dancing once or twice a week," Jack said. "It's always with this salsa group she's part of."

Billy was still listing male "dance partners" five minutes later, when Grant trotted back inside.

"You'd better come with me," he said to Billy. "We're needed upstairs, on the third floor."

Jack Montoya zeroed in on Grant, his gaze alert, his solid-looking muscles tense. "But that's where they took Luz Maria."

"Yeah, it is," Grant said unhappily. "Security's just caught an unidentified white male trying to slip into her room."

CHAPTER TWO

Sleep, along with the mild pain reliever she'd been given, had Luz Maria floating cloudlike somewhere above the pain, high enough to cast the throbbing of her ribs, the pounding of her head, and the raw agony of her throat into shadow. Yet not even the escape of unconsciousness had blunted the fear that hung above her, burning and unblinking as the brutal August sun.

She drifted in a hellish twilight world, her body at rest while her agitated thoughts careened from curve to curve like an out of control toy car around a plastic racetrack.

Someone tried to kill me. Kill me. Kill me.

And he wasn't out to get some random stranger—that was my name he was screaming in between his curses. My name wrapped in profanity while his hands squeezed my throat.

Her breathing hitched, then grew more rapid. Almost imperceptibly, her muscles tensed.

It hadn't been a robbery; he hadn't tried to rip her clothes off, either. Whoever the man was—and she was dead certain, from his iron grip and the tautness of his body, that her attacker had been male—his goal had been murder.

The shock of the realization settled in her stomach like a meal of broken glass, sending wave upon wave of shard-like splinters through her system. Splinters that pierced the bubble of assumptions she had built around her job: that those inconvenienced or offended by her work used angry messages to safely vent their building fury; that after expressing their displeasure, they went on with their lives; that those strangers who imagined they loved her soon came to their senses.

That a few sensible precautions would always be enough—and that it was possible to stop a determined enemy from snuffing out her life.

Her heartbeat quickened, and a prescient warning overrode her body's need for sleep. Hearing footsteps in her room, she forced her eyes open and then struggled to make sense of what she saw.

Not much at first, for the room was mostly dark save for a dim sidelight left on, Luz Maria imagined, so the night nurse could periodically check her vitals. Except that at the moment, someone stood before the light, his solidly male form silhouetted as his arms reached toward her.

Pain awakened in her throat, but nothing could stop Luz Maria from screaming—screaming until the lights came up and the private hospital room filled with people. Two women in printed scrubs struggled to subdue her flailing limbs as a burly black man wearing a security uniform dragged the intruder toward the door.

The ragged scream died on Luz Maria's lips. Sitting up now, she froze, her gaze plastered to the familiar back, her ears tuned to a voice she knew as well as any.

"The security here's a joke. I waltzed right in off the street and straight up to her room without so much as a 'where's your name tag, sweet cheeks?'" He made the complaint sound peevish, almost prissy, but that was Jason Whitfield—diligent, concerned, and flamingly effeminate. "I'm so sorry, Luz Maria. The last thing I had in mind was scaring you, hon."

In an attempt to reassure herself, Luz Maria scanned her friend and coworker, from the light brown hair he kept gelled in short spikes to the wide-set baby blue eyes in a soft, round face totally at odds with the body he worked hard at keeping buff. He worked long hours for Voice of Poverty as well, but tonight he wore a slacker's uniform: tight black running shorts, huarache sandals, and a T-shirt plastered with the logo of some hard rock band from the eighties.

Thank God it's only Whit. Relief flowed through her, though she couldn't yet speak. Whether it was a result of her injuries or the exhaustion that came in the wake of panic, she felt separated from the people all around her, as if she were seeing them through a thick pane of wavy glass.

"Please, don't take him." Her voice was hoarse, barely recognizable to her own ears. "We need to talk. He works with me—he's our head of security."

In reality, the Houston office of the Voice of Poverty's five-person staff was loosely structured, with everyone taking on multiple roles. But in addition to research, Whit—he preferred the name to Jason—handled whatever security concerns came up, mainly because of some sort of a military background. Luz Maria hadn't heard much about his past, but the rumor around the office was that he'd been a casualty of the U.S. government's "Don't Ask, Don't Tell" policy. Whit, who'd come on board VOP around the same time she had, had made it clear he didn't want to talk about it, and that was fine with everyone since he was so good at his job. Though she was not nearly as close-mouthed, Luz Maria could relate to his desire to keep his private life private. After all, her own past was mined with one or two explosive secrets.

Such as Sergio Cardenas . . .

Ruthlessly, she shoved aside the thought, but it was too late. Foreboding had already sunk its barbed hooks into her flesh: the bone-deep knowledge that this evening's attack would unearth the mistakes she had worked so hard to move past. Most likely, the police would be the ones to bring it up—unless someone in VOP's home office had already shared the information with Whit. Or, heaven forbid, some members of the media had decided to rerun old video from their stations' archives.

The guard exchanged a look with the two nurses, one of whom was already murmuring that she needed to go distribute meds to her own patients. The second woman, a middle-aged brunette with smudges of fatigue beneath her eyes, pressed her lips into a flat line. "It's two A.M. Can't this wait until visiting hours?"

Luz Maria snagged the woman's forearm and looked up at her. "Please. It's about the—about what happened tonight."

As the other nurse slipped through the door, the guard shrugged and told the brunette, "You go on about your business, Annie. I'll hang here with these two. Cops'll be here any minute, anyhow. I called when I heard all the commotion, and I 'spect they'll want an explanation."

Looking to Whit, he added, "I'd feel a little better if you'd let me pat you down, sir."

"My pleasure," Whit said with wicked smile. Turning to the wall beside the door, he assumed the position as if he'd done it more than once. Over his shoulder, he said, "I don't carry, by the way. Not weapons, anyway."

The guard scowled, obviously not appreciating Whit's brand of late-night humor. Silently—and not too gently—the larger man carried out a search, mercifully brief, since Whit's shorts and T-shirt offered little in the way of hiding places. As the guard finished, he gave Whit a look of pure disgust. "Sorry I had to do that. You'll never know how sorry. But you can go ahead and talk now."

Luz Maria had barely had time to fumble with the controls that raised the head of her bed and tell Whit what she remembered before two men came into the room, both of them flashing IDs and silver badges. With his wavy red hair, retro narrow tie, and wrinkled chino slacks, the one who introduced himself as William Devlin looked too young to be a cop, let alone an investigator, as HPD called its detectives. But that barely mattered, since her attention immediately gravitated to Investigator Grant Holcomb, who took charge from the first.

Though she didn't put him as any older than his early thirties, there was something about Holcomb that screamed experience. Maybe it was the seen-it-all, heard-it-all sharpness behind his smoky gray eyes, the band collar he'd unbuttoned in response to the night's heat, or the way his dark hair and his face—in need of a shave at the moment—put her in mind of a young George Clooney in a rumpled, tan sport jacket. Whatever the case, she found herself observing him intently as he took the measure of Jason Whitfield.

"You say you're an associate of Ms. Montoya's," Holcomb said as the security guard took his leave. "Business associate or personal?"

Whit smiled, his blue eyes round as moons as he stared back at the man before him. "We're coworkers, sweet thing, at the Houston office of VOP—Voice of Poverty. One of my jobs is making certain our people stay safe."

Some emotion flashed over Holcomb's expression,

and for an instant, his gaze flicked to Luz Maria. She found herself shivering and pulling the sheet up across her breasts as his name echoed through her consciousness. *Investigator Grant Holcomb* . . . Where had she heard of him before?

Holcomb returned his attention to Whit. "Fell a little short tonight, huh?"

Investigator Devlin said nothing, but as he pulled out a pen and a small notepad, his smirk was unmistakable.

Whit pouted, and a muscle twitched at the left corner of his mouth. "You know as well as I do, gentlemen, you can only minimize threats, not eradicate them. Just like you could have—and might I suggest *should* have—posted a guard to minimize the threat of an unidentified individual coming up to this room tonight."

"So, what's your background?" Holcomb asked, keeping the heat on Whit. "Security-wise, that is."

There was a long pause before Whit finally answered, "Marine Corps First Sergeant, Guantanamo Bay."

Luz Maria blinked back her surprise. Jason Whitfield had been in the *Marines?*

"We dealt with our share of . . . *unpleasantness* there," Whit said, his gaze dropping in what looked for all the world like embarrassment.

Investigator Devlin broke in, saying, "You guys really torture prisoners down there?"

Whit shot the red-haired investigator an aggrieved look. Holcomb, on the other hand, shook his head, his lips tightening in what might have been either amusement or disgust.

Devlin smiled at Whit. "Just kidding, sir. Just kidding. Damn fine work our troops do. But what I really want to know is, what brought you here tonight? Ms. Montoya didn't call you, did she?"

Curious, Luz Maria turned her attention toward her coworker. How *had* he known that she was here?

"*I* called him," her brother, Jack, said as he came into the room. "A while back, Whit gave me his card and asked me to let him know if my sister ran into any trouble."

Holcomb's sharp gaze fastened on the new arrival. "I thought you and your wife were supposed to stay downstairs and wait for my all-clear."

Reagan stepped inside and said, "He's never been too good at following directions—particularly those involving Luz Maria. God, Luz, I'm *so* sorry you were hurt. How *are* you?"

But Luz Maria was stuck on what Jack had told the investigators. She stared hard at Whit. "You got my brother to keep tabs on me?"

Whit shrugged. "Who better, sugar? You said he was always butting into your business."

"Luz Maria," Jack said as he made a beeline toward her, "that call about someone in your room scared the hell out of me for the second time tonight. Are . . . are you in pain? Is there anything I can do for you? Anything at all?"

"I'm . . . I'll be okay," she managed before Investigator Holcomb interrupted.

"Hold it, hold it, everyone." He raised a hand as he spoke, but the authority in his voice was enough to silence all of them. "Doctor Montoya and Mrs. Montoya—I mean, Ms. Hurley, you're going to have to excuse us for a little while. Here's my card—we'll touch base a little later. Right now, I need to speak to Ms. Montoya while the details of this evening are still fresh in her mind. Mr. Whitfield, my partner here will talk to you out in the hall."

Jack hugged Luz Maria carefully, kissed the top of her head, and smoothed her now loose hair. "I'll be downstairs, *princesa*—all night if need be."

Reagan hooked his arm and led him toward the door.

"I'll try to keep him there," she told Holcomb before adding, "Be strong, Luz Maria. We're both here for you if you need us."

Luz Maria thanked her, touched that she had come. On the surface, her sister-in-law was invariably helpful and polite, and she'd allowed Luz Maria to play a major role in two-year-old Adam's life. But even so, on an emotional level, Reagan still seemed guarded—wondering, perhaps, if Luz Maria would revert to mistakes now three years past.

Mistakes she would give all she had to atone for . . . as she had tried to do through her work for VOP.

As Reagan and Jack were leaving, Luz Maria called after them, "Could one of you call Kellie, please, and ask her to feed my cat? She has a key to my place."

Reagan turned her head. "Your neighbor? Sure. I still have the number."

Once the couple stepped out through the door, Grant Holcomb closed it, leaving him alone with Luz Maria.

He looked at her from across the room, and something in those gray eyes once more had her shivering.

"Do I know you?" she asked, though she felt certain that if she had met him, she would have remembered—and maybe even flirted with him, unless he had frowned at her the way he was doing right now. He was a good-sized man, maybe six feet two or three, and as he removed his lightweight sports coat, his shoulder holster was clearly visible, along with the butt of the gun that jutted from it.

Apprehension knotted in Luz Maria's stomach, and without warning, a dull throbbing reawakened in her ribs. Something wasn't right here, her intuition cried out. Something just as serious as a metal shopping cart with a masked man running behind it.

"*Do* I know you?" she repeated as the investigator closed in on her.

He stopped at her bedside, too close to it for comfort. From that vantage, he looked straight down, as if she were a bug he was thinking about squashing.

"No, you don't," he told her. "But I think you damned well ought to."

CHAPTER THREE

Grant felt the pounding of his heart, heard the roar of blood rushing through his arteries as black dots clouded his vision. But the harder he struggled to screw the lid back on his temper, the more the heat and pressure built—until he finally erupted.

"Before I made investigator, John Zeman was my partner. For three years, the two of us worked the streets together—three years I trusted that man with my life. Went to his kid's christening, ate barbecue with his wife and his little girls . . . the same family I was trying to spare when I washed my best friend's brains off his bathroom wall. Because of you."

He was still shaking when the torrent eased. He raked his fingers through his hair again and sighed out a deep breath. Now that his vision had cleared, he saw Luz Maria sitting up, her weight braced on her hands and fear shining in a pair of deep brown eyes. Beautiful eyes, he couldn't help noticing, though exhaustion underscored them and they were filmed with tears.

She looked right at him nonetheless, her gaze unblinking and her voice steady, though still hoarse. "I'm very sorry for your loss, but I—"

Without warning, he went off again, despite the knowledge that a woman like Luz Maria Montoya knew a hundred ways to make him pay—maybe even with his job.

"But you *what?*" he demanded. "You get paid to take the word of a pair of fucking crack whores over a decorated veteran officer, a family man, for God's sake, who—"

"I know he was a family man. I thought about it, too, believe me. But what was I supposed to do, let him keep raping women, hurting them so badly, they—"

"The Z-man would *never*—"

"The evidence said otherwise," she argued, "and what's more, I believed those women. And when all was said and done, so did your own department's Internal Affairs Division. And we both know how badly they wanted to find someone else to blame."

Her words carried a quiet conviction that he couldn't help admire—even if she was in the wrong. With sickening clarity, his mind flashed to the rumors of photographs he'd heard about—of the battered female bodies scored by something, the women claimed a shard of broken glass, along the insides of their thighs and all around their nipples. Sick designs carved by a monster, not the man Grant knew.

Luz Maria Montoya, the woman who had taken the charges public, actually *believed* John Zeman did those crimes. Grant couldn't decide whether the idea made him hate her more or less.

"What I was trying to say before you interrupted," she continued, "is that I want another investigator here tonight. A *different* investigator. It's obvious you can't put aside your personal feelings to handle this case. Not that I blame you. It must have been incredibly difficult, living through such—"

Grant's laugh was ragged and utterly devoid of humor. "Save your sympathy—and your reservations. From now on, I promise you, we'll stick to the subject at hand. So how's the neck and all?"

Luz Maria pursed her lips, anger flashing over her expression as she brought her hand up to her throat, where finger-shaped bruises had begun to bloom. "It hurts, what do you think? Whenever I close my eyes, I can still feel him digging into me and shaking. I couldn't breathe, I couldn't scream."

Her gaze sliced sideways, avoiding his. Trembling visibly, her arms twined around her torso. "The whole time, he kept screaming at me, calling me bitch and . . . and . . ." Her attention snapped back to Grant's face. "What do *you* care, anyway? You've as good as told me you're rooting for the other team."

He read the pain in her eyes, measured how it mingled with her courage and her furious, clipped words— and was blindsided by the wholehearted desire to set this right for her, to keep her safe to go on wreaking havoc in God only knew how many other lives. And it wasn't only the whole "to protect and serve" trip. His instinctive response, he suspected, had just as much to do with her beautiful though bruised face and the slender set of curves outlined beneath the bedsheet. God help him, he thought with disgust, his better sense was swimming upstream against a torrent of testosterone.

Even so, he heard himself spouting the whole Joe Friday bit. "It's my job to care, ma'am. Now tell me what happened, from the start. What first drew your attention to this person?"

"The fact that he was racing at me behind a shopping

cart," she began before reclining with a sigh against her pillows and staring toward the curtained window.

As she continued speaking, he interrupted from time to time with questions meant to prize more information from her. In his opinion, she was being honest, especially when she claimed she hadn't recognized the voice—or anything else—of her masked attacker. The only thing she seemed sure of was that he'd called her by name, which indicated the assault was personal instead of random, and that he was a man. But that wasn't exactly a hot clue, since manual strangulation was an almost exclusively male crime.

"I tried clawing at his hands," Luz Maria told him, "but my nails kept catching—I think he was wearing gloves."

Grant glanced at her fingers, whose chipped and torn nails bore witness to her statement. He made a mental note to have a crime tech come in and see if any hairs or fibers remained. It wouldn't be the most bankable of evidence, since unlike a corpse's, a living victim's hands weren't bagged at the scene, but it might help confirm or eliminate a suspect later.

"And then I remembered about going for the eyes." Luz Maria's voice was seriously hoarse now, and exhaustion had settled in more deeply, shadowing her face. "But I couldn't find them. Then everything went black and—"

"So you never reached inside your purse or struggled with him for a firearm?"

She gave her head a shake, then winced at the movement. "Was there a gun?"

"Not that we could find. What about a knife? Do you remember any—"

Her gaze slid to meet his. "Wait—there was a sound, right around the time I passed out. Mostly, all I heard was his screaming at me, but there was this popping, like cracks of thunder or a car backfiring. Could that have been shots?"

"Sounds about right, and there was blood at the scene. Quite a bit more than we think you lost." He tried on a smile. "You sure you didn't bite him, clip a jugular?"

To his surprise, she laughed, a brittle sound that made her cough. Her hand went to her throat, and once again, she grimaced.

"I wish I'd gotten in a bite or two," she told him, her eyelids drooping with fatigue, "but whatever you might think of me, I don't come equipped with fangs."

Grant reminded himself that Luz Maria Montoya, Houston's Voice of Poverty, knew other ways to draw blood. As did he, with the questions he must ask about her private past. Yet when her eyes closed, he decided to let it rest for the time being. Instead he watched her, like the setting moon, slide back down into sleep.

The jet-black ponytail was long gone. The motorcycle, gone, too. Standing at the motel room sink, Sergio Cardenas threw down the blood-splotched towel and ran his shaking fingers through golden hair. Golden as a goddamned gringo's for the past two weeks now. He swore at what he saw.

She had turned him into a stranger, a man he didn't recognize. A man totally at odds with the person who had loved her, the person who had trusted her with everything he was.

The same man whose seed had taken root inside her, once upon a time.

But Luz Maria had betrayed that child, just as she had betrayed him, along with the cause they both held dear. And it was time she answered for those betrayals, no matter what the risk.

And no matter who else had to die to make it so.

* * *

Grant ran into Billy as he was leaving Luz Maria's room. The younger investigator held two Styrofoam cups of coffee, black and steaming.

Though it smelled burnt and bitter, Grant accepted the proffered cup. After midnight, his taste buds were racked out for the night, and the caffeine would keep the rest of him from following suit.

"Thanks," he said, wincing at the realization that there was no sugar in his joe. "So what happened to the Security Fairy?"

"Whitfield?" Billy asked, pulling out his notebook and flipping through the last few pages. "After we finished talking, he went back to the office to gather some files for us. Said he'll be happy to bring 'em by the station in a couple hours."

"Good, 'cause we're heading to Ben Taub's ER to check out that shooting victim."

"I just got off the phone with Ben Taub. Our guy's in surgery, but he's still breathing."

"You get a description? Was he carrying ID?" Grant asked.

Billy nodded. "Yeah, on both counts. White guy, mid-forties, by the name of Anthony Coleman, goes by Tony. That's all I've got for now."

"We'll get more when we go over. So does the name match up with anything Whitfield told you?"

Billy waited through a series of tones and a page for some doctor to report to the ER and then answered. "No, but I can tell you, in spite of the prancing, we could use a Jason Whitfield on every case. First, he gave me a thorough rundown on recent threats, each ranked—and get this, color-coded—in terms of how seriously he took each one."

Grant shook his head in disbelief. "Color coding—Christ. You think they teach that in Marine Corps boot camp?"

Billy ignored the comment. "He told me Miss Montoya's clean. No drugs, excessive drinking, sleeping around. She does go out dancing pretty often, but it's with some social group."

"What about her past?" asked Grant. "He share anything about that?"

Looking up from the pages, Billy gave his head a shake. "Why're you asking?"

With a glance at the door he had just closed behind him, Grant started walking in the direction of the elevators. After pushing the down button, he said, "Because she's got one. A capital P past, in fact. I made it my business to find out when she went after my best friend."

A soft chime interrupted and the elevator doors slid open. The two of them stepped inside the empty car, and Grant started them back toward the ground floor.

"You think it's relevant?" asked Billy, keeping his gaze straight ahead and his voice carefully neutral. "Whatever skeletons are rattling around her closet, I mean. This isn't just some old dirt you want to dredge up to get even?"

As the elevator rattled its way downward, Grant laughed and shook his head. "I may never get a bead on you, kid, but I can say one thing for certain—you've got yourself a set of steel balls, don't you?"

Billy looked his way, his expression inscrutable as ever—compliments, once more, of the Amazing Invisible Eyebrows. "Guess you're rubbing off on me. Pretty soon I'll be the second biggest pain in the ass in Major Assaults."

Grant felt another smile tugging at the corner of his mouth. "As long as you keep in mind who's number one, we'll get along just fine."

The smile faded quickly, but while the two of them made their way to Ben Taub to touch base with the victim's family, the questions in Grant's mind remained.

Could the attack on Luz Maria Montoya be rooted farther in the past than her most recent crusades? Could it, instead, be linked to her affair three years earlier with the dangerous leader of the radical group known as BorderFree-4-All?

The intruder attracted little notice as he passed the first few predawn risers who were picking up their papers or heading out to jog. Even at 4:40 A.M., his friendly nod and business suit marked him as one of them, a hungry, professional go-getter eager to arrive at work before the boss.

He couldn't help smiling, thinking that if they could see inside his briefcase, they would be rushing to lock their doors and dial 911.

The alarm system on the woman's apartment was pitifully simple to disable, despite all the signs beside the front gate that boasted of the complex's "Beautiful Bayou Views and Secure Setting." The deadbolt, too, was easily dispatched with minimal effort—wriggling the tension wrench and lifting pin after pin until his sensitive fingers felt each one snick into place. Patience, practice, and control offered many rewards, access to most residences among them.

Drawing a slim flashlight from his breast pocket, he looked around the space his target called home. In the living room, his beam slid from a sleek, modern-looking sofa in a fiery red fabric to a bare-bones shelving unit that housed a smallish TV and a surprisingly good stereo. Beside it, mounted on the wall, was a rack of CDs. Tex-Mex, he supposed from what he'd learned of her, just as he guessed the furnishings came from the inexpensive European store so many twenty-somethings favored.

The apartment walls were white as eggshell, but his light touched on patch after patch of brilliant color.

Ethnic prints and framed, patterned textiles bloomed like bouquets of tropical flowers, while across the painted mantel of a tiny fireplace, fanciful carved animals stood among framed photographs that he supposed were of family members.

His gaze lingered on the youngest, a bright-eyed toddler smiling as he reached for a balloon. The intruder's gloved hand stretched toward it, but at the last moment he hesitated, then snatched up one of the painted figures, an ornately festooned bright blue lizard with a curly tail and exaggerated claws. After dropping it into his pocket, he turned, eager to investigate the apartment's other rooms . . . and find the perfect place to leave the surprise tucked in his briefcase.

Though he had carefully sealed the mess in plastic, he imagined he could smell it. The heavy, almost sweet stench, the metallic tang that struck far back in his nostrils and brought about the suggestion of its flavor: an echo of the salty flow of blood across the tongue.

At the thought, he had to slow his breathing and carefully wrestle his mind back to its purpose.

"Control," he whispered to himself. His own excitement, all his emotions, were entirely beside the point.

What he had to focus on were Luz Maria's feelings.

Especially when she came home to what he meant to leave.

Mrrr . . . row.

Heart pounding at the unexpected sound, the intruder jerked his gaze toward a bedraggled-looking black and gray cat, who was rubbing his arched back against the sofa and looking up with hungry yellow eyes. The cat meowed a second time, more insistently, while rumbling out a mercenary purr.

"Better yet," the man said as he scooped the large feline up beneath one arm.

Holding his wriggling burden firmly, he hauled both cat and briefcase into the apartment's only bathroom. As he stepped inside, he pushed the door shut behind him, set the briefcase on the counter, and pulled back the Southwestern-patterned shower curtain to expose the empty tub.

The cat squirmed, then scratched his ribs with a rear claw as it pushed out of his grip. With a thud, it landed in the bathtub, where it flattened ragged ears and lashed its tail, a whirring growl vibrating in its throat.

The intruder adjusted his latex gloves, his gaze searching the fingertips for holes. Reassured that he was covered, he flipped open the twin latches on his briefcase, then stared at the agitated cat's reflection in the mirror.

"Don't worry, Mr. Kitty," he said soothingly, "I'll be leaving very shortly. But first, the two of us have one final piece of business to complete."

CHAPTER FOUR

After leaving Ben Taub hospital, where they had spoken with both the wife of the shooting victim and the investigator working on the man's case, Grant and Billy drove back to the scene of Luz Maria's assault to meet Tom Newlin, the head of security for the Ryland Foods chain.

On the way inside the store, Billy said, "Damn shame about that bystander. I hope the poor guy makes it."

"Yeah," Grant said. He couldn't get the image out of his head of those two little boys sitting in the surgical waiting area in their baseball caps. The younger of the two, a towheaded kid around eight, had his knees drawn up beneath a jersey and his arms wrapped around his legs. The ten-year-old had been fiddling with some sort of handheld electronic game, but every time he thought no one was looking, he wiped at his eyes with the back of his hand. Their daddy helped coach both their teams, he'd told the investigators, so he *couldn't* die.

The mother was a basket case, blaming herself for sending her husband out to pick up an over-the-counter medication a doctor had recommended that she take. Though she appeared to be over her illness by this time, she'd been vomiting throughout the evening, after the family took her to a sushi restaurant to celebrate her birthday.

"Some birthday," Grant said as they started toward the staircase a store cashier had pointed out.

Billy shot him a confused glance before saying, "Oh, the wife's. Yeah. Well, maybe the security tapes will show what happened and at least put the guy who did it behind bars."

"That'll be a heck of a lot of consolation." Not for the first time—or even the hundredth, Grant was struck by how little they could do to right the wrongs they saw each day. Sure, they'd keep the man who'd attacked Luz Maria Montoya—probably the same son of a bitch who'd shot Tony Coleman when he'd stumbled into her nightmare—from hurting anyone else. But it wouldn't put a father in those boys' lives or a husband in that woman's bed. Coleman remained critical, and Grant wasn't sure the surgeons could do the trick, either.

Billy hesitated on the steps, then brightened, his blue eyes glowing beneath the store's fluorescent lights. "Maybe the tapes will show that Coleman tried to *stop* the assault."

Grant nodded, understanding the distinction. Even if Coleman didn't make it, it would change his legacy from that of another wrong-place, wrong-time victim to a hero. Grant thought about how, when he'd been about the same age as Coleman's older boy, he would have given anything for even the slightest possibility that his old man's death was heroic—or at least blameless. Unfortunately, his aunts had opted for the brutal truth. Though they were both sweet women who gave raising him their best shot once his mother took off, even now, Grant had a hard time forgiving them their honesty.

When they reached the second door on the left, he rapped sharply, then entered a cramped room. The place stank of grease and cigarette smoke, no surprise since the lone table was littered with overtaxed ashtrays, empty soda cans, and crumpled potato chip bags.

Tom Newlin, head of Ryland's security division, grimaced at the garbage and shook his massive head. A well-spoken African American in his mid-thirties, the man had to be six-six and at least two-eighty. Grant remembered hearing he'd been a linebacker for the University of Texas before a blown knee forced him to reconsider his career plans. Even so, his huge shoulders still strained the confines of the golf shirt he wore with a pair of chino slacks.

"Sorry about the mess," he said as he shook both men's hands. "Our guy better clean his act up if he wants to stay on the payroll."

Grant waved off the apology. "Forget about it." To him, the room looked slightly neater than the average cop's desk. Or *his* at any rate, with the exception of the cancer sticks, a habit he had kicked five years before.

He introduced Billy, who had never before met Newlin, then said, "Let's see what your cameras can tell us."

Grant and Billy commandeered a couple of folding chairs and left the largest seat, a desk model on rollers, for the big guy. All three chairs faced a bank of monitors. Three of the screens flipped through real-time images from CCTV cameras covering the entrances, the registers, and various parking lot and backdoor views. Tom was fiddling with the controls for the fourth while Billy studied a half-eaten donut wrapped up in a grease-spotted paper towel.

"You know I value loyalty," Grant told him, "but you eat that thing and I'm going to have to shoot you."

Boy Wonder slapped on his best "Who, me?" look—

a blank expression that came far too easily for comfort. But before he could work up either a protest or a come-back, Newlin was speaking.

"We have a guard that walks the lot every fifteen minutes and patrols the entrance to the store. A second employee monitors from up here, and the two of them keep in touch by radio. Customer safety is our top priority, just ahead of great food at a great value."

Grant nodded agreeably, waiting for the official corporate spiel to run its course. He had heard it all before—at least a half-dozen times over the past few years—when he'd consulted with Newlin about incidents on one or another of the chain's eight Houston properties. Eager to reduce its liability—and press coverage that would scare off customers—Ryland Foods cooperated fully, and visibly, with police investigations. Newlin put a sincere face on it, enough to convince reporters that he genuinely cared about customer safety.

Yet Tom seemed jittery tonight, and Grant could guess the reason. Somehow, the damned media had picked up on the story, and he and Billy had been advised that the news was already breaking about the assault of a well-known community activist—a woman beloved by many, for all her enemies. Someone would have to take the blame, and if he and Billy didn't find the culprit quickly, both their asses and Tom's job could end up on the line.

"So was it your guy in the booth that first noticed the problem?" Billy asked him after whipping out his little notebook.

Grant watched his partner fish around for his pen, but didn't bother telling him he'd stuck the thing behind his ear. This late into the shift, a man had to take his entertainment where he found it.

Newlin nodded. "That's exactly what happened. He saw a lone male wearing a ski mask rush into camera range, approaching a female customer as she left her vehicle."

Newlin smiled and pointed to his own ear to cue Billy on his pen's location. While Billy swore and retrieved the ballpoint, the security director started the tape. A moment later, he pointed toward flickering images on the monitor and said, "Right there."

"Why's the picture flashing like that?" Billy asked him.

"Lightning," the big man explained. "Didn't ever get any rain out of it, but it played hell with the image quality."

Grant leaned forward, watching as a slender woman stepped out of a boxy compact SUV and pointed what was probably an electronic key toward the little Honda. There was no sound, but they saw the vehicle's headlights flip on and off.

"So the doors were locked and the alarm armed," Billy said. This wasn't exactly hot news, since the vehicle had remained so when they'd found it.

As lightning strobe-lit Luz Maria's white peasant blouse, she pushed her long braid behind her shoulder and started toward the store entrance. Her movements were fluid, graceful, beautiful—the movements of a dancer.

This is the woman who killed John, Grant reminded himself harshly. *She might as well have pushed the goddamned gun into his mouth.*

Even so, he found himself watching her intently, holding his breath in anticipation, his stomach clenching in what felt very much like dread. When it came, the attack was sudden, brutal, the only warning the tilt of Luz Maria's head as she turned toward something out of camera range. And then the shopping cart appeared in the corner of the screen, followed by a dark-clad, man-shaped blur. She reacted swiftly, surprisingly agile as she avoided the cart, but her attacker leapt onto her, slamming her down behind a pickup truck.

While Newlin fiddled with the controls again, Grant pulled an index card and stubby pencil from the pocket of his tan sport jacket and jotted *Ford F-150—silver?* His heart was pounding, though he'd seen more footage of blitz attacks than he cared to recall. Perhaps it was the explosiveness of the violence or the eerie flickering of the footage. Or was he hoping that somehow this time, the man in the ski mask would magically succeed, that he would forever keep his target from destroying another innocent life?

A target that had looked up at Grant with big brown eyes in the hospital tonight. . . .

Nausea slid around his stomach, as much at his undeniable physical attraction as at the wish she had been killed. It was a damned good thing he had two weeks of vacation coming. What the hell was wrong with him tonight?

"Now watch this," Newlin prompted, pointing at the screen again.

The man in the ski mask stood, then raised his arm as the image flickered. His mouth was moving, shouting maybe. Then he ran out of the field of vision, hunching over as if he meant to keep out of sight.

"I didn't see. Did he fire a weapon?" Billy asked.

"Hard to say with the lightning flashes," Newlin answered.

"Did one of the other cameras catch him as he ran off?" Grant followed up. "Did you get anyone else?"

He wanted to see Coleman's part in this. Had that been the man's Ford F-150? That was the vehicle he had reportedly driven off in, wounded, before wrapping it around the light pole on Congress.

Newlin dragged in an audible breath, released it

slowly and noisily as he shook his head. "I'm afraid we missed the rest—including our guy leaving. One of the cameras—number three—was out of service."

"You have footage of that pickup leaving? The one parked in front of the spot where Luz Maria was knocked down?"

Billy cut him a surprised look, clearly noticing Grant's slipup. Normally, they called both victims and suspects Mr. Doe or Ms. Jones, as did most officers. Officially, it was an attempt to sound respectful to any citizen or member of the press who might overhear them. But in reality, it was a mostly unconscious attempt to maintain distance, to keep both suffering and evil at arm's length.

"It belonged to a woman," Newlin said, cuing the tape forward, past the flurry of activity that followed the attack, when emergency lights out-flashed the lightning. Slowing the video once more, he pointed out an older blonde, who wore a towering, honest-to-God beehive hairdo, as she climbed inside the truck's cab. "That's Stacy Boyinton, one of our cashiers. She's gone home, but I could get her number for you."

"That won't be necessary right now." Mentally, Grant cursed his luck. He wasn't overly surprised. Pickups were common in the area and none more so than that model, but he'd been hoping the tape would definitively place Coleman at the scene. Now they'd have to wait for DNA testing of the blood samples taken from the scene and hope for a match—unless Coleman regained consciousness before then. Meanwhile, they would hope the bullet extracted from the man's chest yielded clues.

"What about that camera?" Billy asked. "Camera number three. How long has it been broken?"

Newlin's scowl was fleeting, but Grant could guess he was imagining a reporter asking the same question. Or worse yet, a personal injury attorney for either the Montoya or the Coleman family.

"A work order was put in yesterday for its repair," Newlin answered quickly. Perhaps too quickly.

"*Before* this attack?" asked Billy, his eyes locking onto the much larger man's.

"Yeah," Newlin answered. "Thank God. We've got a time-stamped record of the request on the chain's networked computer system. It went in at four twenty-seven P.M. yesterday."

"Lucky for you all." Billy looked at the former linebacker even harder. "Real lucky."

A telltale muscle twitched in Newlin's jaw and his pleasant, public relations face submerged beneath something stone cold—maybe even dangerous. "If you're implying that I would alter the record to keep the heat off my employer . . ."

Billy rose from his chair and managed a world-class sneer, despite the eyebrow handicap. "Oh, I'm not implying that it's the *chain* you're looking out for."

Grant decided they'd better end the interview right there—unless he wanted Howdy Doody's pen stuck someplace a lot darker than the spot behind his ear.

Rising from his chair, he slipped his index card back into his pocket. "Thanks for the info, Mr. Newlin. Let's go, Devlin, we've got some background checks to run through. The clock's ticking if we want to catch a break before our shift ends."

Once his partner stepped out of the room, Grant made as if to leave, then glanced back over his shoulder at Newlin. "Oh, yeah," he said, attempting to sound bored and irritated. "I know it's a pain in the ass, this hour of the night and all, but we're going to need someone to take a ladder so we can get a quick look at your busted camera."

* * *

"Are you sure there was nothing stronger than Tylenol in that paper cup of yours?" Luz Maria whispered to the dim room as she squeezed the nurse's finger—an action for which she had been awakened, and asked to repeat hourly throughout the night. It was part of what was called a neuro check, used to determine whether the attack had caused an injury to Luz Maria's brain.

"Very sure. Why?" the brunette nurse asked. Her face looked gray, its color leached away by both the fluorescent light and the pearly glow leaking in along the edges of the window's heavy curtains. The long night had nearly ebbed away, like the last traces of a bad dream.

After switching hands to demonstrate her strength on the left side, Luz Maria explained, "All these wild thoughts I'm having—I haven't slept at all since you last came in. I've been worrying more about that darned cop than I have my attacker, even though I haven't committed any crime."

Not lately, anyway. Regret throbbed in time to her heartbeat, a painful pulsing at her throat, a thumping at her rib cage.

"Which cop? *Oooh*, I'll bet I know." Humor brightened the night shift nurse's round face, erasing some of the fatigue there. "That drop-dead gorgeous one. Was it just me, or is he a dead ringer for George Clooney?"

"I didn't notice," Luz Maria lied, even as she decided the investigator was a taller man, and his eyes, unlike the actor's, were smoke-gray. But it was the hatred burning in them that had her feeling so unsettled, not physical attraction.

The middle-aged nurse grinned. "At least we know there's nothing wrong with your vision—or your hormones. But then, that hunk of man could probably jump-start a cadaver."

Shifting back into professionalism, she tucked a palm beneath Luz Maria's left foot and said, "I know you're sore, but I need you to push hard against me."

A moment later, the woman said, "Very good. Now the right one. Oh, and by the way, I was supposed to tell you your brother called to check on you . . . again."

Luz Maria huffed out a sigh. If hospital security hadn't sworn they'd keep an eye on her—and threatened to haul him off—Jack would still be there, sleeping across the doorway to keep her safe.

"Shift change is in a half hour," the nurse said once she had finished, "so I guess this is good-bye. I hope you're feeling better soon."

Luz Maria hugged herself. "So you won't be back tomorrow—I mean, tonight?"

The nurse smiled and opened the curtains, revealing an unimpressive parking lot view, silvery in the cloud-filtered predawn light. "As well as you're doing, you'll be sleeping in your own bed. But if you want, I could call you and wake you up every hour."

A laugh slipped out, surprising Luz Maria and hurting her throat, too. Her hand covered her mouth as she thought how strange—how wrong—it felt to find anything amusing when last night a man had slammed her down and dug his fingers into her neck. A man who'd cursed her, in his harsh and terrifying voice, and shaken her until her world went black.

Dios mío. My God . . .

"What's wrong? Are you in pain—" The nurse stopped short, then said, "It's all right, Ms. Montoya. It's good to laugh, to smile."

Luz Maria looked away, embarrassed to have been read so easily.

The older woman touched her shoulder. "It says you're alive—and you aren't about to let that creep who hurt you win."

45

"Thank you," Luz Maria said. "Thank you for everything."

It was only after the woman left that Luz Maria realized she had forgotten to look at her name tag. Even so, she promised herself she *would* remember what the nurse had told her. Luz Maria meant to take her life back with a will, from its laughter to its daily battles. She wouldn't let one lunatic stop her.

Yet when she closed her eyes in an attempt to rest, Grant Holcomb's face came back to her once more—along with an image of the investigator's big hands settling gently on her neck. He leaned over her and whispered like a lover, his breath warm against her face: *"I washed my best friend's brains off his bathroom wall. Because of you."*

The fine hairs rose along her bruised arms, and her skin prickled as apprehension skated across nerve endings. Her heart thumped in her chest, the adrenalin surging through her system as it all but shouted, *Run.*

She woke with a gasp, though she hadn't realized she'd been dozing. With the sun higher in the east, the room had brightened, but her tangled thoughts refused to follow suit.

Clearly, her subconscious was trying to tell her that Holcomb couldn't be trusted to put her attacker behind bars. Reason enough to want the man off her case, she decided. Reason enough to call his supervisor to discuss her misgivings. After all, she needed this case closed if she hoped to be effective in the performance of her duties. Too many people were counting on her to let a maniac on a mission stop her. . . .

Or the self-doubt that spiked through her at the thought of Investigator Holcomb's accusation.

Already, recriminations were exploding in her head. *What if you were wrong about Investigator Zeman?* And what if she'd been wrong on more than one occasion?

Could it be her own mistake, *her* sins, that had fueled last night's attack—just the way her sins of three years earlier had wreaked havoc on so many lives?

"Stop it," she said aloud, her voice sounding strained and hoarse. If she thought too much about the past, she would lose her will to face the future; she'd have nothing left to give to those who needed her so badly.

After sipping water through a flexible straw, Luz Maria reached for the telephone and dialed the number on the card Investigator Holcomb had left with her. As soon as she reached the lieutenant in charge of the Major Assaults Division, she locked away all doubt and guilt and did the thing she knew best.

She went on the attack.

CHAPTER FIVE

Most of the blood had dripped down the bathtub drain already, but not every drop. Some of it congealed in ugly brownish lumps against the white enameled surface. Some of it made streaks.

All of it, whether in the tub, the drain beneath it, or elsewhere in the bathroom, had begun to give off the sweet-sick odor of decomposition. And though the intruder had closed the doors behind him before leaving, the first few flies had already managed to find their way to the quickly decaying meat inside.

For the moment, their buzzing was almost the only sound in the apartment. Their buzzing and the echo of the dark blood's steady drip.

The intruder smiled as he listened from the spot where he sat waiting. He smiled and pressed his fingertips, again and again, to each of the four corners of the item he'd risked so much to go back inside and pick up. . . .

The photo of the little boy was missing from her mantel.

* * *

Luz Maria had spoken to both Jack and her mama on the telephone within the past hour, yet she didn't share with either that the doctor had just cleared her for release. For one thing, her brother, despite his late night, had to work this morning at his clinic. And her mother's *my poor hija* dramatics had been exhausting, even via phone.

Luz Maria didn't call the Voice of Poverty's office either, though she was certain Whit would drive her home. He would want to check over both her apartment and her vehicle, which Jack and Reagan had dropped at her home after leaving the hospital late last night. The truth was, Luz Maria felt too tired and cranky for conversation, so she decided to take a cab home, pop the sample pain reliever she'd been given, and sleep off her fatigue. Work could wait for now, especially April Walsh, the organization's head publicist and fund-raiser, who would be plotting how to use last night's attack to refill VOP's nearly empty coffers.

The Arabic cab driver earned a good tip because he looked at Luz Maria's bruised throat gravely but withheld his questions during the ride home. Once she punched in the security code from the backseat, he pulled inside the fenced lot and waited without comment while she scanned the area for any vehicle or person that seemed out of place.

Nothing unusual snagged her attention. Though many of the other spaces lay empty at this time of morning, her dusty, gray SUV sat in its numbered parking space. A cadre of blackbirds, common grackles, squawked among themselves in the branches of a nearby ornamental pear tree, no doubt plotting the next move in their ongoing war against the box-shaped Honda's paint job. An elderly neighbor was walking her arthritic dachshund on a strip of yellowed grass, her expression as unruffled as her iron-gray chignon.

After paying and thanking the cab driver, Luz Maria stepped reluctantly from the air-conditioned sedan into a steamy morning. Though it was not yet ten-thirty, the temperature already had to be in the mid-eighties. Humidity weighed down every breath and frizzed her hastily rebraided hair.

By the time she climbed the stairs to the second-floor landing, Luz Maria felt perspiration dampening her temples and collecting at the waistband of her gauzy, ethnic-patterned skirt. *Change of plans*, she thought as she dragged her keys out of her shoulder bag. She would put the nap on hold until she washed her hair, scrubbed her battered body, and sent every atom of last night's horror spinning down her bathtub's drain.

"Mmm," Luz Maria muttered, fumbling the keys in her hurry.

But her anticipation shattered when a hand clamped onto her forearm and a deep male voice growled, "We need to talk. Right now."

Luz Maria yelped in surprise. Yet in spite of her terror, her muscles remembered the hours she'd spent in self-defense training. Her knee rose and then she stamped downward, heel-first, in an attempt to catch an instep or an ankle.

But she missed—or he'd been ready, as he was ready when she tried to tear her arm free to give him a taste of elbow.

"Whoa, whoa," he said quickly. "Police—Investigator Holcomb. It's all right. Sorry I shook you up, there, Ms. Montoya."

Abruptly, he released her, and she rounded on him, unshed tears burning in her eyes. She'd dropped both her shoulder bag and keys, but for the moment she ignored them.

"What the hell are you doing, lurking behind my damned tree?" She gestured toward the oversized potted houseplant she and a friend had dragged onto the covered porch in the hope of reversing its decline. "What do you mean, scaring me to death?"

He kept his hands raised. "Sorry. Sorry. I was so pissed, I didn't stop to think you might be on edge after last night."

"On edge?" she demanded. "On edge? What woman *wouldn't* freak out when a man grabs her on her doorstep?"

He glanced around, as if looking for neighbors charging to the rescue. With no one in evidence, he said, "You're right, but . . . Listen, could we maybe go inside to talk about this?"

Luz Maria the community activist wanted to send him packing so she could call the chief of police, maybe the mayor, and get this *estúpido*, this *idiota* fired. Luz Maria the assault victim wanted to crawl quivering beneath a blanket and let her mama come to coddle and protect her. But Luz Maria the woman watched in fascination while he picked up her shoulder bag and keys and offered her both, his gray eyes begging forgiveness as his handsome face flushed crimson.

And suddenly she was overwhelmed with the desire to invite him inside her apartment, to sit down and discuss with him why she'd felt the need to call his lieutenant earlier and demand that he be taken off her case.

But of course that might have been the hormones talking.

She tried to shut them up, to remind herself of how unsafe he'd made her feel last night. But it was his obvious chagrin more than the way humidity had his blue shirt clinging to his well-developed chest and shoulders that convinced her to hear him out. And something else, something revealed by his missing sport jacket.

"You aren't wearing your gun, are you?" she asked.

He shook his head. "My shift's over, it's too damned

51

hot for the jacket, and I—I didn't think it was a good idea."

As she took her things from him, her face burned at his honesty—and what his words implied. "You . . . you were afraid that you might *shoot* me?"

"Nah," he told her. "Ballbuster like you, I figured you'd probably wrestle it away from me and pistol-whip me halfway to intensive care."

Luz Maria's eyes flared at the insult, and she felt the hairs on the back of her neck rise. But before she could light into him, two things registered: the mischief playing in those gray eyes and the dry humor lancing through his words.

The jerk was baiting her intentionally. Well, two could play at that game. Lifting her chin, she went for what her brother called her *princesa* look, heavy on the haughty. "Investigator Holcomb, I can assure you. If I started on the job, there would be no *halfway* about it."

His brows rising, he asked her, "Are you threatening an officer of the law?"

A yellow leaf cut loose from her fig tree and dropped like a gauntlet into the space between their feet.

Luz Maria made a face. "I'm tired, sweaty, and still wearing the parking lot grit from last night's tango. So you bet your *pompis* I am."

For a few beats, he said nothing, though the beginnings of a smile ticked at one corner of his mouth. "I hear there's a law against that, Ms. Montoya."

"There's also a law against screwing with a community activist," she countered. "I think it's called the law of self-preservation."

And somehow, just like that, both of them were laughing. Though pain shot through her sore neck and ribs, Luz Maria couldn't help herself, struck as she was by the absurdity of this little front porch pissing contest.

"I presume you've come to discuss my call to your

station this morning," she told him once she had recovered. "Come on in and let's talk this out like two adults."

He shot a smile that had undoubtedly made fools of any number of women in the past, the kind of smile that had Luz Maria swearing she wouldn't be so stupid. *Been there, done that,* she reminded herself bitterly.

But Holcomb's voice was breezy as he said, "I thought you'd never ask," then walked straight through the door ahead of her.

The intruder stared at the computer monitor. Watching. Listening. Waiting for the scream.

"How could I have forgotten this?" he whispered. "The power, the control. The totality of domination. In your world, I am omnipotent, unknowable . . . lethal." More of a god than anything they droned on about in the Sunday school classes his grandfather had forced him to attend.

And so very far from the snot-nosed rug rat who stood sniveling and helpless while his own mother had bled out on the bed.

The wait should have been boring as he sat in the unfamiliar office, among a collection of three working computers, an assortment of accessories, and a plethora of technical manuals. Oh, yes, and the bound woman he was using as a footrest—mainly to keep her from getting any ridiculous ideas of escape.

Thanks in part to her presence, he wasn't bored at all. He hadn't planned this little scenario. He'd even experienced a gut-dropping jolt when she'd surprised him coming out of the apartment next door with the photo of the child in his hand. But he couldn't say that he was sorry, now that he had gotten a good look at the young woman, with her springy chocolate curls and expressive blue eyes sending terrified glances his way. Her lower face was hidden by the duct tape gag that covered her mouth and wound around her head. She was far prettier now that he'd removed those skinny little girl geek glasses she'd been wearing. She should be grateful, he decided, that he had dropped them inside his briefcase, into the slot behind the picture of the little boy with the balloon.

Gazing down at her, he used one socked foot to stroke a path along her side, from her rib cage to her middle and down along one lean hip. He liked the way she'd dressed, in a barely there pink T-shirt and a pair of shorts so brief that they highlighted long, tan legs. His toes glided along her smooth thigh, then up along the inside.

She tried to wriggle underneath the desk, and her whimper had his prick straining for release.

Yet he found himself dissatisfied with the woman at his feet. Her hair ought to be longer, darker—a river of black silk, with waves breaking at her waistline. And her eyes . . . the blue was all wrong, like the shape.

He went down to his knees, tearing off another swath of duct tape as he did so. He had to cover up those eyes, that broad forehead, that thin nose. All of them—all wrong, just like the hair.

Her eyes flared, white showing all the way around the irises, and her arms and legs fought uselessly against her bonds. But it was the noise that attracted his attention and made him drop the duct tape.

It was the metallic click of a key turning in a dead-bolt, followed by the light creak of a door's hinges as it opened. Sounds coming not from this apartment's front room but through the speakers of the computer he'd been using to monitor a wireless hidden camera with a built-in microphone. He'd set the device to broadcast, using the unsecured network of a careless tenant in this apartment complex, for it allowed him to keep tabs on his quarry from anywhere in the world with Internet access.

Even from the back bedroom office of Luz Maria's next door neighbor.

With his heart throbbing in his throat and his gaze riveted to the still dark screen, he completely forgot about his captive . . . for the moment.

CHAPTER SIX

Grant glanced around the inside of Luz Maria's apartment, from the lipstick-red sofa to the framed textiles to the weird little Mexican animal figures arranged among the photos on the mantel of the small fireplace. The space was colorful, cheerful, neat—in short, everything his house wasn't.

It also appeared undisturbed, which meant she could safely come in. Not surprisingly, however, she hadn't waited for his say-so, but instead had strode in right behind him, then laid her purse on top of the counter that separated the living room from the galley-style kitchen. Next to the bag sat a combination cordless telephone and answering machine, its crimson message light blinking insistently.

Ignoring it, she called out, "Borracho."

Grant hadn't spent six years in uniform without picking up the Spanish word for *drunk*.

"I may be irritating," he responded with a straight face, though the pet carrier he'd spotted tucked under a lamp table clued him in, "but I assure you, I'm completely sober."

"It's my cat's name. You'll like him. He's a pain in the *nalgas*, too. He's also probably sulking under my bed because Kellie only had dry food for him this morning."

"Tell me about Kellie," he said because it was his job to be nosy. Conveniently, it was his nature, too.

"She lives right over there, next door." Luz Maria pointed, which was unnecessary, since hers was the end unit along this landing. "Kellie Capshaw's a freelance Web designer, works out of her apartment—at least when she's not sneaking off to play nine holes with her little sister. I wasn't sure about her at first—I mean, the sister's so uptight; she's some kind of secretary to the special agent in charge of the FBI field office."

In Luz Maria's delicate shudder, Grant saw aversion. Considering what he knew of her past, that made sense. But in the time it took him to form the thought, Luz Maria's conversation veered back to her neighbor.

"Kellie's great, though. About my age and single, too, so we kind of look out for each other. Share bad date war stories, talk about her appalling taste in music. She likes country better than Tejano, if you can imagine that. *Gringas* and their strange ways."

Luz Maria shook her head in feigned disapproval before opening her whole face to a gorgeous smile, an expression at odds with the ugly bruising on her delicate neck.

Grant wished she wouldn't smile at him, or give as good as she got when he lobbed a smart-ass comment her way. He wanted her to be a bitch, coldhearted and self-righteous. He wanted her to be the *queen* bitch, someone he could hate for the Z-man and for calling to report his behavior from her hospital room last night.

And yet she wasn't, so he couldn't bring himself to

shout at her the way he had planned as he'd driven over. Instead, he said the last thing—the very last thing—he expected.

"I'm sorry for being such a jerk last night. You had every right to ask to have me removed from your case. I shouldn't have taken it in the first place, wouldn't have ever been assigned it if we hadn't had a fill-in supervisor last night."

She looked at him, surprise written in the arch of a delicate, dark brow and the gap between her unpainted lips. But she wasn't a woman who needed makeup, or even a decent night's sleep, to look good in the morning. Noticing her untidy braid, he wondered if she slept that way—and if she'd ever allow a man to unwind those long strands, to run his fingers through them while he . . .

Down, boy. He'd forgotten how damned inconvenient his long-lost libido could prove.

"But I'm not blaming anyone but myself," he rambled. "I should have told the lieutenant all about my . . . history. I should have told him I'm still stopping by Zeman's house a couple times a week, trying to help his wife and kids keep everything together."

An image came to him unbidden: Sherry Zeman, with her soft eyes green as new grass, her smile brave and broken, her slender fingers feathering a touch beneath his jaw. *"I think . . . I think I'm ready to move on, Grant. And I think you could be the one to help me do it."*

Pain shot through him, as if a Taser's prongs had been pushed into his sternum. Shit.

Luz Maria's dark eyes welled with what looked like sympathy. But instead of either asking about the family or defending her actions concerning John, she refocused the conversation on the more immediate matter.

"You frightened me last night. I'd been attacked once in a parking lot already. I couldn't take a chance on having an investigator who felt"—she seemed to struggle for the right word—"who felt . . . *ambivalent* about catching the man who tried to kill me."

He nodded. "I can understand that. And, like I said before, you were right to make that call. But I want you to know you were wrong about me. Dead wrong. I said I'd find the guy, and I will—because I'm that kind of a cop. That kind of a man. I take it seriously, just like the guy who trained me."

John Zeman's name—and his fate—hung in the air between them. Had Luz Maria been his last thought before he stuck the muzzle in his mouth?

But Luz Maria looked confused. "I'm sure you are a good cop. You seem determined enough, at any rate. But I was told you would be taken off my case, that you're planning to be out on vacation anyway, and Investigator Devlin will be—"

"Maybe your case *is* what I want to do with my vacation." Grant wondered if testosterone was interfering with his brain waves, because he couldn't recall the last time he'd said anything so stupid. He already had plans for his time off, beginning with a few days with his cousin Jimmy up at Lake Conroe, where they would zip around on Jet Skis, drown a few worms, and swap lies about women while enjoying some cold brews. First, though, he had to make good on his promise to drop by Sherry's place and help her put together the bicycle she'd bought for Emma's upcoming sixth birthday—even if the thought *did* fill him with foreboding.

Besides, what kind of no-life loser chose to work on his days off? Especially on a case involving a woman who masqueraded as the mouthpiece of morality while destroying other people's lives?

Even if he *couldn't* help thinking about peeling off her white top and finding out what lay beneath that gypsy skirt of hers . . .

She shot a tight-lipped smirk his way, telling him she didn't buy his Dedicated Public Servant story. That she was on to his attraction to her.

His purely physical attraction. He would prove to her it didn't matter, that an investigator relied on only the head north of the equator to do his job.

"While I have you here," Luz Maria said as she perched on one of a pair of counter stools, "maybe you can tell me, did you find out anything last night about my case?"

"We're just starting to go through those threat files your coworker brought us. But we do have a lead as to the possible source of all that blood."

"Who?" She leaned forward, looking anxious.

"A man named Tony Coleman. Name mean anything to you?"

She paused, eyes narrowing in consideration, before her head shook. "Should it?"

"We think your assailant shot him at the scene of the attack."

Her eyes widened, and once more she was on her feet. "My God. Does that mean—was he trying to help me?"

"I was hoping you'd be able to tell me that."

She stopped to think, her gaze drifting toward the ceiling. After a moment, she speared Grant with a panicked look. "I—I can't remember. Did the man live?"

Grant shrugged. "Jury's still out on that question. The trauma team did their bit, but he lost a lot of blood. Still hasn't regained consciousness, last I heard. And there were other injuries as well, from his truck crashing. We think he was trying to drive himself from the scene to the ER."

The color drained from Luz Maria's face, and her knees folded, depositing her atop the stool again. "That poor man . . ."

"Before you go all hysterical on me," Grant said, "we don't know he was trying to save you. We aren't even certain yet that he was there. All we know is he was going out to get his wife some medicine for an upset stomach."

"I'm not 'all hysterical.'" She mimed quotation marks with her fingers. "It's a shock, that's all, and no matter what you think, I have a heart. I was hoping that the man who attacked me hurt himself, too. It would serve the *cabrón* right."

Grant nodded, marking the fact that Luz Maria preferred to swear in Spanish. "And it would make him easier to find, too. But Tony Coleman isn't our guy. No gloves or ski mask in his pickup. No weapon, either."

"Is he—does he have a family?" she asked in a small voice. "Besides the wife, that is?"

Images played through Grant's memory: the two boys sitting in the waiting area, the older one telling them his daddy *couldn't* die. But instead of sharing what he'd seen, he merely said to Luz Maria, "Yeah."

She whispered something in soft Spanish. Not a curse, but what he thought was a prayer—as if she'd sensed the unspoken truths as well as what he'd told her.

Was it possible she cared, that she gave a damn about the impact she had on others' lives? That she had grieved when Zeman took his life, not for him so much, but for the family he'd left behind?

He saw her looking at the answering machine light, and he counted the number of repeating flashes. There were six. Six unheard messages.

Wrestling his mind away from the concept of a professional hell-raiser with a conscience, he said, "Maybe you should play those while I'm still here. Since your attacker knew your name, it's possible he has your phone number—unlisted or not. And it's possible he's called."

At her skeptical look, he added, "Believe me, I've seen stranger things."

Luz Maria glanced downward, then started playing with the tail of her braid, flicking its sable tip between her fingers. A nervous habit, Grant decided.

When she didn't answer, he shrugged. "Don't bother, if there's something you're afraid I'll hear. Maybe a voice from your past that you don't want anyone to know about."

Her dark eyes flashed at his challenge, and he saw both surprise and anger before she mastered her expression. Surprise, that he already knew about her history. Anger that he'd thrown it up in her face. He wondered if fear was in the mix, too, but before he could decide, Luz Maria hit the machine's PLAY button.

The first voice was female and heavily accented. *"Luz Maria, this is Mama. Why did you not call me? I come this morning to the hospital, with Tía Rosario to support me in my hour of need, and they tell me you have gone already. This I must learn from a total stranger, since my own* hija *could not find the time to call—"*

Grant grinned, mostly at Luz Maria's pained look. She hit the button to skip to the next message.

"Hey, Luz." This voice was male, young sounding. *"It's Emilio. You remember, Emilio Hernandez? I heard what happened on the news. Listen, I know we only went out the one time, but if you want me to come stay at your place so you'll feel safe . . . I'd be happy to camp out on your sofa—"*

Luz Maria rolled her eyes and muttered, "Sure you would," then forwarded through two more messages from what sounded like boyfriends she'd blown off after brief relationships.

Grant jotted the names down on an index card under the initials PPE, for Possible Pissed Exes. It was beginning to sound as if it might prove to be a long list.

Luz Maria frowned at him. "You don't need to bother about those guy—"

"You think it was bad last night, just wait 'til next time, Little Looozie," a garbled voice began.

Her jaw dropping, Luz Maria stopped mid-syllable to stare at the recorder. The voice was deep, distorted, like a sound bite from a horror movie.

"Next time I get my hands on your throat, I promise you, we won't be interrupted. Next time, I won't stop squeezing 'til those pretty eyes pop from their sockets. And then I'm going to fuck you there. Makes me rock hard just thinking of—"

Grant crossed the room in two strides and shut off the machine—and the mechanically altered voice.

"Who—who would—who could say such terrible things?" Luz Maria leaned over the counter, hands braced against it as if to keep herself from falling. Bruises stood out on her face and throat, the dark spots highlighted by her sudden pallor.

"You didn't recognize the voice?" he asked, though it sounded electronically altered to him, impossible to identify.

She shook her head emphatically. "God, no. I don't know anyone who would—who could say such filthy . . ."

She covered her face, but not before he caught a glimpse of her tears. The sight struck him like a gut punch, though he had seen more victims weeping than he would care to count. Had learned to block their pain so he could do his best for them. But somehow, Luz Maria's had him reaching out to her, laying his hand on her small, stiff shoulder.

She jerked away as if she'd been stung, turning from him and hiding her face in her hands. Yet she couldn't hide the horror in her voice. "How could anyone be so sick?"

Abruptly, she clapped a hand over her mouth and

dashed toward a closed door along the hallway. The bathroom, he decided.

But after she flung the door open, it was not the sounds of retching that brought Grant Holcomb running.

It was the shattering cacophony of Luz Maria's screams.

Blood was everywhere. Smeared across the mirror. Spattered on the sink and walls.

A few flies buzzed in agitated circles before one dove to rest at the margin of a quarter-sized splotch on the tile.

Abruptly, Luz Maria fell mute, as if someone had used a razor to slice through her vocal cords. Her heart pounded a question through her arteries, so overpowering that she barely noticed when Investigator Holcomb came up behind her.

Where did all this come from? Whose blood could it be?

Her knees loosened at the answer that washed over her. There was but a single source in this apartment—the one she'd supposed was hiding underneath her bed.

"Borracho," she cried. "Oh, my God. My poor ca—"

She clamped down on the word as her eye caught a movement in the mirror, a twitching of the shower curtain.

A strong hand grabbed her upper arm and jerked her out into the hallway.

"Don't go back in there," Grant ordered.

"It moved," she whispered as she pointed at the shower curtain. "Did you see?"

He reached for something at his shoulder, then muttered, "Damn it."

Remembering, she guessed, that he hadn't brought his gun here. Regretting it, too, from his expression.

He turned, then spun her around roughly and gestured toward her front door and mouthed the word, "*Out.*"

He didn't have to tell her twice. If the psycho who had called her—the same man who'd attacked her—was hiding in her bathroom, she wanted to be as far away as possible before . . .

Just outside her front door, Luz Maria stopped in her tracks. Glancing over her shoulder, she realized Investigator Holcomb wasn't following. She didn't see him anywhere, though the hallway wasn't visible from this angle.

Was he confronting the intruder, unarmed and alone?

A noise gave her the answer—the rattling hiss of the shower curtain sliding on its rod.

It was followed by a harsh grunt—and an exclamation.

"Holy shit."

CHAPTER SEVEN

He might have ordered Luz Maria out, but she was behind him in an instant. The sight that met her eyes brought instant relief.

Relief for her cat, at any rate. The ugly silver feline was hunkered down in the bottom of the bathtub, where he was feasting on a bloody mess.

"Oh, Borracho," she said as she bent down and reached for the animal. "My poor—"

"Wait." Grant pointed to the twine someone had looped around the cat's neck. The other end was tied to the hot water faucet. "We'll need to call a team to photograph this—if your animal will quit devouring the evidence."

Though blood caked much of his fur, Borracho didn't look especially unhappy with his situation. Yet. Grant had the distinct impression the tabby would have one hell of a bellyache before the day was over. This stuff smelled none too fresh.

"But he can't eat that—it's disgusting," Luz Maria

said, only hesitating at the warning growl that vibrated in the cat's throat. Clearly, the animal didn't want his meal interrupted.

Luz Maria pointed out a honeycombed white glob, which stood out amid the browns and reds. "Is that . . . ? That's *tripas.*"

"Tripe?" he guessed. He'd never been tempted to try the stuff, which he'd heard lined the stomach of a cow.

She shuddered. "My mother puts it in *menudo.* You know, the soup?"

"I've heard of it." He remembered seeing it on the menu of a Mexican restaurant where he ate. Now that he knew what was in it, he decided that sticking with tacos and fajitas seemed like a good bet.

"So what's this other stuff?" she asked, her nose crinkling with distaste.

"Offal, all of it, probably from a butcher. See, there's part of a liver, and I think those are chicken gizzards. And that's a kidney, isn't—"

Her braid slapped against his arm as she whipped her head around and backed into the hallway. "Ughh. I don't want to see and smell this. I don't want to even hear about it. I just want to take my cat and get the hell out of here."

He glanced over to see her reaching for the doorknob of another closed door off the hallway. "Don't touch that."

She hesitated, her hand only an inch or two from the shiny silver knob. Though she stared down at it distrustfully, she told him, "I have to get some clothes. There's no way I can stay here."

"He might have left fingerprints," Grant told her, though he was more concerned with what else he might have left behind that door. In a break-in, stalkers tended to focus their sick attentions in and around the victim's bed.

"It's not even closed tight. See? Why don't I just push it open with my elbow?"

She was right. The door had been left open a crack, now that he looked closely. Still, Grant shook his head and hurried after her, careful to avoid the bloody splotches that were now part of a crime scene. "No way. Get back from there."

He grabbed her and pulled her back a step. Maybe a little more roughly than he meant to.

"What are you *doing?*" she demanded.

Probably getting my ass on the evening news, where you'll freaking cry to the reporters about police brutality.

But what he said was, "Bomb—he could've wired it."

Grant thought this was unlikely, but his warning had the right effect. She let him hustle her back to the counter stool where she'd been sitting earlier.

Pointing in her face, he ordered, "Stay, and don't touch anything," before fishing a cell phone from his pocket. "I'm calling in crime scene unit officers, and I'll call my partner, too. I don't care if he has gone home for the day. He can damned well drag himself out of bed and get over here to help with this."

"There can't be a bomb." Luz Maria's braid bounced back and forth with the shaking of her head. Her dark brown eyes looked dazed. "There isn't."

Grant fixed her with his sternest cop look. He didn't have time to dance around denial. "He's already tried to kill you. And you heard him threatening you on your recorder. He got inside here somehow"—Grant had seen no sign of a forced entry—"and redecorated your bathroom with gore. Even if it *does* turn out to have butcher shop origins, are you really thinking he's too nice a guy to wire your bedroom door?"

She pushed the heels of her hands against her eyes and said, "This can't be real. It *can't.*"

He'd seen countless victims dissociate from traumatic

events, but Grant couldn't remember the last time he'd wanted to pull one into his arms.

Great idea, dimwit. Why not add sexual harassment to her list of accusations? Let her do for your career what she did for the Z-man's.

The thought doused him like cold water, bringing him back to some semblance of sanity. Turning his back to Luz Maria, he placed the two calls—only to find her gone when he finally glanced back toward the stool.

"Like it or not, you're out of here," Luz Maria told Borracho. Even if it meant disturbing evidence, she wasn't about to allow the cat to eat himself to death simply because he'd growled at her.

After grabbing the more or less clean bath towel from its rack, she tossed it over the big tabby and scooped him up. Careful of her sore ribs, she shifted him to one arm, then cut the twine from his neck with a knife she'd brought from the kitchen.

"What the hell are you doing?"

In the spattered mirror, she saw Grant's big frame fill the doorway.

"Getting my cat," she said over the wriggling bundle. "As it is, he'll probably be puking for a week from this. And . . . and he might be hurt, too. Heaven knows what that sicko did to him. When I leave here, he's going straight to the vet's office."

A paw shot out from the towel, claws fully extended. Luz Maria wrapped it in a corner of the towel before dropping the knife onto the counter. "Oh, knock it off," she told Borracho. "It's not like he can neuter you *again.*"

From the corner of her eye, she thought she saw Grant wince. In sympathy, no doubt. Another time, she might have smiled, but the blood-spattered confines of the room were closing in on her and filling her nostrils with the sickly stench.

Fortunately, Grant stepped aside when she hurried out into the hallway. Maybe he'd seen in her eyes that she was about to lose it.

"All right," he was saying. "Go ahead and take your damned cat. He was mucking up the scene, anyhow."

Good of the man, to give her permission after she had already done the deed. It reminded her of one of those things Jack would do to save face.

Sometimes, she and Reagan even let him get away with it. Luz Maria did the same for Grant now, not out of fond forbearance, but because she didn't want to take the time to argue. Not when every atom of her being was hell-bent on escaping this apartment.

"Can I leave now?" she asked Grant as she swaddled the cat more securely. "I'll go to my brother's house. Reagan should be there with their little boy today."

Luz Maria thought of crashing on their couch for a while, then playing with Adam once she felt human. Her nephew was into building blocks these days and some public TV show about a guy named Bob the Builder. He'd told his dad the other day that he wanted to be a "hammer man" when he grew up.

It sounded like a slice of heaven, à la mode.

Investigator Holcomb's head shook, a grim look settling over his handsome features like a storm cloud smothering the sun. "Sorry, Ms. Montoya. I can't let you go out on your own. It's not safe—and we'll need to have your vehicle checked, too."

Luz Maria saw herself inside her SUV, saw her fingers turning the key in the ignition. Imagined the blast and smoke and fire as they consumed her. Grant's face blurred and her knees weakened.

"Luz Maria," he said sharply.

She blinked at the intensity in his expression, her interest quickening at the sound of her name on his lips.

She wished he would repeat it, wished he would draw her close to that hard body and . . .

She shook her head, bewildered that the seeds of shock and horror would bear such unlikely fruit. Maybe the parking lot assault *had* left her senses scrambled, making her forget how badly she needed to get someplace safe and familiar. And making her forget the tragic consequences of allowing lust to overrule her judgment.

Or maybe the sexy investigator was enough to short-circuit any woman's resolution. Even one he despised.

Investigator Holcomb pressed his palm to the small of her back, then guided Luz Maria toward the living room.

"Let's get you off your feet," he said, his voice little more than a low rumble.

A low rumble that jerked Luz Maria's thoughts once more out of living rooms and into bedrooms. Humiliation stung her face. *He's afraid I'm passing out, that's all.*

So why did his touch seem to burn through the thin layers of her clothing? Why did images flicker through her mind of the two of them on her fiery red sofa, their bodies tangling together, unquenchable as flame?

Borracho yowled and struggled, diverting Luz Maria's thoughts from their insane course. Stepping away from the investigator's touch, she concentrated on sounding steadier than she felt. "Grab that cat carrier, will you? It's tucked away under that lamp table right there. Otherwise, we'll both be wearing claw marks."

As if to prove her right, her pet redoubled his efforts to escape.

Grant grabbed the kennel and flipped it open, then held it while she slipped Borracho inside. The moment he latched the door, the tabby turned and hissed, then tried to bite him through the bars.

"Nice animal," Grant said as he snatched his hand clear.

"Not usually," she agreed, "but believe it or not, he has his moments."

"Those must be *some* moments." Grant lifted the carrier by its handle. "Come on, let's wait out on the porch for reinforcements. It might be a little hot out there, but at least we won't have to worry about touching anything we shouldn't."

As she followed him toward the front door, Luz Maria tried not to think of the one thing she particularly needed to keep her hands off. Swallowing, she dragged her gaze from his rear and wondered who she could call to have her suddenly overactive hormones locked up in a convent.

As Luz Maria turned to close the door behind her, the telephone on the counter began to ring. In the silence of the apartment, it sounded obscenely loud, like a siren long past midnight, a nightmare punctured by a scream.

Grant was there before the second ring, but the caller ID window told him nothing.

"Private number," he read aloud. "Is this a speaker phone?"

She shook her head, a flush rising to her cheeks to counteract the pallor that had scared him in the bathroom. Hurrying beside him, she snatched up the receiver before he could decide whether to let the machine get it.

He leaned close to her to hear interaction with the caller—and hoped it *was* the bastard on the phone. Maybe sheer excitement would get him saying more than whatever he had scripted.

"How do you like having *your* pain exposed, bitch?" the altered voice asked in the same deep, grotesquely garbled tones they'd heard on her answering machine.

"I saw you. Did you know that? I can see you now. And always. I'll see you anywhere you run."

Beside Grant, Luz Maria pulled back her shoulders and raised her chin in defiance. "You think that worries me?"

Grant knew she was feigning the confidence he had so often seen—and cursed—on his TV screen. He had already seen evidence she had been shaken to the core by what had happened last night, as well as by the violation of her home. And now he knew another thing as well: Luz Maria Montoya was one hell of a bluffer.

But after a brief pause, the caller gave a mocking laugh. "Nice try," he told her, "but I could hear the screaming."

So he was nearby. Or else he'd planted a microphone while he was inside the apartment. Grant glanced around, wondering, *Could there be a camera, too?* Spy cameras were readily available, both online and in specialty shops that catered to those paranoid about their nannies or their spouses. And to the technically savvy pervert, too.

Around the department, Grant had heard that an alarming number were turning up in night club ladies' rooms, girls' showers in high school locker rooms, even a local gynecologist's office. Apparently, there was a burgeoning online market for hidden camera pictures.

Somehow, it pissed him off even more to think of some sick bastard getting his rocks off watching Luz Maria's terror.

"I could see you crying, too, my little Looozie." The caller's cruelty seemed to ooze through the receiver. "I'll be happy to lick those tears clean for you, as soon as you send off your boyfriend."

Sonofabitch, thought Grant. The man knew he was here. But at least he hadn't made him for a cop yet. Could be his microphone, if there was one, hadn't picked up Grant's and Luz Maria's entire conversation. Or maybe the caller wasn't the sharpest knife in the drawer. Most stalker types weren't, since their judgment was generally clouded by their emotional shortcomings.

"He's not my—" Luz Maria started.

Grant covered the receiver's mouthpiece with his palm, then put a finger to his lips to shush her.

"He's none of your business," she amended, catching on more quickly than, say, Grant's partner Billy usually did.

"I could kill him for you, Looozie. Get him out of our way so we can be . . . together."

Grant had had enough. Grabbing the phone from Luz Maria, he snarled, "You think you can handle me, you get your sick, pathetic ass over here right now."

A clicking sound rewarded his outburst, followed by a dial tone. Grant swore, mainly at his failure to keep his temper in check. Who knew how much more the suspect would have spilled had he continued threatening his intended audience? But Grant doubted he could keep his mouth shut even if the bastard called back. And if the stupid shit did show up, he was going to have far worse bruises than the ones he'd left on Luz Maria.

She was staring at him, her dark eyes worried. "Maybe you should get your gun now. Did you leave it in your car?"

He nodded. "All right. I'll do that, but he's not really coming. He's a coward, Luz Maria, a man who needs a shopping cart to rush an unsuspecting—and much smaller—woman. A man who slinks around in secret attacking kitty cats with meat by-products."

She laughed, as she had on the front porch before they'd come in. He loved the sound of it, loved the feeling that he had been the one to wring it from her. But he realized he wanted more than laughter from this woman.

He wanted her to cry his name as he made her come.

He clamped down on the unsettling thought, more disgusted with himself than ever. This woman, this freaking *activist* was damned well out of bounds. Touching her—hell, even *fantasizing* about touching her—was the worst betrayal he could imagine. What would Roy Reed, Zeman's good friend and former partner, say? And what about John's widow, Sherry?

Turning away from her, he stalked out of the apartment and trotted down the steps without a backward glance. His heart was hammering by the time he reached his car, an old blue Mercedes roadster that he'd picked up cheap from a guy about to do three to five for—who'd have guessed it—grand theft auto. It was impractical as hell, a two-seater that sucked gas like an SUV, but the convertible had checked out as legal and proved to be in great shape. And even more importantly, the sight of it gleaming in his driveway brought back the day Grant had looked down from a grimy bus window—another of his old man's heaps had just been repoed—and concluded that the Mercedes roadster was class and style itself. Told his mama and his daddy that one day he would own one.

He'd never forget the old man's bitter laughter or the way his mom had pinched and whispered at him not to antagonize his father. She had left a mark that day—and scarred his heart with a desire that had lain dormant until his friendly neighborhood car thief had tossed him the keys.

He used those same keys now to unlock the trunk, where he had left his shoulder holster with his Glock. As he was pulling it on, he finally turned and saw that Luz Maria hadn't followed.

He stood there for a beat, staring into the space he had expected her to fill, wondering at the empty feeling it aroused. And at the prickle of fear behind his neck, followed by the marrow-freezing whisper, *What if there isn't a bomb behind the bedroom door? What if Luz Maria's attacker is hiding there instead, a cell phone in one hand and a weapon in the other?*

Cursing his own stupidity, Grant slammed the trunk's lid and took off for the stairs at a dead run. With every pounding footfall, self-recriminations hit him.

Why didn't you take her by the hand? Or why not, at the very least, leave her standing on the covered porch where you could see her? Are you trying to get her naked—or do you mean to get her killed?

Because by leaving her inside alone, he had left her vulnerable to whatever surprises her tormenter had hidden in her room.

CHAPTER EIGHT

Though she was still reeling from the phone call, it dawned on Luz Maria that there was one thing in her apartment she absolutely couldn't let the police find. She knew they would be searching her apartment for evidence against whoever had broken in. Still, she didn't believe for a second they'd resist the temptation to take her personal file on one of their own investigators— particularly one who had died by his own hand.

Normally, she kept her case files in her VOP office, but she'd been so worried a subpoena could make her most vulnerable sources public knowledge, she'd taped this particular manila envelope beneath the top of her lamp table.

The moment Investigator Holcomb started down the steps, she made a beeline for it, ripped it free, and shoved it deep inside her shoulder bag. With John Zeman dead and the case long closed, she should have burned the contents of that file two years ago. It was an oversight she intended to correct as soon as possible.

Less than a minute later, Luz Maria walked the few

steps next door shifting Borracho's carrier to the opposite hand as she went—the old alley cat felt like an anchor—and knocked at the neighboring apartment door a second time.

What could Kellie be up to? Just the other day, when they'd bumped into each other at the mailboxes, she'd told Luz Maria she had a project deadline that had her all but chained to her computer. No golf for her this week. Had she conked out after pulling an all-nighter? Luz Maria smiled at an image of her friend snoring at her desk, empty cans of Diet Coke vying for space with her equipment.

Luz Maria's head tilted at a faint sound. Had it come from inside?

She turned, recognizing the thump of footsteps on the metal staircase. Grant Holcomb reached the landing and strode toward her, his eyes blazing.

"What the hell are you doing, standing out here? I thought you were right behind me, and then I turn and see—"

Luz Maria couldn't understand his anger. "I was only taking Borracho over to ask Kellie if she could spare a few minutes to run him to the vet. I thought I might be stuck here a while, with the police coming—"

"Don't you get it?" he demanded. "This guy could be anywhere—in one of those houses across the street or down by the bayou looking through binoculars, in a parked vehicle with a scoped weapon in his hand. Hell, Luz Maria, he could be in the damned closet of your bedroom, for all we know. You're in danger—or do I have to play that answering machine message again to get it through your head?"

She closed her eyes and struggled to banish the horrifying images his words set off. As much as she would like to tell herself Grant was only trying to scare her, she couldn't deny that he was right.

And when had her thoughts gotten on a first name basis with the investigator, anyway?

From the parking lot below, she heard car doors slamming. Grant stepped back to take a look.

"It's our crime scene officers," he said, "and my partner's just pulled up, too. Stay with one of us and we'll keep you safe."

Luz Maria wished she felt as confident. With her life whirling out of her control, she questioned everything—including the cops' motivation to keep a troublesome activist out of harm's way. Yet, for the time being, she kept her mouth shut. There was no sense in antagonizing the people who were supposed to protect and serve her.

An armed female member of the crime scene unit waited with Luz Maria on the porch long enough for Grant Holcomb and his partner, Investigator Devlin, to check the entire apartment. Luz Maria shifted from foot to foot and tried not to think of what they might find in her bedroom.

The officer, a stocky black woman with a white streak in her cropped hair, gave Luz Maria a sympathetic look. "Is there someone you'd like to call?"

"I need . . ." Luz Maria shot a last, regretful glance at Kellie's door. What she'd really hoped for was a friendly face, and unlike Jack and her mother, her neighbor wouldn't use this latest incident as more evidence that a career change was in order. "I really should contact my office. Our security officer will want to know what's happened right away."

A knot inside her loosened at the thought of Jason Whitfield. Between his professionalism and his snarky running commentary on her outfits, he always put her mind at ease.

The older woman nodded and blotted perspiration from her face with a folded tissue. She must be dying in that blue jumpsuit she was wearing.

"You go ahead and do that," she invited, "but I'm afraid we can't let you use the phone in your apartment. We'll be checking it for prints—and bugs, too. And I don't mean the kind you spray for."

Luz Maria's first impulse was to argue, to tell her that her life wasn't a 007 movie, with wire taps and heaven only knew what else. But since the impossible had leached into her world already, a listening device probably wasn't such a stretch.

"I have my cell here in my bag." Luz Maria had set her purse on top of Borracho's crate, which she'd been careful to place in full shade. The cat was already mad enough without being cooked, too.

She dug the phone out and punched the speed dial code that Whit had told her to use in an emergency. He swore he kept his cell phone handy at all times.

True to form, he answered on the second ring. "Where on earth *are* you, sweetie? When I went to check on you this morning, you'd already left the hospital. You know you should have called me."

"Sorry—you're right. I . . . I've got some trouble here at my . . . at my apartment." She pressed her fingers to her forehead and forced back the threat of tears. "There's been a . . . a break-in, and he called here."

"Oh, Lord. I should have been with you. I'm out in Clear Lake right now, but I'll get there as soon as I can."

Clear Lake? A far-flung suburb southeast of Houston, it was a place Luz Maria associated with great Gulf seafood, expensive yachts, and nearby NASA. What was Whit doing down there now, the morning after she had been attacked? Before she could ask, he was hurling questions her way.

"Are you safe now, Luz Maria? Tell me you're not calling from your apartment—are you?"

"It's all right, Whit. The police are here. I'll be fine

until you make it." Even if she couldn't quite remember what "fine" felt like.

She ended the call as Grant Holcomb stepped out of her apartment.

"You can come back inside," he said. "Just stick to the living room and kitchen area."

"What about my bedroom? Is everything all right there?" At least she hadn't heard a blast from that direction.

Grant winced. "You'll want to stay out of there until the team's through. It's . . . uh . . . I'm afraid it's pretty messed up."

Her stomach clenched. "Oh, no . . . Is it . . . is it more of that . . ." She winced at the thought of the bloody organs in her bathroom. The smell alone was enough to . . .

But the tall investigator shook his head. "No. It was more on the order of the typical vandalism we see in stalker cases. Drawers pulled out, clothing cut up—particular attention to the . . . uh . . . undergarments."

She ground her fingertips into her temples and wished she'd taken her brother's advice and squeezed the cost of renter's insurance out of her budget. At least she'd left her laptop computer locked up in her Honda, but how was she going to afford the cost of replacing her wardrobe, repairing any damage—even moving out? She damned well wasn't staying where that sick man had been.

Though she didn't think of herself as prudish, Luz Maria felt embarrassed, too, that all these strangers—and especially Investigator Holcomb—would be looking at her private things. She felt stripped to the skin, exposed and violated.

Madre mía, it was boiling out here on this porch.

Grant Holcomb touched her elbow, gently nudging

her toward the apartment door. "Come on in. Your cat's getting hot there, and you should cool off, too."

"Lord knows *I'm* ready for some air-conditioning." Picking up her collection kit, the black woman entered the apartment and joined her colleague, who was already taking photos in the bathroom.

Grant called to the two of them, "That knife in the sink will have Ms. Montoya's prints on it. She took it in to cut her cat free. You can see the twine still on the faucet."

"Jason Whitfield's on his way," Luz Maria told him. "He's going to want to see the—he'll want to see everything."

From the tropical-bright ruins of her salsa dresses right down to her damned *chones*—from the bikinis to her one and only thong. Only sheer determination kept her from groaning at the thought.

Grant scrubbed his hand over his lower face, which needed shaving worse than ever. His eyes looked tired, a reminder that he had worked all night. "Whitfield may be your group's security advisor, or whatever the guy's title is, but he's still a civilian. As such, he can see the scene once we've released it. Otherwise, he'll have to—"

"He'll be here in about an hour," she said, taking traffic into consideration. "You can argue about it with him then."

Irritation flickered across his features. She saw disdain in his face, too, an echo of the same hatred that had alarmed her earlier.

"I'm not spending my vacation arguing with anybody," he snarled.

"No one's asking you to spend your vacation here at all." It felt good to snap back at the big jerk. Waving him off, she added, "Why don't you go on, then? I wouldn't want to make you lose your place in line at Splashtown—or is it the zoo?"

His frown deepened. "Look, I know you probably need to yell at someone right now. But that someone's not me. If you really need to do some screaming—"

Inspector Devlin wandered out of the bedroom. He was wearing jeans with an untucked green golf shirt.

"—you go ahead and talk to *him*," Grant concluded.

"What?" Devlin glanced suspiciously at his partner. "What'd you tell her?"

"Oh, nothing at all, partner. Just that you're my go-to guy if Ms. Montoya here needs to crack some *huevos*."

At Devlin's blank look and Holcomb's wink, Luz Maria laughed, caught completely off guard by his comment. Though it was actually the term for "eggs," it had the same double meaning as the English word "balls."

This guy wasn't just good-looking, he was also outrageous.

And in spite of everything she'd been through—and every reason she had to be on guard—she was starting to like Grant Holcomb very much.

When Grant's official cell phone started ringing, he had the feeling the other shoe was about to drop. One glance at the number clinched it. The area code was southwestern Louisiana.

"Aw, hell." He made eye contact with his partner. "I'd better take this outside."

Lieutenant Marie-Therese Mouton had taken leave to visit Lafayette, Louisiana, where her daughter-in-law had given birth to Marie-Therese's first grandchild. If Mutton—as she was not-so-affectionately known in the department—was interrupting her adoration of the princeling to call Grant, it meant only one thing.

His ass was about to get chewed out by the ragin' Cajun grandma.

As he made for the front door, he noticed Billy look

away. Had the little shit called her to rat him out in an attempt to curry favor? Grant shot a withering look in his new partner's direction, then answered the phone on the front porch.

"Holcomb, what the *fuck* do you think you're doing?" a furious female voice demanded.

"Well, Lieutenant, guess I win the station pool. Everyone else was betting the new grandbaby would've knocked a little of the edge off for a while."

Grant said it to buy time, but judging from the stream of abuse that spewed from his earpiece in response, he would have done better choosing something less incendiary. Maybe a comparison between the size of Mutton's ass and the Astrodome, or a diatribe against women in positions of authority.

Once the shouting more or less subsided, Grant moved the phone back to his ear and said, "Sorry, Lieutenant. Did your daughter-in-law get that package from me and Billy? The little blue blanket with the train?"

The suck-up gift had been Billy's idea, but Grant had to admit it was a pretty good one. As often as he got on the lieutenant's nerves, he could stand to rack up all the positive karma he could muster.

"It's ninety-three goddamned degrees in Lafayette," Mouton shouted. "This kid needs a blanket like I need two assholes. Wait, I've already got two assholes. You and a spare."

"You mean Devlin, right?" Grant watched a second marked squad car cruise slowly along the street.

This time, Mouton managed to ignore him and stay on track. "Explain to me right now why you are on the scene with Ms. Montoya after you were asked this morning to steer clear of her? No more bullshit, and no more setting me off like a goddamned Roman candle. Just a simple answer, Holcomb. Or you will rue this day."

Grant grimaced as, mentally, he gave the roulette

wheel of assorted lies, half-truths, and diversions one last spin. But as Lady Luck would have it, the ball stopped on the truth. After all, this *was* Lieutenant Mouton, and he'd already jerked her around more than a wiser man would dare.

"I thought I was coming over here to give her nine kinds of hell for calling to complain about me—and maybe to bring the subject around again to the Z-man," he explained.

"Grant . . ." She sounded disappointed. Defeated, too, just as she had on the last occasion she had called him by his first name. It was the day she'd met him at John Zeman's, the day she'd walked into that hellish bathroom and asked him—then *ordered* him—to stop cleaning. To get the hell out of there, go home, and wait for a call from one of the department's crisis counselors.

He'd disobeyed her that day. He remembered it so clearly—except that somehow, in his mind, John's bathroom had morphed into Luz Maria's.

"I didn't do it," he told the lieutenant. "I meant to, but I . . . Ms. Montoya was right to be disturbed by my behavior. I told her so, and I apologized."

"You? Apologized?"

Grant grinned, amused by the incredulity in Mouton's voice. "It's been known to happen—on those rare occasions I'm actually wrong."

The lieutenant refused to rise to the bait, instead demanding, "Do you have any idea the trouble that young woman could cause you? The trouble she could make for the department?"

His empty stomach soured. "You think there's any way I could forget?"

The connection crackled, and he wondered if Marie-Therese Mouton was remembering the same things he was. And if they hurt her even half as much.

"No," she said. "I don't. So why? Why the hell are

you still at the scene? I know you were present when a break-in was discovered. And in spite of your incredibly poor judgment—not to mention your defiance of Lieutenant Chapman's order this morning to stay clear of that woman—I understand why you stayed until backup arrived. But you're no longer a part of this investigation. Take your vacation, Holcomb. I suggest somewhere out of town."

"I can solve this case," he said, raising his voice as the crackling grew louder. "I can prove to her that we help *everybody*, not just the rich and white. I can put aside my feelings, Lieutenant. I can damned well show I'm capable of—"

A movement caught his attention. Luz Maria in the open doorway, a bottled water in her hand, the beads of condensation on its slick sides attesting to its coldness. In a fraction of a second, he understood that she'd been bringing him the water. That she'd heard what he'd just said.

Shit.

But Lieutenant Mouton was saying, "Let Devlin worry about it. It's time for you to go home. Now. And don't let me hear about you disobeying another order." Static obliterated her next few words. ". . . don't want to . . . haul my ass all the way . . . Lafayette to start the paperwork on disciplinary actions against you. Serious disciplinary actions. You catch that, Investigator Holcomb?"

"Yeah. Yes, ma'am," he said. "I made that out just fine. I'm on my way, then. Straight home."

When the lieutenant broke the connection, Grant shut off his phone. He wasn't taking any more damned calls.

"I'm sorry," Luz Maria said. "I didn't mean to overhear. I only thought . . . I only thought you might like something cold to drink."

He sighed. "I sure would. You got any Shiner Bock? Might as well make it a beer, now that I'm off duty."

She pushed the water into his hand, then fixed him with her unblinking gaze. "You shouldn't be on this case. We both understand that. We both remember why. But that doesn't mean you're not a good cop. Or a good man."

Of all the things he'd expected from her, understanding was the last. He wanted to tell her to save it for her poor and voiceless. Instead, he wrapped his fingers around the plastic bottle and twisted off its top.

"Thanks," he said quietly. "And damn you, Ms. Montoya."

Her brows flashed upward, a clear question.

"It was a lot easier when I could just hate you," he explained. "A lot less strain on my mental health when I could just chalk you up as some kind of misguided, raving lunatic from hell."

Her smile was gentle, but the sparkle in her eyes warned him there was more than a bleeding heart behind that pretty face. "Would it make you feel better if I told you I'd just spit in your drink?"

He took a swig to show he didn't buy it.

Devlin stepped up behind her, his protective plastic shoe covers crinkling. Though the red-haired investigator had to be ready to sleep after last night's shift, his blue eyes were bright with interest. "You'll want to see this—in the bathroom."

He looked as unabashed as he was serious. Maybe he hadn't been the one who'd called Mutton after all.

"You find the microphone?" Grant guessed.

"Looks like one of those pinhole cameras—wireless," he said. "Bollenbacher found it hidden inside the tissue box."

"Yeah? Wonder if it has audio capability, or if there's

a mike planted elsewhere." Grant started inside, forgetting himself—until he noticed Luz Maria's quizzical expression.

He drew himself up short, then swore. "I'm done here, Billy. That was Lieutenant Mouton on the phone."

The kid's eyes widened. "She called to chew you out from Lafayette?"

"Wonders of technology," Grant murmured before telling him, "You're lead investigator now on this case. You need any help, though, or just to bounce around ideas, ask Investigator McCracken or Sergeant Johnson. But whatever you do, don't bother calling me."

Luz Maria looked as if she wanted to say something. Before she could, Grant turned on his heel and walked away. As his feet pounded down the metal steps, his fatigue began to lift. By the time he reached the roadster, he had started whistling.

Not with the carefree spirit of an officer heading off for two weeks of relaxation, but with the perverse pleasure of a man driving away with the VOP threat files "forgotten" in the trunk of his Mercedes.

CHAPTER NINE

Luz Maria sat on the sofa, her eyes closed and her face tipped upward to catch the ceiling fan's breeze. She prayed to Jesus, Mary, and any saints who might be listening that Detective Devlin was finished asking questions, and that the crime scene unit officers were finished with their work, too. She wanted Whit to hurry up and get there, wanted him to take charge so she could curl up somewhere and sleep.

Somewhere dark and dreamless, where she wouldn't have to see the blood or hear that hideous voice. Somewhere that was anywhere but there. But the person speaking at her front door wasn't Jason Whitfield, or anyone she'd considered calling to pick her up.

"I simply won't take no for an answer. I *must* see her this minute."

Luz Maria groaned at the tone of April Walsh's cultivated but ever-so-insistent voice. The uniformed officer standing at the door seemed unfazed by her demand.

"Sorry, ma'am." The cop sported a salt-and-pepper flattop, a stomach that lapped over his duty belt, and the impenetrable firmness of a veteran people-handler. "I can't let you come inside—and I'm especially not allowing that cameraman."

Luz Maria's eyes sprang open as she blasted off the sofa. Leave it to April to show up with the press in tow—or the usual sorry excuse she rounded up on short notice. A scruffy-looking Anglo guy wearing an unruly beard beneath a graying thatch, round glasses, and ripped jeans pointed a camcorder over April's shoulder at the cop's face. Luz Maria had never liked O'Toole, a freelance cameraman who was always sniffing for footage he could sell to one of the affiliates. Preferably something involving civil unrest, blood, and gore.

She also knew he'd donate a kidney for a shot of the scene inside her apartment. But Luz Maria hadn't the faintest intention of allowing that bottom feeder—or even the Voice of Poverty—to profit from some lunatic's acts.

"I'll talk to them outside, officer." Luz Maria moved so she could catch his eye. "You're welcome to close the door behind me."

He took the hint and did so, effectively blocking any shots the cameraman might get of Investigator Devlin or the crime scene unit officers as they moved from room to room.

"Luz Maria, we could really use that footage." April pouted as she fussed with short, platinum-blond hair that looked as if she'd just rolled out of bed. But then, April was into artfully tousled these days, along with up-to-the-minute skirted suits and sandals that stretched the limits of her trust fund allowance. Today's works of art were strappy, brilliant turquoise, and a far cry from the on-sale footwear Luz Maria could afford. "Is there a window we could peek through?"

"I'm okay, April," Luz Maria grumbled. "Thanks for asking."

April blinked, her green eyes flashing as if someone had just pushed her brain's power switch to the On position. "Oh. Sorry, Luz Maria. But Whit said you were handling it just fine."

"You've talked to Whit? Where *is* he? I've been waiting for him to—"

"He's had some kind of complication. Down in Clear Lake, at the Coleman house."

Luz Maria knew she'd heard the name recently, but she couldn't quite place it. Wait. He was the man who'd been shot last night, the man Grant Holcomb thought could have been hurt by her assailant.

"*Tony* Coleman's house? His family's all the way in *Clear Lake?* So what would he be doing at a grocery store near—"

April waved a perfectly manicured hand in dismissal. "I don't know. That's Whit's department. But he called me to say I needed to come and get you out of here."

"And this explains the cameraman how?" asked Luz Maria before she noticed the camcorder's red light was on. "Turn that damned thing off this minute, O'Toole. In fact, get off my porch."

He backed away a few steps and shot her an aggrieved look before popping the lens cap on his camera. To April, he said, "I thought you told me she'd be thrilled with the publicity."

"You thought I'd be thrilled?" Luz Maria couldn't believe her ears. "With which part—being attacked and nearly strangled or having my place broken into? *Ay, basura!*"

And it *was* garbage. Every bit of it. But she refused to give the gory particulars within the cameraman's hearing. For all she knew, the sleaze was recording her every word for radio.

April heaved a long-suffering sigh. "Stan, would you mind waiting for me in your van?"

He shrugged. "Okay, but if I hear anything wicked on the scanner, I'm like totally out of here."

As he disappeared down the stairwell, April rolled her eyes and mimicked, "Like totally."

"Why do you keep calling that lowlife to shoot VOP footage?" Luz Maria asked irritably. "Does he have blackmail pictures of you with a goat or something?"

Anger flashed over April's face, but a moment later, she recovered, saying, "I guess I deserved that. I suppose you think I'm horribly insensitive." She tried to hug her coworker, a consolation Luz Maria neatly sidestepped, along with April's obvious angling for forgiveness.

Even at the best of times, Luz Maria was none too fond of her coworker's methods. Or maybe it was the woman herself that she resented. Born into an archconservative family whose wealth and influence placed her out of reach of the problems of the needy, April Walsh, with her Ivy League degree and glib, liberal slogans, often struck Luz Maria as insincere. Besides, at the office April always switched Luz Maria's Tex-Mex stations to her beloved classic rock.

"Look, hon," April said. "I . . . I'm sorry if I came off as crass. But VOP is really struggling. As I told everyone at the meeting Monday, we all have to face facts. Unless donations pick up, the Houston office won't last through the end of the year. We've already cut our operating expenses to the bare bones, even salaries."

Luz Maria knew all about the cuts, since she was suddenly having trouble making the payments on her Honda. April herself didn't accept a salary, which was just as well since the little they could offer wouldn't keep her in designer handbags. She only did the work to—actually, Luz Maria wasn't sure why. Maybe so she'd show up on her parents' radar, since both were powerhouses on Houston's philanthropic scene.

"VOP should be supported because of the work we

do," Luz Maria insisted. "Not because of some sick *pendejo's* actions."

Besides that, she was thinking, *are you trying to paint a target on my back by giving creeps the media attention they crave?*

April frowned—or at least that was what Luz Maria supposed she was attempting. Though the blonde was only thirty-one, she'd had Botox treatments that made a mockery of her expressions.

"Don't you get it?" April asked, her voice sliding up the scale in both volume and intensity. "If something doesn't change soon, we won't be doing any more good works. You won't get to help the day care grandma or the baseball player's bastard. You won't get to stick up for hurricane evacuees when scam artists rip them off or save little girls brought here from Mexico or Asia to be whored out to any sleaze with twenty dollars."

Her voice broke, and Luz Maria saw tears gleaming in her eyes. For the first time, she understood that, rich or not, April Walsh really *did* care about the work. And deeply, contrary to her privileged upbringing and her obsession with her personal appearance.

After three years spent working with the woman, it was a revelation, one that had Luz Maria softening her tone—and sharing something she never spoke of willingly. "Once upon a time, April, I let myself be convinced that the ends justify the means. Whatever means were needed. I believed that sufficiently worthy goals could not be tainted. I let expressions like 'acceptable sacrifices' and 'collateral damage' creep into my thinking."

"What do you mean?"

Luz Maria shook her head, refusing to be drawn into sharing more ugly memories. But that didn't stop her from seeing the video footage of the victims being carried out after the bombing of an immigration office in

San Antonio. From hearing Sergio's voice explaining it away, telling her that the perpetrators would be punished, that these radicals' actions did not reflect the true spirit of BorderFree-4-All.

"I mean," she explained, "it's something I'll regret to my last breath. A mistake, a compromise I would give my life to take back."

Luz Maria cleared her throat and fought the sting of tears. God, she was tired. "Don't compromise yourself, April. And don't compromise the Voice of Poverty. Not even to save it."

"We'd only be taking a few pictures of someone's attempt to silence us." April sounded defensive now. "It's not as if we staged whatever went on in your apartment so we could cash in."

Luz Maria shuddered at the statement. She never would have come up with that possibility. Not in a hundred years.

"And people really do care about you," April added. "Why, just since news of your attack leaked out this morning, I've had calls from individuals asking where they can send money. A lot of them are people you've helped in the past."

"And that's not enough for you?" Luz Maria asked, even as she wondered if April had been the one who'd tipped off reporters.

April's head shook, but the artfully tossed hair didn't budge. "Those people don't have any money. Not *real* money, anyway."

The comment infuriated Luz Maria, pushing her to voice a question that had been bugging her for years. "If things are really that bad, why don't you ask your mom and dad to help us? Can't they organize another one of their galas, shake some of those corporate money trees they've been cultivating?"

April's eyes narrowed, warning Luz Maria she had crossed a line. "They have their causes, I have mine."

Luz Maria decided a change of subject was definitely in order. "Uh, let me step inside and talk to the detective in charge. If they're about finished, I really would like to get out of here, if you're still up for giving me that ride."

The fire in April's green eyes was banked, but her tight smile gave off the frozen fumes of dry ice. "I can do that, Luz Maria. Any place you want."

Like a lot of cops working in the fourth largest U.S. city, Investigator Grant Holcomb felt the need to retreat from Houston at the end of each shift. But thanks to urban sprawl, the damned city was coming out to meet him, splaying arms of commercial development and traffic toward the little house he'd bought outside the small town of Magnolia. So far—and he hoped like hell it lasted—the pretty little town, with its huge trees, gently rolling pastures, and peacefully grazing horses had pretty much survived. Yet it was changing daily as well-heeled suburbanites snapped up the five to twenty-acre "executive ranchettes" being offered in the area.

Grant swung off a dirt road and onto the long, pea gravel driveway of the tan brick, older three-bedroom he called home. Situated in the middle of five mostly wooded acres, the one-story house had been in foreclosure three years earlier and Grant had recognized it for the bargain that it was.

He and Jennifer had had big plans when he'd first bought it. Plans to remodel the dated kitchen and two bathrooms and to replace the small windows with larger ones so they could look out at the birds and deer. She would shit a brick if she saw that he hadn't even gotten around to replacing the ugly, rust-colored carpet from the eighties, that he hadn't done a damned thing except to keep the place from falling down around his ears.

But Jennifer no longer had a vote, since the wedding hadn't quite happened the way they'd planned. Hadn't happened at all, to be specific.

Grant swore and dropped the VOP file box onto his dust-coated coffee table, scattering a stack of magazines, unsorted mail, and a crime novel he'd been reading. Every now and then after a long night, fatigue got him thinking about her, about the life that never quite got off the ground. Like that was doing anybody a god-damned bit of good.

After a shower, a shave, and a breakfast of cold pizza from the fridge, which he ate standing over the sink, Grant felt halfway human. A few hours of sleep clinched the deal.

He would have slept longer, but the file box sitting on his coffee table tugged at his dreams like a magnet, one he had no ability to resist.

He had to see if it was still there, among the three years of scribblings from the nutcases and the lovelorn, the angry and the manic. He had to know if Jason Whitfield had considered it a threat. And Grant knew he'd damned well better find it before Billy Devlin showed up—or worse yet, an officer from the Internal Affairs Division.

But in spite of his anxiety, or perhaps because of it, Grant started from the front of the files, where the most recent communications were arranged in chrono-logical order.

As long as he had them in hand, he told himself, he might as well see if any of the written, e-mailed, or phone-logged threats looked serious. What he found impressed him, not the array of messages, which ranged from pathetic to unnerving, but their meticulous orga-nization. Each one had been stapled behind what appeared to be a computer-generated cover form that included the date and time of receipt, a checked box from the list of categories—Inappropriate/Unusual Interest, Hostile/Aggressive Communication, Threatening Act/Words Reported by Other, Rambling/Incoherent Message, or Other Concern—along with the signature of the VOP staff member who had received it. In addition, a series of boxes categorized the communicator, from anonymous to what someone, probably Whitfield, termed a "Frequent Flyer."

At the bottom of each numbered form, Grant found a summary paragraph and a threat level assessment, printed in blue, orange, or red, which seemed to indicate increasing severity. Though Whitfield's form and terminology didn't precisely jibe with Grant's police department training, they'd clearly been created by a professional.

Grant's stomach knotted at the realization that a guy this organized would have made copies—had probably even typed and backed up computer transcripts of every suspect communication.

Including the one that Grant had written almost two years before.

Luz Maria didn't wake up until a tongue lapped at her ear. Frank Lee's slimy tongue, to be specific.

Grumpily, she pushed his long white head away and murmured, "Dooooon't."

The retired racing greyhound merely wagged his tail and grinned, showing teeth that could use brushing. Not that she was volunteering for the job. Her sister-in-law's pet had major dog breath.

Luz Maria rolled to put her back to him, but he snuffled in her ear again, then added quiet whimpers.

"Déjame en paz," she demanded, but the greyhound refused to cut her any slack. The dumb thing probably

wanted to go outside. Since Luz Maria had insisted that Reagan go ahead and take Adam to a birthday party as planned, the dog had no one else available to bug.

"All right, all right. You win, Frank." Luz Maria rolled off the sofa and stood stiffly. But before she could tell him that Borracho didn't have to bother her every time he needed to pee, the greyhound had achieved his true mission.

Sprawled upside down across the overstuffed blue sofa, the big lummox parked his head on her pillow and heaved a contented sigh.

"Well, I'll be darned," she told him. "I never figured you were smart enough for treachery."

She thought Borracho would approve—if he weren't currently in cat hell, being bathed and checked out by the vet who would board him for a few days. But before Luz Maria could worry too much over her pet's unhappiness, she heard a creak from what sounded like one of the wooden steps to the old bungalow's front porch, followed by the unmistakable sound of footsteps.

Her body tensed and her gaze shot to the clock that hung above the television. It was only three-thirty, too early for Jack to be coming home from work, and Reagan had said she wouldn't be back until at least four-fifteen. Besides, neither of them would come to the front door.

The greyhound rolled over and his ears stood straight up, trembling to their tips. Luz Maria knew better than to expect him to morph into a fierce protector—she'd never even heard him bark—but his alertness put her on edge.

She glanced next at the alarm panel and saw the comforting red flash that indicated it remained armed, as her sister-in-law had left it, and the deadbolt was still locked. Even so, her heart pounded as horrible images pulsed through her mind: the flash of the shopping cart with the masked face just behind it; the bloody scene inside her bathroom.

Trembling violently, Luz Maria snatched her cell phone off a lamp table, then debated whether to dial 911 first or make for the kitchen, where the back door—the only other exit—lay.

Before she made up her mind, she heard a soft tap at the front door. At the knock, Frank Lee rolled off the sofa and trotted toward the sound. Though he didn't make a peep, the white dog raised his hackles instead of wagging his tail.

The second knock was firmer, and followed by a buzz.

Cautiously, Luz Maria crept toward the peephole. A psycho wouldn't really ring the doorbell, would he?

Standing on her tiptoes to see, she peered out—and loosed the breath she had been holding. She made short work of both the alarm and deadbolt before opening the door and lighting into Jason Whitfield. "You scared me half to death, Whit. Why didn't you call me back? And where on earth have you been, anyway?"

A smile lit his baby-blue eyes. "Glad to see you, too, sweetie—and why don't you trying looking at your cell phone?"

She glanced at its screen and read, SEVEN MISSED CALLS. Most, if not all, from Whit, she'd be willing to bet.

"Sorry. I was in the shower," she said as she let him inside. "By the time I dried my hair and dressed, I was so exhausted I probably could've slept through World War Three."

Luz Maria had put on a pair of drawstring shorts and a T-shirt, both of which were Reagan's. The fit was a little off—the taller, more athletic Reagan had at least twenty pounds on her—but Luz Maria was grateful to feel clean.

"Ooh, aren't these old wood floors to die for?" Whit asked as he scanned the living and dining rooms, from the toy box in one corner to the curtained windows behind the big oak table. "And don't you worry another minute about missing my calls. I had an inkling you'd be here, so I came as soon as I could."

"The house has an alarm," she told him, knowing he was mentally critiquing her security as well as the decor. "Deadbolts on both doors, too."

"April never should have left you here alone."

Luz Maria could almost hear him thinking, *Pinhead*, or something equally unflattering. Everybody in the office had picked up on Whit's disdain for April's role in VOP. Even more than the others, he seemed to resent the need for both publicity and donations. Or maybe he was just bugged by her embarrassingly pushy attempts to set him up with every unattached gay artist she befriended.

"You can have your fairy painter boys," Whit had been heard to snap at her once. *"Leave me to my big, strapping . . . never mind that. Just stay out of my love life."*

"Reagan was here when she dropped me off," Luz Maria said to placate him. "And would have been here still, if I hadn't run her off. I couldn't sleep with her hovering over me, and Adam—he's my nephew—was all excited about his day care buddy's *Bob the Builder* theme party. I didn't want him missing it."

Whit's round face grew somber. "So they'll say you were a good aunt in your eulogy?"

Her stomach knotted. Whit could be hilarious, with his snarky comments and eye-rolling during April's fundraising pep talks, but when it came to security, he had a way of casting every risk in the bleakest light. Including those that sane people preferred not to think of.

"You don't get invited to a lot of parties, do you?" she asked.

He smirked. "That just goes to show what *you* know, sweet cakes."

"So where the heck have you been all this time, anyway? At home?" That would explain his change of clothes, from last night's shorts and T-shirt to this afternoon's sockless deck shoes, sharply creased blue jeans, and a barely wrinkled Hawaiian shirt in muted colors. To her knowledge, this was as dressed up as Whit ever got.

He ran a palm over his light brown spikes, but the gesture hid neither fatigue nor aggravation. "April didn't tell you?"

"She said you'd gotten held up in Clear Lake. Something with the Coleman family. Would that be Tony Coleman's family? The guy the cops think was shot in the Ryland's lot?"

"The very one," Whit said. "He's still critical, by the way, but for now he's hanging in there."

"I hope he makes it. But these people live in Clear Lake? Were they visiting friends in town or something?"

"That's what I was trying to find out," Whit said. "After I got back from dropping off files at the police station—I had to copy the past couple of months' worth first—I ran home, changed, and headed over to Ben Taub Hospital, but Mrs. Coleman had left to take her two boys home."

"How did you find out they lived in Clear Lake?" The way Luz Maria understood it, medical personnel were required to guard such information closely.

"There's this ICU nurse I've known a few years—fabulous dancer, I might add. He let it slip how he hoped the woman would be okay driving down there, since she was so exhausted and upset."

"So you tracked her down somehow?" she asked.

"Sure did. There weren't many Anthony Colemans in the phone directory, so it didn't take long to narrow the field to the one with two school-aged sons. Then I drove down there."

"Why, Whit? If what I understand is true, the man's in no shape to give any information yet, and his wife's already upset enough without a bunch of—"

"Coleman's a baseball coach. Kids' teams—both of them. The little boys were telling everybody at the hospital."

"That poor family . . . ," Luz Maria whispered. She didn't remember her own papa, who had been killed by renegade human smugglers while crossing the border into Mexico, where he'd been traveling to visit his mother. She'd been Adam's age when it had happened.

"He's also a huge pro baseball fan." Whit followed up the statement with a pointed look.

Luz Maria's heartbeat quickened, and she felt weak in the knees. "Don't tell me . . ."

Whit gestured toward the sofa—still dogless for the moment—and she moved to sit down. Whit took the matching blue chair across from it and leaned forward, his elbows resting on his knees, his feet planted on the oval braid rug.

Waiting, she supposed, for her to process what he'd told her—and to connect the dots with the single case that had caused more backlash than any other in her three-year career with VOP. This past May, Trey-Don Peterson, a talented young third baseman in his third season with the Astros, had been burning up the outfield, and his bat had never been hotter. Nor had his popularity, since he was a local boy who'd made good.

But the local boy had a secret that didn't mesh with the nice guy image the team was trying to project to its fans. Not only had he fathered—and subsequently refused to acknowledge or support—a child out of wedlock, he had done so with his own first cousin, who had been sixteen at the time.

Luz Maria had attempted to deal with him personally. The one time she had managed to get past his gatekeeper "assistants" and actually speak to the man, he'd been by turns defensive, defiant, and threatening. When he finally realized those tactics wouldn't shake her off, the idiot had made a pass at her, treating her as if she were some besotted groupie who could be appeased with a good—

She shuddered at the thought. Unfortunately, going public with her accusations had done more than get Peterson traded. When a losing streak ensued, VOP's and particularly Luz Maria's names became mud everywhere from call-in sports talk radio shows to bars and barbershops all over greater Houston.

And furious calls, letters, and e-mails followed, heavier than spring rains blown in off the Gulf. Threats, of course, came with them, enough that Whit had sat out in his car watching her apartment for several nights. When the Astros began winning again a few weeks later, most fans forgot their anger, and when Peterson tested positive for steroids for his new team in early July, the consensus shifted. From sportscasters to sportswriters to average Joes at the ballpark, Houstonians were glad that VOP's campaign had run the "dirty cheater" out of town.

Most of them, at any rate. A few continued to insist that the "unfair exposure of his youthful indiscretion" had driven a potential Hall of Famer from the game.

The irony of it was that Luz Maria had gotten hooked on the Astros as a kid, when her school awarded nosebleed-level tickets for perfect attendance throughout the school year. All through school, she'd savored each of her rare visits to the Astrodome, where she'd feasted on Dome Dogs and rooted for the first of the legendary Killer Bees. Years later, she'd been thrilled by her visits to the new park, nicknamed the Juice Box for its affiliation with Minute Maid, and ecstatic when the team took its first National League Pennant.

But since the Peterson incident, she couldn't even think of her team without getting a sick feeling in her stomach.

"Was there a letter?" Luz Maria asked, referring to Whit's threat files. "Or a phone call or an e-mail?"

Long ago, she'd given up reading them if she could possibly avoid it. She needed to stay fearless to remain halfway effective. If that meant keeping her head in the sand to some extent, she would rather live in ignorance than a state of constant terror.

Whit ran a palm over the greyhound's head while the dog sniffed him. "My gut says there was at least one, but I can't be sure yet. You know that most of the really ugly stuff comes in anonymously. I'm going to do some research, see if I can connect him to the routing of some anonymized e-mails or get a match to one of the phone numbers our caller ID unit recorded."

"If you don't have a recorded threat, what makes you believe Tony Coleman could have been the man who hurt me? That *is* what you're thinking, right?"

Frank Lee wandered back to the sofa and jumped up beside Luz Maria. But she was too intent on Whit's answer to protest when the thin dog laid his white head across her knees.

"His wife got flustered when I showed up at the house and asked her to explain why Mr. Coleman would drive at least forty-five minutes to pick up her medicine when there's a grocery store open just over a mile from their house."

"Maybe she's just upset about what happened," Luz Maria countered as she automatically stroked smooth fur.

"She seemed okay, almost friendly, when I got there—when she figured VOP was checking on her husband to determine whether we might be partially liable for his injuries. They're a middle-class family living in a modest, older neighborhood. And Coleman's a self-employed contractor with no medical insurance."

"*Are* we liable?"

Whit shook his head. "Not a chance, hon, but it got me in the door—and let me see the signed baseball in the display case and the Astros pennant on the wall. When she couldn't come up with an answer to my question, she went from flustered to nasty in no time and asked me to leave—even threatened to call the cops on my 'faggot ass' before I could get out the door."

Luz Maria winced at the name, but that didn't keep her from playing the devil's advocate. "People can act strangely—and rude, too—when they're under a lot of stress."

Whit shrugged. "And some people don't even need that much of an excuse. But I was curious, so I stopped by the library nearest the Coleman's and logged onto the Net. I found comments on an online sports forum that look like they're from our guy."

"What kind of comments?"

"Not overtly threatening, but hostile. And there was a post from the forum moderator warning him about his language. Then, later, there was something that led me to believe he'd been suspended from the board. The moderator could have deleted some of his more inflammatory posts as well. I've e-mailed the guy to check into it."

Luz Maria left off petting Frank to massage her throat. "So if he's the one . . . if he's the one who—who choked me, I don't get it. Who shot *him?*"

Could it have been the same person who had threatened her this morning on the phone? Could she really have two stalkers at the same time? Luz Maria grappled with the concept.

Whit shook his head once more. "I don't know. Maybe the police will get that from the security cameras."

"No. Detective Devlin told me they didn't see Mr. Coleman, but one of the parking lot cameras wasn't working."

"Of all the incompetence," Whit grumbled.

"And what about that mess in my apartment?" Luz Maria asked him. "Do you think he might have broken in *before* I was attacked?"

"Makes as much sense as anything. If I could get a look at your apartment, now that the police are through with it—"

"Reagan called a service. They clean up places where there's been crime and trauma scenes. Can you believe there's a need for businesses like that?"

The light in Whit's eyes dimmed. "Unfortunately, I can. Have they been in yet?"

"I'm not sure," Luz Maria answered. "She said something about meeting them there with the key, but I was half-asleep already. I can't remember whether she was going before or after the birthday par . . ."

A thought struck her with such force that she lost the thread of what she had been saying. A horrible thought that had her digging her ragged nails into her own palms.

"What's wrong?" Whit asked her, standing as he did so. "You look like—My lord, honey, you're whiter than the dog. What is it?"

A feeling of nausea swamped her. Though she wanted to discount the thought, wanted desperately to dismiss it, intuition forbade denial.

"It's Kellie—Kellie Capshaw. My next door neighbor, and my friend. Last night, Reagan called and asked her to go into my apartment and take care of Borracho. I *asked* her to call Kellie. *I* sent her over there. And this morning, this morning she didn't come to her door. She didn't answer, even though I knew she had a project she should have been working on at home."

Whit looked concerned, but he said, "Please, calm down, Luz Maria. There could be a hundred explanations."

"There could be." Luz Maria grasped his statement like a lifeline, even as she punched buttons on her cell phone. Her fumbling fingers forced her to start over twice, but finally, Kellie's home phone began ringing . . . and ringing and ringing until the answering machine finally picked up.

CHAPTER TEN

The paper shredder growled a warning, and the document trembled, as if in mortal terror.

Grant hesitated, staring down at the machine he'd bought to destroy documents a criminal could use to hijack his identity. Occasionally, his glance traveled the short distance to the paper he was holding. The blue ink script looked familiar, but larger and more slapdash than his usual hen scratch.

Cursing, he swiveled his chair in the opposite direction, affording him a view of the untidy spare bedroom that housed his desk, computer, and a bookcase holding a collection of paperback crime novels—the long-running interest that had lured him into police work. But it was the cork bulletin board that drew his notice, or the photos he'd pinned up with thumbtacks. One was of his aunts, Judy and Lorraine, grinning with their speckled trout catch on a South Padre Island beach. The two were so hooked on that stretch of southern Texas, they had sold the Houston home they shared and moved into a beachside condo. As much as he loved the women who'd joined forces to help raise him, Grant's attention turned to another photo: John Zeman clowning for two tiny, blond daughters at a backyard barbecue while his wife Sherry laughed and clapped her hands together.

It was a lousy picture, partly blurred and partly out of focus. A throwaway, really, or it should have been. But Grant had picked it up the day before the street whores' lies aired on television, the day before Luz Maria Montoya had shoved them down the public's throat.

And only three days later, he'd been out of his damned mind when he wrote the letter, only hours after John's body was taken to the morgue. Consumed with guilt so strong he couldn't contain it inside his head. Even today, he fought a running battle against self-blame and loathing. He damned well should have guessed what the Z-man meant to do, should have recognized the warning signs. He'd never forget his confrontation with Roy Reed, John's former partner from the Sex Crimes Division, who had arrived on the scene and backed him into a corner of the Zeman's kitchen, then screamed into his face, "What kind of fucking detective misses the clues his own goddamned partner lays out? What kind of sorry excuse for a friend lets down Zeman's wife and little girls?"

Even now, the accusations echoed through Grant's mind in a waking, never ending nightmare. Roy Reed's beefy, reddened face, bellowing like a wounded bull, goring Grant with every word.

With a sigh, Grant reached for the paper shredder and switched off its power before wiping beads of moisture from his forehead. That day, his guilt had twisted itself into a rage so white-hot it threatened to consume him. A rage he'd diverted from himself and, more alarmingly, John, then willfully locked onto a safer target—a woman he had never met in person. A woman who had robbed his good friend of the will to live.

If Grant had crossed a line that day in writing and mailing the letter he now held in his sweating hand, he had done so in the heat of the moment. If he crossed a second line years later in an attempt to cover his ass, he would lose something that counted for more than sanity, maybe even more than his survival. Without integrity, he was no better than the vilest of those who'd threatened Luz Maria. And no better than his old man, after all.

His perpetually *unemployed* old man—which was exactly what Grant was going to be once Jason Whitfield came across his name. He had probably remembered it already, or he'd found it as he went through his records while working to figure out which wacko was trying to murder Luz Maria. Sure, Whitfield would start with the most recent and persistent, but he would eventually work his way back to the cop who'd been both mad enough and dumb enough to sign his real name to the letter.

I'm good and screwed, goddammit.

So what the hell should he do now? Grant figured he could try calling Mutton, if he wanted to chance throwing himself on the lieutenant's mercy. But considering the tone of their last conversation, he would be better off phoning the attorney the union kept on retainer.

You saw how much good the union lawyer did John Zeman. In spite of the outdated air-conditioning system, a chill passed over Grant, and for just a moment, he smelled blood and brains and gun smoke.

A split second later, his phone rang.

He stood staring at it, his gut warning that a two-year-old pile of shit was about to hit the fan.

And then he reached for the receiver, to accept his fate with whatever dignity he could scrape together.

Reagan fished through her purse for the key to Luz Maria's deadbolt. The techs from CSC, Inc.—short for

Crime Scene Cleanup—hadn't yet arrived, but they should be there any minute. They'd better be on time. Patty, mother of the birthday boy, was watching Adam, but judging from the amount of sugar the kids had happily inhaled, the woman would soon need all the reinforcements she could get. And since Reagan had forgotten to recharge her cell phone, she was anxious to get back as soon as possible.

"Aha," she said as her finger hooked the key ring.

She stepped around rust-colored smudges in front of the doormat—probably blood tracked out of the bathroom by the cops. Without thinking any more of it, she unlocked the apartment door. Most people, she imagined, would squeamishly wait outside for the cleaners, but a brief rain shower earlier had turned this part of town into a steam bath. Besides, Reagan wasn't afraid of a few giblet drippings; the crime lab would have removed the nastiest of the butcher shop gook for testing. Heaven knew, she'd seen worse things.

But the smell that hit her as the door swung open froze the seasoned paramedic in her tracks. Though it rode a wave of refrigerated air, the odor was as overpowering as it was recognizable: the distinctive stench of violent death.

Instinctively, Reagan took a step back. But not before she saw the golf club lying outside the entrance to the kitchen. And not before she spotted the first blood-soaked clumps of hair.

Still, she didn't scream yet. Not until she heard the garbled voice.

"We're sorry. The customer you are trying to reach is unavailable," the canned voice told Luz Maria for the third time.

"Where *are* you, Reagan?" Luz Maria asked the mindless drone. As desperate as she was to have someone find

Kellie—and Whit was on his cell phone now, asking the cops to do a welfare check—Luz Maria didn't want Reagan and Adam anywhere near what could turn out to be a . . .

No. She couldn't think it. *Wouldn't.* She concentrated on what Whit had told her, struggled to convince herself that Kellie was taking a long shower, swinging a driver on the links, sleeping with earplugs after a hard night's work. *Anything* but missing, hurt, or even murdered.

Yet the images cascading into Luz Maria's mind were not of death, but life. Of her brother coming into this home, his eyes lighting like candles as he swept his wife into his arms, then building block towers on the rug so Adam could happily crash them down with his toy car. Though Jack spent day after day battling illness, injury, and the side effects of poverty, he shed that stress with each homecoming and with every bit of laughter he shared with his young family.

Could it be a family Luz Maria had unintentionally put at risk? Bad enough that three years earlier she'd nearly ruined his career by passing medical records to the media that supported BorderFree's aims. All for a man not worthy to wipe Jack's spit from the sidewalk . . . Cold ripples fluttered in the pit of her stomach.

If anything happened to his wife and child . . .

Whit clicked a button on his phone to break the connection. "They're sending a couple of officers to her apartment to check things out. It'll be all right. You'll see."

He tried to pat her hand, but Luz Maria hugged herself, squeezing back apprehension. "Will they go inside if she's still not answering? Would they force open the door?"

"I can't be sure, but maybe, in light of the break-in at your place. Especially if they see anything suspicious.

Or the manager of the complex could volunteer to let them in."

Luz Maria thought of how often the leasing agent had emphasized the words *comfort* and *security* when he'd shown her the unit. "He'll probably cooperate, if only to get the police cars out of the parking lot before most of the tenants make it home from work."

Even so, the news of Luz Maria's break-in would soon spread, especially if the media caught wind of it. Or more likely *when*, considering April's attitude this morning.

"Should we drive over there?" Luz Maria asked him.

Whit shook his head. "Not a good idea. You've been all right here so far, but if you go near the apartment now, you could end up leading him back."

"But what if Reagan and my nephew—"

"The police will be there soon."

"*How* soon?" Luz Maria demanded. She'd heard so many complaints about response times since the recent change in dispatch systems. "How can we be sure they consider this a priority? Besides, you identified yourself as VOP staff and gave them my name, too. So maybe they'll drag their heels on purpose, or dispatch some cop who hates me."

Grant Holcomb's words jabbed at her memory, painful as the headache that sometimes followed ice water downed in haste. "*I washed my best friend's brains off his bathroom wall. Because of you.*"

But Whit was the one who grimaced, probably with the knowledge she was about to turn her considerable nagging skills on him. Back when she was still a social worker, she'd acquired a nickname—the Piranha. Her brother always argued that a belt sander was a more accurate comparison, though Reagan made an excellent case for fire ants, which, once disturbed, would swarm up inside clothing to sting and sting, even after victims knocked their tiny heads off. But everyone, from her family to her friends to coworkers, agreed on one thing: Luz Maria was relentless when she put her mind to it.

The downside of the reputation came in the hate mail, name calling, and threats with which she and Whit so often had to deal. But on the upside, people often caved before her dogged persistence.

She could see this was going to be another such victory when Whit shook his head and muttered, "All right, all right. I'll check on her—but you're staying locked up in here with the alarm *on.*"

But for some reason, her coworker's pout got to her in a way it never had before. Maybe it was the last straw of antipathy, heaped onto her already creaking camel's back. Or maybe it was a delayed reaction to the fact that someone—maybe more than one someone—hated her enough to try to kill her. And possibly enough to hurt others who happened to be close.

Whatever the reason, the first crack snaked along the monolith that formed Luz Maria's will to fight for justice. A crack that splintered, branching out into a vast network of fault lines.

CHAPTER ELEVEN

Grant was halfway to Sherry Zeman's place, an older brick one-story in Houston's Oak Forest neighborhood, when his cell phone rang again.

"Christ, Sherry," he muttered to himself. "Give it a damned rest."

She had called him at home about an hour earlier to remind him about the bicycle, then phoned again as he left the driveway to ask if he'd mind helping her clean out the pine needle–clogged gutters, as long as he was coming. Helping Sherry clean gutters meant climbing the rickety ladder while she smiled up at him and held his glass of iced tea, since she was afraid of heights. She was afraid of spiders, too, and yellow jackets and tiny garter snakes barely bigger than night crawlers. Even the briefest glimpse could earn Grant another phone call, after which he'd come to the rescue, grateful beyond words to have something, anything, to assuage his throbbing guilt.

So his own annoyance with her weakness came as a surprise.

But it wasn't Sherry's soft voice on his cell phone. Instead, it was Steve Petit, a buddy from his academy days. Though he'd done well as a rookie cop, the West Texan had quit halfway through his probationary period when he was offered a shot at his first career choice, the FBI. The last Grant had heard, Steve was working out of the San Diego field office.

Once Steve had identified himself, Grant broke into a broad grin. "Whatcha doing? Slumming? I thought you Feebs never lowered yourself to conversing with the local talent. Unless, wait a minute—you need somebody to do the actual investigating, Cowboy?"

Before he'd been bitten by the law enforcement bug, Steve had been some kind of junior bull-riding phenom, with his own blue jean endorsement deal, a fan Web site, and everything. Yet for some unknown reason, it infuriated him when someone had spread that bit of gossip around the academy. So naturally, some smart-ass saddled him with the unwanted nickname.

It was a damned wonder he was still on speaking terms with Grant.

"Don't have time for the standard bullshit," Steve said. "Just calling to give you a head's up—has to do with that informant you asked me to look into a while back."

Grant's heart pounded. The one and only time he had called in a favor from his old friend, it had been to check out the spokeswoman for the Voice of Poverty. He'd heard talk she had once been the target of an investigation by a domestic terrorism task force, but he'd needed to know if there was anything he could use to get her to ease up on John before his partner . . .

By the time the information came, it had been too

late to find out if he really could have stooped to black-mail. John Zeman had permanently checked out.

"Are you still interested?" Steve asked.

"What do you have?" If it was more of the old shit, how Luz Maria had cooperated with the Feds, rolling over on the murderous bastard she'd been seeing, Grant didn't want to hear about it. But if there was some new twist, something that might explain last night's attack, the threats, and the mess in her apartment . . .

"Sergio Cardenas is back inside the U.S. After a tip got us checking some surveillance video from the Tijuana border crossing, we're fairly confident he came in on a forged passport, using the name Rogelio Izquierda—"

"At least we know he has a sense of humor." *Izquierda* was the Spanish word for "left," as in leftist, which pretty much described the man's extremist politics.

"Yeah." Cowboy's voice gave no hint he found the alias amusing. "And we're pretty sure he's heading straight for Houston, if he isn't there already."

"Could be he's gunning for his old girlfriend," Grant suggested. Had Cardenas figured out it was Luz Maria's secret testimony that had dealt BorderFree-4-All such a devastating blow? Though she'd only been peripherally involved, Luz Maria had heard enough to put away several members of the group—including at least one of the bombers of the Immigration and Naturalization Office in San Antonio.

Pillow talk, Grant figured. That was how she knew. The thought struck him like a hard fist.

"I've been monitoring the Houston news sites," Steve said. "I saw she was attacked. We'll be sending a couple of special agents to investigate."

This was the part where Grant should mention he'd

gotten his ass kicked off the case. But Petit was speaking strictly off the record. He'd clam up in a heartbeat if he had to talk to Devlin, or any cop he didn't know. Which would leave HPD completely in the dark, as the Feds were notorious for keeping their own counsel.

"Are you coming?" Grant asked casually. "'Cause if you are, I've got some information that hasn't hit the case file."

When his phone beeped, Grant at first mistook the sound for the low battery warning tone. But he'd charged the thing while he slept, so he realized it had to be the damned call waiting. Grant ignored the interruption, figuring Sherry could survive clogged gutters for another fifteen minutes.

"I'll do my best," Steve said, "but they may work it out of the Houston field office, budget considerations being what they are."

"Just mention 'terrorism' and they'll charter you a whole jet."

"Domestic terrorism isn't as romantic these days. The pro- and anti-immigration nuts haven't made as many headlines lately."

"Thank God," Grant said, "but I know what you mean about priorities."

"Listen, if you could just pass on to me what you have now, I'd be happy to treat you as a confidential source," Petit promised.

"No offense, Steve, but I'm on some pretty thin ice as it is, and anything I gave you would mark me like the dye pack in a bank heist. You get yourself sent out here, I'll cut you in. Otherwise, it's official channels all the way."

The phone resumed its beeping, and this time, Grant glanced down in annoyance at the screen. But it wasn't

Sherry Zeman's name that caused him to abruptly tell Cowboy he would get back to him later.

It was the flashing letters that read *L MONTOYA*.

In her years as a first responder with the Houston Fire Department, Reagan Hurley had seen things that would curl the hair of a lot of ER doctors. Even Jack, who'd done time in a busy Houston trauma center, had never accidentally crushed a charred human arm with a fire boot. He'd never cut down the bloated body of a fifteen-year-old who'd hanged himself in a masturbatory experiment gone horribly awry, nor had he hosed away the effluvia resulting when the miracle of birth took place inside a moving ambulance.

For the most part, she handled the work with grim professionalism, and sometimes even—when there were no grieving relatives in earshot—the gallows humor that kept emergency workers sane. But on her day off and in her own sister-in-law's apartment, Reagan hadn't been prepared to find a scene like this one. And the shock had barely sunk in when that sick voice scared her half out of her wits.

She still hadn't figured how the bastard did it. Probably, he'd jury-rigged a sound-activated device to play the recording. The door opening might have been enough to start it—or her own gasp of horror when she'd first seen the hair.

As she stood waiting in the doorway for the swelling sounds of sirens, she wished she'd gone no farther into the apartment. But, bloody or not, the clumps of brown curls didn't guarantee their owner wasn't breathing, so after Reagan spotted the microcassette recorder, she went in to see if someone needed help.

The nude woman she spotted in the bedroom was

clearly dead. No need to check a pulse with the face taped over completely and the skull caved in.

Reagan shuddered, clamping her hand over her mouth with one hand even as the other reached for the inhaler in her purse. After two puffs, she heard the first siren, followed by the keening of a second.

But instead of relaxing, she agonized about Luz Maria. Reagan was no expert on criminal psychology, but it seemed obvious to her that this poor girl had served the killer as a less than satisfactory substitute for the woman he hated. The shorn hair, the covered face, the hideous arrangement on Luz Maria's own bed: all were clear as crystal. And in case he'd been too subtle, the recorded threat was as unequivocal as it was brief.

"Next time, I'll have you."

Though the words shook her, they also intimated that the killer was long gone. So Reagan risked remaining inside long enough to dial 911.

She'd meant to leave right afterward. Would have left, had she not spotted the gaping kitchen drawer. Not the one holding knives, as she might have expected, but a drawer containing stationery, stamps, and Luz Maria's address book, open to the M page.

Luz Maria's mother was listed, along with only one other Montoya: Jack. Reagan's gaze locked onto her own address, lying as naked and exposed as that poor woman in the bedroom.

"Oh, God," she breathed. Her mother-in-law would still be safe, working at her herb shop for the next few hours, but Luz Maria was alone—and completely un-protected.

Frantically, Reagan dug Investigator Grant Hol-comb's card out of her purse and started dialing. It took her a few tries to reach him, but when she did, she quickly rattled off the circumstances before giving her address and demanding that he get his ass right over to look after Luz Maria.

Reagan thought she might have shouted, but she didn't give a damn. All she cared about was getting Jack's sister a protector before the sick son of a bitch who'd murdered this girl got hold of her, too.

CHAPTER TWELVE

Call Billy or the station. Hell, dial 911, Grant told himself when Reagan Hurley broke off the conversation.

But the terror in her voice was so sharp, her concern for her sister-in-law so palpable, that before Grant knew what he was doing, he was making a wheel-squealing U-turn on West Forty-third Street, to the bleats and honks of several vehicles. Flooring the Mercedes, he put the blue roadster's overpowered engine to the test. As the convertible zipped onto the loop, he told himself he was far closer than Billy—and that by the time he explained the situation to somebody at the station or in dispatch, he could be there.

So let a patrol car meet you. Not a bad idea, since he didn't have his weapon. He never took it to the Zeman place—not around two curious little girls and a widow still traumatized by a gun's handiwork. Traumatized because of Luz Maria Montoya's accusations, he reminded himself.

Yet he didn't slow his speed, didn't call for backup. He told himself he didn't want to explain his involvement—

especially not to Mutton when she caught wind of it. It wouldn't *be* involvement if he passed the buck now, but the truth was, Grant was as hooked as any redfish who'd ever swallowed the damned lure. He had to know whether the killer was Sergio Cardenas or one of those people whose threat file was still sitting in his home office—himself excluded.

Curiosity might have hooked him, but Grant couldn't quite beat back the suspicion that the memory of Luz Maria's face, of her tight little body and her fiery wit, was reeling him straight into disaster.

Ten minutes later, he pulled into the driveway of a neat white bungalow that reminded him of a bygone era. Behind the emerald lawn, a riotous mass of flame-colored lantana framed a front porch with its own honest-to-God swing. He felt as if he'd driven into a lemonade commercial. For damned sure, this place was a real home—one that made a mockery of his own sorry abode.

The thought of anyone's murder taking place here didn't set right. The possibility it could be Luz Maria's had him swearing, "Not on my damned watch."

At the sound of the car door slamming in the driveway, Luz Maria peered carefully out past the curtain. But instead of Reagan's bright red Jetta or Whit's brown sedan, she spotted a little car she didn't recognize.

The man climbing out was quite another story.

She raced to the front door to meet Grant Holcomb. Yet something in her hung back. The police never came with good news, did they? They came to say there had been a terrible accident or someone close was dead.

Despite her fear, she raced through the steps of disarming the alarm system and opening the deadbolt, then the door. By the time she finished, Grant stood before her, his fist poised as if to knock.

He expelled a noisy breath, the kind that slipped out when a man's worst fears had proved unfounded. "You're all right," he said.

"Are Reagan and my nephew okay?" With panic knotted painfully inside her, Luz Maria searched his face for an answer.

Grant nodded, but his features were inscrutable. "She just called me. We need to get you out of here right now. Gather up your things and let's go."

"What? I can't do that. Why would I—"

"I'll explain it on the road."

Luz Maria stared at him, fear swelling inside her. "Something's happened, hasn't it? I—I want my brother. I want Whit—"

He grabbed her arm, hard. "Where's your purse? And you'll need shoes, too."

She tried to pull away. "You're hurting me. And I don't take orders from a—"

"A woman's dead," Grant told her, his gray eyes as intense as a big cat staring down its next kill. "And your sister-in-law thinks the killer knows where you are right now. She begged me to get you out of here before he comes for you."

"Dead?" Luz Maria's voice shriveled. She felt dazed, disoriented, but she was already turning her head, looking for her sandals. Searching for the strength to survive this new horror.

"I don't know who she was. But she was found in your apartment. In your bedroom."

When Grant let go of Luz Maria's arm, she shoved her feet into her sandals and went for her shoulder bag, which she'd left on the kitchen counter. Frank Lee got under her feet, as he was prone to do when any of his people seemed upset.

"What about the dog?" Luz Maria asked Grant. "Should we take him, too?"

"Sorry, there's no room in my car. We'll have an officer come and keep an eye on the place. Besides, you're the one this guy wants. He's escalated way past hurting an animal that isn't even yours."

Luz Maria stroked the sleek, white head. "It'll be okay, boy."

Thinking of Borracho in her bathtub, she breathed a silent prayer that her words would prove true.

As they left, she reset the alarm and deadbolt. Her mind hummed with white noise and vibrated with the effort of not thinking, of not picturing someone lying dead in her apartment or Reagan and little Adam finding her there.

Grant opened the passenger-side door of his car and reminded her to duck her head as she climbed in. He backed out of the driveway, then headed out of the Heights neighborhood.

After a time, he made a phone call, but the words slipped past her in a steady current, as meaningless as water rushing over pebbles. Luz Maria turned and pressed her head against the side window. She had a vague impression of the silver underbellies of the low clouds, but her eyes refused to focus on the homes and corner businesses that blurred past.

But when they turned a corner, something shifted. Her skin prickled as if an electric charge surged through her, and disquiet skated across her nerve endings. She'd been so frightened about Kellie, Reagan, and Adam, she hadn't spared a thought for her own safety. Now, the realization crashed down on her that she had just left a locked house on the say-so of an off-duty investigator who'd been ordered to keep his distance from her. *He could have made it all up—from Reagan's call to the body in my apartment. He could be taking me anywhere, this man who blames me for his partner's suicide.*

Though the car's AC labored against the afternoon's heat, a drop of perspiration slid along the grooved channel of her backbone.

She realized Grant had put away his phone and was speaking to her. "Did you hear me, Luz Maria? I asked if you're okay. You look like you're fading."

Even before his words sank in, her stunned brain processed his concern. Real concern. Since she was already in his car with him, Luz Maria decided to trust her instincts, at least until she knew more.

"I'm fine," she said. "But what else did Reagan tell you? I . . . I need to hear it all."

"First of all, where are we going? Is there someplace you'd like me to take you?"

Luz Maria thought a moment before saying, "My mother's, I suppose. Her house is at—"

"Your sister-in-law called me because she found your address book—open to the M page. Is your mother . . . ?"

Luz Maria shook her head. "That would be Mama's old address. I never thought I'd see the day, but she remarried last year—a carpenter named Espinosa. They're living in his house off Oxford. Neither one will be there for a couple of hours, but I have a key, and they would want me to make myself at home."

After forcing herself to focus on their surroundings, she added, "Take a right here, then the third left. And tell me about Reagan. Please."

He hesitated, a frown tugging the corner of his mouth. Finally relenting, he said, "All right, Luz Maria. I'll tell you what I know. She went inside to wait for the cleaning crew, and she saw a golf club lying on the floor. There was hair, too, clumps of brown curls."

Luz Maria pressed her hands over her eyes, felt the scalding tears. Grant wasn't making up this story, hadn't invented it to lure her. "It . . . it has to be my neighbor, Kellie Capshaw. She plays golf, and she has curly brown hair. She didn't answer her door this morning when I knocked. I was worried when I couldn't reach her by phone later, so I asked Whit to go check on her just a little while ago."

"That body could be anyone's," said Grant, but the investigator didn't sound as if he believed that any more than she did.

"What about Reagan? Did she have her little boy with her?" Luz Maria knew her sister-in-law had seen a lot of terrible things, but Adam was so innocent, so cocooned by love.

"She didn't say. But she'd already called nine-one-one. Help was on the way."

"Whit should be there by now, too," Luz Maria said. "I should call him."

But she didn't do it, *couldn't*, because she couldn't stand the thought of telling him—of telling anyone—what had happened. Some irrational corner of her mind insisted that speaking the words would make them real, that if she kept them locked inside her, the body could turn out to be a stranger's after all.

Once she'd given somewhat shaky directions to her mother's, she abruptly changed the subject, if only to keep herself from imagining the scene in her apartment. "When Whit came by, he told me Tony Coleman and his family live in Clear Lake."

Grant did a double take. "Clear Lake?"

"Yes, and Coleman's quite the Astros fan. Whit thinks he might have made some nasty posts to an online forum after the Trey-Don Peterson trade."

"Interesting," Grant said. "But what's your take on all this? You think this thing's about baseball?"

"It's the fourth house on the right," she said, "the little yellow one with the palm trees in the front yard. And no, I don't think it could be baseball. You said this guy was badly hurt, right? So he surely didn't call to threaten me from the hospital this morning. And there's no way he could have gone back to my apartment after the police left."

"All that's true, but he is someone to consider. Especially if he has a buddy working with him. Maybe a like-minded individual."

As he spoke, Grant slowed but passed the house.

"Why didn't you turn in?" Luz Maria asked.

"I'm making the block so I can have a look around."

He reminded her of Whit, a man she sometimes teasingly referred to as the "Queen of Overkill." But with the horrors of this past day scoring her heart like razor slashes, Luz Maria couldn't imagine ever laughing off his—or even her brother's—concerns again.

She waited patiently while Grant slowed down and peered into open garages and through clumps of shrubbery. Several times, he leaned so close her nostrils filled with the clean male scents of soap and aftershave. Scents that blindsided her with a throb of unexpected hunger.

He pulled into the driveway alongside the house, an area sheltered from view by a thick stand of oleanders covered with white blooms. As the car stopped, his gaze slid toward hers, traveling from thighs to eyes with a heat that sent a bead of moisture trickling between her breasts.

"I'm staying here with you," he said. "You won't be safe alone."

Though his words were perfectly professional, their intensity warned her he had caught the direction of her thoughts. Maybe out of the corner of his eye he'd seen her glance from that square jaw to the flex of bicep as he'd shifted into neutral and applied the hand brake. Or perhaps he'd heard her suck in a startled breath. It was even possible that after three years of keeping her hands and hormones to herself, she was leaking pheromones like a punctured aerosol can.

Luz Maria looked away, heat suffusing her face. Was she so frightened, so desperate for an ally that she'd unconsciously tried to trade sex for protection? Or was it worse than that? Was this proof she had a penchant for picking the worst men possible?

"It's okay to be scared," Grant said before doing something she would never have expected: he climbed out of the car, then went around and opened the door for her.

Looking up at him, she blindly grabbed her shoulder bag before accepting his hand. In spite of the cloud cover, she felt as if she were being drawn into a sauna.

"I really don't need your help." Heat or not, her voice froze over at the realization that they stood too close together, and an image of where their simple, hand-to-hand touch might lead.

She stepped back, terrified she would do something crazy to keep from thinking about the woman lying dead in her apartment.

Grant looked at her oddly, and something closed off in his expression. But he hid it quickly, shrugging and explaining, "You're still pale, Ms. Montoya. Don't need you passing out on me before the cavalry gets here."

"The cavalry?"

"You can't be left alone again. Not even for a minute."

Luz Maria turned from him and started toward the back door. She mounted the three concrete steps, digging for the key with trembling hands. *Caray*—where the devil was it?

Grant moved behind her. "Ms. Montoya—Luz Maria. There's something else I need to tell you."

Finally, she pulled the key out of a zippered pocket. But something in his voice made her hesitate to use it. Still keeping her back to him, she grasped the handle of the screen door. "What?"

"Why don't we go inside first, where it's cool?"

She nodded stiffly, dread clutching at her stomach. Whatever he had to say, it wouldn't be good news.

The screen door, unlocked as always, opened with a creak. But before Luz Maria could use the key to let them inside, she saw a Manila envelope tilted against the base of the heavy, wooden door.

Her name was written on it, in huge, red block letters.

Luz Maria backed away, as if she'd found a copperhead coiled to strike. And found herself bumping against the unyielding wall of Investigator Holcomb's chest.

CHAPTER THIRTEEN

"I take it your mama doesn't usually leave you notes here," Grant said, though her reaction left him no doubt.

Luz Maria shook her head. "Are you kidding? She's too busy leaving guilt trips on my answering machine to bother writing. It's not from her, and it's not from her husband, either. Somebody else left this here for me."

"Someone else who guessed you would come here." Grant placed a hand on her thin shoulder, meaning to gently move her aside so he could get a closer look. But instead, he found himself giving her a reassuring squeeze.

Couldn't have her going to pieces, he told himself—though he knew damned well it was bullshit. Knew that sometime late last night, he'd stepped over a line and couldn't find his way back.

"Better let me see it," he said. Still, he was almost surprised when she moved aside.

"All . . . all right," she told him, "but be careful. In case it's something . . ."

Her words trailed off, as if she were afraid to imagine what might have been left for her. And it was her fear that surprised him most of all.

For so long, he'd thought of her as a force of nature, like one of the minor league tornadoes that spun off of spring thunderstorms and hopped about the county, wrecking a mobile home here, a subdivision's roofs there. Once in a while, somebody got hurt or even killed, but it was more a matter of bad luck than malice. Luz Maria Montoya didn't care who she destroyed.

It was tough getting used to the realization that she was only one small, very human woman. It was even harder dealing with his gut-level attraction to her. Christ, all she had to do was turn those drop-dead gorgeous brown eyes his way and he started hardening like concrete. He prayed she wouldn't look down and see what she did to him.

"I could call for backup, but I'd feel pretty idiotic if it turned out to be something from your mama after all," he said. And his ass would likely be suspended for not taking her in to the station in the first place. "Why don't you stand back and let me—"

Her head shook, flipping the loose black braid over her shoulder. "No. If you're going to see it, I am, too."

He could have—should have—argued that they were dealing with a sophisticated criminal, one smart enough to booby-trap an envelope with God only knew what substance. But it occurred to Grant that this stalker wasn't out to simply kill his quarry. Otherwise, he could have shot her from a safe distance in the parking lot last night.

"If it's from our guy," he said as he pulled a folded handkerchief from the back pocket of his jeans, "it'll be all about the terror. Everything he's done so far has been designed to scare you more than—"

"I have every right to know," she said, sounding

more like the indignant Voice of Poverty he was used to from TV.

Grant used the back of his hand to wipe away the sweat that was running into his eyes. As the central air-conditioning unit kicked on, he wished they could do this in the house, but they couldn't risk entering until he saw what was in the envelope.

He used the handkerchief to protect any prints, though in his heart Grant knew this guy was far too bright to leave them. His breath held, Grant tipped the envelope away from the door. No protruding wires. No suspicious bulge. Good.

He picked the thing up, then balanced it on the railing at the right side of the steps and used the blade of his pocketknife to prize up the envelope's flap. Puckered with the afternoon's humidity, it opened easily enough, so he tilted it, his body partly blocking Luz Maria's view.

A photo slid out, just a small one, of a little boy smiling as he reached for a balloon. A ballpoint pen had dug black indentations where the eyes were, and across the white wall background, meticulous block letters warned, "NOWHERE TO HIDE."

"It's . . . it's Adam," Luz Maria whispered as she stood on tiptoe to peer over his shoulder. "My nephew—Jack and Reagan's son. This . . . this picture was above my fireplace. That *cabrón* must have taken it from the apartment."

He shoved the picture back inside the envelope, but he didn't put it down. "Come on. Let's get in the car."

She let him steer her, her movements listless as a sleepwalker's. Once they were both inside his Mercedes, he started it and cranked the AC as high as it would go.

Grant backed out of the driveway, his heart sinking with the realization that he was the only investigator holding all the pieces. If he took what he knew to his superiors, he'd not only wind up on the wrong end of a disciplinary hearing, but Billy—or whoever ended up with this case—would lose access to Grant's FBI source. The Feds, too, would be hampered, half-blinded by the layers of interdepartmental rivalry and pride.

And they were dealing with a goddamned genius of a killer. A professional, if Grant were any judge.

A terrorist who'd had three years to plan his revenge.

Grant suspected that even Lieutenant Mutton would have a tough time staying pissed if he brought in one of the FBI's most wanted fugitives. And if he somehow managed to embarrass the Feebs in the process, he'd probably get a goddamned commendation.

Or so Grant tried to convince himself as he headed toward his own house in Magnolia.

Though it was only a little after three o'clock, the Friday afternoon exodus from Houston was already threatening to clog I-45 North. While Grant jockeyed for position, Luz Maria listened intently as he laid out his plan. By the time he finished, they were jammed up short of the exit to the beltway, near a stretch of freeway overlooking a down-at-the-heels strip center and an old high school sports stadium. Ahead of them, the sun had broken through the clouds, and heat waves shimmered off the concrete road surface.

"You're sure about this?" Luz Maria asked Grant.

"Not completely, but it'll give us both time to sit back and hash this out together. You'll be safe there, and once I tell you everything I know, you can decide exactly what you want to do."

Luz Maria felt punch-drunk, hammered by both physical exhaustion and this onslaught of disaster. It was hard to think, but one thing came through clearly: she couldn't risk her family's safety by staying with either Jack and Reagan or her mother. Kellie's murder—she'd given up the fantasy that the body was a stranger's—

proved that the bastard stalking her was dangerous to anyone for whom she cared.

And worse yet, he seemed to know her well enough to predict her every move.

Well, he wouldn't predict this one. Luz Maria couldn't have imagined it herself.

"I'll go with you," she told him. "But only if you'll tell me everything you've found out and everything you're thinking."

His glance flicked out toward traffic, but not quickly enough to keep her from seeing what a dangerous idea that was. That just as she was, he was harboring some thoughts that didn't bear discussing.

Yet he nodded his agreement, so she acted on his earlier suggestion, calling Jack at work to tell him he needed to meet an officer at his house.

"I just got off the phone with Reagan. She's with the police at your apartment," he said. "Is someone there with you? Are you safe?"

"I'm fine," Luz Maria answered. "But what about Reagan and Adam. Are they all—"

"Reag's all right, just a little shaken. And Adam's great. Our friend Peaches picked him up from the party and took him to her place."

"Then he wasn't with her when she found the . . . ?"

"No. Thank God, he wasn't. Listen, I'll meet you at the house. You're there, right? With the officer?"

"I'm going somewhere safe. That's all you need to know now."

"Luz Maria, you can't possibly—"

"He left a photo for me at Mama's. Adam's photo, Jack, and he meant it as a threat."

Jack made a sound like a man punched in the stomach. "That son of a bitch. When I find out who—"

"I can't risk your family, or Mama and Eduardo, either. Have their house checked out, Jack, to make sure nothing else was left inside. And I'll be back in touch when it's safe."

"Luz Maria, please, be reasonable. The police can—"

"I love you, Jack," she told him before breaking the connection, then switching off her telephone. She had to, or he'd call her back a thousand times. With his protective instincts triggered, there would be no convincing him to back off.

Finally, they made it to the beltway, where the pack of cars dispersed into something approaching highway speeds. Yet Grant's tension towered over Luz Maria like a huge black thunderhead. Did he already regret his offer?

She didn't bring it up, though. Couldn't, with her own doubts and fears commandeering her attention. The effort of speech seemed insurmountable, and since he said nothing to her, she rode in silence, keeping her gaze fixed on the traffic and the businesses and the new upscale subdivisions that had popped up since she had last visited this section of the county. More accustomed to the small, Depression-era houses built inside the Loop and on the East End, Luz Maria was appalled by both the sheer number and the size of these new monuments to suburban excess. Her mind wandered to those she spoke for, who mainly lived in rundown apartments or tumbledown shotgun shacks with rats only slightly smaller and far nastier than Borracho. Some of her clients didn't even receive services as basic as trash pickup and running water, a neat trick the city pulled off by selectively annexing areas with fat tax bases, such as the outposts these yuppies were creating. By making unincorporated islands out of pockets of poverty, the city was left with cash enough to serve the needs of *those who mattered*. Just thinking about the injustice whipped her into a white-hot fury, burning away a little of the terror and exhaustion of the past two days.

Grant passed one last set of yuppie farms, then turned onto a narrow unpaved road. As the little car jounced along, a cloud of dust rose in its wake, a smoke signal beckoning the clouds to ease the heat with another of the late afternoon showers that had been popping up all week.

"Sorry it's a little bumpy," he said, speaking his first words to her in forty minutes. "County doesn't get around to grading it too often."

Luz Maria smiled at a trio of spotted Texas longhorns grazing in a fenced field, at a windmill's lazy spin above a stock tank where a mare drank with her foal. A rangy yellow dog trotted along the roadside, and the occasional older, one-story brick home nestled amid a cluster of outbuildings. There were trees, too, not the carefully groomed specimens coddled like hothouse flowers by the affluent, but the haphazard jumble of pines—their needles rusty with the stress of August's heat—and hardwoods that marked this area as the country. The real country, not the too-perfect micro-ranches dreamed up by developers.

But gradually, the pastures gave way to thickening woods, and Grant turned off onto an even narrower, deeply shaded track. On either side of the Mercedes, tangles of vines rose far above their heads, where they crowded out the possibility of sunlight.

"What is this?" she asked, her eagerness dissolving into apprehension as awareness of their isolation set it.

"This is my place," Grant said flatly. "It's set kind of far back from the road."

He wasn't kidding. To Luz Maria, the rutted driveway seemed to go on forever, but eventually, they pulled into a clearing of sorts, where a pair of huge oak trees submerged a modest tan brick house in a pool of shadow.

Luz Maria attempted a smile to hide her nervousness. "Bet you don't get a lot of trick-or-treaters."

"All the more candy for me," Grant said with a disarming waggle of his brows.

He pulled into an open carport, then stepped out of the roadster. Luz Maria hurried to follow suit before he could do the door-opening routine again. Better to keep him at arm's length, to remind him this was a temporary alliance based on necessity and nothing more. Even if her hormones *were* sending up flares at the thought that somewhere inside his house, Grant Holcomb had a bed.

And she'd bet her next month's rent that the man knew how to put it to good use.

He let her in through a back door, and she sighed as she stepped into the house's cool interior. He flipped on a fluorescent overhead fixture, which bathed the kitchen in flickering white light.

"Sorry about the mess," he told her, though he sounded none too troubled. "It's the maid's year off."

Luz Maria glanced from the harvest-gold countertop stacked with newspapers and what she hoped were clean dishes to cabinets finished in a hideous avocado green. The linoleum floor was coming up in places, and the autumn leaf wallpaper had faded in the sunlight that streamed through a bare window just above the sink.

Though she wasn't exactly Martha Stewart, Luz Maria was bowled over by the room's sheer ugliness.

As if he'd read her mind—or expected the reaction from anyone with a matched set of X chromosomes—Grant added, "My decorator's fled to Hungary seeking asylum. Word is, they don't want her, either."

Luz Maria laughed hoarsely, a rusty sound that took her by surprise. It was a nice, big kitchen anyway, and the round oak table where he tossed the envelope was not only clean, it appeared to be a well-made antique with a pretty set of matched chairs.

"Want something to drink?" he asked. "You sound like you could use one."

She thought longingly of a light beer—she had a weakness for Corona—but asked instead for water. He grabbed each of them a bottle from the refrigerator.

A refrigerator whose dark-brown surface was festooned with crayon drawings. Loopy orange flowers. A house watched over by a smiling sun. A long-eared creature probably meant to be a dog.

"You have kids?" Luz Maria burst out before she could stop herself. She'd never considered the possibility that Investigator Holcomb might have a wife and family. She didn't know why such a thing should trouble her. Maybe it was the idea that a woman, any woman, would tolerate this kitchen.

Grant's expression sobered. "John's girls drew those. Emma and Sierra."

John Zeman. Of course. Unease tightened its noose, setting the bruises throbbing at her neck.

Sitting at the table, she opened the water bottle. Though she longed for cool relief, she found it almost impossible to swallow.

"I'll make a couple phone calls soon." Grant pulled up a chair and took a swig from his own bottle.

She watched his Adam's apple work, caught sight of a few stray chest hairs at the neck of his dark green T-shirt.

"I know a guy in homicide who's on today," Grant continued. "He might be able to tell me what they've got so far on the murder investigation."

Homicide. Murder. The words went off like bombs inside her skull. It seemed impossible that such terms had become part of her life. *How? Why? Oh, Kellie . . .*

"Before . . . before I found the envelope at Mama's place, you were about to . . . about to tell me something." Luz Maria struggled to string the words together. "What did you mean to say?"

"You want a sandwich or something? Some chips?"

"No, thanks."

"Maybe you'd be more comfortable in the family room."

"You're stalling," she accused.

He frowned and lived up to the accusation by taking another long swig from his water. Once he'd had his fill, he set down the empty bottle and looked her in the eye.

"Sergio Cardenas has come back to the United States. The FBI thinks he was heading straight for Houston. My money's on a more specific destination: you."

Though Luz Maria's eyes were dark, Grant saw the pupils dilate. She grabbed the table's edge as if to keep herself from sliding to the floor, and her lips moved in what appeared to be a futile attempt to form speech.

One thing was for certain: she hadn't been in contact with her former lover. Grant recognized the theatrics of feigned shock and horror. This was the real deal.

"I know about your testimony," he said. "The gist, at any rate."

"S-sealed," she managed weakly. "They said it would be sealed. Th-that no one would ever know. Especially not Sergio. *Santa Maria*, do you think he's the one? The one who killed my neighbor?"

"If the FBI's right about his whereabouts, I'd say it's a strong possibility. Cardenas has experience using terror as a weapon, as well as planning and orchestrating complex crimes. He's used to killing, too." Grant's gaze snagged on the flowers Emma Zeman had drawn for him, so he added, "But I guess you know all that, right? Since you were sleeping with him."

How many nights had he dreamed of saying those

words to her, of pushing even further to call her a whoring snitch, a hypocrite with fucking nerve to cast the first stone at anybody on the planet. Yet now that God or the devil had offered him the chance, the words coated his mouth with a taste like rancid grease. And when her head drooped forward, tears dripping onto the smooth oak surface, he felt not victory, but a gut-shriveling sensation suspiciously like shame.

"He told me," Luz Maria started, "he told me they were a dangerous splinter, the ones who bombed the immigration office. He said they had been dealt with—that BorderFree-4-All had never condoned violence. . . . I had no idea at the time that he had planned the whole thing, that the group I thought was only out to raise awareness of the plight of poor immigrants was killing innocent people to get their point across."

Shaking her head, she pulled a tissue from her pocket to blot her eyes. "He told me many things. Things I was stupid and idealistic and in love enough to swallow. It took a lot to wake me up to the truth. And my involvement cost me more than I can ever tell you."

"Who else did it cost?" In spite of his distaste, he wasn't willing to let her completely off the hook. "How many others did you hurt?"

She didn't flinch when he stared at her. Nor did she look away. Instead, she straightened her spine, her face arranging itself into the semblance of some ancient warrior goddess. One who had lost battles but could never truly be defeated.

"I don't owe you an explanation," she said. "There are others who could make that claim, but you're not one of them."

He admired the coolness of her answer, but as she swept an errant lock of hair back, a tremor in her left hand hinted that Luz Maria's toughest critic might be her own conscience.

He told himself he was letting it go for now so he could get back to the current problem. Not because he pitied or, worse yet, respected her. His lust could be explained away as a case of misfiring libido, a curse of the male tendency to want any attractive woman within reach. But anything more than simple physical attraction was a betrayal of John Zeman. He had to remember that at any cost.

Luz Maria took a delicate swallow of her water, her gaze losing focus, her mind clearly elsewhere. A frown played at her full lips, the perfect complement to her sultry eyes.

Goddammit. He *had* to drag his mind out of the bedroom. And yet he couldn't help wondering—exactly how messy had he left it? Would she be disgusted if he took her . . .

Luz Maria said, "I don't think it was Sergio, not in the parking lot, at least. I would have known his voice. Even after three years, I can't imagine I'd forget it."

"People can sound different under stress," Grant said, but he was skeptical as well. Jumping and cursing Luz Maria, then choking her unconscious didn't sound much like the style of a master planner. But if it was his aim to terrify . . .

She shook her head. "It wasn't him. It couldn't be. I'm sure he's forgotten all about me by now. If he hadn't, why wouldn't he have come for me before?"

"Maybe he only just found out," Grant suggested. "I know your testimony was sealed, but sooner or later, these things have a way of leaking. After all, *I* heard."

She arched a delicate, dark brow. "You sure you didn't call him?"

"Oh, yeah," Grant said dryly. "He gave me his number. One-eight hundred-RATFINK."

A smile eased the strain around her eyes. He found

himself wishing he could keep her happy, if only for the improvement in his view.

But her smile died when his telephone, mounted on the kitchen wall, started ringing. A prescient sense warned that it could only bring bad news.

CHAPTER FOURTEEN

Luz Maria's heart sank as Grant walked from the room with the handset from the cordless unit.

His voice carried down the hallway. "No, I haven't seen her. Haven't heard from her, either—but then, I imagine I'd be the last person on earth Ms. Montoya would call for help. Did you ask Jason Whitfield?"

She heard a door close as he shut her off from the remainder of the conversation. But his words lingered, reminding her of Whit, who was probably beside himself with worry.

She pulled her cell phone from her shoulder bag and turned on the power. As she waited for a signal, she decided to listen to any messages—Jack had probably left a dozen—before calling Whit to set his mind at ease.

But the cell phone wasn't showing any bars. Dammit. She must be in a dead spot.

Standing, she walked into and around the dining room and living room, even up and down the hallway. But no matter where she tried, she still couldn't get a signal. As long as she stayed here, she would be dependent on Grant's landline.

She glanced around the living room and judged it as slightly more inviting than the kitchen, with its oversized and cushiony tan sofa and recliner and guy-friendly big-screen TV. The coffee and lamp tables might be cluttered, the blinds dusty, and the dingy walls dull, but the real abomination was the rust-colored shag carpet.

She imagined Whit's commentary on Grant's taste but the exercise did little to distract her from the conversation taking place behind the closed door. Would the caller know something about Kellie? Had the police discovered how she'd died or whether she had suffered? Had they called her sister, Bobbi, to ask her to come identify the . . .

Luz Maria paced the room, her arms folded tightly across her midsection and her vision blurred with fresh tears. What right did she have to hide here, out of touch, while others dealt with a death that had occurred because of her? Did she even deserve the safety of this shelter?

"For the wages of sin is death"—Father Renaldo's voice echoed from her childhood—*"but the gift of God is eternal life in Christ Jesus our Lord."*

A snippet of memory tumbled from a long-locked closet of her brain. One of the nuns—Sister Mary Catherine, with the bulbous nose and angry eyebrows—had pinched nine-year-old Luz Maria when she'd failed to correctly recite the verse—a forewarning, perhaps, that this particular snatch of scripture would someday come back to haunt her.

For three long years, she'd worried that it would, and she'd lived with the anxiety. But how could she have guessed that when death finally did come, it would fall upon her neighbor—and threaten a little boy she loved as deeply as if he were her own?

As her knees grew weak, Luz Maria staggered to the sofa. Closing her eyes tightly, she fought to think of something else. Of getting the petition completed in time to force a hearing that might put a stop to Tex-Rid's planned incinerator. Of helping an eighty-seven-year-old former hotel maid from the Fourth Ward replace her window air-conditioning unit—the third stolen over the past two summers—before the sweltering heat stewed poor Mrs. Washington in her own sweat. Of working with April on a new fund-raising plan.

But Luz Maria's efforts fell far short, pebbles pitched against a monster. The monster whose bed and whose goals she had once shared.

Sergio had lost the goddamned car in traffic, but it was the car itself that pissed him off most. A fucking *Mercedes*, of all things. He should have known Luz Maria would sell out. Should have known she'd go for a broad-shouldered gringo with an expensive European sports car.

Hypocritical bitch. For all her talk of helping the poor, she had been sucked into the world of the movers and the shakers. Oh, he knew all about the pathetic little sideshow she put on for the media. Slapping Band-Aids on the symptoms. Helping a sick *niño* here, an old black grandma there, and putting herself on display for pampered white socialites who bought themselves a good night's sleep by preening in their finery while donating to the cause.

As if the Voice of Poverty was a *real* cause, one that addressed the root cause of *their* people's—not just any people's—problems: the immigration barriers that marginalized *la gente* while supplying overfed Americans with nannies, housekeepers, laborers, and lawn crews grateful to work long hours for low wages, without the possibility of benefits or retirement plans. And economic disenfranchisement was far from the worst risk. With illegal immigration routes straying farther and farther into the remote desert to avoid the Border Patrol's stepped-up enforcement, hundreds of his people were dying every year.

And yet this news, when it made the papers at all, was tucked into a brief column many pages behind the latest exploits of a blond heiress famed for her stupidity. Even though this summer, the hottest in a decade, was taking more lives every day.

As events from Oklahoma City to the Twin Towers had proven, there was but one way to make an impression on the complacent U.S. public. And thanks to Luz Maria Montoya's fucking treachery, the efforts of BorderFree-4-All had been set back years.

But the time of hiding and licking wounds had ended. The time had come for rising from the ashes to revive, energize, and recruit freshly enthusiastic individuals for his group. Because in three short weeks, they had a job to do, on the anniversary of the day that had brought the great American machine to a stunned standstill.

But first, Sergio meant to deal with Luz Maria—and he would, soon, thanks to the resources of his associate and the license plate number he had managed to record.

Grant was digging himself in deeper and deeper, but of all the questionable things he'd done these past two days, lying to Billy Devlin felt the worst. Hadn't Zeman taught him that partners could bullshit anybody else, but they had to shoot straight with each other? Roy Reed's red face flared up in Grant's memory, screaming out his accusations in John Zeman's kitchen.

Yet here Grant was, covering his first lie with another

after it became apparent that Billy—who was racking up some serious overtime today—had already talked to Reagan Hurley.

"Yeah, Ms. Hurley did call me," Grant said as he paced the cluttered confines of his home office. "I knew Mutton would have a fit, but I was so close, I swung by her house. Far as I could see, Ms. Montoya was gone already. Before I left, I walked around and checked the doors and looked in windows. Place looked secure, no sign of forced entry or a struggle. I'd say she left of her own volition. You sure she didn't go to her office? You checked with the VOP staff, right?"

With Billy, it always paid to ask.

"Of course I checked. What the hell do you think?" the younger man snapped. "She's not there."

"Someone's grumpy." Grant reasoned that Devlin would get suspicious if he wasn't treated to at least a little sarcasm. "Did little Billy miss his nappy?"

Ignoring him, Billy said, "Listen, no one's seen her. And it's her next door neighbor who's dead. A freelance Web designer by the name of Kellie Capshaw. Her sister, Bobbi Capshaw—she's a secretary at the FBI field office—was bringing by some takeout for her as the body was wheeled out of Ms. Montoya's apartment. Woman went ballistic as soon as she saw the inside of her sister's place. Definitely some struggle there—hair on the floor, too, just like the clumps found at Ms. Montoya's. Course, Eagan from homicide can't call it a positive ID yet, since they went ahead and bagged and transported her with the face still taped up. Didn't want to screw up any evidence."

"Her face was taped?"

"Duct taped—my guess is he couldn't get off unless he could pretend he had Ms. Montoya. The vic was nude and in Montoya's bed."

In the years he'd worked the streets, Grant had made a lot of cases, bad cases featuring the ugliest of crimes. In major assaults, he'd investigated things that were in some ways even worse, because their recipients survived to suffer. But this one kicked hard, partly because he knew how desperately Luz Maria wanted the miraculous news that the dead woman was a stranger. But mostly because he was imagining what would have happened had Luz Maria been inside the apartment when this sick son of a bitch came calling.

"So she was sexually assaulted?" Grant asked.

"Hard to tell. There were a lot of splattered fluids, what with the head trauma. If she didn't suffocate from the tape, the cause of death was likely a five iron to the cranium."

Grant searched for some scrap of comfort he could offer the woman he'd left waiting in his kitchen. "If her eyes were covered, at least she might not have seen it coming."

He found himself hoping, too, that Kellie Capshaw had died, or at least passed out, before she'd been raped, before she had felt much pain or terror.

"I'm going to work with Eagan and his partner on this—and the FBI's all over it, too," Billy said. "They're charging in like the wrath of God on account of this neighbor being the sister of an FBI employee, and with Cardenas under suspicion for it. Whether it's us or the Feds, we're going to find this bastard before he gets to Ms. Montoya."

Too damned late, Grant thought. The killer had already gotten to her with this murder and his threats, not to mention her assault.

"Have at it, man," Grant told him. "But don't keep calling here to pick my brain. Remember? I'm on vacation. *Especially* if Mutton or anybody else asks."

He disconnected and hoped that numb nuts knew a big hint when he heard one. Yet even if he was as clueless as Grant suspected, Billy would still have to come out here once he figured out his vacationing partner had "accidentally" taken home the VOP threat files.

He wondered what would happen when Devlin recognized Grant's own name and handwriting among the letters. Would loyalty tempt Billy to make that particular piece of evidence disappear? Or would Devlin call him on it or go straight to the brass?

Grant wondered, too. What was the right answer? What *did* partners owe each other? If he had discovered evidence John Zeman was hurting women—even lowlife addict prostitutes—what would he have done about it?

The questions dug in so uncomfortably, he dismissed them. Zeman *wasn't* guilty, no matter what Internal Affairs had ruled.

Putting aside that dilemma, Grant turned to a more immediate concern. Should he share with Luz Maria the devastating news about the circumstances of her friend's death? Or should he tell yet another lie today—this one, by omission?

CHAPTER FIFTEEN

The cushions shifted, alerting Luz Maria that someone sat beside her on the sofa.

Grant. She knew it without opening her eyes. The air itself vibrated with his presence, and his scent called to her like cinnamon *pastelitos* hot out of the oven.

She jerked upright, her face heating with the realization that she'd succumbed to sleep while she'd been waiting. And worse yet, she'd been dreaming. Dreaming of Grant doing things to her that were probably illegal across the Bible Belt.

And there he was, sitting right next to her, leaning forward, his big hands folded and his arms resting on the faded knees of jeans that hugged all the right places. . . .

Wake up, idiota. But scolding herself did nothing to ease the anticipation coiled tight inside her stomach or the prickling tension of her skin.

It was Grant's expression that jarred her back to reality, with his mouth pressed into a grim line and his features set as if in concrete. But the look in his eyes hit her hardest. Somber, guarded, a cop bracing himself to mete out the worst of news. Every last trace of smart-ass attitude had been stowed out of sight.

Luz Maria's legs uncurled and she braced her bare feet against the floor. With her heart punching at her chest wall, her body prepared for fight or flight.

"What is it?" As much as she feared the news, the wait to hear it was unbearable.

"You were right," he said, "about your neighbor. It's not official yet, but the investigators are almost positive the victim's Kellie Capshaw."

"You said *almost*. So there's still doubt?"

He unclasped his hands, and his gaze locked onto hers. "I'm sorry, but your friend's dead. Murdered, from the looks of things."

She glared at him. "You're just saying that. To punish me for John Zeman. You made up this whole thing and isolated me out here to torment me—"

"Don't go there, Luz Maria." He laid one hand over hers, and a callused finger stroked the inside of her wrist. "Denial's a blind alley—a pocket full of pain. You know it in your heart. You've known it from the first."

Luz Maria went dead still, afraid even to breathe. Nonetheless, the walls of emotion closed in, crushing out her last remaining hope.

But not her fury, which turned inward. "This . . . this is all my fault." She snatched her hand away from his, launching herself to her feet. "It's because of what I do."

Grant stood as well and looked down at her, his expression stone-cold sober. "No. It's because of what some maniac did. He's the one who killed her."

Grant's words were a cool breeze wafting through the pine boughs, something that ought to bring her comfort on this blazing August afternoon. Yet somehow, his consolation ignited fury like a lit match tossed on a gas-soaked haystack.

"*Chale!* If I didn't spend my life sticking my nose in everybody's business, trying to shove my version of justice down all of Houston's throats, Kellie would be alive." Though her bruised neck throbbed and tears choked her, Luz Maria couldn't stop the venom bubbling up inside her. "If I didn't raise hell on the evening news, your friend Zeman's little girls would be . . . would be putting pictures . . . on their . . . on their own papa's fridge."

"In a lot of cases, Houston *needs* a public conscience," Grant conceded. "God knows, money talks loud enough around here to drown out anybody who's not shouting."

"How can . . . how can I be anyone's '*voice*'"—she made angry quotations—"when I can't even fix myself? How can I—oh, God, why didn't that *cabrón* just finish me last night instead of . . ."

Grant stepped nearer—too near—to grab her flailing wrists. Staring down into her face, he told her, "Because *this* is what he wants. Luz Maria Montoya doubting herself, too terrified to speak for fear of what he'll do or who he'll hurt next. This asshole's out to scare you, out to shut you up and put you in what he sees as your place. The question is, are you gonna let him, Luz Maria? Are you going to let this bastard *win?* Or have you only pretended to be a fighter all these years?"

She wanted to tell him that all her life, she *had* been faking courage, and never more than these past three years. She wanted to tell him about Kellie, too, about her dubious taste in music and her hilarious, self-deprecating stories of being the only girl in her high school's all-dweeb tech club, her ill-fated attempts to fit into the corporate world, and her straitlaced sister's tireless attempts to whip her sorry golf game into shape. But with each attempt, Luz Maria's efforts splintered into sobs that shook her body.

And just that quickly, Grant was holding her, rubbing her back, rocking on his feet, and whispering, "Shh, shh," while he let her cry it out.

As she wept, the feeling took root that his arms were all that was holding her together, that if he let go of her, she'd surely fly to pieces. She nuzzled into his embrace, letting her body soak in his strength, her parched soul take in the nourishment that only human contact offered.

When his fingertips stroked the hair along her temple, a layer of pain peeled back, taking with it the burden of coherent thought. When he gently tilted her head backward, it seemed so very natural, felt so very right.

She had only a split second to take in the intensity of his expression, the conflict building like thunderheads in the clouded field of his gray eyes. And then his mouth was on hers, his kiss fierce and possessive, his hands pulling her close enough to feel his impossible hardness against her—impossible unless he was wearing a gun she hadn't spotted.

Whatever it was, it felt like just the right caliber.

Greedily, she kissed him back, her every nerve firing with the touch of tongue to tongue and the pulsing against the point of her hip. *Híjole*—that was no gun, and one of his hands was skimming her side, sliding up beneath her T-shirt, squeezing her breast and sending the word *Yes* blazing like a meteor across her consciousness.

But with consciousness came conscience, and hers roared back with a vengeance, screaming that she had no business enjoying this man—enjoying *anything*—while Kellie lay in a morgue somewhere and her family and coworkers worried themselves sick about her well-being.

Blistered by the intrusion of reality, Luz Maria jerked back and pushed at Grant's shoulders.

"What in God's name are we *doing?*" she demanded as

she extricated himself from his embrace. "This is . . . this is insane."

For a moment, he retained a blissed-out, heavy-lidded look of passion that made her want to stop fighting her own desire and ask directions to his bedroom. But before she could say anything, Grant blinked hard and his jaw clenched until she heard his teeth grind.

Raking his hand through his short hair, he turned his back to her, his head bowing and his powerful shoulders trembling visibly. When he swore aloud, she knew she was not seeing his frustration, or the fury of a man whose lust had been denied.

She was watching another example of rage turning to self-loathing, exactly as her own had a few short minutes earlier.

Grant slammed the front door behind him as he stormed out of the house and stalked up the driveway. He had no destination in mind, no goal whatsoever except putting distance between himself and Luz Maria.

What the hell had he been thinking? Never in his life had he tried to kiss a victim, or anyone connected to any of his cases. It was unprofessional as hell—the kind of behavior she'd be well within her rights to broadcast all over the evening news.

And it had gone a hell of a lot further than a simple kiss. Hell, he'd had his tongue halfway down her throat and his hand inside her bra by the time her reluctance finally cut through the haze of his desire. If she hadn't stopped him, he would already be inside her, pumping between those sweet thighs for all he was worth.

He groaned aloud and fought to switch the channel of his overheated brain. It scarcely made a differences, for he still felt the peaking nipple of her warm breast and the way she'd writhed against him, kissing him with all the fire he'd sensed in her from the beginning.

At the start, she'd wanted him, too. He was certain of it. Either that or she'd been flat-out desperate to push thoughts of her murdered neighbor from her mind.

And he'd been right there, moving in on her emotional upheaval—taking advantage of proximity and power, just as she'd accused the Z-man of doing with those prostitutes. At the thought of John, he groaned again, the last of his desire crumbling into ash.

How could he have pounced on Luz Maria Montoya, of all people, after what she'd done? Could he have made a worse decision?

She had it well within her power to put his career beyond any possibility of salvage. But it hurt far more to think of his coworkers' anger and disgust, especially those who had worked with John, too.

And what in God's name could he say to Sherry Zeman when she asked if it was true? How would he explain to her that he'd been late to put together a bicycle for her daughter because he was busy trying to nail the woman responsible for John's death? Especially after he'd brushed aside Sherry's hesitant overtures by saying he was still getting over Jennifer's desertion.

He was over that already—and good riddance to the woman, if she couldn't tough out his depression in the months following John's death. *What happened to John is terribly sad but it's over,* she'd kept telling him, her voice so simultaneously perky and dismissive he could have strangled her. *This is our time for celebration, our time to think about the future instead of wallowing in the past.* And then she'd whip out some damned catalog and demand his opinion on cocktail napkin imprints or reception table centerpieces even when she knew he didn't give a rat's ass, even when she knew he only wanted to be left alone.

She'd replaced him within six months, found a willing stand-in—some power company executive she worked with—for the Jennifer Southwick Bridal Extravaganza she'd been planning half her life. Knowing her, she'd simply changed the groom's name and the date, then gone on as if she'd never walked out of his life three weeks before their own planned nuptials.

Though Grant's path lay in shadow, the interlaced canopy of trees held in the day's heat, steeping him in perspiration. The mosquitoes found him, too, conspiring with the humid air to turn him around, to drive him back toward the only solution he could think of, daunting as it was.

He had to apologize to Luz Maria. Apologize, and somehow convince the media mouthpiece to keep silent.

Luz Maria thought of going after Grant, but she had no words of comfort. And with her own emotions swirling, she couldn't be sure whether she would curse him or beg him to come back to finish what he'd started.

She didn't dare go to find him—not with desire threatening to overtake her better sense. Because she did want him, pure and simple, in a way she hadn't wanted anyone since . . .

She went to find the phone instead. Heaven knew, it was a safer bet.

She located it in a small home office, which proved as cluttered as she might have imagined. Snatching up the cordless handset, she started dialing, then switched the phone off.

It still made good sense not to broadcast her location. Though she had serious doubts about the wisdom of staying here, she didn't want Grant getting suspended, or even fired, for trying to keep her safe. After a moment's consideration, she punched in the code that would block this name and number from caller ID, then dialed Whit's cell phone.

She got his voice mail and left a simple message, saying she was somewhere safe and not to worry. She promised a return call later, then once again blocked the phone's identity and called the VOP office.

Strangely, no one answered. Had everyone cut out early because it was a Friday? Luz Maria dismissed the thought. Surely the office would be buzzing with all that had happened these past two days. She couldn't imagine them all out at happy hour while she was missing in action.

After leaving a message at work as well, she dug the number of April's cell phone from her purse and tried it. On the third ring, VOP's public relations and fund-raising manager answered with a tentative, "Yes?"

"Where is everybody?" Luz Maria asked without preamble. "I tried the office, but—"

"Luz, where are you? Everyone's been looking for you. We've been scared out of our minds that that horrible man has you."

By now, Luz Maria was holding the phone several inches from her ear. She'd never heard her coworker so upset.

"I'm really sorry," Luz Maria told her. "I called as soon as I could. And I thought that my brother would've let Whit know I phoned to tell him I was safe."

"He did call—called the office, too, but he said you sounded strange. He was afraid someone might have been forcing you to make that—"

"*Forcing* me? Since when has anybody been able to make me do anything?" Luz Maria rolled her eyes. Things were scary enough without Jack going into Big Brother mode. "Please, tell everyone I'm fine. I'm safe where I am. Are you at home?"

"No, I'm at Mama Bellini's. We all are."

Luz Maria felt her forehead furrow in confusion, not only that the "frantic" VOP staff had gone to the little

Italian eatery across the street, but that April seemed so frightened. She sounded close to tears, and April *never* cried.

"What's going on? What's happening, April? It's more than me, and more than my neighbor, isn't it?"

"Someone—oh, God, Luz Maria. We had a drive-by shooting at the office, just a little while ago. The police are still there, gathering evi—"

"A drive-by shooting—at VOP?" Luz Maria echoed. "My Lord. Was anybody hurt?"

She thought of Whit's phone, which he always kept on; thought of how she'd only connected with his voice mail. An idea occurred, so horrifying that she barely noticed Grant standing in the doorway looking at her.

"Did that bastard shoot Whit, April?" she demanded. "Tell me right this minute—is Jason Whitfield dead?"

CHAPTER SIXTEEN

Grant's heart pounded as Luz Maria dropped like a stone into his desk chair. The desire flared anew to touch her, to soften whatever fresh shock had pummeled her.

He struggled to rein in his instinct while she found her tongue again.

"Thank God—thank God no one was hurt, at least. What do you mean, Whit was? I thought you said—" Luz Maria nodded, then paused before adding, "Oh, that makes sense. I'm glad it didn't hit his eye. Is the cut bad?"

Flying glass, Grant guessed. Before he'd reached the doorway, he'd heard something about a drive-by. The gunman must have taken out at least one window.

Luz Maria loosed an audible breath. "That's good. I'm glad he won't need stitches. Was anyone else—? Good. So tell me how it happened. Did anyone see the shooter? What about the car?"

Grant wanted desperately to snatch the phone away, to take over questioning the witness. But if Luz Maria hadn't mentioned him, he'd do better to keep out of this. Besides, he'd probably get more information by allowing the conversation to play out and then asking her about it. Presuming she was still inclined to speak to him.

As she talked with someone Grant figured must be a coworker, he didn't bother to hide his eavesdropping. But Luz Maria gave no sign she cared or even noticed. Clearly, her attention was centered on getting more details—and later, on deflecting questions as to her whereabouts.

"I'll check in again later," Luz Maria promised. "But it's safer for everyone involved if I don't come back until the police arrest whoever's doing these things. I'm sorry, April. I have to go now."

Breaking the connection, she swiveled the chair and looked at Grant. "There was a drive-by shooting at the VOP office."

"So I gathered," he said. "But nobody was hit?"

She shook her head. "A piece of window glass nicked Whit's neck. He's okay, though—and even better, he got a look at the car."

"He get the plate number?" If anyone would have thought to write it down, it would have been the hyper-organized Whitfield.

But Luz Maria's head shook once again. "He couldn't make it out, but he got a pretty good description. Tan Camry, maybe four or five years old."

Grant's hope fizzled like a damp fuse. "There must be thousands in the area—*tens* of thousands."

"Loose trim on the passenger front door, a missing hubcap on the same side." A smile played over the mouth whose taste still haunted him. "There was a bumper sticker, too, one supporting the—"

"Let me guess. The Houston Astros."

She nodded, pointing at him. "Bingo."

"Interesting. Wonder if this guy's a buddy of Tony

Coleman." Surely, even a rookie investigator like Devlin would know to question Coleman's wife—or better yet, the man himself, if he was talking. They had to get a lead on any known associates.

"Did Whitfield see the shooter?"

Luz Maria said, "April said he couldn't be sure, but he got the impression the person might've had short, blond hair."

"Blond, huh? Male or female?"

Luz Maria shrugged. "She didn't mention anything about that. Because of the calls, I'd just assumed—but I guess it's a mistake to do that."

Grant managed what he hoped would pass for a smile of his own. "First thing they teach investigators, the dangers of tossing out any possibilities that don't fit your going theory."

"Do you even have one? The way you talked before, I thought you were pretty convinced we were dealing with . . ." She took a deep breath, a tic tugging her lips into a frown. "With Sergio Contreras."

"I'm not dismissing that idea yet. Our suspect's definitely sophisticated, maybe enough to steal a vehicle that would lead cops to look elsewhere. But we can't discount the Coleman angle either—or anybody else you've pissed off lately."

She made a face and said, "I'm so relieved. For a minute there, I was worried you had absolutely no idea."

He smiled at her sarcasm before sobering abruptly. The bizarre circumstances were blurring boundaries he'd never butted up against before. To remind himself of the most important of them, he glanced at the hazy photo of the Zeman family.

"What happened earlier—I was way out of line, Ms. Montoya," he said. "I'm sorry, and I give you my word, I won't forget myself again."

Her frown deepened, and to his astonishment, she waved off the apology. "It's Luz Maria, Grant. I think we're well past the formalities. And don't beat yourself up over it. I was upset and you were trying to be a human about it. If I hadn't been half out of my mind, I would've never, um . . . you know, brushed up against you that way."

A flush tinged her cheeks, cluing him in that her apparent nonchalance wasn't telling the whole story. Luz Maria Montoya was embarrassed by their little grope-fest, probably too embarrassed to mention it to anyone.

Grant ought to feel relieved and damned well ought to keep his mouth shut. But as Lieutenant Mouton would attest, discretion had never been one of his better qualities.

"I'm not some horny teenager. I'm an officer of the law," he said. "No matter what you did, I damn well ought to know better. And I do, I swear it. I've made some dumb-ass moves in my life, but I've never, ever done anything so—"

"Maybe you'd better quit while you're ahead," she suggested, amusement dancing in her dark eyes.

"Right." He felt heat suffuse his own face, and he floundered for something else to say. Anything that would lead them away from this particular topic. "So, uh, you'll still stay for a while?"

"You still want me?" Luz Maria asked, then hastily added, "I mean, do you still want me *here?*"

As he looked at her, it occurred to Grant that he'd probably want her *anywhere*, but he swallowed back the thought. "Sure, you can stay. So long as no one knows where you are."

She shook her head. "I didn't tell a soul. I didn't want to risk it. I even blocked the ID on my outgoing calls from your phone."

He was impressed, but not surprised. He'd long since

figured out the beautiful Latina was nobody's fool. "Very good thinking. For one thing, I kind of like my job. Most days, anyway. And it bears mentioning that this stalker appears to have no trouble with locks and seems to know his way around electronics. Bugging your office or your family's phones wouldn't be much of a stretch—especially if we're talking about multiple perpetrators working as a team."

Her gaze darted to the floor, and he imagined she was trying to recall anything she might have said on the telephone that would give her away.

Moments later, she looked up again. "Whoever's doing this, I'll help in any way I can to stop him—or them. But I won't put my family or my friends in any more danger than I have already. Even if it means I have to let them worry for a little while."

"You know I want to help you," he said. "For one thing, the faster we get this solved, the faster I can get back to my vacation."

But Grant wasn't thinking about swapping lies and fishing with his cousin. How could he, with Luz Maria sitting there, gazing up at him with those gorgeous, long-lashed eyes? And he found himself wishing she had stuck with her long skirt, for her slender legs were proving one hell of a distraction. For damned sure, if he didn't quit ogling, she wouldn't believe one word of his ridiculous claim.

The phone rang, making them both jump. They stared at it through two rings, until Grant reached for the handset. Whatever news was coming, ignoring it wouldn't keep it at bay for very long.

"Holcomb," he said, as if he were still at work.

"You sorry son of a bitch."

Recognizing Devlin's voice, Grant grinned. "Well, golly gee whiz, partner. I love you, too."

Billy cut straight through the bullshit. "You took the damned files."

"What files? Aw, hell. The ones Whitfield gathered for us . . . I left 'em in my damned trunk, didn't I?" Grant hoped he sounded more innocent than he felt. "I'm really sorry. You want to come out here and pick them up?"

That ought to buy him some time. Billy had gotten lost both times before, once when he'd come to watch a game and once to give his roommate and a conquest a little breathing space. Trent, the playboy roommate, was the reigning poster child for STD awareness.

"I'm not driving all the way out there. Some of us have to work tonight, remember? Besides that, *you* took the files. *You* bring the damned things back."

Grant rolled his eyes. What a baby. "All right, all right already. I'm not going near the station, but I'll drop them by your apartment. I've got to run an errand in town, anyway."

The more he thought of canceling on Sherry, the guiltier he felt. Instead of calling her with some lame excuse for his lateness, he might as well go make a start on assembling the bicycle. The gutters could always wait, but Emma's big day was on Sunday.

Once he hung up, Luz Maria furrowed her brow. "You're leaving me alone here?"

He nodded. "Yeah, I'm going to have to. My partner needs those VOP files, and I need to pick his brain to see what's happening. Besides that, it'll be safer if Devlin doesn't come by and figure out you're here."

"Safer for *you?*" A spark of censure had crept into her voice.

In the hopes of stamping out that ember, he shrugged. "Every person who knows is one more person who might tell someone else. And before you know it, our little secret's not a secret anymore."

"So you think I'll be okay alone?"

"I don't see how anybody could possibly guess I'd do

such an idiotic thing as to bring you here to my place."
He nodded and felt a wry smile pull at the corner of his
mouth. "Besides that, I have an alarm system I'll turn
on, and I'll leave you with one of my guns. Let me get it
for you."

Her nose crinkled. "I don't do guns. Statistics tell us
we're more likely to shoot a friend or family member
than—"

"Statistically, most people don't have sicko killers
stalking them. You'll keep the pistol, Luz Maria."

Her stare burning into him, she swallowed audibly,
then took a deep breath. "You never told me how my
neighbor died. What did he . . . what did he do to Kellie?"

Grant shook his head. "We can't really say yet, not
until the autopsy's been—"

"*Déjate de pendejadas,*" she said. "Don't give me
that . . . that garbage. I know you heard something. You
just don't want me freaking out on you. But I have the
right to know, Grant. She was my friend."

He sighed. "I'll tell you after I come back, once I've
had the chance to talk to Billy. I'll know more then,
and . . . and you won't have to be alone with it."

Her eyes narrowed. "I don't like being patronized."

He leaned over her and whispered conspiratorially,
"Well, here's a little secret. *I* don't care what you like."

"You should," she advised. "Because rumor has it I
can be a real pain in the *pompis* when I don't get my way."

"That might be your public image . . ."

"Or it just might be the truth."

"I don't know. There are a few who'd contend I have
pain-in-the-ass behavior down to a science," he boasted.
"I suspect you may be a lightweight—at least when no
cameras or microphones are in sight."

She flashed a smile, but her brown eyes gleamed a
challenge. "Nice theory, but I wouldn't bet on it. At
least, not with more than I could afford to lose."

As she stood, he held her gaze, but a realization blazed through his consciousness like a streak of lightning.

I think I have already.

Normally, his associate preferred to e-mail Sergio from a newly activated, disposable account. But this evening, for the first time, he received a return call after posting his encrypted request for information.

"Sybil here. I know you don't pay me to give advice," the woman began without preamble, "but you might want to reconsider, if you're thinking of taking out a cop."

Sergio nearly dropped his cell phone onto the still steaming Chinese take-out carton resting on the hotel room bed. And it wasn't only Sybil's softly feminine voice that had taken him aback. There was no way in hell that classic Mercedes was an HPD vehicle. So what was Luz Maria doing in an officer's private car?

Instinct told him his first guess had been the right one. Luz Maria was screwing this guy, cop or not. Compared to her other sins, this betrayal was minor, yet somehow the idea struck him to his core.

"I'll need the name," he said. "The address, too."

The infamous hacker hesitated long enough that he snapped at her, "Funny time for you to grow some scruples, now that your payment's cleared."

He hated dealing with mercenaries, whose attachment to the cause ran no deeper that their pockets—or in Sybil's case, the electronic purse strings of her anonymous offshore accounts. He'd heard rumors that she had enough money tucked away to buy one of the island nations for her very own, yet still she stayed active in the riskiest of ventures. Such pointless greed; yet it served his purpose.

"It's hardly scruples," she said, her soft voice dripping scorn. "It's self-preservation, that's all. I like keeping a low profile."

He chuffed a laugh; he couldn't help it. "Like the FBI's most wanted list?"

"What's that old saying? You know, the one about the pot calling the kettle black?"

"You don't have to worry about this information coming back to bite you. And this cop doesn't need to worry, either. He's not my target—never has been."

As he jotted down the name and address Sybil gave him, Sergio didn't elucidate.

Even though he knew he'd take out anyone who stood between him and the woman he'd once loved.

Sherry Zeman met Grant at the front door of the one-story redbrick house she and John had bought after their marriage, then added onto as their family grew. Nestled among mature oaks in a gracefully aging neighborhood, the Zeman house was set off by azaleas that bloomed a welcome every spring and beds bordered with daylilies that kept the spirit going throughout each endless summer. Though it was by no means ornate, the place was nicer than anywhere Grant had ever lived.

Nicer than you deserve, too, the way you let down her husband. The memory of his mother's voice was like a blast of hell-hot air, though more than sixteen years had passed since the woman ran off with a man she'd met two weeks earlier—only two months after Grant's father had been shot dead. *Now wipe your big feet so you won't track in any dirt.*

"Sorry I'm so late," he told Sherry, though her green eyes showed no reproach, only enormous relief that he had made it. Since the suicide, she took nothing for granted. "I had to drop some files off at Devlin's, and before that, I got tied up with—"

"You already apologized on the phone. It's all right. Come on in." Smiling a welcome, she stepped back from the door to let him inside, and he noticed she'd taken more care than usual with her sandy-colored, chin-length hair. She wore a pretty, halter-style sundress that flattered generous curves. "I wish you'd come around back, Grant. You know how the girls and I— well, you're practically family by now. Definitely a backdoor guest."

As if to underscore her statement, a scrabbling of paws preceded squealing cries of, "Uncle Grant, Uncle Grant."

A chocolate-brown streak beat Sherry's daughters to him with a leap that knocked him two steps backward. Ox had been an impulse gift, a lab mix puppy he'd talked Sherry into letting him bring the girls last summer. The animal shelter people had neglected to tell him the "mix" part of the pup's pedigree must include a liberal sprinkling of elephant. The galumphing menace had quickly grown into his huge paws—and out of the girls' first name for him: "Fluffy."

The girls giggled as Grant fended off Ox's tongue and dropped the dog's paws from his shoulders to the floor, where they belonged. "Sorry, bud," he told Ox with a friendly ear scratch. "The only kisses I want are from two very special young ladies."

Squatting down to the girls' level, he opened his arms wide. Emma and Sierra filled them, throwing their arms around his neck and smacking their lips against his cheeks with such exuberance that Ox whined and wriggled in frustration.

Grant scooped the girls up, one in each arm, and nuzzled each soft blond head. "How are my best girls?"

"Just leaving," Sherry answered for them.

At the same moment, he spotted Sherry's sister Donna in the living room doorway with car keys jingling in her hand. Donna glanced first at Sherry before smiling at him.

Grant's stomach tightened. Something was in the air

this evening—something that smelled a lot like a conspiracy between the set of sisters.

"Oh, Mommy, can we please stay? I wanna play with Uncle Grant," begged three-year-old Sierra.

A rush of pleasure blindsided Grant. God, they were sweet kids. John had no idea how much joy he'd thrown away in a single, desperate moment.

"Hey, Grant," Donna greeted him. Though the redhead struggled with her weight—she carried at least fifty pounds more on her small frame than her younger sister—her bubbly personality had always drawn more than her share of lovers. None of whom she had bothered marrying, since she preferred to devote her energy to the trendy fashion accessories she designed.

The three thousand square foot Memorial area palace she'd bought recently attested to the fact that designing expensive ladies' handbags paid far better than police work. Grant didn't hold it against her, though. She was too nice to resent.

"The princesses and I are about to head over to my place, where we fully intend to swim in our underwear, stay up *way* past bedtime, and maybe even . . ." After a dramatic pause, Donna's voice dropped to a near whisper. ". . . maybe even skip our baths."

A cheer went up from the two girls, who squirmed until Grant put them down.

Within minutes, Donna, the girls, and even Ox—who was sure to swamp everyone by belly-flopping into Donna's pool—vanished, leaving the house quiet but for the soft strains of jazz Grant now heard playing in the background.

"Come inside, Grant," Sherry said.

Though the light was dim, he saw two patches of color stain her cheeks. They were softly rounded, almost like a child's. But there was nothing childish about the light floral perfume she wore, nor in the glances she flitted his way—when she could bear to meet his eye.

Oh, God. He *so* did not want to deal with this tonight. Especially not with Luz Maria Montoya waiting in his house and with the burden of the bad news he needed to deliver.

"I'm so glad you could come," she said as he followed her through the dining room. A light tremor in her voice betrayed her nervousness. But there was determination there, too, the resolve of a woman who meant to make her play this evening or die trying.

Grant felt sick with remorse. Sherry was sweet and pretty in her own way. Unlike the more outgoing Donna, she was an old-fashioned, loving mother who kept a warm, inviting home and wanted nothing more than a man to worship and to care for at its center. No one would blame Grant—on the contrary, he would be much admired by his coworkers—if he stepped into John's place and took his partner's family as his own. He already spent so much time over here, a couple of the guys had dropped less-than-subtle hints that it was about time for him to do the right thing by her.

Yet though he cared very much for Sherry, Grant couldn't summon anything but despair at the thought of bedding her, or of walking down the aisle—and into the delusion that John's ghost would not always stand between them. She deserved one hell of a lot better, even if she didn't know it.

"Um, I think we'd better get working on that bicycle," he said. "Before it gets too late."

If he acted oblivious enough and dragged things out long enough, maybe he could put off hurting her one more night. But when disappointment touched the corners of her mouth, he said reflexively, "You look nice tonight. That's a pretty dress you've got on."

Pleasure lit her whole face, making her eyes glow like

little Sierra's on those occasions Grant pulled a chocolate kiss out from behind his back. "I—ah, thank you,
Grant." She sounded so damned grateful that it nearly
broke his heart. "The bike box is in the family room. I
spread out a sheet for the parts and brought the tools inside. I thought . . . it's too hot in the shop, and the mosquitoes have been awful."

She led him inside the family room, where his gaze
touched on the mantle above a small brick fireplace.
John and Sherry's wedding photograph was still there,
along with some of the hand-carved duck decoys Zeman had spent so many hours crafting in his backyard
woodshop.

Turning to Grant, Sherry spoke all too quickly, more
color rising to her fair face. "Can I offer you a glass of
wine? I . . . I picked up a nice bottle of Merlot. But I have
some white chilled, just in case you'd like that better."

Since Grant had never known Sherry to drink, he pre-
sumed the purchase was for his benefit. Nausea stirred
his empty stomach as he thought of Luz Maria—
thought of how it would destroy Sherry if she ever
guessed.

An impulse gripped him to rush out to his car this
minute, to get Luz Maria the hell out of his house and
his life. Then to drag his ass back here and make himself feel something for this beautiful, loving woman.
Anything besides the pity and remorse that he felt now.

The struggle to make his mouth form words felt
Herculean, like the effort to slog through deep sand.
"To tell you the truth, I've got a killer headache," he
lied. "And I'm running on about four hours' sleep. You
think that maybe we could take a rain check?"

With the light in her eyes dimming, she pulled at
her dress's shoulder strap self-consciously, an act that
drew his eye to one full breast. Swallowing hard, he
looked away.

"I should . . . I should have known." Her voice broke, but she covered her disappointment quickly, clearing her throat and going on. "I mean, I should've realized you'd be tired, since you worked last night. Would you like—maybe something to eat would make you feel better. I could make you a nice—"

"Maybe a couple of aspirin," he suggested. Sherry was an amazing cook, but he couldn't stand the thought of her doing one more thing to please him. "With some water—yeah, some ice water would be great, thanks."

She nodded, then hurried off, her steps lightened by what she clearly thought was the opportunity to win his approval. The fictitious pain in his forehead grew so real, Grant bolted for the bathroom, where he splashed cold water on his face and fought back an urge to vomit.

Several minutes later, he heard Sherry's light tap at the door. "Are you all right, Grant? Is there anything I can get you? Anything at all that I can do?"

He glanced up at the window, seized with a desire to smash it out and scramble through it, then climb into his damned car and drive off to parts unknown.

Instead, he took a deep breath and murmured to himself, "Get a goddamn grip, Grant."

To Sherry, he called, "I'll be right out."

After all, they had a soon-to-be six-year-old's bicycle to assemble.

After a second, longer nap on Grant's sofa, Luz Maria awakened to a room painted in the bruised shades of late dusk. Pushing herself into a sitting position, she strained her ears, wondering what sound had roused her.

For several minutes, she sat completely still, listening to . . . what was that? Almost, but not quite rhythmic, and so soft it took all her concentration to detect it.

She hugged herself, realizing for the first time what she *didn't* hear. No cars in the street, no faint but friendly thump of bass from a neighbor's stereo. No ticking clock or humming air-conditioning. Instead, a sterile silence that made the downy hairs rise along her arms. And that faint tapping—shouldn't Grant be home by now? He'd been gone for hours already.

Luz Maria rose, then crept to the window and used her fingertips to raise one dust-filmed blind slat. Moments later, she allowed the breath she had been holding to slip free.

"It's only a little rain," she told herself as her vision adjusted to the gloom beneath the front yard's canopy of tree limbs. Moisture blackened thick trunks, and closer to the ground, the tender leaves of bushes shuddered as the fat drops struck them.

And off to the right, a staccato flash of tiny lights drew her attention to something larger, moving through the undergrowth.

With her pulse throbbing at her temples, Luz Maria's gaze twitched to the handgun Grant had left her. Though he'd placed it on the coffee table no more than six feet from the window, in her perception, the distance stretched into an unbridgeable expanse.

Out of the corner of her eye, she caught another movement. She looked again, squinting into the near darkness . . . and swore at the sight of a deer—three deer—browsing among the sparse, late summer grasses. As she watched, the fairy lights of fireflies waxed and waned in quick succession—and reminded her she'd spent far too much time inside Houston's city limits.

"Some fearless crusader you are," she chided herself, "scared half out of your wits by Bambi *y la familia*."

The air-conditioning restarted, drowning out the raindrops. Eager to banish her jitters, Luz Maria hurried to switch on lights and turn on the television, which was in the midst of a comfortingly familiar commercial break.

As tension eased its grip, her stomach asserted its needs with a noisy growl, so Luz Maria went to the kitchen to see what Grant had on hand. He'd told her to help herself to anything he had out there, but as Luz Maria surveyed the contents of the fridge and pantry, she found very little that appealed to her. One thing was certain—a man had done the shopping, stocking the place with frozen pizza, canned chili, chips, summer sausage, and not a fresh vegetable in sight.

At last, Luz Maria decided on an unopened box of fruit and granola cereal. After finding a spoon and pouring milk into the bowl, she carried it back to the sofa and hunted for the remote control, eager to avoid the nine o'clock newscast that was starting. But by the time she found the remote, tucked between two cushions, she was already too late.

Her own face was staring at her from the screen, above a graphic that read "File Footage." Unable to look away, she set down her untouched bowl.

"We have breaking news on a shocking new development in the case of well-known Voice of Poverty activist Luz Maria Montoya, who was assaulted late last night in the parking lot of a Memorial area Ryland's Grocery."

The news anchor, a slender redhead with a carefully crafted girl next door image, affected a look of sympathy generally reserved for mudslides killing hundreds. Luz Maria's hand froze on the remote, her stomach clutching with sheer dread as the screen image shifted to a shot of the parking lot of her own apartment complex. A shrouded form was being loaded into the back of an unmarked white van with tinted windows.

"Late this afternoon," the news anchor said solemnly, "police officials confirmed that a nude female body bound with duct tape was removed from the apartment of Ms. Montoya, who had been released from Hermann Hospital earlier in the day."

Nude. Bound with duct tape. The words detonated in Luz Maria's mind—along with the knowledge that her friend might have been raped. Her stalker's ugly words rose like ghosts to haunt her: *"Next time I get my hands on your throat, I promise you, we won't be interrupted. Next time, I won't stop squeezing 'til those pretty eyes pop from their sockets. And then I'm going to fuck you there."*

"Oh, Kellie . . ." Helpless tears flowed freely, coating Luz Maria's face with their damp heat.

But the anchor—and the bad news—were relentless.

"Though relatives have not yet officially identified the remains, the case is under investigation by members of the homicide division—"

As the redhead launched a teary-eyed retrospective of Luz Maria's "selfless heroism," the saint-in-question cursed a bilingual blue streak.

"Idiota," Luz Maria railed as she clicked off the TV. "Why are you telling everyone I've been killed?"

Didn't reporters have a responsibility to check these things before they reported them?

Luz Maria muttered through clenched teeth, "April. April Walsh—if you were the one who called the television stations . . ."

She couldn't come up with a vile enough threat, but she swore to herself she'd think of something. Fire ants on the floorboards of April's Porsche, the heels sawed off her Manolos . . .

Her anger wound down like an untended clock. Doubt spilled into the vacuum, filling it with both fear and self-recrimination. Yet a tiny island stood out, a single spot where she could stand to keep her head an inch or so above the driving waves.

It was the memory of Grant telling her, *"This asshole's out to scare you, out to shut you up and put you in what he sees as your place. The question is, are you gonna let him, Luz Maria?"*

"No," she swore aloud as she summoned the outrage that had always been her gift—or her curse, if anyone asked Mama. "I can't let him do this."

Her stubbornness served her well, allowing her to choke down a few bites of the cereal before giving up and throwing the rest down the disposal. But with full darkness shrouding the house, her courage finally failed her when she heard an electronic beep—the first chirp of an alarm system as it warned that one of the house's doors or windows had been opened.

CHAPTER SEVENTEEN

He came in through the side door, stepping into a dark kitchen—but not so dark that he couldn't make out Luz Maria's silhouette.

As Grant reached for the kitchen light switch, he asked, "What are you doing standing here in the da—?"

Overhead, the fluorescent fixture flickered to life, illuminating Luz Maria's outstretched arms, as well as the gun she pointed toward the center of his chest.

"I thought you didn't believe in those things." Grant kept his voice low and calm, though his heart had crowded into his throat and his right hand tingled with the instinctive need to reach for his own weapon.

"Oh, my—my . . ." The gun's muzzle sank below the level of the counter. A second later, so did Luz Maria.

Moving quickly, Grant punched the security code into the alarm to quiet its beeping, then dropped the bag he'd brought in on the kitchen table. Afterward, he squatted beside Luz Maria, who was slumped on the linoleum, her eyes dazed and her expression vacant.

Carefully, Grant extricated the handgun from her

unresisting fingers and reached up to lay it on the countertop. "It's all right," he said softly, though he wanted to ride the wave of adrenalin pounding through him, wanted to shout, *"Are you insane?"* then haul her straight back to her family, where she rightfully belonged. He'd been thinking about it all the way back here from Sherry's—or at least until he'd heard the top-of-the-hour news update.

Grant took a deep breath, struggling to regroup. "I'm really sorry I scared you. If I hadn't had my head up my—I mean, if I hadn't been so distracted, I would've thought to call the house on the way in."

When she didn't answer, he added, "Listen, I can understand why you're spooked. Under the circumstances, anybody in their right mind would be. Luz Maria—Luz Maria, can you hear me?"

Ever so slightly, her chin bobbed, and her lost look cleaved him to the bone. In self-defense, he dragged his gaze away, then frowned down at the floor. It needed sweeping. Mopping, too, judging from the way his shoe was sticking. For damned sure, it was no place for Luz Maria.

Reaching under and around her, Grant scooped her up. His left knee popped as he rose—a little souvenir of his days playing high school football—but he carried her easily to the living room, then sank down on the sofa, Luz Maria still in his arms.

Bad idea, he realized. Because no matter how he told himself he was only concerned about the possibility of an undiagnosed concussion or the onset of shock, her bottom atop his groin had Grant's blood rushing away from his brain, which needed every molecule of oxygen it could get.

Sliding out from under her—hopefully, before she noticed what was going on—Grant cupped her jaw and looked into her brown eyes.

"Talk to me. Tell me you're all right," he ordered, just before a horrible suspicion plunged his lust into cold water. "You didn't—you haven't taken something, have you?"

He shouldn't have left her alone—not even for a minute. As a cop, he'd seen both men and women crack when stress became intolerable, had seen too many attempts to silence anxiety with pills and alcohol, with razor blades and nooses. His mouth dried as he remembered forcing open Zeman's door—the back door—after he'd heard the single shot that told him John was already past help. Yet even after that hard lesson, Grant had left Luz Maria here with his gun, along with the contents of his medicine cabinet and whatever she carried in that big purse.

Could some part of him have done such a thing on purpose, in the hopes that she would . . . ?

He clamped down on the thought, refusing to complete it. Refusing to accept that he would ever sink so low.

Luz Maria sucked in an audible breath, her eyes focusing on his face and her spine straightening. "Of course I didn't take anything. How could you think that?"

Relief surged through him at her spark of indignation. He should have known Luz Maria was no suicide. She might be distraught, but there was strength in her, too, the mettle of a woman tough enough to regularly square off against Houston's most powerful. He found himself admiring that strength, so at odds with Sherry Zeman's weakness.

Guilt swamped him. If Sherry had been shattered, Luz Maria was the one who'd wielded the sledgehammer. And he had been the damned fool who'd caught on to John's state of mind too late.

"Sorry," he said to Luz Maria. "You weren't looking so good, that's all. Uh, that didn't come out the way I meant it. What I should have said is, you look pretty shaken up."

"Sorry. I'm so sorry." Moisture glimmered along the rims of her eyes. "I'd been watching the news, and I was upset. But I . . . I might have shot you. Damned guns— see, I told you they were trouble."

He tried on a smile, hoped like hell it would mask the way her tears affected him. She might be tough, but the thought of shooting him left her horrified. That unexpected softness stirred his protective instincts, but then, he'd always been partial to a woman who wouldn't derive too much enjoyment out of killing him.

"Maybe the real problem's nervous females," he said lightly. "Just who did you think was coming through that door? With his own key, I might add."

She sighed. "It was stupid, I know. But I didn't hear you drive up, and when that alarm beeped—"

"Have you eaten, Luz Maria?" He still didn't like her pallor. And heaven only knew, she could use the distraction.

"*What?*"

He shrugged. "You know, that thing most people do with food?"

Smiling, she closed her eyes and shook her head. "You have an answer for everything, don't you?"

"Nope. Still haven't figured out why I brought you along on my so-called 'vacation.' Now, did you eat or not?"

She shrugged. "I gave it a whirl. Didn't work out too well."

"I missed dinner myself," he told her, still amazed at the resurrection of his appetite once he had left Sherry's, "so I stopped and picked up something from my favorite little hole-in-the-wall place. And somehow, I had the feeling you might be hungry, too."

He'd bought the food with the thought that a decent

meal might bolster her. She'd need all the strength she could muster to deal with more bad news.

"I appreciate the thought. But really, I couldn't—"

Ignoring her, he said, "It's been brought to my attention on numerous occasions that my kitchen's not chick-friendly."

"You mean '*woman*-friendly,' don't you? I thought you cops were getting training in PC-speak lately." She smiled as she spoke. "But now that you mention it, after looking at your kitchen, I'm surprised you haven't died of malnutrition."

"Surprised or disappointed?"

"Depends on what you brought home." She sniffed the air and added, "Something smells like—"

"Tripe soup?" He shook his head. "Sorry, they were all out of *menudo*."

"Thank goodness," she said.

The bright notes of her laughter lifted his mood and beat back his exhaustion. It felt nice, having someone respond to his line of bull with something other than annoyance.

"I brought you a pint of homemade veggie soup—good for anything that ails you," he said. "And a salad, too. Soup-and-salad combos are chick foods, right?"

Nodding, she said, "*Women* like them, too. So what are *you* having?"

He stood, then he offered her his hand. "Come to the table, and you'll find out. I might even share, if you're nice."

She hesitated, her eyes clouding. "This . . . this doesn't feel right. Talking, joking . . . I heard that Kellie was found nude, and taped up."

His heart sank, and he urged her, "Come on, Luz Maria. You need to eat. *I* need to eat. Can't we let it be that simple, for just a little while?"

She placed her hand in his, yet still, she hesitated.

"On the news, they made it sound like I'm . . . like *I* was the one murdered."

He thought of all the times a victim interview or a crime scene or the news that one of his "slam-dunk" cases had crumbled in the courtroom had gotten him so worked up, he couldn't eat or sleep. He remembered, and repeated, the Z-man's sage advice. "Shove it in a little box. Snap a padlock on it. Otherwise, you'll end up sick or drunk or burned out—because it takes strength to win."

Something eased in her dark gaze, and she let him help her to her feet and lead her to the table. He pulled the chair out for her, then got her a clean plate, bowl, and utensils—though normally, he'd figure that Styrofoam and plastic were plenty good enough.

"Would you like soda, or maybe a beer?" he asked her.

She shook her head. "How about some water?"

After he checked a glass for spots, he got her ice and water from the dispenser on the fridge door, then decided to forego the Shiner Bock and have the same. He was having enough trouble handling the strange brew of his emotions without throwing alcohol into the mix.

By the time he'd unwrapped his chicken salad sandwich and opened the pickle and the bag of chips that had come with it, he saw that Luz Maria was only playing with her salad, flipping the lettuce idly with her fork.

"So," he began without preamble, "if you were redoing this kitchen, would you put up new wallpaper or paint it?"

She blinked back what looked for all the world like tears. "*What?*"

"Come on, help me out here," he said, feeling desperate to take her mind off her circumstances. "Do I go with wallpaper or some green paint?"

She wrinkled her nose. "Green?"

"What about something in a nice pink? And what about wood flooring, or do you think tile's better?"

"Is this part of your new 'chick'-friendly kitchen program?" Once again, she made quotations with her fingers, while what might have been amusement glinted in her eyes.

His knot of apprehension loosened. This beat tears by a long shot.

He told her, "A man could do worse than luring pretty ladies to come check out his—"

"Appliance options?"

"Exactly."

When he snatched a bite of sandwich, she ate a forkful of her salad. He offered her his jalapeno-flavored chips.

"You might want some of these. All that healthy stuff'll kill you."

She took a couple, then asked, "Did your partner tell you anything—anything we didn't know about the . . . ?"

He shook his head. "Food first," he insisted.

Because once that particular box's hinges creaked back open, he feared it would be a long while before Luz Maria would eat or sleep again.

She forced herself to watch as Grant devoured his dinner, forced herself to chew and swallow, just as he did. The salad and the soup eased a little of Luz Maria's shakiness. But even so, she finished less than half of each before pushing plate and bowl aside.

"You don't like it?" Grant asked.

"It tasted good. I just can't—" She stopped herself, head shaking. "But thank you. Thank you very much. You've been awfully kind. Especially considering the way you feel about—"

"I don't hate you, Luz Maria. I can't." Using a paper napkin from the take-out bag, he wiped a crumb from his mouth. "I would have thought that was obvious after what happened earlier."

Her heart sped up, and she dropped her gaze. "I do appreciate what you've done. But if you're looking for some kind of, uh, physical . . . repayment, I can't."

He laughed. "Don't worry. This isn't arms-for-hostages here—or soup-and-sandwiches-for-sex. I told you before, that was a real bad move on my part, one I won't be repeating."

She looked up. "Arms for *what?*"

He waved it off. "Forget it. You were probably just a tiny thing then. Unless you were already leading protest marches back in preschool."

"Oh, sure, but at the time, I was focused on more substantive issues—like boycotting creamed spinach."

He grinned at her, and she was struck by the surreal fact that she truly *liked* him, though her occasional battles against abusive and prejudiced officers had left her wary of those who stood behind the badge. Perhaps that was a prejudice in its own right—one that she should reexamine. But not with this man, and especially not now, with so many factors splintering her attention.

One shard pricked her conscience, causing her to straighten in her seat.

"I need to call that TV station. I can't have people thinking I'm dead."

"Surely, your brother will let the rest of your family know you're okay," Grant said. "And the people you work with know it's not you, right?"

"I did talk to April, but I know lots of other people, too." She rose from her seat, then started for the phone. "I can't let some irresponsible report upset them."

As she reached for the handset, he said, "Maybe you ought to rethink that for the moment."

Something in his voice gave her pause. "Why? What is it?"

He frowned and pushed back from the table, then stood, an act that forced her to look up at him.

"My partner's gotten hooked on this case, too, so he did a little online research while he should have been sleeping."

"And?" she prompted.

"And he found this Web log, a list of 'sightings' around town—along with a few notes on upcoming appearances."

"What kind of sightings do you mean?" A sick chill stole over her, telling her that whatever it was, she wasn't going to like it. "Whose appearances, Grant?"

"*Yours.* This—this blog, it's supposedly a site for your supporters—'fans,' is what the thing says. But this information that's been posted—it lists places where you shop and take your laundry, nightclubs where you've been spotted dancing, meetings where you're scheduled to appear."

"But who would post such things?" she demanded. "Who would even know them?"

"Someone who knows *you*, Luz Maria—someone who knows you very well."

CHAPTER EIGHTEEN

"Leave it alone, Jack," Reagan told him as he sat with the cordless phone in hand, his fingers poised to dial the number on Grant Holcomb's card.

He frowned up at her from the bed, where he was sitting beside a digital clock that read 11:47 P.M. Shirtless, he wore nothing but a pair of boxers. Normally, Reagan would slip into bed to personally express her appreciation of the view—but tonight the tension between them blew that possibility straight out of the water.

"They *have* to find her," Jack said, his eyes dark with concern, "and if it takes me calling every cop I can think of every hour of the damned night to demand it, that's what I plan on doing."

"Luz Maria's got the right idea, keeping us out of it," Reagan argued. "Or have you forgotten what happened the last time we both got sucked into the consequences of her—"

"That was a long time ago, a terrible lesson, and a regret she'll carry her whole life. We've gone over this before. You told me—hell, you've told *her*—you forgive her. But I'm starting to wonder, will you ever *forget?*"

"This . . . this bastard threatened Adam. *Our* Adam." Reagan's nose stung and her vision blurred with unshed tears. But worst of all was the fear radiating at her center, a dry ice chunk of terror she hadn't known in years.

Jack put down the phone and went to her. He pulled her into his arms, stroking her bare shoulders and whispering, "Ah, Reag, I never should have told you that, never should have scared you. You know I'll keep our son safe."

She pushed herself away from him abruptly and straightened the ribbon-thin strap of her pajama top. "I've seen—I saw today—what that man's capable of doing. That woman in the apartment—if you'd gotten a look what he did to her . . ."

"It's what he wants to do to Luz Maria. My little sister. The sister I helped raise."

"She's all grown up now, Jack. And dealing with threats is part of what she does. She has a staff—and a very capable security officer—to help her. The cops are on this, too, in a big way. Even if they wanted to, they can't afford to let anything happen to Luz Maria—not with this much media attention." Reagan moved to the bed and picked up the telephone, then dropped it back into its cradle. "So let them do their job now. Without interference."

"If something happens to her, what will I tell Mama? I promised her Luz Maria wouldn't be hurt."

Grabbing her robe, Reagan set a precedent in their marriage. She walked out of their bedroom and firmly closed the door behind her, unable and unwilling to argue out this issue—or perhaps sensing there was no way either one of them could win.

A few minutes later, Reagan sat on the edge of Adam's bed. The train-shaped nightlight cast the sleeping child's form in a friendly glow. Yet in spite of the gentle susurration of his breathing, her son's usual face-down sprawl painted a far uglier scene in Reagan's mind—the broken body she'd found earlier in her sister-in-law's bed.

"Not here," she whispered to herself as she leaned forward to pick up Snorty, the stuffed elephant Adam had knocked to the rug in his sleep. Ever so carefully, she lifted her son's slumber-heavy arm and tucked his favorite friend beneath it. "Never here, in this house."

Yet she couldn't stop thinking of another time, three years earlier, when Luz Maria's actions had invited violence inside. True, the younger woman had never meant for it to happen, and truer still, she could not have foreseen the collision of madness and ambition that would cost all of them—Jack, Reagan, and Luz Maria herself—so very much. But even so, her foolishness had sparked the conflagration.

There was a hitch in Adam's breathing before he rolled onto his back and his long-lashed brown eyes fluttered open. "Mommy?"

Reagan smoothed the fine, light brown hair back from his forehead, then crawled into the bed and gathered his small body into her arms. "How 'bout you and me and Snorty have a real long cuddle?" she asked. "Mommy needs a little Adam fix about now."

He murmured something she couldn't quite make out, but before she could say another word, she heard his soft snores.

She only wished she could drop off half as easily. Instead, Reagan was left thinking about Luz Maria. Whether or not Jack bought it, Reagan *had* forgiven her, won over because her sister-in-law clearly judged herself so harshly and did so much good for so many in her struggle to make amends for her mistakes.

Down the hall, Reagan heard the bedroom door

creak open, heard the heavy tread of Jack's familiar footsteps, followed by the click of Frank Lee's toenails, in the hallway. She watched from Adam's bed as her husband approached them, a pillow and a light throw tucked beneath his arm.

For several moments, they stared into each other's faces, and though the light was dim, she felt his apprehension as keenly as her own. Bending forward, Jack kissed Adam's temple before untangling the top sheet and pulling it over both his wife and child.

He leaned over Reagan's ear, so close she felt his lips move when he whispered, "I love you both so dearly. More than I can ever tell you."

She turned her head, quick enough to capture the taste of his lips. He lingered for a minute as they both poured all their emotions into that one kiss.

When he broke it off, he lay down on the braided rug beside the bed, where she understood he meant to spend the night. The dog curled near his feet, a sleek white ball of greyhound.

That was the moment Reagan realized Jack had one thing right. She never would forget the way danger could spill over from one life to another, the way the ripples could swell to devastating waves during the quiet hours of darkness.

She shifted slightly, allowing one long arm to dangle off the bed's side so she could take her husband's hand.

How could she possibly risk forgetting when she had so very much to lose?

Luz Maria regretted turning down first the beer and then the sleeping pill that Grant had offered after giving her a second piece of bad news. Hours later, in the darkness of his guest room—the neatest and most thoughtfully decorated room in the house—she lay awake, her mind churning with the implications of what he had told her.

Tony Coleman was dead. Without ever regaining consciousness, he'd coded at the hospital, and in spite of the frantic efforts of the staff, there had been no putting Humpty Dumpty back together again. Just as there would be no questioning the man about the things he'd seen or done the night of her attack.

"What killed him?" Luz Maria had asked. "Was it the bullet or the crash?"

Grant had only shrugged his shoulders and said that was a question for the medical examiner.

She wondered if had Coleman died because he'd been trying to kill her in that parking lot or because he'd tried to stop her murder. Either way, would his friends and family lay the blame for his death at her doorstep?

Her mind painted moving pictures, images in which she tried to escape the office of the Voice of Poverty, only to trip over body after body. A prone form that must be Coleman's. Kellie, nude and bloody, her china-blue doll's eyes staring up in accusation. John Zeman, crumpled with his service weapon in his hand and a gaping hole blown through the back of his head.

Unable to bear the sight, Luz Maria jerked her gaze upward, only to realize that the field of corpses extended as far as she could see, like a grisly battlefield scene. Except that instead of nameless soldiers, she knew far too many of these fallen—along with the one voice hurling accusations as devastating as grenades.

Luz Maria jolted awake, heart pounding so hard she was certain it would burst. *Ave Maria Purísima*.

But no holy intercession vanquished the images of her own family members, from Mama to Jack and little Adam, lying broken among her coworkers and friends, even some of the men she'd briefly dated.

And nothing could erase the memory of Reagan Hurley pointing to her face and screaming, *"I knew you'd do this to us. I knew it all along."*

Luz Maria sat on the bed's edge, her body shaking and her arms folded across the oversized Astros T-shirt that Grant—the smart-ass—had given her to sleep in. Not that she'd risk closing her eyes again tonight, convinced as she was the nightmare lay in wait, poised to pounce the moment she drifted into darkness.

Desperate for light, she groped for the lamp she remembered on the nightstand. In her hurry, she sent a small electric clock toppling to the floor.

She picked it up and squinted at its softly glowing hands, which marked the time as 3:30 and told her she must have slept far longer than the few minutes she'd imagined. After replacing the clock, she felt for the lamp once more, this time with more caution. But before she flipped the switch, a muffled thump made her head turn toward the wall behind her.

"I'm right next door to your room," Grant had told her after getting her clean towels. A softness came into his gray eyes that belied the wink he'd offered with the sleep shirt. *"So if you need anything—anything at all—I'll be right there."*

She'd thanked him and quickly closed the door behind her, embarrassed that the first need that sprang to her mind was the last thing either of them could afford.

Something thunked again, and Luz Maria strained her ears. Had the sound come from the same direction, or was someone moving through the darkened house?

She withdrew her hand, suddenly wary of the light she'd craved. Her ribs and throat throbbed an alarm, and her brain screamed a reminder. The intruder who had twice broken into her apartment had alerted no one and left no sign of forced entry. Yet he had left calling cards, the second—Kellie's body—even ghastlier than the first.

This time, Luz Maria wondered, would he leave her corpse behind? Would he first rape and torment her, as his calls had said he would?

Her hands knotted so tightly that she felt her ragged nails cut into her palms. If he had really come for her— if the thumping was not Grant going for a midnight snack or branches stirred by rising winds, as she prayed—Luz Maria would be damned if she was going down without one hell of a fight.

CHAPTER NINETEEN

Grant sat up in his bed, his eyes wide and his breathing fast and rough, as if he'd just chased down a suspect.

At the thought, his sweat-soaked skin crawled, tight with chill bumps. For he *had* been chasing someone—a mysterious figure who'd disappeared among mist-shrouded trees. With only the full moon's light to guide him, Grant had followed—into a nightmare so vivid he half expected he bore the welts left by the branches he had run through and the cuts of the thorns that snatched at the gray T-shirt and boxers he had worn to bed.

For damn sure, his foot and left arm hurt, leading him to believe that in his thrashing, he had repeatedly bumped the wall beside his bed. He'd suspected it had been a mistake to shove it over to make room for his weights and treadmill, and now he had proof of it, he thought as he rubbed the point of his elbow.

He sat up straighter as some sound—more a subtle shifting of the silence than anything discernible—put his senses on alert. More details from his dream came back: the clumps of long black hair clinging like cobwebs to the rough bark, the screeches of an owl morphing into Luz Maria's shrieks of terror. Finally catching up with the person he'd been chasing, spinning him around to punch him—and seeing it was Billy Devlin, who'd started shouting, *"He's getting away. And he has her with him."*

That was when Grant woke, tangled in the coiled mess he'd made of his sheets. But no matter how bad, a nightmare could be brushed aside. The barely detectable creak, however, had him rising, feeling for the shoulder holster he'd slung over the bedpost.

Someone was moving through the house. He reminded himself it could be Luz Maria, up to use the bathroom across the hall. But no light showed beneath his closed door, and when he slowly opened it, the dim illumination of the moon slanting through his blinds allowed him to make out the dark and gaping bathroom doorway.

He glanced to his left but saw no light spilling from the kitchen, either, no telltale flickering from the living room TV.

"Grant."

He jerked toward the whisper of his own name, his movement so swift, the gun in his right hand banged into something solid.

"Ow, what was that? You hit my sore ribs," Luz Maria said in quiet tones.

Pointing the Glock's muzzle downward, Grant asked, "What the hell are you doing, creeping around here in the dark? Don't you know I could have—"

"I heard something—something thumping. I thought there might be—I was afraid there was someone in the house."

Grant considered for a moment, though the memory of the thin T-shirt he had given her to sleep in proved a powerful distraction. Was she wearing it now? Did she have on anything beneath it?

He wrenched his thoughts back on track—and off of Luz Maria's slender curves.

"You were hearing me, I think. I . . . uh . . . I guess I was having some kind of bad dream." No need to go into the disturbing details. "My bed's close to the wall, and I think I might've banged up against it. Sorry if I scared you."

"I wasn't scared."

The quaver of her denial belied the statement, but he wasn't about to call her on it. Especially not with the evidence of his own concern in his right hand.

Besides, even if he had felt inclined to tell her to quit acting like a girl, the sounds of crashing metal from outside the house would have changed his mind completely.

Luz Maria raised an arm to cover her eyes when Grant flipped on the hall light.

"Damned dirty swine," he swore as he raced toward the kitchen.

Luz Maria followed, though her glimpse of his gun made her want to run and dive beneath the bed where she'd been sleeping. She wished she'd stayed at Jack's house or checked into a hotel or had herself locked up inside a jail cell. She'd been wrong before to think of fighting—wrong to think of anything but hiding from the murderer.

Another crash pulled her attention toward the darkness of the backyard. After flipping on both the kitchen light and an outdoor floodlight, Grant fumbled with the deadbolt.

"Don't you think you should call someone for backup, or whatever you guys call it?" Luz Maria asked him.

But it was too late. Grant had already thrown the back door wide and rushed forward in his bare feet.

As she hesitated in the doorway, she heard another clatter of metal from beyond the ring of light. The sound was followed by a crack as loud as any thunderbolt—the report of Grant's handgun as he fired once and then again into the trees beside the carport.

Ducking back inside, she heard an inhuman squeal and Grant shouting, "Stay out of my damned trash cans, or you're breakfast! Y'all hear that?"

Curiosity overwhelmed caution, prompting Luz Maria to peek out in time to see several low, dark shapes disappearing into the underbrush.

"What . . . what *are* those?" she called to Grant, who was still pelting them with threats of violence.

He stopped and glanced back her way, then grinned sheepishly, as if he'd forgotten she was present. "Those? They're renegade pork chops, smashing up my trash cans for the third time this damned month."

"You mean . . ." Still peering off into the moonlight, she struggled to make sense of it. "You mean they're *pigs?* Real live pigs?"

He nodded solemnly. "Yes, ma'am. Feral hogs. Years ago, farmers around here used to turn their swine loose every fall to feed on acorns in the woods. Only sometimes they'd miss rounding up the dark ones, so now we have these wild black pigs that root up everybody's gardens, break into feed bins, and generally act like a pack of teenaged vandals."

Luz Maria's knees grew weak as the tension drained from her limbs. "*Idiota.* You scared me half to death over some *pigs?*"

He shrugged and grinned. "Didn't want you thinking life out here in the country's boring."

She couldn't help herself; she started laughing. "Grant Holcomb, I can't imagine it stays dull long *anywhere* you are."

He laughed, too, and just like that, their gazes caught. Warmth crept toward her face as she noticed the way his gray T-shirt clung to a well-developed chest. At the same moment, she saw him looking at her bare legs.

And she could swear that in the sudden silence, she heard the sound of his hard swallow.

Desperate for a distraction, she said, "You . . . you didn't hit one of them, did you?"

"What?" A little of the mist lifted from those storm-gray eyes. "Oh, no. I fired over their heads. Just to scare 'em off."

What she needed right now was something to scare *her* off. But the memory of her nightmare lingered, along with the understanding that the weight—and waiting—of the remaining hours of darkness would combine to crush her flat. Despite the night's heat, chill bumps prickled along her arms and the fine hairs stood upright.

Shaking her head, she whispered, "I don't . . . I don't want to sleep alone, Grant."

A breeze ruffled his short hair, and all at once she wished to touch it, to touch *him*, if only to keep the night at bay for a few hours.

His throat worked as he stared at her for an unbearable interval. In that time, she saw the naked desire in his expression—saw him struggling to mask it, preparing to turn her down.

"Please," she said, desperate to derail his better judgment. "I know what I said earlier, but I need—"

She never got to finish, as he took two swift steps and pulled her close to his already rock-hard body, then crushed his mouth to hers with the force and fury of a man possessed. She opened her mouth to take in his tongue, a thrill of fear arcing through the pleasure—and the certain knowledge that she had pushed him beyond control. There would be no recalling her invitation, no gentle explorations or gradual escalation—nothing but this white-hot explosion of mouth-to-mouth and body-to-body contact.

Already, his hands were sweeping up beneath her T-shirt and he groaned deep in his throat at the discovery that she had taken off her bra. Pushing her against the door frame, he pulled up the shirt and sucked an erect nipple into his mouth while his knee parted her legs and his free hand made for her damp panties.

Dear God, he was going to take her right here, in the open doorway, where all the creatures of the darkness could watch them. And she was not only powerless to stop him, she'd scream with the agony of frustration if he tried to walk away. It had been so long for her, so damned long. . . .

His knees bent, his kisses dropped, and she moaned as his tongue laved her navel. At a crackling sound— maybe one of his knees—he gave a grunt, then hoisted her over his shoulder in a fireman's carry that left her rear end exposed to the night's eye.

"What are you doing?" she demanded as he closed the door and turned the deadbolt.

"I think we need a little change of venue," he said and carried her straight back to the room where she'd been sleeping.

This time, the fear that surfaced screamed a warning that he meant to drop her back in her bed, then walk straight out the door. But his hands, fingering her thigh, convinced her he had no intention of taking the high road.

He leaned forward, rolling her onto her back on the mattress. As he stood straight before her, the light that spilled in from the hallway limned a body so fine and taut that her mouth watered at the sight. She didn't move, could scarcely breathe, as he stripped off his T-shirt and finally the boxers to reveal a thick shaft, long and gently curving—and begging for her touch.

She dragged her gaze away to stare a question into his

face. Doubts fluttered in her stomach, yet every cell wept with longing for the wild passion he'd stirred in that open doorway.

"You want out?" he asked, his voice rough with need. " 'Cause if that's what you're thinking, you damned well better say so. Right here, right now, before things go one bit further."

She pushed herself into a sitting position, her movements slow and her mind roiling with all the reasons she should stamp down on the brakes while she still could.

At her hesitation, he frowned and raised an index finger. Then he turned on his heel and marched out, leaving Luz Maria more alone than she had ever felt before.

The rumors were all true, Grant decided. He *was* a first-class shitheel. Because instead of locking himself in his bedroom as he should have—or even getting dressed and jumping in the car to drive away—he was digging through his dresser drawer, his mind full of the heat and taste of Luz Maria.

There it was. Pulling out the box of condoms, he walked back to the guestroom. But some last misgiving gave him pause enough to stop outside the open door and rap it softly with his knuckles.

Time stretched out, a silken thread that ran from his heart to the woman watching so intently from the bed. She sighed, maybe with relief at his return—or was she grateful that he'd given her a minute to clear her head? A minute in which she'd decided to let sanity prevail?

She sat up, her gaze never leaving his—except for the moment when she peeled the T-shirt off and tossed it to the floor. Even in the weak light, her skin gleamed with a light sheen of perspiration, and her eyes glowed like candles as she reached toward him in invitation.

God, she was gorgeous—gorgeous and clearly desperate for his touch. Grant's hardness intensified, growing more painfully urgent with each heartbeat. He couldn't remember ever having been so aroused. Not in his horniest high school days, not even with his fiancée, whatever the hell her name had been.

He didn't even bother trying to resist, but instead knelt beside the bed, then reached in to fondle one of her small, high breasts and locked his mouth with hers, tongue thrusting in anticipation of what he meant to do.

The effect was electric, pulling his hand downward where he plunged two fingers roughly into her hot, moist cleft. Judging from the moan deep in her throat, it turned her on as much as it did him. She arched her neck, encouraging him to trail kisses down the slender column, then to suckle both her breasts.

He'd meant to take his time, to make what was sure to be a one-time encounter last as long as possible. But she was stroking him, too, sliding her grip up and down his length and whimpering, "Now, Grant, please. Come into me right now."

He barely managed to rip open the condom wrapper, to sheath his cock in latex and register the light scent mingling with the musky odor of desire. A moment later, he was on the bed and in her, with every flex of his hips heightening his pleasure.

He felt her broken nails on his back—focused on their sharp discomfort to keep himself from instantly exploding. But she pulled him along, encouraging him to pump faster, harder as she bucked against him, matching his rhythm thrust for thrust.

He withstood it until she cried out, calling his name

as her core spasmed, enveloping him in a wave of pleasure so intense that he gave himself up to it, his own shout mingling with hers.

If he burned in hell for this, so be it, for this memory of heaven would sustain him—though it could last no longer than the coming of the dawn.

CHAPTER TWENTY

The first two times, Grant ignored the ringing of his home phone, lost as he was in the warm haze of another round of mind-blowing sex and the almost forgotten comfort of waking with his arms twined around a woman's sated, sleeping body. Had it ever felt so good before? Had he ever known such wholehearted contentment as he'd felt at the soft sounds of Luz Maria's sighs?

Yet the third time the distant phone rang, his eyes flew open as he came back to himself—as well as to dismay and disgust about what he had done. But it was worry and not guilt that had him springing from the mattress and rushing bare-assed to answer by the fourth ring.

"Holcomb here," he said, glancing at the clock above the microwave. It was seven-twenty A.M., which meant that Billy's shift had ended. Was he calling as a courtesy to let Grant know he'd found the letter in the VOP threat file?

"You said you'd talk business if I could get to Houston." Special Agent Steve Petit's West Texas twang, along with his annoyance, came through loud and clear. "Funny how you didn't mention you'd be on god-damned vacation. *Or* that you'd quit answering your phones."

Grant winced and groped for something to placate his FBI source before it dried up for good. "I'm still working the case, Cowboy. And I still have information you can use in your investigation."

A hummingbird hovered outside the kitchen window. The tiny voyeur peered inside. An instant later, it was gone, zipping among the scarlet blossoms of the trumpet vine that clung to a big pine tree.

As Grant tracked the darting movements, he tried not to think of Luz Maria, sleeping naked in the bed they'd shared throughout the night. Tried not to think about returning for another taste of nectar.

"The agents working on the Capshaw murder will definitely want to hear from you, but I'm not sure I'm going to need your help on the Cardenas case," Steve told him, "seeing as how we've drawn a bead on a car rented by our 'Rogelio Izquierda.'"

Grant recognized the alias Sergio Cardenas was believed to be using. "You found a car?"

"Not yet, but we've pulled up rental records out of San Antonio. I'm being sent there to check it out."

"So? It's only a three and a half, four hour drive. Maybe he rented the car there, then came to settle the score with his old girlfriend in Houston."

"According to their records—and the associate on duty—the vehicle was rented yesterday, sometime around six-twenty, by a man fitting Cardenas's description. Long black hair, tied back, about five-ten and Hispanic."

"Rented where? One of those places over by the airport?" Grant filed away the new information, then tried to shoehorn the car rental among yesterday's events. Six-twenty. If he could get the ME's estimate for the time of death of Luz Maria's neighbor, maybe he could make the timeline work. Cardenas could have killed Kellie Capshaw, then hopped a flight to San Antonio. He would have Billy check records of incoming commuter flights from Houston.

Presuming Grant could "advise" his partner without raising his suspicions . . .

"I know what you're thinking," Steve said, "but I have a hard time figuring our target made such a detour. For one thing, our sources tell us other members of BorderFree-4-All appear to be heading to San Antonio as well. And surely you haven't forgotten the group's connection with that city?"

"They're planning another terrorist attack . . . ," Grant guessed as he thought of the bombing, three years past, of the immigration office.

"That's the general idea." Steven lowered his voice. "We've got half a dozen agencies all over this, working to track down the principals before the deadline."

"There's a deadline? Then you have specific threats?"

"I really can't go into—"

"Listen, you want to play the one-way street game, call somebody who isn't on vacation," Grant warned. "And I'm not going out of my way to talk to some agent I don't know. I've got too much to lose if it gets back to the wrong people."

He didn't even want to imagine Mutton's reaction.

"Not on the phone," Steve told him. "Maybe we could meet before I leave this afternoon to head for San Antonio. I'm not sure our cases are connected, but if there's even the slightest chance you have something we could use, I can't risk leaving without hearing you out."

A warning shuddered along Grant's backbone at the strain in Cowboy's voice. This wasn't typical FBI grandstanding, not this far from the cameras. Something even bigger than the murder of the sister of an FBI employee was in the air, something with an urgent deadline.

Grant's gaze slid to the calendar, turned to August, hanging on the wall. In the lower right corner, a smaller one showed September. This year, the eleventh would fall on a Monday. A Monday now less than three weeks distant—the anniversary target date for every two-bit radical organization in the country and beyond.

"So what time do you want to get together?" Grant asked him.

The two of them agreed upon a hole-in-the-wall Greek place, as well as an early afternoon time. Afterward, he left a message on Billy's voice mail before slipping like a ghost back inside the guest room. For several minutes, Grant simply stood there, watching the splay of shiny hair across the pillow, the slim curve of Luz Maria's arm as it lay utterly relaxed atop the ivory sheet.

I never should have touched her. I never will again.

As if Luz Maria tasted the bitterness of his thoughts, her long lashes started twitching. Behind the lids, her eyes moved; her breathing sped and roughened. Tension tightened both her arm and the sleek calf that showed beneath a lighter fold of cotton. Her dream, he sensed, was turning into a nightmare.

So wake her up, he told himself. *Or walk out of the room and close the door so you won't hear it.*

He continued watching, torn between the two thoughts, yet unable to imagine himself doing either.

Until at last he climbed into bed beside her and drew her back into his arms.

It was nearly ten A.M. when Luz Maria lifted Grant's heavy arm off her waist. After picking up her purse, she crept naked to the bathroom. She would have made it faster, except she kept looking back over her shoulder, stealing tender glances at the man who'd loved her not only once but three different times during the night.

She shivered with pleasure, thinking of the way he'd made her body sing, the way he'd driven every worry from her mind and forever altered her definition of true passion. Not that she had much basis for comparison, since for all the men she'd dated, Sergio Cardenas had been her only other bed partner.

With the memory came a pang of guilt—and disgust at the realization she'd turned her heart and loyalties inside out for a selfish lover whose rare efforts to satisfy her needs had been geared to using her to achieve his own ends. And who had badgered and manipulated her into having unprotected sex.

Tears welled at the memory of the child she had lost—a miscarriage she was certain her own sins had set in motion. Sniffing back the moisture, she buried the pain deep.

After closing the door behind her, Luz Maria used the bathroom, then dug into her shoulder bag for her hairbrush, her travel toothbrush, and please, God, let there be a tampon, since her period had started. She ended up taking out everything, from her reading glasses to the file she'd removed from her apartment to various key rings and her wallet, before she came up with not only one, but a pair of plastic-wrapped white cylinders.

Sighing her relief, she whispered, "Thank you," to the patron saint of feminine protection.

She was enjoying a long shower when she heard a tapping. The door opened a crack and Grant called, "Luz Maria? You okay in there?"

Her heartbeat knocked painfully at the sound of his voice. With the coming of the daylight, would he remember how he'd blamed her for John Zeman's death? Would he despise her for seducing him and further risking his career?

She pushed past her nervousness, telling herself his voice betrayed nothing but friendly concern. Maybe the old adage had it wrong, and the way to a man's heart wasn't through his stomach but an entirely different organ.

"I'm fine, Grant," she managed. "My neck's feeling a lot better."

She knew it was a stupid thing to say, but once she dressed and had the chance to talk to him face-to-face, perhaps she could find some way past this awkwardness.

"Come on out when you're ready," he said. "I'll get some breakfast going. Do you eat eggs?"

"Do you have salsa?"

There was a pause, long enough that she thought he'd left the bathroom. But finally, he answered, "Sure," before she heard the door close.

After drying and dressing in the same borrowed clothes from yesterday, she met Grant in the kitchen. His back to her, he stood at the stove, and the scent of the eggs and cheese he was scrambling together mingled with those of toasting bread and the pot of coffee he had made.

She filled both of the mugs beside the coffeemaker. "How do you take yours?"

"Huh?" He shot her a distracted look. "Um, black with a couple of teaspoons of sugar. I'm afraid I don't have any of the fake stuff, but there's milk in the fridge if you want it."

After finding the sugar bowl, she doctored both of their coffees, then lightened her mug to make the *cafe con leche* she craved. By the time she carried the mugs to the table, Grant was bringing out silverware and plates of eggs and buttered toast.

"Thanks," Luz Maria told him, trying not to mind that he hadn't made eye contact. "Looks great."

He held up an index finger. "Almost forgot the salsa."

He returned with an unopened jar a moment later, and the two of them sat down to eat. For several minutes, the only sounds were the clinking of forks against plates and the quiet thunking of the mugs each time they were set back on the table.

Finally, Luz Maria couldn't stand his distance any longer. After choking down a last mouthful, she said, "It's obvious you're uncomfortable having me here. So why don't you just drive me back to town this morning? I promise, I won't mention where I stayed last night. Or what went on here."

Over the curve of his mug, he looked at her intently. After putting down his coffee, he said, "I don't want you to go. It's still not safe."

"You can hardly bear to look at me, let alone say anything beyond the minimum."

"Sorry, Luz Maria. I'm just trying to sort some things out in my mind. But I promise, I haven't forgotten last night. I'm pretty sure I never will."

It hurt to swallow, as if a bit of eggshell had caught in her throat. Yet defiance colored her words. "I won't say I'm sorry it happened."

That prompted a wry smile. "Did I seem like I was fishing for an apology last night? And last night, later? And then again early this morning?"

She smiled back and felt her face heat with a memory so searing, she couldn't meet his gaze. "What happened—it's not something I do a lot. What I mean to say is, I don't—"

"You don't sleep around," he finished for her, then took both of their mugs back to the coffeemaker. "I know that. You forget, I've investigated you. Thoroughly."

She thought about his knowledge of her testimony, about the way he'd thrown her relationship with Sergio back in her face. Yet she knew almost nothing about him.

"Were you ever married?" she asked.

He looked surprised, but recovered quickly, shaking his head. "Almost, but she wised up in the nick of time. Not long after I bought this house for the two of us to . . ." With a shrug, he clamped down on what was clearly a painful memory.

"And family?" she asked. "Do you have any?"

"Two aunts and a few cousins," he said. "Maybe a mother. If she's still living."

She cocked her head. "How could you not—"

"Look, if you're finished with the twenty questions, I've got a couple of things in Houston that I need to take care of. For one thing, I need to pick some brains about your case. And then—listen, you want another cup?" His chin jerked toward the half-full pot.

She shook her head, a feeling of unease tightening her stomach. Something was different about him this morning. Strained, no matter how he tried to reassure her. "So you're leaving me alone again?"

He nodded. "I'm sorry. I know it's hard on you, but if you don't feel safe with the alarm on and the gun—"

"No gun," she said. "Don't you remember what almost happened last night?"

"Honey, my brain's still stuck on what *did* happen." He followed up the statement with a wink.

"I hate to break it to you, but that *isn't* your brain, Grant," she pointed out.

"I can go talk to my neighbor, next place over, see if he can stay with you while I'm gone. He's a good old boy, a retired cattleman. Still runs a few head for old time's sake. But I'm sure he's finished off more than a few coyotes in his day."

"No. No, I'll be fine, especially if you don't mind me checking my e-mail on your computer while you're out. But before you go into Houston, I'm going to need you to pick me up a couple of things from the store. You *do* have stores out here, right?"

He grinned. "Maybe not the Galleria, but we have stores, yeah. So what do you need?"

When she told him, his grin withered, and he said, "Aw, shit. Now I remember why I'm not married."

Though Grant wasted no time picking up the items Luz Maria wanted, he spent his minutes in the store looking back over his shoulder. It would be distressing enough under normal circumstances if anyone he knew caught him with tampons and women's panties in his basket, but the last thing he could afford was for someone— and a surprising number of cops lived in the area—to figure out that he was harboring Luz Maria.

As Grant approached the checkout lanes, he made a beeline toward the rack containing today's newspapers and grabbed a copy of the *Houston Chronicle* to cover his purchases. As the sheaf tilted, the City & State section edged out—enough for Grant to catch the headline reading HAS A VOICE FOR POVERTY BEEN SILENCED?

"Shit," he muttered as he studied the two photos. One showed a close-up of Luz Maria, eyes fiery as she stood behind a clutch of microphones and railed against the injustice *du jour*. In the second, two Harris County ME techs loaded a shrouded form into a van. The caption beneath it read, "The body of neighbor Kellie Capshaw is removed from the apartment of missing Voice of Poverty spokesperson Luz Maria Montoya."

Unable to stop himself, Grant skimmed the text, his teeth gritting as the report ticked off details the investigators would have been better off keeping from the public to help them weed out the inevitable false confessions. Though the article mentioned only that the body had been bound and "officials were awaiting autopsy results," Grant found the description of the scene he and Luz Maria had found in her apartment troubling. The goddamned reporter had everything, from accurate accounts of the threatening phone messages to the entrails in the bathtub to the surveillance camera subsequently removed from the apartment.

Somebody had to have leaked the information. Someone very close to the investigation. If he were still on the case, Grant would be asking the uniforms and crime scene techs—even his partner—some hard questions. But as he skimmed further into the article, its slant changed his mind. The focus quickly came around to the "war of terror" against the Houston office of the Voice of Poverty, including yesterday's drive-by shooting and what appeared, according to fund-raising chair April Walsh, to be "a concerted effort among Houston's mostly conservative elite to choke the organization into silence, not only by shunning its fund-raising efforts, but by boycotting its supporters."

The charge seemed pretty wild to Grant, but a lot of people, particularly those who felt marginalized, got off on conspiracy theories. If the local media outlets latched onto April Walsh's theory the way Grant suspected they would, VOP would soon be awash in donations from individuals, groups, and especially businesses afraid of being labeled elitist—or worse yet, racist—and subjected to a boycott of their own.

It was a brilliant strategy on Walsh's part. So brilliant Grant made a mental note to question Luz Maria about the woman. Could she have wheedled details from one of the investigative team members, then leaked the story to the press? Or was she capable of going even further?

Grant glanced one last time at Luz Maria's picture. Could she have somehow been involved, too? His instincts told him no, that she wore her passions on her face for all the world to see, that she held nothing back.

Yet once upon a time—a time not so long ago—she had kept dangerous company. And dangerous secrets, too. Only a lunatic would trust a woman like that.

And only a total fool would take her to his bed.

"Are you ready, sir?" asked the gnomelike, gray-haired woman at the register.

"Or do you maybe want to read the rest of the damned paper while we all wait?" the yuppie behind him asked as he made a show of checking his diamond-rimmed gold watch.

"Sorry," Grant grumbled as he tucked the paper back into the handbasket and slid it to the checker.

He ended up lucking out, seeing no one he recognized and spotting no vehicles behind him after he gassed up and left the Wal-Mart twelve miles from his house. He seriously doubted that Sergio Cardenas—or any possible stalker—would be able to track down Luz Maria. What really had Grant sweating was the file he had spotted on the bathroom counter this morning. Clearly, she hadn't realized he'd removed the folder's contents, then replaced them with a handful of blank printer paper he'd grabbed out of his office.

Bad idea, he told himself, but the moment he'd spotted the name *Zeman* on the scrap of paper jutting from the file, he'd had to know what had convinced her to publicly accuse John. Part of him was certain that looking was a terrible idea, understood it might mean the destruction of the fragile bond he'd formed with Luz Maria. But if there were even the thinnest hope that he could move beyond his partner's death, that he could forgive not only Luz Maria but himself for what had happened, Grant sensed it was in those stolen pages. Pages he had not yet dared to open.

He would drop off Luz Maria's things—and hope to God she hadn't yet missed the contents of the file.

Or he might very well have cause to regret his insistence upon leaving a loaded gun with her again.

* * *

Sometimes, when a man was both wise and fortunate, experience kicked in where adrenalin left off. Experience enough to realize that a night hunt in unfamiliar territory favored quarry more than predator, and that a decent meal and a good night's sleep would give him the advantage when the time came.

But neither wisdom nor good fortune conferred the gift of patience, and right now, the predator's was at its end. To wait longer meant the risk that she would move once more, and knowing she was hunted, Luz Maria was smart enough to find someplace he couldn't find.

Someplace even better hidden than the shadowed house deep in the woods.

CHAPTER TWENTY-ONE

After he placed the bag beside her on the desk, Grant made an excuse, telling Luz Maria he had to hurry into town if he wanted to meet his partner to talk about the case. She was working at his computer, where she'd logged onto her e-mail to review some work-related messages.

She peered at the screen intently through a pair of funky reading glasses painted as gaudily as parrots. "We're never going to make the hearing deadline if I can't get a fire lit under this petition drive," she murmured, her fingers flying across the keyboard. "And what kind of *imbéciles* e-mail a person to ask her if she's really dead?"

"You're going to melt down that poor computer," he warned. "It's used to hunt and peck."

"What? Oh, sorry, Grant." Her smile was apologetic as she looked up at him. "I tend to get a little carried away when I get into—you're leaving now?"

"Yeah, sorry. I've really got to run." He ducked toward her, feeling like a fraud as he touched his lips to hers. Weird, how he could make love to her, how they could give each other the most intimate of gifts, yet neither knew how to act around the other.

It was especially difficult since he was so anxious to get back to his car and find a quiet spot to look at her file on his partner. He counted his blessings that Luz Maria had connected to her e-mail rather than checking her purse and realizing what was missing.

After jotting his cell phone number on a sheet of printer paper, he added his neighbor's name and contact information. "If you need anything at all, you call me. But if I can't get here quick enough, here's Ike Fenton's number. I phoned him while I was in the car and told him you're a lady friend who just might have some trouble from an ex who won't let go."

She frowned. "*Am* I?"

He paused, one foot already out the doorway. "Are you what?"

Another smile warmed those brown eyes. "A lady friend—sounds so old-fashioned."

Grant shrugged and dredged up another term he'd heard during his patrol days. "He's eighty, so I figured he'd prefer that to *mi vieja*."

Her nose crinkled. "I'm *not* your old lady."

"No," he said seriously. "No, you're definitely not that."

Their gazes locked, and an uncomfortable silence reigned as they grappled with what the hell they were to each other. He was grateful when Luz Maria looked away first, distracted by a soft chime signaling that she had another e-mail.

Taking the coward's way, he slipped out and called back, "I'll be in touch soon."

He double-checked the doors and set the alarm before climbing into the Mercedes and pointing the car's nose toward the city. But he didn't get two miles before he pulled into the parking lot of the public library.

Since he'd broil inside of two minutes without the air-conditioning, Grant set the brake and left the car idling. He hesitated, thinking he could still turn back, could probably replace the file in Luz Maria's shoulder bag without her knowing that he'd had it.

He could leave Pandora's box locked tight.

What do you hope to find in there? Lieutenant Mouton's voice pulsed through his conscience. *Evidence that John was innocent—or ironclad proof that he was guilty?*

Unable to stop himself, he pulled the manila folder out from beneath the passenger side seat. His hands trembled like a drunkard's, and on some level, he knew he was making a mistake, knew that he was feeding an unhealthy obsession. Nothing good could come of this—nothing.

Just like that, he flipped it open, promising himself he would only look at the top page. Lying to himself, he knew already.

The notes inside were written in neat script—Luz Maria's, he decided. He skimmed through an account of the day she'd met with a prostitute named Shanti Starr—or at least that was the woman's street name. Or the girl's, unless he missed his bet. Luz Maria had recorded her age as eighteen, but she'd circled a question mark next to the notation, which made sense, as every runaway teenaged hooker in Houston claimed to be of age when dealing with anyone she thought of as authority.

Though he had heard about the photos and seen the media accusations—Luz Maria's accusations—Grant had never known the names of the women who'd come forward. But then, as John's partner, he'd never been privy to the details of the Internal Affairs investigation—and

Lieutenant Mouton had forced him to take leave after he had found the Z-man's body.

He shoved aside the ugly memory and flipped to the next page, but a packet of photographs distracted him, sliding out onto his lap. Without letting himself think, he dumped out the pictures and let his gaze fall onto the first image. Shock rolled over him in sickening waves. It had been one thing to hear the accusations against his partner, but seeing this . . .

This particular hooker was undeniably a girl, for one thing. Even with her face in profile, he saw that her small nose and smooth, deep caramel-colored skin had a clear, unfinished look, as if she had not long been on the aging streets. Her hair was worn in cornrows, the red-gold tips of which brushed the tops of her bony shoulders. The large, deep brown eye he saw was downcast, the lashes long and curly, wet with what might have been tears. The name Shanti Starr was written in red permanent marker along the white border at the bottom of the photo.

But it was her small, ruined breast that drew his gaze and held it. Someone had mutilated it—someone who had clearly taken pleasure in his handiwork. Someone like a master woodworker.

Grant closed his eyes, trying to erase the image of the pretty African-American girl with her hideous slash and puncture wounds. No more streetwalking for Shanti—not with that hideous pattern of puckered, half-healed scarring radiated in a discordant pattern all around the nipple.

Zeman wouldn't have done that. The man married to the gentle Sherry and father to two small girls, the man who could take a cedar block and make a thing of beauty from it, could never mutilate a young girl's body. Gritting his teeth with effort, Grant forced himself to go through the other photos, flipping through shots of the unfortunate Shanti's other breast and inner thighs, where huge W's—presumably for "whore"—had been gouged deep into the flesh.

There was another woman, too. Grant could tell from the lighter skin tone and thicker body type, though in this instance, the photographer had avoided capturing the face. Only the word "Petal" was written on the lower border. Petal's wounds appeared less recent, the scarring more purplish than red. Nonetheless, the slashes had healed badly, as if she had received little medical attention, and the pattern of injuries clearly suggested the same perpetrator. As did the notes Luz Maria had taken regarding the two women's complaints.

Not that either would have come forward to do any complaining on her own. Apparently, Luz Maria had tracked them down following a phone tip. Her notes remarked on the pair's reluctance, as well as on their shifting pattern of prevarication under questioning. She had underscored the word "terrified," and jotted something about the women's obvious nervousness when shown a photo of Investigator Zeman. In another spot, Luz Maria had jotted a ten-digit number. Beside it, she had written, "Pay phone?"

Grant swore. In two years' time, those two women could be anywhere, particularly since their disfigurement had forcibly removed them from the sex trade. Without their last names—hell, without any *real* name or address whatsoever, his chances of tracking either of them down were slim to none.

And Slim had just saddled up his horse and ridden out of town.

But if looking at this file was dangerous, visiting those women could be fatal. At least to his career, and very possibly to his sanity as well.

Grant Holcomb looked out his windshield, beyond the parking lot and up into the bands of cumulus clouds already building with another day's moist heat. Shrugging his shoulders, he muttered, "*What* career, you moron?"

Because once any thread of his involvement with Luz Maria Montoya was pulled—from the two-year-old threat he'd left in the VOP file Billy now had to his meeting with Steve Petit—the rest of his story would unravel. When Internal Affairs figured out he'd been sleeping with the enemy instead of taking care of Sherry as he ought to, the department wouldn't have to fire him. Word would leak out to his fellow cops, who would be sure to let him know in a thousand ways that he was well and truly finished on the force.

Even after scrolling past those messages from members of the press and people whose names she didn't recognize, Luz Maria still had at least two dozen e-mails she could not leave unanswered. Some were messages of concern from city council members and other highly placed individuals who would put priority VOP projects on back burners if they thought she was out of commission. She quickly fired off assurances that she was well and remained attentive to her ongoing commitments.

Not that it was true . . .

How could she hope to focus with four unread messages from Jack alone, along with others from April, Whit, and most of her coworkers, close friends, and even past clients she'd grown fond of? Overwhelmed by subject lines screaming, *Call me*, *Urgent*, and *R U OK*, Luz Maria settled on the only one that wasn't riddled with exclamation points or red flags: *Please phone Juanita re: Tex-Rid Incinerator*, it read. Since the time stamp indicated that Carol Jarvis, the most senior member of VOP's staff, had sent the e-mail before the parking lot assault, Luz Maria used the computer's mouse to highlight what appeared to be a routine message.

You're stalling, her conscience insisted. Luz Maria felt guilty, but still, it was far easier to deal with the work-related e-mails than the glut of personal notes sure to flay her already raw conscience over her friends' and family's worry.

She double-clicked Carol's message, which included a phone number for Juanita Reyes, the day care grandma downwind from Tex-Rid's proposed incinerator. In spite of her own problems, Luz Maria was curious. Had the *piojo*—she still thought of Tex-Rid's lead attorney as a blood-sucking louse—threatened to get the state on the woman about her small, but unlicensed, operation? With the señora's poor command of English, it would be simple for a couple of white men in ties to convince her she would do jail time if she didn't drop her complaints. Luz Maria had faced this sort of intimidation on more than one occasion. She was willing to bet that if *the suits*'—as she called her corporate and governmental foes—warnings about the horrors of prison didn't do the trick, they'd next threaten to have the INS look into Juanita's family members' immigration status.

"Dirty *cabrónes*," Luz Maria mumbled, reaching for the phone as her mind clicked through possible end runs around their threats. First, though, she would have to convince Juanita this was a war worth waging—not only for herself and the handful of children she nurtured, but for the entire community, if Tex-Rid continued its usual pattern of ignoring air pollution standards.

"*Aló,*" Señora Reyes answered. When she recognized Luz Maria's greeting, she exclaimed, "*Ah, mi angelita. Estoy tan feliz que tú llamaste.*"

The friendly greeting didn't surprise Luz Maria as much as the older woman's tone. Her voice sounded as smooth and sweet as the delicious *flan de coco* she made, not alarmed as if she'd been the victim of intimidation—or heard the news about the violence against Luz Maria. But then again, the long-widowed señora lived in a homey little world of her own making, a place where time was measured by the burning of saints' candles and the soaking of corn husks for *tamales.* Unlike Luz Maria's mother, who ran a thriving herb shop and busied herself dispensing advice to family, friends, and loyal customers—including, occasionally, Juanita—Señora Reyes could barely name the current U.S. president, much less the events of the day.

"I have very glad news," the older woman said, joy bubbling through her heavily accented English. "Those men are buying me new house, only six year old, in place no too far, away from bad smoke. They take me in big car, big black Cadillac, show me good new trailer—*carísimo.*"

Luz Maria wondered what the señora's idea of "very expensive" would be. For forty-two years, she'd lived in the same four-room shotgun shack. Surrounded by waves of blooming color and permeated by the smells of wondrous cooking, she kept the little house meticulously clean, but it was poor, too, with its steps rotting, its carpet threadbare, and shingles flaking from the roof like dandruff. It wouldn't take much to dazzle her. A ride in a luxury car and a free six-year-old trailer would seem like a winning lottery ticket to a woman who had spent a lifetime making do.

"That's very nice," Luz Maria commented as she wondered how she could possibly convince Señora Reyes to pass up this unexpected miracle.

"You didn't sign any papers, did you?" Luz Maria

asked her, then repeated the question in Spanish when the older woman made confused sounds. If the *piojo* had tricked her into endorsing whatever agreement they'd drawn up, undoubtedly in some sort of legalese that even native English speakers would have trouble comprehending, the Voice of Poverty would face an uphill—and expensive—battle undoing the damage. If it was even possible.

"*No, yó no firmé,*" the older woman claimed. "I tell them I wait for you to see house, to see *los documentos.* I let them know I trust only you, *mi angelita,* like your mama tell me."

Though she had never understood Candelaria's hold over the Mexican immigrants who trekked to her *yerbería* from all over Greater Houston, Luz Maria breathed again. "That's very good. *Está bien.*"

Señora Reyes laughed. "They no think so. They try make nice, but man with the—how you say—*lentes para leer*—"

"Reading glasses."

"*Sí,* he say better decide quick or no more trailer."

"I'm sure he did." Luz Maria felt her forehead furrow. Was the *piojo* an attorney or a high-pressure used-car salesman? "I'll come over there tomorrow if that's all right, and we'll talk about it."

"And you drive me, I can show you my trailer, too. This man, he leave me key. Only six years old, *señorita*—with the pretty wallpaper in the kitchen and central air-conditioning."

As Luz Maria ended the call, her hopes faded. With Señora Reyes already referring to it as her trailer and the lure of central AC instead of the rickety window unit that left her and the children she watched sweating, what possible chance could something as intangible as the greater good stand? Luz Maria certainly couldn't offer her a new home—or anything except a legal battle she wouldn't even understand, a battle that might last longer than the seventy-three-year-old woman had.

Doubts rippled through Luz Maria, doubts she'd rarely felt before. *Am I doing the right thing here? Is manipulating an old woman into fighting a VOP battle any less reprehensible than bribing her for profit?*

She wasn't sure she knew the answers—and she damned well didn't know if she was willing to allow others to pay the price of her own need to battle the world's wrongs. Others such as Kellie Capshaw, who'd never railed against a damned thing in her life.

And if anything happened to little Adam . . .

The thought was so painful that Luz Maria reflexively clicked on one of Whit's messages. Maybe he would have more news on the investigation, perhaps something that would allow her to keep her promise to visit the Señora Reyes by tomorrow.

Luz Maria clapped her hand over her mouth as she took in the few words: *Call me right away. It's about your mother.*

Oh, God. Was that why there were all those messages from Jack? Had the same lunatic who'd left her a message at her mother's house gone after Mama and Eduardo when he couldn't find his target?

Without opening another message, Luz Maria grabbed the home office extension and began dialing Whit's cell phone number. Again and again, she had to start anew, her hands shaking so violently she had trouble hitting the right digits.

Once she dialed correctly, Whit answered on the first ring.

"Luz Maria," he said. "Tell me you're all right, hon. We've been out of our minds worrying about you."

"What's happened to my mama?" she demanded. "Please, Whit, tell me."

"God, Luz Maria. I'm so sorry—"

"No. No, Whit. You can't mean that—" Hot tears coursed down her face, burning like rivers of acid.

"No," Whit's voice rose. "Your mama's just fine. I'm sorry I had to scare you like that, that's all."

"You—are you kidding, Whit?" Luz Maria heard her voice sliding up the register and felt her heartbeat hammering. "You mean you *lied* to get me to check in? You lied about my *mama?*"

If Whit were here, she'd rip his head off with her bare hands. She'd never been so furious.

"It's my job to make sure you're safe, sweetie. And I'm truly sorry—"

"Don't you 'sweetie' me, *pendejo*, and you can save your apologies for . . ." Luz Maria thought about the drive-by shooting at VOP headquarters, then remembered what April had told her. "Are you . . . are you all right? April said you were hurt."

"Takes more than a little glass to put me out of commission," Whit said. "Now tell me, where on earth are you holed up? The police want to talk to you about—do you know about the body found in your apartment?"

"Kellie . . ." Luz Maria felt her gorge rise at the thought of what her friend must have suffered.

"I'm so sorry, dear heart. This is . . . this is getting way too scary. No one would blame you if you wanted to take some time away, even look for a less visible position in—"

"*I'd* blame me," she said, recalling Grant's words. "I'd never forgive myself if I let this *cabrón* win."

For several moments, Whit said nothing, but Luz Maria could have sworn she heard his fear for her safety crackling on the open line. Before she could ask if he was still there, he launched into a question.

"So where are you? I'll need to tell the homicide investigators something."

"I can't say," Luz Maria told him. She couldn't allow Grant's job to become the next victim of a man who had already killed her neighbor—and possibly Tony Coleman as well. "But I am somewhere safe, and I'll call the police as soon as—"

"*Where?* Have you checked into a hotel? You're not using your real name, are you?" Tinged with barely contained panic, Whit's questions picked up speed. "Tell me you're not alone right now."

Luz Maria took a deep breath, not knowing where to start. "I'm with someone I trust," she started. *Or at least I will be when he gets back.* "But I won't endanger this person, or anybody else, by saying where. And I *will* call the police as soon as I can. Do you have the homicide investigator's number? Or should I call the investigator working on my assault?"

"Oh, God, no. Whatever you do, don't call Grant Holcomb."

She shot out of the desk chair, alarm pulsing through each synapse. "Why not?"

Though she tried to keep the question casual, anxiety strained the words. She prayed Whit wouldn't notice—or if he did, that he wouldn't put two and two together.

"Because Grant Holcomb could be trouble," Whit said. "Yesterday, I heard he'd gone out on vacation. But later, someone let it slip that he was taken off your case. I got curious—something about that guy rang a bell—and checked my backup files . . ."

"And found out he was Investigator John Zeman's partner," she supplied. "He—uh—he mentioned it to me. But he seemed professional enough."

"Don't trust him, Luz Maria. Don't trust him for an instant. When I went back and checked our records, I found Holcomb's name, all right. I found it in our threat files."

"*What?*"

"He wrote a letter to you two years back, right after his partner was found dead. An orange-level letter, with his name signed to the damned thing."

Luz Maria could not believe what she was hearing. "He *threatened* me?"

"Not specifically, but the language was pretty rough."

"You didn't report it to the police?"

"No," said Whit. "You know I only routinely do that with red-level assessments. At the time, I mentioned it to you, and you said let it go. He was probably only grieving, blowing off a little steam. Do you recall the conversation?"

Though Luz Maria tried, the memory wouldn't come. But then, at the time, she would have seen it as routine. As her family was forever pointing out, she was in the business of pushing the wrong buttons. Often, in the process, she pushed basically decent people beyond the limits of control.

All for a good cause, she tried to tell herself. Only this time, the thought reminded her of Sergio's assurances about "acceptable risks" and "the greater good." Was she still thinking like her former lover, still sacrificing one set of innocents in favor of another?

Or was Grant Holcomb, the same man who had made love to her so sweetly, still a very real threat to her safety?

"I have to go now," she murmured.

"Luz Maria, honey, why don't you come and stay at my place? I'd feel so much better if—"

"Take care of the other VOP staff members—and watch out for yourself, too. I'll call you later, Whit," she said an instant before she broke the connection.

From someplace outside, she heard what might have been the clatter of a metal trash can overturning . . . or possibly the slamming of a car door in the driveway.

CHAPTER TWENTY-TWO

Luz Maria hurried to the window, where she looked out through a gap near the blind's left edge. A tree trunk blocked her vision, so she lifted one slat with a finger and peered out toward the empty carport.

From this angle, she couldn't see the trash cans, nor did she spot any sign of animals. If the pigs had returned for a visit, maybe something had frightened them away—or they'd discovered Grant was fresh out of appetizing garbage.

Whichever was the case, Luz Maria wasn't about to go out looking for them. For one thing, Grant hadn't given her the code to deactivate his alarm system. But even if he had, the thought of venturing outside into the isolation that surrounded Grant's house made her skin prickle and the fine hairs rise along her arms.

The thick trees and the undergrowth could hide far more than wildlife. Unnerved by the thought, Luz Maria glanced toward the pistol resting next to the computer.

Her mind recalled the horrible moment last night

when she'd been so damned scared she'd nearly shot Grant dead. At the thought, she felt her stomach plummet, and her world's axis wobbled.

No way was she touching that thing again without good reason. If she saw something suspicious, she'd run back and get the gun—and dial 911.

After taking a deep breath, Luz Maria crept from room to room, until she ended up at last at the big, bare window above the kitchen sink.

She frowned out at the emptiness, hope fading that she would spot a deer, a stray dog, or any kind of animal that might explain the sound she'd heard.

A breeze bent the fragile stalks of grass and ruffled leaves in every shade of green. Luz Maria glanced up at the patches of gray behind the tree limbs. Could a thunderstorm be brewing stronger winds? The sky flashed, as if to bolster the idea that a trash can lid might have been blown from its perch.

That was it, she decided as the still distant thunder growled a threat. Unused to the country and unnerved by circumstances, she had jumped to conclusions—just as she had last night when she'd been frightened by the little band of deer.

She blew out a long breath, one she hadn't realized she'd been holding. Which explained why, when the back door exploded open, Luz Maria lacked the wherewithal to scream.

"Why the hell didn't you tell me about that goddamned letter?" Billy Devlin demanded.

Grant winced and downshifted, then moved the cell phone several inches from his ear. He was lucky he hadn't run into the median, the way his partner was screaming at him.

But strangely, Grant felt something like relief course through him. Ever since he'd given Billy the VOP threat file last night, he'd been on edge, waiting for the other shoe to drop.

"Do you have any goddamned idea what kind of position you've put me in?" Billy continued.

"Yeah," Grant told him. "I do . . . and I just want to say I'm sorry. It was a long time ago, and I couldn't think of how to tell—"

"Are you *apologizing?*" The younger investigator all but screamed the question. "I could lose my fucking *job* for this. I could end up so far down Lieutenant Mouton's shit list, I'll need a team of plumbers to pull my head out of the sewer."

"What the hell do you mean?" His scheduled meeting with Cowboy forgotten, Grant glided to a stop along the side of the beltway. As he did, his car bumped over the black remnants of somebody's blown-out tire. "You aren't telling me you destroyed it—are you?"

Lightning pulsed among the banked clouds to the west, and a few windblown drops of rain splattered against the windshield.

"Hell, no," Billy answered. "You think I'm destroying evidence for you? Is that what you're expecting?"

"Of course not. So why are you afraid of getting—" Grant thumped the steering wheel as it came to him. "You didn't report it yet, did you? You found it last night, but you didn't pass it on . . . to anybody."

"I decided to give you one chance to explain it first."

Grant didn't know whether to feel gratitude or irritation. Gratitude that Billy apparently felt some measure of loyalty, and irritation that he hadn't been smart enough to cover his own ass.

"I appreciate it," Grant said, "and as soon as I finish meeting my source, I'll swing by your place so we can discuss—"

Billy grunted in the negative. "No deal. I said I'd give

you one chance, and that's ending as soon as Lieutenant Chapman returns the call I left on his voice mail."

So his partner *had* hedged his bet, leaving a message with their temporary supervisor.

"Listen, Billy. This source—he's FBI, and he's not going to wait. You stall on this other thing and I'll share what I—"

"Lieutenant Mouton pulled you off this case, remember? And considering what's in this letter with your signature, that's looking like a pretty good idea to me. If there's somebody I should interview, you need to turn it over."

"He's not gonna talk to you. You know how those guys are. Any of the other Feebs find out he's sharing information—"

But Billy wasn't budging. "You can either get your ass over here right now or hope like hell that Chapman doesn't get back to me. Because I've already pushed this, sitting on it while I tried to figure what was right."

"So what *is* right, Billy? Denying me a couple hours to give you something that could break this case wide open?"

"You're famous for your bullshit, Holcomb. So let me tell you, I'm not bullshitting you right now. You've got one hour. Get here."

Grant tried to argue, but the line was dead. In hanging up on him, Billy had broken more than the connection; he'd cured Grant of the suspicion that his partner was as stupid, young, and naive as he looked.

Billy Devlin had finally come into his own.

Before Grant had time to figure out whether to call his partner's bluff or push it by first squeezing in a visit with Cowboy, his cell phone rang with yet another interruption.

An interruption that would cause him to miss his appointments with both men.

* * *

Luz Maria spun, turning away from the horrifying glimpse of the blond stranger bursting through Grant Holcomb's shattered door. She bolted toward the office, adrenalin exploding through her system, propelling her toward the only thing she could think of that might save her: the gun she had foolishly left on the desk.

Staccato images flashed through her mind. The shopping cart as it rushed toward her. Her own gore-spattered bathroom. The shrouded body—Kellie's body—as it was loaded into the ghost-white van.

But the man's voice was what made her stumble. The familiar voice that shouted, "Luz Maria! Damn it. Luz Maria, don't you fucking run from me."

CHAPTER TWENTY-THREE

Even as his car roared down the beltway, Grant was phoning the house—and praying that Luz Maria had simply triggered his home alarm by stepping outside for some reason. He pictured her looking out the window, her attention captured by the deer that roamed the area or the slant of sunlight through the thick trees. He saw her opening the door, then realizing too late he'd neglected to leave her the code that would prevent the system from automatically dialing his cell phone.

A growl of thunder discouraged the idea that she'd decided on a walk, as did the dark clouds gathering above Magnolia. Grant floored the roadster, darting around the slowing traffic to zoom toward the exit on the shoulder. He ignored the angry blare of horns—though in other circumstances, he would have agreed that his driving deserved worse punishment than honking—and zipped off the ramp toward his home.

Meanwhile, the phone he'd caught between his ear and shoulder rang until the answering machine picked up. After waiting impatiently for the beep following his message, Grant shouted, "Luz Maria, pick up. If you're there, answer the phone. Damn it. Hurry—get the phone."

But Luz Maria didn't. Or she couldn't, so after a moment's hesitation, Grant dialed 911 and asked to be put through to the Montgomery County Sheriff's Department.

The shock of hearing Sergio's voice tangled Luz Maria's feet. By the time she recovered from her stumble, he was only steps behind her in the hallway.

Her perception took on facets, like a wasp's eye. One window replayed her single glimpse of his face. Another decoded its fury, while still another measured her progress as she launched herself toward the door of Grant's home office.

She made it there ahead of Sergio, but as she slammed the door, his foot wedged against it so it wouldn't close completely.

Inside the office with her, the phone began to ring. Luz Maria ignored it, intent as she was on forcing the door shut. She heard herself screaming—and Sergio shouting something, cursing her in both Spanish and English, demanding she stop fighting.

She might as well have, for all the good it did her. When he hurled his weight against the door, the top hinge broke loose, canting it so suddenly that she was forced to step back before wood struck her head.

Twisting around, she caught sight of the gun. Her hand strained toward it and her body followed.

But her leap fell short.

Grant's car popped over another bump in the rutted dirt road, making him feel he'd left behind his stomach. Still, he barely slowed as he made the sharp corner that took him down his own drive.

Dry, golden needles rained down from the pine trees as the wind tousled their crowns. Fat drops of water followed, bursting against the windshield like blood spatter from a gunshot.

As Grant flipped on the headlights to see through the deep gloom, he thought of Tony Coleman's blood staining the Ryland's parking lot. He remembered both Billy and Reagan Hurley telling him about the bound girl found dead in Luz Maria's bedroom.

Fear took hold, cramping Grant's organs, streaming from his pores. Would he find Luz Maria murdered, bleeding in his own bed? Over the course of his career, he'd seen plenty of dead bodies, but never one he had made love to only hours before. And, God forgive him, never one he had taken to his own home and sworn he would protect.

As he skidded to a stop beside the brick house, thunder cracked and the rain abruptly went from smattering to torrent. It was coming down so hard he couldn't see the shattered side door until he was out of the car and nearly on it, his Glock in his hand.

He fought the urge to scream Luz Maria's name. Though he'd seen no other vehicle, he thought it possible the attacker was still inside, too distracted by whatever he was doing to hear Grant coming.

Was the filthy bastard raping Luz Maria even now? Or had he already smashed in her skull?

Jesus. Grant's stomach spasmed once more as he stepped past the splintered door—a door that only a strong man could have broken.

He knew damned well he should wait for backup, knew damned well anyone inside would hear him crunching over the broken wood and glass. But there was no fighting the horrendous images that drew him—even when his wet shoes slid on the linoleum and he fell hard on his right side.

A loud *crack* preceded a thunk against the cabinet door beside the stove. But it was the acrid scent of gunsmoke that sent reality arcing through him. When he'd landed—his finger on the trigger—he'd shot his own damned kitchen cupboard.

He pushed himself upright, ignoring the cut on his right hand and the fact that the intruder would have to be stone deaf not to have heard his entrance. All thoughts of stealth abandoned, Grant charged through the house, from the empty living room to the hallway leading to the bedrooms.

He stopped at the first door, that of his home office. It swung inward from the top, and the desk chair had toppled onto its side. Papers littered the floor, offering mute witness to a struggle. His spare gun had vanished from the desktop.

With the pulse of his own heartbeat hammering his eardrums, Grant raced to each bedroom in turn. Since both looked as he had left them, he checked out the bathrooms and the dining room. But nothing was amiss there either, so he turned back to the office, barely registering the desperate prayer that he was muttering, a prayer that somehow, despite the evidence, Luz Maria had escaped and was hiding somewhere safe, his pistol in hand.

As the sound of approaching sirens swelled outside the house, Grant used his foot to move one of the papers—it was an old credit card bill of his that needed shredding—off of something it half covered on the floor.

It was a snakelike length of rope—it looked like cotton clothesline—and beside it, something even more alarming. A roll of silver duct tape, its gummy, torn end loose.

When the sheriff's deputies found Grant, he was in the bathroom heaving up his last meal, his weapon lying on the tiled floor beside the toilet. He had barely finished vomiting when the two men kicked aside his Glock and cuffed his hands behind his back.

"You have the right to remain silent," the beefier of the two men started. "If you give up that right, anything you say can and will be used against you in a court of law. . . ."

CHAPTER TWENTY-FOUR

Luz Maria hurt. A constellation of injuries vied for her attention, from the rope digging into her bound ankles to the wrists tied tight behind her, to her face, with its carpet burn from the desperate struggle in the office. But adrenalin pushed her past physical discomfort, insisting she get herself out of the backseat of the moving car before it was too late.

She lifted her head off the tan seat cushion, where she'd been pushed facedown. Sergio might have left her powerless to flee or fight, but she'd rubbed her duct-taped mouth against her shoulder until she'd worked the gag loose.

At first, she'd screamed—until Sergio slowed the car and pointed a pistol at her over the seat. "Scream once more and I'll kill you—and that's not what I'm here for. Now shut up, you faithless *puta*."

He's taking me out to some dirt road to rape me, just the way he did Kellie. With rain sluicing down the car's windows, revulsion cascaded through Luz Maria's every cell, and her mind reverberated with the echo of his vile threat on the phone. *They'll find me dead, too, when it's finished—unless I come up with some way to stop him*, she thought.

As they started moving, she closed her eyes and forced herself to take deep, slow breaths. Her only weapons now were words and a clear mind. Sergio would not expect reason from a woman, a girl, really, who had once let passion rule her. Who had let *him* rule her, with the fiery illusion he called love.

She tried not to remember the way it had burned her, the way it had singed so many others. Still, she felt her fury rise, pushing past her fear.

"Why'd you kill her, Sergio? Why did you murder Kellie Capshaw?" Though it started weak, her voice gathered power. "Was she just a little 'collateral damage' on your way to me?"

Out of the corner of her eye, she thought she saw his head jerk toward her. Then the car swung left, and she struggled to keep from sliding off the seat.

Before she recovered from the unexpected turn, Sergio asked, "Why would I kill—who the hell is she?"

"My neighbor—or have you already forgotten?"

"All I want are answers, Luz Maria. It was never my intention for anyone to die here."

"How can you say that, *asesino?*" she demanded.

"If you're going to call anyone a murderer, you'd better look a little closer. Or don't you count the three members of BorderFree-4-All gunned down by the Mexican *Federales* after the FBI tipped them off about us? And what about our child, Luz Maria—could it be you've forgotten him? Or was it my baby *girl* you butchered?"

Shock spilled through her. How could he have known she had been pregnant before he'd left town, one step ahead of the authorities? And why did he accuse her of—did he imagine she'd had an abortion? "What are you talking about?" she demanded. "What in God's name—"

After wheeling to the right, Sergio slammed on the brakes and shifted the car into park before whipping around and shoving a sleek, black handgun in her face. "Don't you play dumb with me. Don't you fucking lie— and certainly not in God's name, not after the sins that you've committed."

"But I—" Luz Maria clamped down on the denial, her mind whirling with both terror and confusion. None of it made sense, not even the part about the *Federales* killing members of BorderFree-4-All. She'd read about the raid in the paper some time around last Christmas, but she'd never imagined it had anything to do with testimony she'd given more than two years earlier.

"I don't understand." Disoriented by the accusations, she spoke more to herself than Sergio. "There was an accident that day you left—a man ran me off the road. I broke my left arm, and I had a miscarriage. A *miscarriage*, Sergio. It was . . . it was horrible. I wanted to die myself."

"*Mentirosa,*" he shouted, pounding something, maybe his own hand, against the dashboard as he called her a liar. "I saw the medical report. I *saw* it, damn you. I was worried enough about you to call a contact at the hospital and have her fax your information."

Luz Maria thought of how, not long before her "accident," Sergio had manipulated her into committing the same sort of crime. Had he been sleeping with that woman, too, telling her he loved her? Filling her head with lies about his so-called "bloodless" revolution to help their people?

Not that any of it mattered to her anymore, with Sergio about to kill her for a procedure she'd never had, a procedure that—Luz Maria gasped, blindsided by a memory from the days she had interned as a social worker within the hospital district. She heard, as clearly as if the lead social worker stood beside her speaking, the warning never to use a certain clinical term when dealing with a client, a word which often caused extreme emotional reactions.

"On the medical report, it said I'd—" she began.

"It said you'd had an abortion." His voice trembled with fury, as did the weapon he held. "That you murdered my child."

"A spon—" Choked by fear and sorrow, Luz Maria's vision blurred with tears. "A spontaneous abortion—it's what the doctors call miscarriage. *Idiota*—you came back here and killed Kellie, you shot at my office, all because you couldn't comprehend a stolen medical report?"

She jerked as the pistol's barrel smacked into her forehead. Her ears rang with a blow that swelled to drown his curses. Her vision blurred, like the watery world outside the car's windows.

When she could finally make out words again, he was telling her, "I didn't kill your neighbor. I didn't hurt anybody—except maybe the guy I had to shoot to jack this car. I just needed—I had to see you, Luz Maria. I needed to understand why you would . . . why you would do that to our child. To *my* child."

"You broke into my apartment and left butcher shop gore in my bathroom. You used some kind of device to change your voice so you could make threats on the phone. Damn it, Sergio, you jumped me in a parking lot and choked me halfway to hell—"

"I didn't—"

"And you shot up my office, too, in *this* car. Why? So you could *talk* to me about an abortion that never happened? About a life that never had a chance—one you wouldn't have wanted or acknowledged even if things had turned out different? Or was it really so we could *talk* about some raid that didn't even happen in this county? Have you lost your mind? Your methods may be all wrong, but I used to think you stood for something."

"I *do* stand for something, Luz Maria. A cause I could have sworn you understood. Or have you forgotten about your father and the thousands like him, killed crossing this country's borders? Dying for American hypocrites and their illusion that this country's economy isn't fueled with blood."

She heard the conviction in his tone, but his arguments had long since ceased to move her.

"You're completely delusional," she said, "if you think for one minute that murder can convince this country to examine its collective conscience—or change a single law."

She turned away her face so she wouldn't have to see what he'd become—and so she wouldn't have to see the death bearing down on her.

And it surely would: one final penance, a leaden key that would at last unshackle her from the guilt chained to her heart.

But instead of a bullet, he had questions for her.

"Who's trying to appeal to anybody's conscience? What's the point when fear works so much better—and when terror, *mi tesoro*, works the best of all?"

As the car rolled to a stop, fresh panic tore through Luz Maria. She made one last-ditch effort to pull free from her bonds, an effort that was cut short when a second blow to her head plunged her into blackness.

The more Grant argued with the deputies that they needed to forget him and find Luz Maria quickly, the rougher they became, muscling him out into the kitchen and demanding he explain to them what had really gone on there.

He took a deep breath and tried to see the scene as they would, in response to a call about a possible break-in and attempted homicide against a woman. With no woman in sight, of course they'd want to check out the sole man present—especially considering the shattered door, evidence of a struggle, and the fresh blood oozing from his hand. He forced himself to look straight ahead, afraid a stray glance would lead their attention to the fresh hole in his kitchen cabinet, but there was nothing he could do to hide the lingering scent of gun smoke in the air.

And if they brought out an evidence team, it wouldn't take long to come up with proof that he had slept with Luz Maria.

Which made him the likely suspect if she were found . . .

A vision rose of Luz Maria's warm, supple body, cold and stiff with rigor mortis. How could he worry what might happen to him when she was out there somewhere with that lunatic?

"If you'll take out my wallet, you'll find my badge, department ID, and a driver's license bearing this address." He forced himself to speak calmly, in what seemed like slow, underwater motion, as his heart pounded out a message of impatience. "As I was trying to explain, my alarm system's set to call my cell phone if a door or window's opened. It was raining hard when I ran in, so my shoes slipped on the floor and I cut my hand on the debris."

Even now, the deputies were dripping, and beyond the broken door, rain hissed against the flagstones leading to the kitchen entrance. A brilliant flash gave only an instant's warning before a crash of thunder rent the air.

All three men flinched at the close strike, and at the earsplitting blast of static from the radio one of the deputies carried. Just beyond the carport, the top half of a pine tree toppled from its splintered base.

"Jesus, that was damned close." The bulkier deputy

used both hands and one foot to push the broken door shut.

Strictly speaking, Grant knew the lawman shouldn't touch it, but considering the weather, his partner didn't seem inclined to argue.

Instead, the smaller man, a white guy with brushy, salt-and-pepper hair and nicotine-stained teeth, used two fingers to remove the wallet from Grant's back pocket. After flipping it open, he nodded, but his expression said he was reserving judgment.

Grant understood that, too. It was a sad fact that cops were no more immune to bad behavior than any other group of people. Since these two didn't know him personally, they couldn't take anything he said at face value. But that wasn't about to stop him from trying to get help to Luz Maria.

"Look guys, call my partner. Call my station. Turn on the goddamned news if that's what it takes. Luz Maria Montoya was here when I left—now she isn't. And from the looks of this place, I'm guessing the same maniac who killed her neighbor has her. You've got to put an APB out—slender Hispanic female, twenty-six, long, black hair and brown eyes." He struggled to recall her brother's description. "Five-three, a hundred and five pounds."

The salt-and-pepper deputy, whose nametag read D. BOOREN unclipped the radio from his belt, but he looked so skeptical, so devoid of hope, that Grant could almost hear him wondering what the point was. Even if Luz Maria remained in the area, the odds of locating her with an unknown assailant were tiny. And the odds of finding her before it was too late . . .

No. Grant refused to think about that. "He's living out a fantasy, something he's imagined doing a long time. These guys get excited. They lose their heads and make mistakes."

The heavier man shrugged. "It happens," he admitted, glancing at his partner. "If scum always thought straight, we'd never catch a break."

Salt-and-pepper nodded, then moved to radio in the request. But first, he waited while another call went out. A call from a breathless-sounding officer reporting the pursuit of a gold Toyota Camry reported stolen in Houston.

Intuition flared, and Grant insisted, "That's him—that's gotta be our guy. A witness reported a tan Camry fleeing the scene of a drive-by at Ms. Montoya's office yesterday. Four- or five-year-old model, missing passenger-side trim and hubcap, Astros bumper sticker—I'm telling you, it's him. We have to go."

The deputy involved in the chase reported his location, on a rural road less than five minutes from Grant's house.

"Come on." Grant strained against the handcuffs. "We can catch him, I know it. We can still save her—please."

The bigger deputy jerked his arm to keep him still. "That cowboy shit might fly for you in Houston," he said gruffly. "But out here in the county, you aren't calling the shots."

Grant glared, in no mood for a jurisdictional pissing contest. "Listen, jackass. He's already assaulted Ms. Montoya once and murdered another young woman. And if I'm right, he's on the FBI's Most Wanted List on charges of domestic terrorism—a suspect by the name of Sergio Cardenas."

The deputies exchanged a look so incredulous that Grant seriously considered adding aggravated assault of an officer to his growing list of problems.

"He's probably armed," Grant pleaded, opting for the saner course. "Your fellow deputy could get hurt."

"They'll be dispatching other units on another frequency," Big Boy explained, but in his eyes, Grant saw the fuse of the man's patience burning too close to the powder.

Still, Grant pushed it. "Please."

He was interrupted by a squawking from the radio. "Shots fired. Shots fired," cried the deputy. "Officer needs assistance—*now*."

CHAPTER TWENTY-FIVE

Red lights flashed in the rearview mirror as the big Ford interceptor steadily gained ground.

Sergio tightened his death grip on the wheel. He would be damned if he'd let these locals catch him with what might prove to be a body—damned if he'd allow this little detour to deal with Luz Maria to cost him everything he had planned for the past three years.

He was so close to putting together the splintered fragments of BorderFree-4-All and shoring it up with fresh recruits, including his half-brother, Rogelio. Nearly blinded by a bolt of lightning, Sergio sped around a corner with the sinking realization that he'd gotten himself lost on these back roads.

In just a few short weeks, he would bring the people's cause to the forefront, would scar the American psyche with a reminder that its sins could not forever go unpunished.

And yet he'd gone running after a woman whose punishment could easily have waited or been left to others. Maybe Luz Maria had been right about his state of mind. With the rain pouring down faster than the wiper blades could clear it, Sergio realized—perhaps too late—he'd been insane to take the risk.

The flashing lights drew nearer, the white patrol car's big engine easily outpacing the Toyota's. Sergio had turned off the AC in an attempt to coax more horsepower from the stolen sedan. It hadn't achieved much, other than heating up the vehicle's interior and sending a stream of stinging sweat into his eyes.

Soon, he was bound to have worse problems. His pursuer—who must know this wooded territory—had surely called for backup. And the car was edging to Sergio's left, almost close enough to nudge the Toyota's rear wheel with the Ford's front bumper and cause him to spin out, maybe to nosedive into one of the drainage ditches that flanked the rural road.

Sergio couldn't let that happen. He lowered the driver's side window, sending a spray of cool rainwater across his face and shoulder and into the backseat. This elicited a groan from Luz Maria—along with a rush of relief that he hadn't killed her when he'd struck her with the gun. Bad enough he'd allowed obsession to carry him this far, to a place where his ideals were compromised by car theft and wild shots into the VOP headquarters. Bad enough she'd pushed him far enough to strike a woman in the first place.

As the deputy's car closed in, Sergio reached out the window with his right hand and blindly fired behind him. The Ford swerved and dropped back, and Sergio felt desperation flare.

Shooting at a cop, abduction, and carjacking. Assault, too.

If he let them catch him, he was screwed now, out of action. He was the only one with all the pieces of the plan he'd put together. His September strike against customers of businesses that exploited illegal immigrants would fail. The synchronized bombings of restaurants and grocery stores would never happen; the suffering of laborers who were treated like modern-day slaves would continue unabated.

Because of *his* sins, his obsession . . .

But in the end, it wasn't Sergio Cardenas's obsession that cost him. Nor was it the carjacking, the abduction, or the shots he'd fired in the white heat of emotion.

It was a far smaller transgression that finally took out one of the FBI's most wanted: his failure to buckle his seatbelt at the outset of his final, wild ride.

A hydraulic whoosh followed by the creak and whine of metal stressed past its endurance. The shatter of glass, a murmur of deep voices. Rough texture and darkness—something thrown over Luz Maria's face to protect her from the extrication.

Pain, beyond endurance. Pounding in her head but sharpest at her shoulder. Lesser discomforts, too, her body on the floor, wedged awkwardly between the backseat and the front, hanging just above the pancaked roof.

A louder voice came to her as the firefighter's coat was moved away from her face. "We're going to get you out now. But first, you need to let me put this collar around your neck—what's that on your wrists?"

Alarm shot through the rescue worker's professional calm, and his deep-set blue eyes widened. He was seeing the bindings, Luz Maria realized. Understanding she hadn't been a willing passenger.

He withdrew his curly, dark head from the car, then returned quickly, some kind of cutting tool in his right hand. "Don't worry, miss," he told her. "We're going to get you out of here. We'll take care of you."

Though his ruddy face was weathered, the concern in his expression reminded her of Grant Holcomb. Troubled by the thought of the detective, by something—she could not remember what—that Whit had said about him, she looked away. Her gaze slid toward the driver's seat, toward the cluster of red globules, like the crimson seeds of pomegranates. There were clumps, too, gray and viscous. Clumps with strands of blond hair sticking from them. One detached itself, to splash into the few inches of water flowing over the mashed roof.

"Don't look there," the firefighter told her. "Look at me and tell me—what's your name?"

Sergio's dead, she realized. *I was seeing Sergio's blood and his brains.* When the car flipped and slid on its roof, she'd been saved by rolling from the backseat to the floor. Saved by the strength of the front seat backs that had held the car's roof off her. It would have smashed into her head had she been sitting.

Dizziness washed over her, and her body's pain receded. She'd been saved by this rollover, yet she felt far too shaken to know gratitude. The effort to think was like the struggle to push a stalled car up a hill.

"I need you to stay with me." The firefighter's command grew firmer. "I need to know your name."

"Luz Maria," she murmured. "Luz Maria Montoya."

"That's great, Luz Maria. Can you tell me what day this is?"

He finished sawing through the rope binding her hands, and this fragment of freedom eased the throbbing of her shoulder. Ignoring his question—who *cared* what day today was—she struggled to crawl toward her rescuer. Her mind flooded with the need to get away from Sergio, to get away from death.

"It's okay, Luz Maria," the firefighter told her. "Just let me immobilize your neck, and we'll—"

Her panic must have changed his mind, for he ended up pulling her out through the window and onto the weedy slope that formed part of a muddy ditch. She fought to rise—to run as far and fast as she could—but her bound ankles made it impossible.

A second firefighter restrained her, told her, "Please, miss, let us help you," while the first squatted in his high boots and began working at the coils around her feet.

She glanced back, saw Sergio's limp arms and upper body hanging from the driver's side window. Saw what was left of his skull, tilted on his neck at a horrifying angle. Felt the world dissolve, changing from gray into a blackness as vast and deep as any ocean.

Yet a welcome voice lapped at its shores. Grant's voice, unmistakably, calling her name over and over. Grant's hand—she was certain of it—grasping hers and telling her, "Hang on."

She surfaced for a moment, lost in time and place, but anchoring herself to his hand with a death grip—and an urgent whisper: "Don't let them take my baby. Don't let me lose this child."

CHAPTER TWENTY-SIX

Three days after he'd watched Luz Maria being loaded into an ambulance, Grant's insides still felt like a sack of broken lightbulbs. Lieutenant Mouton's return to Houston to personally "counsel" him—which had turned into a shout-fest and suspension pending a disciplinary hearing—wasn't the only thing bothering him. The vacation-turned-suspension came as a relief, considering the cold shoulder his fellow officers turned toward him when he walked into the station—and the news that John's old partner, Roy Reed, had come by looking for him. Clearly, the details of the incident in Magnolia had spread throughout the station and beyond. *All* the details, including the fact that the activist blamed for his partner's death had spent the preceding night with him.

God help him if the brass found out what he was digging into now. It could happen, he knew, since he'd relied on a street source from his patrol days to track down the working girl once known as Shanti Starr. She had changed her name, he'd learned, to Niqua Bates, but after two years' worth of botched attempts to walk the straight and narrow, she was back—scars or no scars—to turning tricks out of her apartment.

Grant had been promised an exclusive on the information, but greasy Jimmy Koznoski would forget that part as soon as he came down from the crack he'd undoubtedly scored within five minutes of taking Grant's money. If the opportunity came up to sell out his benefactor, he'd do it in a heartbeat.

Part of Grant prayed the snitch *would* talk, that the blue brotherhood would hear about it and assume Grant had only been using Luz Maria to get information to help him exonerate or even avenge his late partner. And that the brotherhood would keep its mouth shut around Mutton and any IAD investigators who came calling.

It sounded unlikely, even to Grant. He had made plenty of enemies over the past two years, run off a lot of partners who couldn't hold a candle to the Z-man. Somebody, somewhere, would rat him out. But even that beat being thought a traitor to his partner's memory.

Grant found Shanti in one of the Southwest side's scarier complexes, though it took five minutes of pounding on the door of her apartment before she answered.

Peering through the chained door, which looked and smelled as if someone might have recently mistaken it for a urinal, a slender, young black woman squinted in a shaft of morning sunlight. Rhinestones sparkled across a low-cut, pale pink tee, spelling out JUICY. Mentally, Grant rearranged the glittering stars to form the word LIAR.

This two-bit street whore might have fooled a naive young bleeding heart like Luz Maria two years earlier, but Grant had years of experience distinguishing false victims from the real thing. And he'd known John Zeman far better than the Internal Affairs investigators who'd rushed to judgment in his case.

As she sized him up, Shanti's caramel-colored face soured.

"What the hell you mean, poundin' like that at this hour?" she demanded. "You tryin' to get yourself shot, fool?"

Grant was well aware that most of the tenants here spent their nights drifting through the Sharpstown neighborhood's streets—and making them more dangerous year by year. His work experience had taught him that morning was the best time to talk to one of the residents without the interference of an audience.

The welcome wagon wasn't exactly rolled out for any lone cop on the premises.

He flashed a pair of fifties. "I thought we might talk."

Her deep brown eyes regarded him appraisingly. "You the police, ain't you?"

He didn't bother to deny it. In this complex, a white man wearing a sport jacket meant only one thing. "Just want a little information. Off the record."

"Show me," she said. "Not just the damn badge, neither. Any fool can buy one of those. I wanta see that ID they give you."

He pulled out his wallet, slipped out the photo ID and passed it to her through the opening—along with one of the fifties. The door closed and he waited, wondering what the hell he'd do if she decided not to let him into the apartment. Considering what she'd supposedly been through at the hands of another cop, Shanti might be too terrified to take a chance with him.

Apparently, the thought of the other fifty he was

holding won her over, for less than a minute later, Shanti unchained the door and confirmed, "Just questions, right? No way I'm workin' at this hour."

Once he nodded, she stepped back to let him inside a cramped and dimly lit room dominated by an open sofa bed. Its tangled sheets, along with the fuzzed condition of her reddish braids, bore testimony to the fact she had been sleeping.

He saw only two other doorways, one leading to a narrow kitchen and the other, he supposed, to a bathroom. The entire unit had to be less than four hundred square feet. There was air-conditioning, at least, but a noisy oscillating floor fan augmented the system's weak efforts.

She went to a battered square table and switched on a Tiffany lamp—probably a fake—whose glowing glass mosaic made it the single point of beauty in an otherwise depressing place. Sensing her pride in the piece—and wanting to get Shanti Starr on his side—Grant said, "I like the dragonflies. It's very pretty."

"My man give me that. He's gettin' me out of the life any day now, just as soon as he finish with his sentence." She smiled, showing at least one missing front tooth and another broken off at an angle.

Grant's expression must have shifted, for her own clouded as she added, "Hey, a woman gotta understand, even a good man have a temper if she push him too hard."

Since advising her otherwise would never change her mind, Grant made his point fast. "Like John Zeman had a temper?"

Shanti jerked back, eyes flaring in clear terror. She thrust the fifty toward him, then threw it when he didn't take it fast enough to suit her. Her skinny wrist was trembling as she backed up against a wall.

"I thought you was here about that murder, that

brother got shot last week in the 'partment upstairs. But I won't take no money to talk 'bout what that pig did—talk about the way he cut me." The dragonfly lamp's glow caught the moisture gleaming beneath her eyes, the jittery movements of her hands as they darted to cover her long legs—hidden by blue jeans, despite the heat—and her smallish breasts.

Grant shook his head and placed the second fifty next to the lamp's base. The first, he left untouched on the floor where it had fallen.

"I'm not here to hurt you. I'm not here for revenge. I only want to hear it from you. I only need to understand," he said, as if that were really all he did need.

"I don't want to tell that story," she cried. "You know the kind of men I get here? The kind that don't care what I look like, since it all feels the same in the dark anyhow. Or . . . or sometimes I get me some brothers want to pay me just to see the way he do me. Just to see them ugly scars. Sometimes they spit on me, then walk right back out that door. The lookin's worse, though, like I ain't nothin' but some freak show. Like I ain't nothin' human."

"I have to know." Grant pulled a photo of John Zeman from his pocket.

She recoiled at the movement, as if she had expected him to draw his gun, to shoot her.

"Please, Shanti—or Niqua." His words trembled, as if he were the one frightened for his life. "Just tell me, was it *this* man? Was he the guy who cut you?"

For several moments, she stood staring at the picture, huffing through an open mouth, her face growing slick with a flood of tears and mucus. Then she covered her face, as if to hold back her escalating sobs.

Since he could get no other answer, Grant left her

that way, with both an apology and the two fifties on the table. Afterward, he climbed into his car and headed toward his breakfast meeting, though he already felt full to overflowing, weighed down with regret.

"The guys understand about the letter," Billy explained almost apologetically. The two of them had come to an out-of-the-way pancake house in a north side neighborhood where they were unlikely to be spotted.

Grant struggled to push the memory of the prostitute's sobs out of his mind. It was like trying to ignore a fist-sized hole in the center of his chest or to attempt a goddamned Texas two-step on a floor slick with his own blood.

The sound of shattering refocused his attention. At a neighboring table in the restaurant, a grubby-looking preschooler had knocked his glass of soda to the floor.

Like a man awakening in a strange hotel room, Grant glanced around the restaurant, an older place that attracted a mix of retired couples, badly dressed obese folks, and a young family with more kids than they could handle—including the dark-haired boy already howling for another Coke. As Billy had promised when he'd suggested it, what the place lacked in atmosphere, it more than made up for in anonymity.

"I mean," Billy added, "everybody at work knows the hell you went through back when Zeman—well, when he did what he did. What they can't deal with is the idea of you screwing that Montoya woman, especially while you're seeing Sherry Zeman."

"I got that," Grant said, thinking he'd been lucky to avoid getting his ass whipped by the two detectives who'd stopped by his place yesterday for what they'd termed a "friendly chat."

"I've never been involved with Sherry," Grant told Billy, just as he'd told the duo yesterday. "I've just been helping her through a bad stretch."

"For two years?" Billy challenged. "And you better get it through to *her* you're not involved, man, 'cause that's not how she's telling it around the other guys' wives."

Grant swallowed back a curse when he saw the waitress coming. Though still in her teens, the Hispanic girl—Guadalupe, according to her name tag—made him think of Luz Maria, in spite of the coffee-stained apron over her form-fitting pink dress and her flirtatious smile.

But nearly every woman he saw prompted thoughts of Luz Maria, who was supposed to have been released from the hospital yesterday. Luz Maria, who had told Jason Whitfield and her brother Jack that she didn't want to see Grant. Who had suffered a concussion and God only knew what else during her abduction and the subsequent car wreck.

What the hell did she mean about a baby? Though she'd appeared anything but pregnant when the two of them had made love, could he have been wrong about her? Could she be carrying some other man's child?

The thought rattled the shards inside Grant, slicing away at something vital. Why was he so upset? Over a woman he'd hated until a few days earlier? A woman who'd scared the hell out of him when he'd seen her lying in the grass and mud, spattered with another's blood for the second time in days?

Billy threw a crumpled napkin at his face. "You going to order or you going to sit there staring at that menu 'til the lunch rush?"

"Oh, sorry," Grant said. "I'll have the number three combo, with the eggs scrambled."

Why should his breakfast be any different from his life?

"And some more coffee when you get the chance." He glanced down at his mug to see she'd already refilled it.

"Don't mind him," Billy told the waitress as he tapped a finger to his temple. "*Poco loco.*"

Guadalupe giggled, then blushed at Billy's wink before she turned to all but skip back to the kitchen.

"Who're you calling crazy?" Grant asked. "You're the moron making time with jailbait."

"She's gotta be at least eighteen." Billy frowned as he doctored his coffee with enough sugar to induce a diabetic coma. "But better jailbait than the woman who made your partner's wife a widow. Or were the guys back at the station right? Was sleeping with that bitch just part of some grand plan to pay her back for—"

Grant nearly went across the table at him. "Don't call Luz Maria Montoya that name. You damned well know better. You've met her, too. You know she isn't like that—isn't at all like what I thought two years ago. Whatever she said, whatever she did about Zeman, was because she thought she was right. Sincerely."

Billy snorted. "That good in bed, huh?"

Grant pushed his chair out from the table, was on his feet in half a second. "Goddamn it—you, too, Brutus?"

"Huh?" His partner drew back, then shook his head before asking, "You want to hear about the blood or not?"

When Grant didn't answer, Billy added, "Come on, man. I'm sorry. You're right. She didn't seem like a bad person. It's just—I'm worried about you, that's all. First, that letter, and then, this—I still can't believe you took her to your *house.*"

Grant heard the exasperation in his voice. Yet it was nothing compared to the solid wrath of Mutton. And his own sense of bewilderment was even worse. Had some defective gene sprung up in him, the legacy of a father who had gone from bad to worse until that terrible, last day when . . .

Even as a criminal, the man had been a screwup. Was Grant finally, in spite of all his efforts to avoid it, living down to the man's example and his mother's expectations?

The thought dropped him back into his bench seat. Who was he to blow up over his rookie partner's jibes?

Besides, he meant to pry some information out of Howdy Doody. "You were talking about the blood found at the Ryland's lot where Luz Maria was assaulted, right? So what's the story? Was it Coleman's, after all, or Sergio Cardenas's?"

"Coleman's," Billy said. "Feds stepped in and ran the DNA test in a hurry. They're horning in on every angle of the investigation, but at least they're able to wave the magic wand over the usual lab backlog, and the special agent in charge is making an effort to deal us in."

Grant nodded. With the sister of an FBI employee murdered, a fugitive on the Most Wanted List involved, and whatever intelligence the Feds had on some kind of planned terrorist attack, every string imaginable would be pulled in this case.

Billy sipped his coffee before adding, "I heard the mayor's in this, too, pushing the police chief hard to get the case closed. He doesn't want anyone accusing the department—or his administration—of slacking off on any case involving Ms. Montoya or the Voice of Poverty."

"Getting back to our favorite rabid baseball fan, do we know any more about how Coleman died?"

"ME rushed the autopsy, too," Billy explained, "ruled it as a homicide, result of the initial bullet. Looks like the guy showed up to confront Ms. Montoya at the wrong time. Homicide figures Cardenas is the perp. They're looking for solid evidence to place him at the scene . . . but they're not really working that part of the case as hard as you'd think."

Grant shook his head. There were a lot of things Billy Devlin still had to learn about how investigations really worked. "Dead suspect's as good as it gets for them. No flight risk, no defense attorney, and no screaming press or prosecutor riding your ass for a confession and nine kinds of corroborating evidence. The brass and the mayor are all smiles, and the Feebs'll be happy enough to lay another murder at Cardenas's feet, as long as they can close out the Capshaw case. You know how it is. There's always a dozen other investigations clamoring for attention."

An endless chain of human misery, he thought dejectedly.

Billy screwed his face up, more evidence that even with his handicap, he could muster an expression in a pinch. "Back to the Capshaw case—we did get some hair and fingerprints out of both Ms. Montoya's and her neighbor's apartment. But the thing is, none of 'em matched up to Sergio Cardenas."

"What about semen?" Grant asked. "Any collected from the body?"

He shut up as the waitress set his plate down, her pretty face crinkling in exaggerated revulsion.

"Sorry," he told her. "You can take a cop out of the station . . ."

Billy touched his head again and whispered conspiratorially, "Some days he likes to pretend he's a fireman, too."

Giggling, Guadalupe set down Billy's pancakes and sausage patties and scooted off again, her pink hem fluttering around slim thighs. Thighs Grant's partner was watching too intently.

"Jailbait," Grant warned again. "I've got a twenty says she's sixteen."

"Huh?" Billy unfolded a piece of what looked like an order pad. With a triumphant grin, he showed Grant the phone number the girl had slipped him. "Well how 'bout that? And she's at least eighteen—I have a sixth sense about these things."

Grant snorted, then snatched the paper from his partner's hand. "Probably the number to Dial-A-Prayer—see, if you look real hard, there's an extension for the patron saint of lost items. Maybe he can come up with your eyebrows."

"Or *your* sanity." But Billy's answering smile quickly faded. "And to get back to your question, yeah, they did find semen in the victim. DNA should be back any time."

"It'll be Cardenas," Grant predicted. "To my way of thinking, it all fits. He spent a long time planning his revenge against Luz Maria. Long enough that he started out real careful. But as things got away from him, his organization started to unravel. By the time he assaulted and killed Ms. Capshaw, the sick son of a bitch had lost it completely."

"So where are his fingerprints?" asked Billy. "Cardenas wears latex gloves but not a condom? I mean, this guy's been keeping one step ahead of everything the Feds could throw at him for years. Seems to me he'd know enough to avoid leaving physical evidence."

"This is personal," Grant countered, "a crime of passion. The two of them were lov—they were involved—before she turned informant. He's bottled up three years' worth of rage. I'm telling you, he cracked."

Still, Billy looked mystified. "Sorry, but I can't picture it. What if it wasn't him at the apartment? What if somebody else—"

"Look, Devlin. There are a lot of our best guys on this. Investigators with a hell of a lot more than a week and a half's experience under their belts. And the Feds are all over it like fire ants on a dropped hot dog. My advice is sit back, watch, and learn from this one. And absorb the lesson that when it comes to human behavior, one and one don't always make two. There are always questions we can't answer. It doesn't make us wrong about the main point. Sergio Cardenas murdered Ms. Capshaw, same as he shot Coleman. He'd kill anybody standing between him and Luz Maria."

While Billy finished breakfast—Grant had lost his appetite completely—the younger man continued to feed him the forbidden fruit of information, including the technicians' opinion that the grocery store parking lot security camera outage was due to normal wear and tear instead of vandalism. That, along with the time-stamped repair request, should make Security Chief Tom Newlin and Ryland Foods' attorneys happy. Billy also mentioned that the origin of the Web log listing Luz Maria's activities remained a mystery, its source untraceable as yet.

"Probably unrelated," Grant commented. "After all, the woman *has* pissed off a lot of people. If it makes you feel any better, why don't you run a check on Montoya's coworkers? It's crossed my mind the Web log may be an inside job—maybe motivated by interoffice rivalry or something. Probably not related to Cardenas—except as a tool he used to find her faster."

But as Grant left Billy to chat up the waitress, he couldn't stop thinking about his partner's doubts. What if there really was something else in play here?

Candelaria Esmeralda de Vaca Montoya whisked into the spare bedroom, her short arms straining beneath the loaded breakfast tray she set down on the nightstand. "You feel much better, *mija*, once you fill your stomach with good things from my kitchen."

The tiny woman withdrew a handkerchief from the bodice of her embroidered white gauze dress and made a show of blotting the perspiration from her brow.

Luz Maria pushed herself into a sitting position and surveyed her mother's largess in horror. "Mama, you could fill an entire *family's* stomachs with all this. Including all the aunts and uncles and *abuelos.*"

Her still aching head swam with the kaleidoscope of scents and colors: a platter heaped with scrambled eggs, chiles, and chorizo, covered with melting cheese and salsa; a tropical fruit salad; fresh, warm corn tortillas; a small pot of coffee; a glass of orange juice. Even at her hungriest, she'd barely make a dent.

"It was nice of you to arrange to open the shop late this morning," Luz Maria tried, having already lost the argument that she was well enough to take care of herself. "And you were so thoughtful, making all this wonderful food, but I'm really not that—"

"You no want?" Her mother snatched up the whole tray, groaning loudly about her back. "I feed to dogs. Maybe dogs appreciate my hard work—or bad-tempered cat of yours."

Borracho rose from his spot near Luz Maria's feet, then turned his back on both of them to wash his striped back with haughty indifference. The tabby was still angry about his stay at the vet's, where Jack had picked him up last night, and in no mood to be bought off with anything less than Chicken Nibblets.

"Please, put it down," Luz Maria begged. With her wrenched shoulder still tender and her heart sore, she was no match for her mama's theatrics. For heaven's sake, the woman didn't even *have* dogs. How was Luz Maria supposed to deal with her?

Her own tears surprised her, though they shouldn't have. Ever since the accident, she'd been leaking like a colander. Hearing Kellie's screams, seeing Sergio's broken body drooping out the car window . . .

Her mother set the tray back down and sat on the bed's edge, then gathered Luz Maria into her arms. For once, Candelaria didn't accuse, didn't turn the situation around to focus on *her* suffering. Instead, she hummed a tune Luz Maria remembered from her childhood, from a song about a little white dove with black eyes. As her mama rubbed Luz Maria's back, the older woman whispered, "This will pass, I promise. It may seem like it will kill you, but with each scar, the *corazón* beats stronger. This is something I have learned."

Luz Maria leaned her cheek against the short, still-dark curls and thought of how her mother had been widowed in her early thirties, how she'd been left, heartbroken, to raise two children in a country where she barely spoke the language.

Though she had done plenty of complaining, she had somehow survived it—cleaning houses seven days a week, growing traditional medicinal herbs in the backyard of their rental house and selling them to others unable to afford modern doctors. And in time opening the *yerbería*, a shop where she sold enough herbs, incense, candles, and assorted paraphernalia to make a decent living. Two years ago, she had even surprised herself by finding love, with her gentle, patient carpenter, Eduardo Espinosa.

Straightening, Luz Maria looked into her mother's eyes and said, "At least it wasn't your fault. At least you weren't the one who caused Papa's death. The one who had a hand in so many others."

She wondered just how many. Did she stop with Kellie or go on to Sergio and the three members of BorderFree-4-All gunned down in Mexico? Did she count Tony Coleman, shot either while attacking her or perhaps while interfering with an attack by Sergio? And what of John Zeman, who had taken his own life and left behind a family? How far did the ripples travel, once she tossed a stone into still waters?

And how would she ever cast another?

Her mother picked up Luz Maria's hand and squeezed it. "Always with you, it is the bad thoughts—these feelings of *responsabilidad*. Tell me why is it you imagine God has put you in charge of the whole world? Why can it not be enough to find a good *esposo*, a husband like *mi* Eduardo, and use up all this being responsible on children? Why not some more *nietos* for your *mamá?*"

Oh, no. Once her mama got wound up on the subject of grandchildren, there would be no stopping her. Luz Maria had hoped she'd simmer down after the birth of Jack and Reagan's son, but no. Now she harassed the couple about the importance of adding to their *familia* before thirty-one-year-old Reagan became "old woman with the shriveled eggs." Apparently, Candelaria would not be satisfied until both her children produced enough grandkids to fill a stadium.

Come to think of it, knowing her mother, that wouldn't do it, either.

"I don't want to be responsible for anyone right now," Luz Maria told her. "Not kids or a husband, not even the people who come to VOP for help."

Her mama nodded sagely. "This is good. You let those strangers take care of their own *problemas*. And your eggs have time, a few more years at least, so you take this Galveston vacation, like Reagan tell you. Then you come back, live here with me, get good, safe new job—maybe help me at the *yerbería*—and then husband."

267

"*Mama.*" Luz Maria massaged her forehead. At the moment, the best thing about the Galveston suggestion was that, though the island city was no more than an hour south of Houston, her mother never ventured down there.

When a car door slammed outside, Luz Maria was profoundly glad for the diversion.

"This must be your Señor Whit," Candelaria guessed, though the room's sole window lay shrouded behind a pair of tasseled curtains. "So good, he come take care of you while I go work in shop. He is single man, too. And very nice to look at, for a gringo."

"Please don't start on poor Whit," Luz Maria said as her mama headed for the bedroom door. "I explained to you, he's gay."

Candelaria swatted away the concern as if it had no more substance than a fruit fly. "Such foolishness. I have seen this man. Pretty girl like you change his mind lick-splittedly."

As Luz Maria tried not to laugh at her mother's fractured English idiom, the doorbell rang. Quickly, her mama excused herself with the admonishment that her daughter was to, "Eat now or when I come back, I swat your *pompis.*"

Luz Maria did smile this time, at the thought of how many times her mother had repeated—though never carried out—this same threat. Though Luz Maria had improved considerably, she'd always been a picky eater, with a tendency to latch onto those foods she did enjoy and insist on eating them exclusively—much like her surly cat.

Yet despite the constant warnings, she had not died of "the *mala*nutrition," as her mother put it. Luz Maria figured a vitamin deficiency didn't stand a chance of killing her, not considering the enemies she'd been able to sidestep over the past few years.

Including the one her smiling mother ushered into the bedroom.

"Look, Luz Maria," Candelaria all but sang. "This is your day for handsome visitors, no?"

Grant Holcomb, wearing a pair of chino slacks and a short-sleeve polo-style shirt, had the grace to look sheepish. As well as good enough to eat . . .

Luz Maria crossed her arms over her breasts and glared at him. "When you came to bring my purse back to the hospital, Whit told you I don't want to see you. Jack told you, too. Since I know this isn't an official visit, what the hell do you think you're doing, showing up—"

"*Claro que sí*, Luz Maria," her mama interrupted. "Is plain as nose on face that *Investigador* Holcomb comes to speak of matters of the heart."

Grant's smile slanted, lending him a rogue's charm.

It isn't fair, thought Luz Maria, *that he has to look so damned good.* And what in heaven's name had he said to her mother, to get her on his side in thirty seconds?

Come to think of it, the way Candelaria had been carrying on about grandchildren, it would not have taken much more than the twinkle in his gray eyes.

"I leave you two alone," Luz Maria's mother said, "to work out your *problemas* and share my humble breakfast."

"It smells delicious, Mrs. Montoya," Grant said earnestly.

Luz Maria felt her scowl deepen, and she muttered, "What a suck-up."

Her mother left, closing the door behind her—and probably racing downstairs to light a couple of prayer candles.

Without an invitation, Grant dragged up a wooden chair and sat beside Luz Maria. Borracho—ever the model pet—hissed at him before jumping off the bed to crawl beneath it.

Luz Maria wished that she could do the same.

"Why didn't you tell me?" she asked, her arms still crossed and her gaze lowered. "Why didn't you let me know it was always about your partner? Why didn't you tell me before we slept together?"

"Because it wasn't about him then," Grant said quietly. "Because being with you, getting to know you, changed things. And because making love with you was one of the best things I've ever—"

"You should have told me all about that letter—the one you sent after your partner—"

"You're right about that. Absolutely."

When she glanced up at him, she saw his shoulders slump as he picked at a hangnail. Avoiding her eyes, she decided.

"And I could tell you'd been through that file, the one I had in my purse. The pages were all turned around and out of order, so don't even try denying—"

"I'm sorry, Luz. I'm so damned sorry. Once I saw his name on it, I . . . I had to know all of it. What the department saw fit to keep from me. I wish I'd never seen it, but for my own sanity, I had to—"

He cut himself off with a curse, then shook his head and asked her, "Haven't you ever done something . . . something so stupid and so terrible you'd give anything you had to take it back? Or at least to pretend it never happened?"

A flash of comprehension caught her off-guard, like a glimmer of heat lightning at the corner of her eye. And just that quickly, she understood the way it was for him, the way it had been since John Zeman's death.

"Yes," she told him quietly. "I think you know I have."

His gaze met hers, the pain in it so palpable, it tempted

her to look away. Yet she did not until he asked another question.

"Is it—is it something to do with a child, Luz Maria? A child you're carrying?"

She threw back the sheet covering her legs, which were bare beneath a pair of cotton shorts. Swinging her feet to the floor on the opposite side of the bed from Grant, she stood. Borracho yowled, then tried to scratch her, since her heel came down on the black tip of his tail. But Luz Maria couldn't spare the tabby any sympathy, not with her muscles trembling as she stared at the crucifix hanging on the wall.

"Why would you ask me that, Grant?" Her head was pounding once more, a souvenir of her concussion.

"After the accident, when I showed up, you said something to me. Something about not losing this baby."

The cross wavered in a haze of unshed tears.

"I must have been confused," she told him. "That was the other accident."

"Your accident three years ago?" he asked, reminding her how much he knew of her past.

Nodding, she admitted, "I . . . I miscarried afterward. But Sergio thought—he got the idea that I'd had an abortion."

"Is that the real reason he came after you?" Grant asked. "Was it that and not the testimony?"

"To him, that was the worst betrayal. He was furious, insulted—as if he would or could have stepped up to be a father if I hadn't lost the baby."

"So before—you turned him in knowing you were carrying his child?"

Tears streamed down unchecked now. Why was he making her relive this? And why didn't she simply stop explaining and start demanding that he leave?

But something in her responded to his unhealed wounds, as well as to the memory of the intimacy that had bloomed between them like a flower growing up through cracked concrete.

"I had to go to the authorities," she said. "My brother finally made me see how Sergio's actions hurt people. How I'd been manipulated into doing things that . . . But it wasn't just manipulation. It was *me*, making bad decisions. The worst decisions of my life."

Grant came up behind her, touched two fingers to the delicate skin inside her wrist. "So we're a couple of screwups, so what now? Are we both supposed to spend the rest of our lives being sorry? Burn ourselves out helping other people, trying to settle up with God or fate or guilt?"

She turned to look at him and murmured, "I'm not sure I'm helping anyone."

"And I'm not sure I have it in me to make it up to Zeman's widow, to replace the husband she might still have if I'd paid enough attention."

"The funny thing is, back then, with Sergio, I was so damned certain I was doing right. And as far as I know, he never questioned himself, not for a single moment." She wiped at her eyes. "But now—God, Grant. Sometimes I want to find myself a surgeon and pay him to cut out my conscience like a cancer. What good is it, anyway, all these questions? All these doubts? What good is it doing either one of us, to—"

Grant's head shook. "I can't answer that, but I can tell you one thing. I've known people without any conscience—I've arrested plenty of them. And if you could somehow get rid of yours, you wouldn't like what you had left . . . and I wouldn't be here like an idiot, risking whatever's left of my career to ask if I can see you."

"You—you're asking me out?" She could hardly believe what she was hearing. "As in to dinner?"

His gaze drifted to the tray of cooling food on the

nightstand, and he smiled at her. "Maybe we could start with breakfast, see where that will lead us."

She swallowed hard, then nodded. If nothing else, he could help her eat enough to get her mama off her back.

And then she could explain to him the thousand-and-one reasons why seeing him could never, ever work.

CHAPTER TWENTY-SEVEN

"Are you completely out of your mind?"

Though Whit's words vibrated with fury, his expression was alarmed. Concerned. For her.

Meteor-bright shame streaked across Luz Maria's consciousness, the realization that once again, her actions were causing those who cared for her to worry.

But even so, she strained to listen for the sound of Grant's car door slamming and his engine roaring to life. When Whit threatened to call the chief of police if Grant didn't get the hell out in a hurry, the investigator had merely nodded and turned to leave—though not without giving Luz Maria a wink and smile that could mean only one thing.

She hadn't heard the last of him. Not by a long shot.

"He's all right," she explained to Whit. "If you'd talked to him instead of bursting in and firing off threats, you'd see that."

"I do see. I see a man who wants to worm his way into your confidence—not to mention your bed." He fussed with the collar of one of his more flamboyant Hawaiian shirts, his fingers pulling it away from the small bandage on the side of his neck.

With a shake of his head, he continued. "Don't you get it, hon? Here's a man so gorgeous he could take his pick of just about any woman in Houston, yet he goes after the one he blames for his partner's death. The one he's threatened in the past."

Doubt nudged its way past the sense of well-being that had taken shape as Luz Maria and Grant shared her mother's food. She had rarely felt such ease in talking to a man, even laughing at his stories about stupid criminals. Perhaps because with him, there was nothing she was hiding, nothing she was holding back and praying would not be discovered.

Grant knew her mistakes, knew every shameful secret. Yet instead of reflecting and magnifying her self-loathing, he'd seemed more determined than ever to get to know her better. Could his interest be an act, his acceptance a deception? Was this chance to accept each other's past shortcomings and build something strong and lasting, something every bit as solid and healthy as her brother's relationship with Reagan, no more than wishful thinking? Or was he conning her as deftly as Sergio had three years before?

"You're right," she told Whit, her body slumping as if someone had let the air out of her. "It makes no sense, his coming here. I know he's been suspended, so it can't be about the case. It's just that—"

"Did that knock to the head shake loose your memory?" Whit demanded. "In this city, *you're* the Voice of Poverty. To fulfill that role, you have to be fearless, you have to be outspoken, and you damned well have to use good sense to stay alive. I can assess the threats. I can advise you about sensible precautions. But I cannot and will not do my job if you won't listen to the obvious, if you won't—"

"I'm finished with it, Jason."

"What?" He could not have looked more stunned if she had smacked his temple with a two-by-four. On several past occasions, Whit had peppered her with everything from pouts to warnings, even threats to quit when he thought she'd taken his recommendations too lightly. But she had never given any indication that she could be backed down.

Luz Maria shook her head, flipping her braid from one shoulder to the other. "I've been thinking these past few days. I can't live like this."

"But, Luz Maria, you're—"

"You said it yourself, Whit. The Voice of Poverty has to be fearless and outspoken. How can I be either of those things now, after what's happened this past week?"

If she thought she'd get an argument, she was mistaken. Whit only nodded, his wide-set blue eyes sad. "I'm sorry, sweetie, but I'd be a liar if I didn't tell you this comes as a relief. I hope I'm not out of line in saying this, but you've been drawing way too much of the wrong kind of attention. Maybe it's because you're so young and pretty. . . ."

Luz Maria felt herself flushing as she murmured, "I don't know about that, Whit."

"Have you told anybody else from the office?"

She shook her head. "I was waiting, just to be sure. My sister-in-law's mom and stepdad own a condo in Galveston that they've been kind enough to offer. I thought I'd drive down there tomorrow and spend some time regrouping, figuring out where I go from here. I—uh—I will warn April. I'll call her after you leave. Then I'll put together an official letter of resignation while I'm down there."

She tried to smile at her friend as she told him, "Who

knows, Whit? Maybe the powers that be will see fit to put you in the spotlight."

"Fat chance," Whit shot back with a smile. "Too many skeletons in this boy's closet. Starting with that hunk of a sailor down in—"

He stepped back suddenly as Borracho emerged growling from beneath the bedspread's fringe.

"What's got into him? You hurt my feelings, Borracho buddy. I thought we were good pals."

On more than one occasion, Whit—who had two cats of his own—had made an effort with Borracho. But privately, Luz Maria thought his "friendship" with her cranky feline was doomed to remain one-sided.

"Don't mind him," Luz Maria explained, "he's still out of sorts about his bath and boarding—and I *did* step on him."

As he emerged, the tabby's tail lashed back and forth in irritation. Instead of clawing or biting anybody, however, the cat jumped up beside Luz Maria on the bed and snuggled next to her, his back muscles rippling with pleasure when she scratched him. He was having one of his rare "moments," Luz Maria decided. But still, the nasty little sucker never took his evil gaze off Whit.

Whit just smirked and shook his head.

"I was a little worried about you running down to Galveston alone," he told Luz Maria, "but you'll be fine, as long as you take your attack cat with you."

"I plan to—my mother can't handle him, and the vet as much as told me he wasn't welcome back there. Something about biting the hand that fed him."

"I'd offer to take him home myself, but I can't bear the idea of Mitzi and Maxine getting chewed up by this reprobate." Whit pointed down at the big tabby—though the security director kept a respectful distance. "But I'll tell you what, Borracho. You see Detective

Holcomb slinking around, you can go ahead and give him no fewer than ten toenails—right across the eyes."

The moment Grant got out of his car, he heard them. The damned pigs had come back for his trash cans.

Anger with himself surged past his frustration over the Luz Maria situation. How many times did he have to clean up garbage before he finally got around to building a secure enclosure for the containers?

Swearing at the nuisance, he stormed out of his carport and raced around the corner . . . only to have a metal lid smash into the side of his face.

He went down hard and fast, landing on his ass and staring up in astonishment at the thick-bodied man who stood above him. Roy Reed's beefy face was no less ruddy, nor his expression any calmer, than the last time Grant had seen him—in the aftermath of Zeman's funeral, when John's former partner from the Sex Crimes Unit had taken a swing at Grant and told him he had a lot of fucking nerve to show up.

Reed tossed the metal lid to one side and growled down at Grant. "Now that I've gotten your attention, *traitor*, can you give me one goddamned reason I shouldn't leave you stuffed in these cans with the rest of the freaking garbage?"

Grant rubbed at his jaw as he picked himself up off the ground. He was several inches taller than the forty-something Reed, but John's former partner made up for the height difference in sheer bulk—not to mention a propensity for fury rumored to be a side effect of the Body by Steroids. Beneath his tight T-shirt, muscled hillocks trembled. One, showing beneath the sleeves, bore a tattoo of a bulldog that read *Semper Fi-do*.

The Marine Corps background didn't surprise Grant any more than the buzz-cut, salt-and-pepper hair. Both the military and the police force drew their share of assholes—fortunately a minority—who lived for the chance to exert power over others. The only surprise was that Reed had lasted so long in the department.

"I guess you shouldn't try it," Grant glared as he answered, "because I might have something to say about it. In a language even you could understand."

He spat out something salty. He hoped it was only blood and not a tooth. But he could worry about the damage later. At the moment, he had to concentrate on avoiding more.

If he could steer clear of an all-out brawl, he would. Even if he ended up beating the hell out of Reed, Grant knew he'd come out the loser with regards to his career. Not to mention falling even farther in the opinion of his fellow officers.

Raised as he had been, Grant had learned to fight young and fight dirty. But he would still probably get pounded in a contest with Reed. With his own guilt to fight as well as his muscle-bound opponent, Grant saw a future stuffed inside a trash can as a very real possibility.

Sweat popping from his skin, Reed moved in closer, breathing in Grant's face.

Since Grant doubted this was a good time to recommend the man pay more attention to his oral hygiene, he tried another tack. "Look, Roy. It's hotter than hell out here, and thanks to you, I could use a couple aspirin. You want to come inside in the AC and hash this out? How 'bout some iced tea or a cold brew?"

"The only thing I want to do is leave you in a bloody heap, you goddamned traitor. What the fuck do you think you're *doing*, looking out for that Montoya bitch? After what that cunt did to Zeman?"

"Hey, man, there's no need for the language."

Reed shoved him. "What? You going pansy on us now, too?"

Grant's hands knotted into fists and his voice iced

over. "I know you were John's friend, same as I was. But you *don't* want to push me again, you no-necked, shit-for-brains psychopath—"

Later, Grant acknowledged it probably hadn't been his wisest choice of words.

"What the hell happened to your face?" Special Agent Steve Petit asked Grant over dinner that evening.

Grant rubbed his jaw, which was still throbbing from the morning run-in with the man he'd come to think of as 'Roid Rage Reed. Though Grant had given a surprisingly good account of himself, Reed had driven home the point that he considered Grant a "total fuckup" who needed to go to Sherry Zeman on his hands and knees and beg forgiveness for his betrayal. And he'd better have a goddamn diamond ring—not one of those lame-ass fake ones either—in his pocket.

Grant was going to have to have a serious talk with Sherry—and soon. He was fresh out of unbruised cheeks to turn.

"Ran into a door," he told Cowboy, not wanting to get into his life as a pariah.

Grant had been surprised when Petit had called and asked him if he knew a decent place for chicken-fried steak. Though he didn't say as much, Cowboy's friendly manner hinted he was still willing to spill details from his investigation. What Grant didn't understand was why. It wasn't as if he had anything to offer the Feebs—especially since he was officially cut off from all further information.

Still, he'd taken the hint and talked Petit into meeting him at Wunsche Brothers, a historic Old Town Spring café first built as a saloon. Though Grant usually avoided the touristy area north of Houston, it was far enough from both home and work that they would be unlikely to run into anyone he knew. For another thing,

Grant figured it would do him some good to drown his sorrows in a cold beer and a plate of artery-clogging ecstasy chased down with cream gravy. And maybe a slice of the chocolate whiskey cake as well.

The hostess led them to a corner table Grant had pointed out. As they were seated, Cowboy eyed the rustic décor, which mostly consisted of neon beer signs and photos of old trains.

"This place is real Texas," he said after letting out a sigh of deep contentment. "All you see in Southern California are the plastic imitations. And that goes for the women, too."

He grinned and used his hands to indicate a pair of pointy breasts. Tall, lean, and blond at thirty-two, with the same slightly chipped front tooth from his days riding bulls, Petit wore ironed jeans and a black Jack Daniels T-shirt.

"You sure you're a real Fed?" Grant asked. "You still dress like a human and haven't been reprogrammed to PC-speak."

"I revert in my off hours—among old friends, at any rate."

Instead of getting right to business, the two of them talked trash awhile—local yokels versus the mighty Feebs—and enjoyed a beer before putting away the better part of a pair of chicken-fried steak dinners.

Finally, Petit pushed back from his plate and said, "I've heard a few things, Holcomb. Things that worry me."

Grant, who'd given up on finishing his meal as well, frowned at him. "Sorry, Cowboy. I figured somebody would've already broken it to you about Santa and the Easter Bunny."

Ignoring his remark, his old friend frowned. "Word is you got yourself involved with the wrong lady. Or maybe I should say got yourself caught getting involved."

"Let's just say I know better now." Grant tried to sound

adamant in the hopes he could convince Pettit—and himself. "It was a one-shot thing. Temporary insanity."

The insanity part he was sure of; it was the "temporary" part that worried him—along with the deepening itch to keep seeing Luz Maria Montoya. Only the thought of Lieutenant Mouton's ultimatum stopped him, the clear warning that the next time he was caught defying orders to stay away from her would surely put the last nails in the coffin of his career.

And other voices came back to him from his teen years, when he'd been fired from his first job as a valet parking attendant after he'd yielded to the temptation to take a hot, sleek Corvette for a spin. He'd been ruthlessly jerked back to the straight and narrow the night he'd overheard his aunts whispering together: *God help him, he's his father all over. That man never could learn to color in the lines—or hold down a job, either.*

"Un-huh." Cowboy kept his murmur noncommittal. "Well, just in case it's more than that, I thought I'd clue you in that the semen in Kellie Capshaw's body didn't match up."

Despite his effort to look uninterested, Grant felt the blood drain from his face. "To Cardenas, you mean?"

Pettit nodded. "Right. He may have abducted Luz Maria Montoya, and ballistics matched the gun he carried to the bullets found at the scene of the VOP drive-by shooting, but we have no physical evidence he was ever in her place. Once Cardenas was excluded, we were left with an un-sub."

The sinking feeling reached deep into Grant's chest. An unidentified suspect had the entire investigation back to square one—and confirmed his inexperienced partner's hunch.

Luz Maria Montoya was in as much danger as ever.

He thought of how she'd told him she planned to spend sometime in Galveston, alone.

But even as it sank in, Pettit's phrasing registered as well. "You said you *were* left with an un-sub. Meaning that you have something now?"

Cowboy nodded, looking him directly in the eye.

"I do," he said, his voice dry as the West Texas dust bred into him. "Unfortunately, I do."

CHAPTER TWENTY-EIGHT

The bitch thought she was safe now. They all did, thanks to Sergio Cardenas and his well-timed meltdown.

Stupid, every one of them—despite his slip-up with the girl who'd chosen the wrong moment to step out of her apartment. The girl who hadn't looked enough like the first one, or like Luz Maria, either, for that matter.

But in spite of their stupidity, they might just turn out to be right after all. Her nightmare could be over— as long as she'd learned something about the nature of the enemies her work made. As long as she walked away from it right now and never looked back. It would be safer that way for him, smarter, he supposed.

So for the time being, he would sit tight, monitor the situation—even though something in him craved the rush of power he had felt when he had smashed the golf club down through Kellie Capshaw's head.

And his prick hardened at the thought of the hole in one that followed, the cooling of her body as he pumped himself inside her.

So much *power*, feeling a death he'd dealt on purpose.

Such absolute control, with no one there to blame him for a stupid accident that wasn't even his fault.

An image splashed through his mind: his thin legs kicking in his favorite footed Spider-man pajamas. His hands bagged and taped until the cops could test for gunshot residue.

Why didn't the bitch tell me it wasn't a goddamned toy gun in her purse? It was Mama's fault, anyway—her fault—so how can I be sorry, no matter how often Grandpa looked at me that way in the hellish years that followed?

As he headed home that evening, Grant gritted his teeth in frustration as he mentally replayed his argument with Cowboy.

"She deserves to know, goddammit," Grant had argued. *"You have a responsibility to warn her."*

"If we haven't, you can bet your ass we've got good reason," Pettit had insisted.

Grant had demanded to know what reason could be good enough to keep from Luz Maria the fact that Kellie Capshaw had been raped and presumably murdered by a thirty-three-year-old predator named Kevin Vallens. Previously, the man had served five years for the aggravated sexual assault of a prostitute. It wasn't his first brush with authority, either. Before his arrest in Houston, the Army private had been discharged in San Antonio under a cloud of accusations—Cowboy's source in the judge advocate's office had told him there probably would have been a long stint in military prison if a young Hispanic woman who'd claimed Vallens beat and raped her hadn't disappeared before she'd been deposed. There was a sealed juvenile record as well, in Dallas County, which the feds were attempting to get a court order to have opened.

Grant had never before heard of Vallens, but that came as no surprise. The Houston area was a hot bed of paroled sex offenders, any one of whom could have become fixated on the beautiful activist so often featured on the evening news. Grant's dinner formed a greasy lump in his stomach at the thought.

Cowboy refused to share the FBI's reasons for failing to disclose this new information to Luz Maria, but Grant had his suspicions. The Feds suspected she was somehow in on this. Between her past involvement with a leader of BorderFree-4-All and what some of the hide-bound old-timers within the bureau would consider her "subversive" activism, they would never completely trust her. He could well imagine one of the dinosaurs, far more concerned with Kellie Capshaw's murder than the fate of the still-living "troublemaker," arguing that someone like Luz Maria could be romantically entangled with Kevin Vallens, too.

"It's bullshit," Grant argued. *"There's no way she's involved."*

"We have some of our very best, most senior people on this. If you know what's good for you, you'll stay out of it."

But Grant couldn't stay out of it, not with Luz Maria's safety at stake. Nor with the memory of the raw passion that had flared between them. Forget his aunts' words and Mutton's warnings. If it cost him his career, so be it. He had learned from John Zeman's death that there were worse fates than getting fired. Such as living with the knowledge that a life he might have saved had slipped through his fingers.

As he pulled into his long, dark driveway, he decided he would make a trip to Galveston—as soon as he found out exactly where Luz Maria was staying. He might reach Luz Maria's sister-in-law, Reagan Hurley, at the fire station where her ambulance was housed. Maybe he could convince the paramedic of his desire to help. For certain, that route made more sense than trying to talk to Luz Maria's brother, Jack, or Jason Whitfield, both of whom had decided Grant was evil incarnate.

As he made the slight turn toward the carport, the roadster's headlights glinted off the bumper of a van parked by his house. The sight so surprised him—both the house and vehicle were dark and he was not expecting company—that it took Grant several moments to recognize the silver Chrysler, despite the telltale bumper sticker supporting a kids' soccer league that stressed fair play and another that read BACK THE BADGE.

Grant sighed as he pulled into the carport and killed the engine. Once he'd turned off the headlights, he banged his forehead against the wheel twice while he asked himself, "Why me?"

But he knew why. For two long years, he had allowed, even encouraged, Sherry Zeman to grow dependent on him.

Telling himself he'd put off this discussion far too long already, he sucked in a breath and climbed out of his car. As he approached her van, the door opened, and the dome light illuminated Sherry, wearing a flowered top with short, ruffled sleeves over a pair of cropped pants.

A moist trail down her face gleamed in the weak light, and her swollen eyes indicated she had been crying for a while. He had to look away or he would cave in on the spot, begging her forgiveness, her hand in marriage—whatever it would take to stanch those tears.

I'm sorry, John. Sorry I couldn't take better care of her. Just as he was sorry for the doubts crowding into his subconscious since he'd been crazy enough to track down Shanti Starr.

"I've been calling and calling you," she told him. "Why haven't you called me back?"

"I'm sorry." Though Grant felt like a first-class shitheel, he refused to compound his sin with excuses. Yet fear pricked at his resolve, prompting him to add, "It's not an emergency, is it? Are the girls all right?"

Fresh tears sent a mascara-darkened stream down her round cheek. She swiped at it with a clump of crumpled tissue she held in her hand. "Emma and Sierra are fine. They're spending the night with my sister." Her voice went husky with emotion. "It's not the girls, it's—it's us."

What "us"? he wanted to demand, but it seemed cruel to ask her out here with the darkness weighing on them. He invited her inside and led her through the recently repaired door.

As he flipped on the lights, she glanced around the kitchen, a reminder that he'd never invited either her or the girls to the house before. Whenever she had asked, he'd put her off with excuses about remodeling—excuses she would now realize had been lies.

But she didn't remark about the ugly room. Instead, her gaze locked onto the refrigerator, with its covering of her daughters' crayon drawings.

She drew in an audible breath, as if to marshal her strength. "You know what they asked me last night, after their prayers? They wanted to know if it would be all right to call you Daddy sometimes, to pretend a little. Because they don't remember having a father. Well, Sierra doesn't, and even Emma was so little when—"

"Please, don't." Grant closed his eyes. Sometimes, he had been guilty of the same thing. Pretending they were not John's daughters, but his own.

"I could have sworn you—don't you *love* us, Grant? Don't you love the girls, at least?"

He sighed, feeling their silky hair against his lips when he'd last kissed their blond heads, smelling their baby shampoo as he had set them down to let them go to Donna. To let them go . . . could it be forever?

"Come into the living room. Please, Sherry. Let me get you something to drink."

"No!"

It was a shriek of pain, a cry that sliced clean through Grant's soul. Sherry's fists were clenched and her face burned red as she leaned toward him. For as long as he had known her, she had been a quiet woman, unfailingly gracious. For her to lose control like this—he hadn't seen it since John's death.

"I *do* love your family." Grant heard himself floundering, struggling to salvage something, *anything* from this disaster. "And I care for you, Sherry. I care *about* you, and I want you to be happy. I'll always be your friend."

He winced at that last sentence, at the realization that Jennifer had lobbed it his way the day she'd dumped him in favor of a less damaged groom. Sherry didn't take it any better than he had.

"It's that woman, isn't it?" A snarl of distaste marred her pretty features. "That horrible little Mexican who—"

"Don't do this, Sherry, please. You're better than this."

"It's true what they're saying, isn't it? You're sleeping with her, aren't you? The bitch who killed my John."

"Your husband—my friend and partner—killed himself," Grant said. "Luz Maria didn't do it any more than I did."

In the silence, he saw her face darken, saw it sink in that he had not denied a relationship with Luz Maria. Watched a heart splinter into pieces and wished that he could bear the pain of it for her.

"We did do it, Grant. We're responsible, too," Sherry erupted. "If you'd come to the house five minutes sooner, or if I'd paid enough attention to what he was going through instead of worrying so much about what people would think about the accusations—"

"You're better than this," Grant repeated, though she was naming the same self-recriminations he had lived with for the past two years. But this time, for the first time, he heard the pain and grief and buried anger in them, the futility and wrongness. "Blaming yourself or me or Ms. Montoya can never bring John back."

"She's the worst of all. She spread those filthy lies in public. On the news where all our friends, our families, where *everyone* could see. That . . . that witch destroyed him, and over what? The accusations of two *whores?* And you're defending her now? *Protecting* her?"

The raw hatred in her voice shook him, but it occurred to Grant he should have seen this coming. Though he had never taken her on anything she might construe as a date, never touched her except in the most innocent context, she had been talking to other cops and their wives, using their sympathy to pressure him into a marriage born of guilt. A marriage that would eventually hurt not only the two of them, but the children they both loved.

Her behavior reminded Grant of something John had once mentioned in passing, that his wife was in general all things sweet and willing, but when she didn't get her way, she didn't always fight fair. And on those occasions when he didn't buckle, he'd swear he could find Sherry's picture in the dictionary underneath the entry for "passive-aggressive."

But that didn't diminish her pain, nor did it ease Grant's sadness at the words he had to tell her. "John should have fought those charges, should have stayed strong for you and the kids. But he slid into the darkness, and worse yet, he hid it well. No one could have guessed he would—"

"He *didn't* hurt those women," she insisted.

She might have her human failings, but disloyalty had never been among them.

"I've always supported John," Grant said, though the photographs he'd seen nagged at him, the carvings on the breasts and thighs of those young women. He wished he'd never taken them from Luz Maria's purse. And the memory of Shanti Starr's sobs, raw and wounded, tore through his conscience like a twister, leaving wreckage in its wake.

"The Montoya woman deserves to die," said Sherry, as if she'd guessed the direction of Grant's thoughts, "for what she did to John. For what she—what she's doing to us—my daughters, too. I . . . I wish that man had killed her, that man from the news."

Grant wanted to stop her, to insist she didn't mean it. But one look at her convinced him that, at this moment, she did.

The surge of fury didn't last. Framed by tear-clumped lashes, her green eyes leaked fresh moisture and her hands crept to her mouth.

"I'm so . . . I'm so sorry," she said. "I don't—of course I don't want anyone else dead. It's just . . . I'm so angry. At myself, for being such a blind fool. And at you, too, Grant. You must have known how this would hurt me."

Fresh shame washed over him. If he'd had the guts to tell her from the first moment he had guessed she saw him as a replacement husband, if he'd had the morals to keep his hands off the one woman she blamed for John's death . . .

God, he was a bastard. Even worse than his old man, shot dead by a convenience store owner while attempting an ineptly planned holdup.

"I'm sorry, Sherry. So sorry I can't be the man you need. When I walk into your house, John is always there, you know?" *Always there dead in the master bathroom, blood and hair and bits of bone spattered on the walls. Always waiting to be washed clean.* Grant's eyes burned with the thought. "When I look into your face, you're still his wife. And in my mind, you always will be."

Her expression softened into sadness. "Then maybe you've been looking in the wrong place, Grant. Maybe you've forgotten I'm no more than a woman, a woman with the same needs, the same desires . . ."

To his horror, she began unbuttoning her top.

He turned away, head shaking as he did so.

"Please, Sherry, please, don't do this. Let me take you home."

For several moments, she said nothing. Still, he did not—could not—turn to look.

Finally, she cried, "Go to hell, Grant Holcomb. You and that Montoya bitch both."

When the door slammed seconds later, Grant blew out a long sigh.

CHAPTER TWENTY-NINE

"This had *better* be important," Reagan Hurley growled into the phone. Still half asleep during a rare quiet hour after midnight at the station, she was irritated as hell at having been roused by the firefighter assigned to the night watch. An HPD investigator by the name of Holcomb was calling, he'd explained.

But even before Holcomb answered, apprehension awakened, kick-starting her heart rate into overdrive. "Has something happened?" she asked. Surely, cops didn't call at this hour—she squinted at the office clock, which gave the time as 1:22 A.M.—with good news.

"I'm not sure," Grant Holcomb told her. "That's where you come in."

In spite of the scare he'd given her, Reagan fought the urge to yawn. She'd been on duty since six-thirty A.M., and the ambulance had responded to so many calls she'd lost count.

"What do you mean?" she asked, a moment before she remembered something Jack had told her about Holcomb. Her fatigue dissipated, leaving in its wake the sharp taste of suspicion. "Weren't you kicked off this case over that deal with your old partner?"

"Yeah," the detective admitted. "That part's true, but so's this. The Feds have information about the murder of Kellie Capshaw. Information they haven't shared with Luz Maria."

"What information?"

"Sergio Cardenas didn't kill your sister-in-law's neighbor. The non-excluded prints in Luz Maria's apartment and the semen from the body didn't match the samples taken from Cardenas."

"So whose were they?"

When Holcomb told her, she swore, then added, "But this bastard could still be after Luz Maria. Why hasn't the FBI warned her?"

"My source won't say, but I think they suspect her of having some involvement. Either a romantic link or maybe some sort of publicity stunt—"

"That's bullshit. I know Luz Maria's history, but I know *her*, too," Reagan insisted. "The woman might be a thorn in a lot of people's sides, but she's got ethics. And since that mess with Sergio, she's been seriously gun-shy about relationships."

Reagan thought about Grant Holcomb, an attractive man by anybody's standards. Recalled his clear concern when she had called from her sister-in-law's apartment and begged him to take Luz Maria to safety. Then Reagan remembered the other thing she'd heard about Holcomb. That part of the reason for his suspension involved taking Luz Maria to his own home, where they had spent the night together.

Could it be that the activist and the partner of a man who had taken his own life after her public criticism had found some common ground? Did that explain why Holcomb was calling the station, risking whatever was left of his career to pass on a warning?

"I'd like to check on her," Grant said. "At your parents' place in Galveston, if you would help me."

Reagan knew what Jack would say if she asked his advice. Knew beyond doubt that her husband would warn off Holcomb, then race down to the island condo to protect his little sister—whether she wanted it or not. But Reagan thought she heard something in the investigator's voice, an emotion she could not discount.

And unlike Jack, she saw Luz Maria as an adult, more than capable of making her own choices. Reagan wasn't going to take one this important from her.

So she said, "I'm not giving you her address, not under the circumstances. But I will call her right now and pass along your number, along with what you've told me. If she wants to contact you, she can."

"Listen, Ms. Hurley—"

"No, *you* listen, Investigator Holcomb. That's the best offer you're getting," Reagan told him. "The only offer."

She prayed that it would not come back to haunt her, or drive a wedge into her marriage to the finest man she'd ever known.

Six days later

If you keep very still, Luz Maria told herself as she peered through the peephole, *maybe he'll go away for good this time.*

Then she could get back to her e-mail to the director of the Florida Coalition for Farm Worker Rights and forget all about Grant Holcomb. On the round, glass-topped table in the breakfast area, her laptop sat open, her acceptance of the job she had been offered only a click away.

Ignoring the knock was undoubtedly the best idea

Luz Maria had had all week. Yet she watched disconnected as her fingers undid the deadbolt, felt her foolish heart thump at the bright, metallic jingle of the chain as it fell free.

The door opened, and behind the broad-shouldered silhouette before her, the lowering sun glinted off windshields in the nearly full lot. The warm breeze brought her the unseen Gulf's scents and the *quok-quok-quok* of distant shorebirds.

But it was the sight of Grant that made her smile, damn him, though she had asked him not to come back the last two times he'd driven here.

"I can't believe you made another two-hour drive here from Magnolia," she said.

He flashed a grin so incorrigible, it made her wonder how many teachers, as a kid, he'd driven to retirement. "Who says I've been commuting? I'm still on vacation, after all. Well, sort of."

She couldn't believe what she was hearing. "You're staying on the island? Where?"

"Let's just say close enough for comfort."

She thought about the old hotel next door. Scheduled for renovation, it was plastic palm tree hideous. But if he'd taken a room on the correct side, he would have a direct view of her borrowed condo, the next to the last apartment on the second floor of a sixty-unit building. "You mean close enough to watch me."

His gaze turned serious, and he shook his head. "To watch out *for* you. There's a difference."

With a sigh, she stepped back and let him inside, since asking him to keep his distance hadn't made much difference. The least she could do was tell him in person she'd be leaving Texas, heading for an anonymous position in a place where no one knew her name. A place where she wouldn't need him or Whit or anyone to watch her back for her.

He breezed into the upscale second-floor unit as if he belonged there. Across from the door at the condo's rear, huge windows and a balcony overlooked the street and just beyond it, the top of the sixteen-foot-tall seawall built to protect much of Galveston from the hurricanes that had wreaked destruction on the island city. Past the seawall lay the Gulf of Mexico, its light chop deep blue-gray and sparkling, the outline of an offshore oil platform hazy in the distance.

She wished in vain for an even stronger barricade than the concrete wall to protect her from her tidal wave of want.

"You're looking good," he told her once he'd locked the deadbolt. "Healthy. Bruises fading, and I like it when you wear your hair loose."

She felt a flush warm her face. "I washed it a little while ago. As soon as it's completely dry, I'll pull it back again."

"Don't hurry on my account."

A smile warmed his gray eyes, which dropped to take in her gauzy, coral-colored, sleeveless blouse and matching skirt. Though its hem skimmed her ankles, she shivered, feeling naked to his gaze.

"You slipped out today," he said, the smile fading.

"I had to have some clothes," she said, ignoring Borracho, who rubbed against her leg to remind her it was nearly time for Chicken Nibblets.

"I told you I'd take care of that." Displeasure roughened his voice. "All you had to do was call my cell phone."

"And I told you no one knows I'm here, no one but my family and a couple of VOP people."

"*I* didn't have any trouble tracking you down."

"Only because my brother hadn't mentioned to his wife that you'd sent me hate mail." If Reagan's work schedule hadn't kept her out of the loop regarding that letter, she surely would have refused to pass on Grant's late-night message.

Luz Maria thought she saw Grant flinch at the mention of what he'd done. Inside her, something softened— a part of her that had moved beyond their past mistakes. They had moved, too, beyond the error of lovemaking. In his previous two visits, he had made no move to touch her. Even though she almost wished he would.

"Look," she said. "I understand you're worried about this Vallens guy."

She had been, too, at first. Since Grant had told her of the sexual predator who had broken into her apartment, then killed Kellie, she'd had nightmare after nightmare. He must have been the person who'd had his hands around her throat in the parking lot of Ryland's, the man whose voice had sounded nothing like Sergio's to her. Certainly, it had not been Tony Coleman. Grant had also told her, when he'd last come, that enhanced tape from the surveillance system of a shop across the street had picked up what the broken camera had missed: the moment Coleman, the baseball fan who'd meant to have it out with her, had confronted the masked man choking her instead.

It was an ironic act of heroism that had cost a man who hated her his life.

"Surely, he's moved on by now," Luz Maria said of Vallens. "I can't imagine he would stick around the area with the police and FBI all over this case."

At least that was what she told herself each time she woke, heart racing.

"I think you underestimate the power of obsession."

As he spoke, Grant's gaze bored into her, leaving her to wonder if that was what lingered between them. Obsession, sparked by their one night together and by their need for secrecy.

What else could it be? Surely this compulsion she felt to be with him, this desire to talk to him and touch him no matter what Whit and her brother thought, was nothing as solid and as wholesome as real love.

Grant broke eye contact first, his glance jerking toward her open laptop at the table. As if he somehow guessed her e-mail's contents would put an end to any chance of a relationship.

Before he asked—before she had to tell him—she said, "Let's go for another walk, Grant. I'm in the mood for mango ice cream."

He had discovered it on their walk during his last visit two days earlier, in a beachside shop crowded with skaters, bicyclists, and sunbathers. She'd ordered a vanilla cone, as always, but he'd persuaded her to try a taste of his.

At first lick, she'd been hooked. Or maybe it had been his presence and the easy rapport between them as they'd strolled both Seawall Boulevard and the Strand, an old stretch of downtown that had given itself over to tourist-centered shopping.

Their time together had been easy for her, anyway. She had noticed that Grant remained vigilant, in spite of the vacation-like atmosphere and the tropical heat shimmering between them. Though he laughed and joked with her, he continually scanned the crowd, his sharp gaze challenging any man resembling the description he had found of Vallens on the Texas Sex Offender database online. Unfortunately, five foot ten inch, hundred seventy pound white males with brown hair and blue eyes weren't exactly rare, so she had watched him tense at least a dozen times. It would have been easier if a photo had been available, but Grant had explained he didn't dare push his luck by asking the authorities about it. Particularly not with his disciplinary hearing coming up in a week's time.

At his hesitation, she said, "Come on, Grant. Nothing happened last time. I told you, no one knows where I am."

An insistent knock made her jump, and Grant turned toward the door.

He pulled a weapon from beneath the lightweight blazer he wore over a white T-shirt. With his free hand, he waved her toward the kitchen, away from the exposure of the windows, as he looked out through the peephole.

"You expecting a delivery?" he asked.

Luz Maria couldn't push words past the sudden lump in her throat. The unexpected sight of his pistol had brought back the memory of Sergio, pointing his weapon toward her chest.

"Did you send out for dinner, or—"

"*Claro que sí*—surely, that's from April." She remembered an e-mail she'd had earlier from the VOP publicist. Something about paperwork Luz Maria needed to sign. "She said she'd send a courier with my separation packet—it's an agreement not to disclose details of my work with Voice of Poverty."

She managed a grin. "Somebody in the national office has this paranoid delusion that I might sell off VOP's trade secrets and turn lobbyist for the forces of oppression."

Grant snorted and said, "That'll be the day," before unlocking and cracking open the door.

"Yeah?" he asked as he peered outside.

Fortunately, he kept his gun out of sight, because Luz Maria was almost certain the pimply Asian teenager who had her sign for the package would wet himself if he spotted the weapon.

Grant tipped the courier, then locked the door behind him and insisted on checking out the padded envelope.

"So you're sure," he asked, "sure you're leaving VOP?"

She nodded, sighed, and got the hard part out of the way. "Not only VOP, Grant. I'm leaving Houston, too. For a job in South Florida. I'll . . . I'll be researching legal remedies of issues affecting the health and living conditions of migrant farm workers."

Surprise flickered across his features. "Researching? Then you're—"

"I've had enough of cameras. From now on, I'll work behind the scenes."

"I mean, you're really going? What about your family? All your friends and—" Though Grant cut himself short, his unspoken words spilled like drops of blood to stain the space between them. *What about the two of us?*

A moment later, he shook his head as if to dismiss the insane thought. Returning his attention to the envelope, he said, "This isn't paperwork. There's something hard in here, and—"

Luz Maria snatched it away, suddenly impatient with his caution. "Oh, come on, Grant. That's April's handwriting all over it. Now, relax and let me see it."

She tore open the flap. Instead of the stapled sheaf of papers she expected, her fingers found an angled edge. Slipping out the clear plastic case, she looked at the shiny silver DVD inside. A lime-green sticky note on the outside read: *Play me, Luz Maria!* Again, she recognized her coworker's neat print.

"Looks like a video," she told Grant before heading to the player beneath the flat-panel TV in the living room.

She powered on both screen and the connected stereo speakers, then slipped the disc into the DVD player. It took some fiddling with buttons—Grant had to help her with it—before Bob Marley's voice flooded the condo with a reggae tune about redemption. An instant later, the picture showed a trio of little African-American girls grinning, two of them sporting missing front teeth. As the music faded, the three sang out, "Thank you, Luz Maria."

The image shifted to an old Anglo man in a wheelchair, his back straight in an army uniform festooned with decorations. "Thank you, Luz Maria."

Her eyes filling with tears, Luz Maria let Grant lead her to the sea-green sofa as the video went on and on, a stream of people of all colors and all ages, each of them thanking her for the help she'd given and the fights she'd led. A montage followed. Interspersed with clips from Luz Maria's fiery speeches before the television cameras, the sequence began with the demolition of the dangerously rundown Las Casitas Village apartment complex on the East End and ended with the erection of what Grant took to be a home for battered women and their children.

"April Walsh did this, our PR and fund-raising director at Houston VOP." Luz Maria wiped at her face as she spoke. "She must have spent days and a small fortune putting this together. I'll bet she had O'Toole's help, too— that sleazy cameraman she keeps on a string. About time he quit muckraking and did something worthwhile for a change."

"April Walsh is the heiress, right?" Grant asked.

Luz Maria wasn't surprised he knew of her. In addition to their conservative political efforts, April's parents had spearheaded the formation of a trust that would cover the college education of the children of police officers and firefighters who died in the line of duty.

Luz Maria nodded as April appeared on screen. Stylish as ever, the blond woman wore a crisp, white-skirted suit that highlighted her tan. She stood near the sign of the Voice of Poverty's Houston headquarters. It was pockmarked with a couple of bullet holes, courtesy of Sergio's drive-by visit.

"We so appreciate everything you've done." April's green-eyed stare was direct, intense—as if she were speaking to Luz Maria from across a table instead of in a video. "But we ask that you consider all those things you haven't yet . . ."

A new montage followed, and the music shifted to Tracy Chapman lamenting the world's rape, asking how we can stand aside. Luz Maria stared dry-eyed at the screen. As Borracho wound around her legs unheeded, one unsettling image chased another. It began with a sweating, wrinkled woman weeping in a dim house as she fanned herself with a piece of folded paper. It continued to an aerial shot that glanced off a sign reading TEX-RID INCINERATION and pulled back to show a huge ring of dead vegetation that wreathed a site capped by a plume of brownish smoke. In a third scene, preschool-aged children swung on dilapidated—and dangerous-looking—playground equipment while in the background, gangbangers fought with knives.

"Not real subtle, your friend April," Grant said. "Next thing you know, she'll zoom in on the puppy-kickers."

Luz Maria looked at him, a feeling of clarity taking hold, as if she had just awakened from a dream. It was then she understood that Grant had spent his last two visits speaking to a shadow, drawn to the illusion that she might allow him to take care of her.

"Every bit of it is real," she said, "and there is so much more I can't begin to list it."

"Your friend's manipulating you," Grant warned, "and in the slickest way possible. Look, I didn't want to mention this until we knew more, but my partner called me. He's found evidence she's making regular payments to Max O'Toole. And the guy's not only a freelance camerman, he's got a record. Trespassing convictions, charges of assault . . ."

Luz Maria waved off the admonition as the video ended with Tom Petty's musical refusal to back down. "O'Toole's a lowlife—nothing he'd do to get a story would surprise me, and April has plenty of money. It's no skin off her teeth to keep someone in the media on retainer so there's always footage available for the networks.

"And as far as I'm concerned," Luz Maria continued, "this refusal to accept my resignation is just April being stubborn. She's gone right on scheduling things in my name, announcing my appearance at next week's hearing over the Tex-Rid incinerator project and a press conference that I know of, even though I've told her and told her I won't be coming back. She probably had the video made as an insurance policy earlier, so she could soak up some sympathy donations in case I kicked the bucket."

She smiled and shrugged her shoulders, then added, "But that's April for you. Always thinking about VOP's bottom line. And she's not exactly off-base. We *are* in deep financial trouble."

"You aren't letting her change your mind, are you?" Grant asked. "She's using you, don't you see? You don't want to be a sucker for this load of sentiment."

She didn't answer, but instead let Petty's lyrics reverberate through her heart. Could she, too, stand her ground? She thought of Señora Reyes, who had—even though Luz Maria had never gone back to see her—somehow concluded that turning down the Tex-Rid lawyer's offer of a trailer was the right move. Was the day care grandmother braver than the self-proclaimed spokesperson for the poor?

"You told me you were through making a target of

yourself," Grant insisted, "through looking over your shoulder and wondering which loved one might be hurt next."

Luz Maria used the remote to turn off the entertainment system. But she sat staring at the blank screen while she fought a tug as strong as the moon's pull on the tides.

As if he sensed her battle, Grant said, "It doesn't have to be an all-or-nothing proposition. You can still quit VOP but stay here. Around Houston, anyway."

Still seated on the sofa, Luz Maria gestured toward the folded classifieds section of a newspaper that sat beside her laptop. "I would, but it seems the only jobs I'm qualified for are waitress, part-time receptionist, and professional hell-raiser."

"I think you're selling yourself short." A wry grin skated across his handsome features. "Let's not forget Hooters girl or exotic dancer."

She buried her awareness of how close they were sitting by gesturing toward her small breasts and saying, "With *these?* You've got to be kidding."

"They're perfect, if you ask me."

"Fortunately, my mouth is big enough to compensate," she said. "And that and a heart are all I need to remain the Voice of Poverty—"

"No," he said, so quickly and firmly that it stunned her. "I can't let you. I won't."

"Excuse me—you can't *let* me?" Her indignation mushroomed into outrage. "Who do you think you are?"

A look of pure exhaustion washed over his features. "Nobody, Luz Maria. Just a washed-up cop. Just the son of a dead robber and a runaway mother. Just a man who keeps waking up with nightmares about finding you dead at the scene of that wreck, your skull smashed like Kellie Capshaw's and Sergio Cardenas laughing over your corpse."

Her anger vanished, condensing into tears that trembled on her lashes as he spoke.

"Just a man who thought that this time, love could turn into something real, a highway that can go in both directions." Grant shrugged, defeat written in the gesture. "But I've been wrong before on that count. And it's not as if I've got a lot to offer any woman. In another week, I may be as unemployed and far from prospects as my old man ever was."

She leaned in close, until she tasted his mouth, until she recalled how she had dreamed of his kiss to dispel her own dark nightmares. A spark of hope leapt from his lips to hers, a flare of need that pulled the rug out from under her hard-won equilibrium.

She fell hard, following her instinct, running her palms beneath his jacket to feel the muscles of his chest. When her fingers grazed the shoulder holster, she jerked away with a reflexive gasp.

His gaze seared hers, and she said, "I'm sorry," without knowing whether she apologized for flinching or for daring to kiss him in the first place. For certain, she would be kissing him still had it not been for her reaction to the gun.

Without a single word or taking his eyes off her, he shed both the blazer and the weapon, then laid them on the sofa's end. Like startled birds irresistibly drawn back to the rice field, her fingers moved back to his chest to reach up beneath his shirt.

She felt his lungs expand, heard his breathing quicken.

"This *is* a two-way highway, Grant," she swore. "As crazy and as sudden as it seems."

He took her hand and led her from the room, with its bank of windows. Led her to the bedroom and closed Borracho outside.

Left alone, the tabby wagged his tail in annoyance at the delay in his dinner. While outside, a birdwatcher on the seawall lowered his binoculars, no less irritated than the feline he had once tied in a tub.

CHAPTER THIRTY

Reagan Hurley stood before her bedroom mirror and smoothed the satiny emerald of the sexy little number Jack had bought for her birthday last weekend. *Talk about your self-serving gifts.* She smiled at the thought and sipped her glass of Chardonnay.

Not that she minded a bit, ready as she was to enjoy a rare night alone with her husband—for as long as he could dodge the on-call bullet, anyway. Her mother-in-law had insisted on keeping Adam for an overnight full of home-baked *galletas*, as she called her cookies, and playing with Eduardo's hammers.

"Since it seems he will be my only *nieto*,"—if Luz Maria was the Voice of Poverty, then Candelaria could surely claim the title of the Voice of Martyrdom—"I must spoil this baby while I can."

If Adam heard her call him a baby, he'd throw a fit she wouldn't soon forget. At two and a half, he had decided he was ready to be called a big boy, his dependence on nighttime pull-up diapers be damned. Chuckling, Reagan glanced impatiently toward the open bedroom door.

If Jack was going to do his part in making Adam a big brother—and fulfill his mama's dreams of another grandchild to cuddle—he was going to have to get off the phone.

With all that had happened to Luz Maria of late, Reagan understood her husband's renewed need to check on the younger sister he had all but raised. What she didn't understand was his strained voice on the telephone, the anger she heard all the way from the kitchen.

On her way out of the bedroom, Reagan tripped over the white greyhound, who had decided the hall rug was a cozy place to lie.

"Darn it, Frank Lee," she scolded him. "The one time you don't sneak onto the couch or someone's bed . . ."

The dog's look of chagrin took the heat out of her words, and the sound of Jack's voice shut her up completely.

"What the hell are you doing there, Holcomb? With all the trouble you're in—where's my sister? Put her on the phone."

Reagan's stomach clenched. She hadn't mentioned the message she'd passed on to Luz Maria, nor the growing suspicion that her sister-in-law had something going with the hot detective.

"I don't give a damn if she's in the shower," Jack said. "I want to speak with her. Never mind—I'm driving down there right now."

Reagan pinched the bridge of her nose. Of all the . . . So much for the romantic evening they'd planned.

Jack met her in the hallway, his look of irritation melting into deep regret. He fingered the ends of her blond hair, which she'd let grow long enough to skim her shoulders. "You look amazing, Reag. But I'm going to have to drive down to the condo. That son of a bitch Holcomb's there with Luz Maria. At this hour—while she's showering."

"Jack." Exasperation lanced Reagan's voice. "If your sister wants a little fling, who are you to stop her? My lord, after everything she's been through, doesn't she deserve a chance at some kind of normal life?"

"This isn't about some 'little fling' with him. It's about his partner."

"I'm not sure it is," she argued. "Not anymore, at least."

Jack raked his dark hair out of his eyes, exposing a look that had shifted to suspicion. "Who have you been talking to?"

Oh, shit. Here it comes. Reagan winced, then admitted, "Him—her. Both of them, actually, last week."

"And you didn't feel this was worth mentioning to me?"

Though she knew he would disagree, that had never before stopped Reagan from expressing her opinions. Shaking her head, she said, "I didn't really think it was any of our business. Luz Maria knows the facts, right?"

"Do *you?*" he demanded. "Know all of them, I mean? I know we talked about the man's suspension and the fact that he had no business going near my sister after what happened with his partner. But I saw a copy of his letter. Whit showed me."

She blinked, lost. "What letter?"

"The *threat* he sent Luz Maria after John Zeman's suicide. He swore he'd see her pay for it, and you damned well decided to play matchmaker?"

She closed her eyes, her heart sinking. "I didn't know. I'm sorry. Look, Jack, give me two minutes to pull on some clothes. I'm going down there with you."

"No thanks, Reagan," he said. "I think you've done enough."

Her temper sparked and crackled—how the hell could she have known? But before she could say something she would likely regret later, the cell phone clipped to Jack's belt rang in the tone assigned to his on-call service.

Frowning, he hesitated through the first ring, then answered on the second. He was only on-call for his clinic one night every other week, and he had never been one to shirk his duty to his patients.

He walked out to the kitchen, where he spoke in low tones while Reagan went into the bedroom to change into a pair of denim shorts and a sky-blue T-shirt from the gym where she worked out. Jack might *think* he was leaving her behind while he drove down to Galveston to play Super Brother. But she damned well wasn't letting him leave angry—or alone.

As she finished dressing, he came into the bedroom, a grim look on his face. Frank Lee's tail beat like a drum against the door as he stared up at his master and wagged out his hope for an ear rub.

"I have to meet an ambulance coming into the ER," Jack told her as he unconsciously obliged the grey-hound. "I have a toddler in respiratory distress. It may be the croup again, but I'm afraid it could be bad enough this time to deprive his brain of oxygen. The mother's a single mom, way too young. She's scared to death and—"

"You don't have to explain your job to me," she said. It was one of the things she loved about him, his dedication to his largely low-income patients. "Listen, Jack, I'm driving down to the condo. I'll talk to Luz Maria, make sure everything's okay and that she understands—"

"You don't have to do that."

"I want to. Contrary to your belief, I *do* care about your sister. I've come to consider her a friend."

Jack leaned forward to squeeze her in a firm hug and kiss her temple. "I'm sorry, Reagan. What I said before—

I didn't mean it. I know I can be a little much when it comes to Luz Maria."

She smiled at him. "What do you mean, 'a little?'"

He smiled back and they wished each other a safe trip before their lips brushed briefly.

In a few short hours, Reagan would wish to God they'd lingered over that last contact, or forgotten the demands of life and slipped back to bed as they had planned.

Grant stepped into the bathroom where the shower hissed and steam swirled around the top of the glass enclosure. Inside, he could make out Luz Maria's body, only partly shrouded by the mist.

Leaning back against the counter, he crossed his arms and watched. Damned if this wasn't a better view than anything ESPN had to offer.

Luz Maria's hand squeaked against the glass as she cleared a patch at eye-level. "I see you out there. Ogling."

At the suggestion in her sweet voice, he felt a stirring south of the equator. God, she had him hard and ready as a randy teenager again.

But instead of acting on the impulse, he decided he owed her a warning.

"Don't know if you heard the phone ringing, but I picked it up." *Like a dumbass*, he added to himself. He'd been blissed-out, half-asleep in the wake of their lovemaking, not thinking about how bad it could be for his department hearing if he were caught with her.

"So who was it?" Luz Maria asked. She didn't sound concerned.

"Your brother. And he sounded pissed."

"Oh, Jack," she said in fond exasperation. "I'll talk to him, explain you're not *el diablo*. You know, the devil. Don't worry. I've been calming my big brother down— or stirring him up—all my life."

Moving closer to the shower door so he wouldn't have to shout, Grant told her, "I'm not worried. I just thought you should know he's on his way. Right now."

Luz Maria popped open the door, gave his nude—and very appreciative—body the once-over, and grabbed him by the wrist. As she pulled him inside the steamy glass box with her, she wrapped her arms around his neck and grinned up. "So you say Jack's coming? Well, let's see if you and I can't just beat him to it."

His mouth met hers, then parted her lips for a kiss that sent pleasure jolting straight down to his cock. A groan rose from his chest as her soapy hands slid down his back, along and over his ass cheeks to pull him closer. He felt those flame-tipped painted nails of hers, felt them digging into his flesh—a pain that scratched the surface of an unimagined pleasure.

With his own hands slipping over her breasts and his mouth moving to graze at her sensitive neck, Grant pressed her small body against the shower wall. She grunted in surprise, then arched back her head and murmured his name.

It was the sound of absolute arousal, and though he had taken his time with her earlier, in the bedroom, Grant felt like a damned volcano, hotter than hell and ready to erupt at any second.

So ready that when she slid down to her knees to take him in her mouth, as he had taken her before, Grant had to fight the urge to thrust. He turned the streaming water to cold to make himself last. But even then, the moist heat and motion of her sweet mouth and her fingers cupping his balls were more than he could bear. When he was sure he couldn't last another second, he stepped back, then pulled her gently to her feet and stared into dark eyes dilated with pure passion.

"I want to come inside you," he said urgently. "I need to get so deep, so close, that you forget your name."

She draped her arms around his neck and leaned her head into his chest, let him rub the hard nub of her pleasure, then stood on tiptoe as he pushed the head of his shaft inside, then thrust into her core.

Excited as they both were, they found their rhythm quickly. And it was good, so damned good that all too soon, he felt her body spasming around him, saw bursts of light exploding in his vision as he cried out, "Luz Maria," and spilled himself inside her. . . .

Only moments later, he was wondering how he could stand to give her up if she left him—and whether his reluctance to let her go, his deep need to possess her, was the reason that for the first time in his adult life, he hadn't even thought to grab a condom.

CHAPTER THIRTY-ONE

As she climbed from bed, where she and Grant had collapsed after the most incredible shower of her life, Luz Maria wished she had resisted temptation long enough to call Jack's cell phone to discourage him from driving down this evening. With her body sated by lovemaking and her mind more at peace than it had been in days, she was in no mood to fend off her brother's attempts to protect her from her faulty judgment.

At least her judgment when it came to men.

With a frown, she slipped back into fresh underthings and the still clean, coral-colored outfit she'd worn earlier.

Glancing back at Grant's sprawled—and still deliciously naked—form, she reached for a pillow and popped the top of his head.

One gray eye slid open. "I'm warning you, Luz Maria, you don't want to end up on the wrong side of a pillow fight with me."

"In your weakened condition," Luz Maria told him, "I'm pretty sure that I could take you."

"You really want to take that chance?" As he grabbed another pillow, he propped himself up on one elbow, a look that made her mouth water and her thoughts slip back to all the things they'd done together. Her skin quivered at the memory, and she wondered how she'd made it to the age of twenty-six without ever realizing how fantastic sex could be.

But her brother would be here soon, and she cared too much about Jack's feelings to start something with Grant that promised to keep them in bed longer.

"Maybe you'd better get dressed," she said, "unless you'd like to experience the Mexican-American version of a shotgun wedding."

Grant's grin broadened. "Right now, that doesn't sound like such a terrible idea."

She scooped up his clothes and tossed them his way. "I'm not joking. And I wish you wouldn't, either. Not about that. Not when . . ."

"Not when *what?*" His expression grew serious. As he started dressing, he said, "We can make this work, Luz Maria. I'll figure something out."

"Like what?" she asked. "This—this thing between us—it just complicates the situation."

He shook his head. "Some things are worth fighting for. The question is, do you believe we're one of them? I do. It amazes me how it's happened, how fast and hard and totally I've fallen for you, Luz Maria. And how dead sure I am that this time, it's the real thing. I love you and I want to be with you—and damn the consequences."

I love you, he had told her.

She fought the urge to reassure him she felt exactly the same way, though she was brimming over with emotion. Love *couldn't* steal up on two people so quickly, not the kind of love worth getting Grant fired. Not the kind of love worth giving up her life's work to appease him.

Sooner or later, they would come to hate each other

for it. Maybe not in the first glow, with the heat of sexual passion to distract them, but inevitably. Eternally, until resentment smashed to pieces all the hope they had left.

Her brother might think she was still a child, but her affair with Sergio three years before had tempered her heart with the searing shame of the relationship's destruction. She'd been cruel to give Grant any hope, a fool to make love to him. And the fact that they'd done so without protection—had she learned nothing from her earlier, unplanned pregnancy?

But she couldn't make herself tell him she regretted it, so instead she simply nodded, then asked abruptly, "Are you hungry? Would you like me to call out for a pizza?"

His head jerked in her direction, and something dimmed in his eyes. Several heartbeats later, he exploded. "That's it? I bare my soul to you, and that's all you have to say?"

She fingered the damp tip of her ponytail. "I'm sorry, Grant. I just can't—I'm not ready to deal with this right now. It's too much to take in, after everything that's happened—and I really haven't eaten anything since breakfast."

He opened his mouth with a look that warned her he meant to press his case. But he hesitated, then shrugged, turning away from her. "I could eat, I guess. And then we talk, Luz Maria."

Her stomach gave a nervous flutter that had nothing to do with hunger. "I'll call in the order, then. I have the number in the kitchen."

He said nothing, and she understood how deeply she had hurt him. It bothered her far more than she could handle, so she turned and left the room.

And screamed at the sight of a face pressed to the window beside the condo's outside door with hands cupped around the eyes to better see inside.

* * *

Grant came running, wondering what the hell had gotten into him that he'd left his pistol in the living room, where anyone on the back landing could spot it. He'd been a fool to let his libido distract him—or the promise of something more than another round of the best sex he'd ever had.

But at the moment, he pushed aside the sting of rejection to scan the living room, entryway, and kitchen, then to glance at Luz Maria, to see where she was looking. Following her gaze, he focused on the window, where he saw nothing but the gray sky and the parking area behind the three-story bank of condos. An SUV pulling in from Seawall Boulevard had its headlights on against the evening gloom.

"There was someone out there." Luz Maria pointed to the window. "I—I saw this face, staring in."

Grant grabbed his gun and pulled it from the holster, releasing the safety as he did so. In three long steps, he reached the front door and flung it open, looked right and then left.

And spotted a woman making for the outdoor staircase, her sandy-colored hair fluttering as she fled.

"Sherry?" He had to be mistaken. What would she be doing here?

But the sound of the name stopped her. She turned toward him, her face lit by a security light, her cheeks shining with tears. She looked a mess, her bob disheveled and her cropped pants and striped top rumpled, as if she had been sleeping in the outfit.

"What's going on?" he asked as he strode toward her. "How did you find me?"

But the real question went unspoken. What in God's name was she thinking?

"I . . . I still know detectives," she said, her voice steeped in equal parts defeat and desperation. "Investigators on the force. You . . . you used your credit card for the hotel room."

Grant's heart sank, and not only at the pathetic picture the woman painted. Who from the force would she have asked to help her? Lieutenant Mouton, or worse yet, her husband's former partner, Reed? Grant could almost hear the thin ice beneath him cracking.

"So you followed me from there?" he asked. "Why, Sherry?"

Shaking her head, she cried, "That woman already took John from me. I couldn't stand to let her take you, too. I . . . I couldn't . . ."

"I'm so sorry."

The voice came from behind him. Luz Maria's. Quiet and sincere.

He heard her bare feet approaching, heard her add, "I've never had the chance to tell you this in person, Mrs. Zeman, but I deeply regret what happened to your husband. If there'd been any other way to stop him—"

"They were whores," said Sherry. "Even if he did sleep with them, they were still lying whores who—"

"I believed them," Luz Maria said as Grant absorbed Sherry's admission.

Even if he did sleep with them, she'd said. How could he not have known his partner had been sampling the wares of prostitutes? Had John gotten a taste for them when he had worked sex crimes, many of which involved hookers? Had he really exposed both Sherry and his little girls to the risk of the diseases hookers carried?

Grant's stomach soured—along with his faith in Zeman's innocence. Between Shanti Starr's reaction to John's photo and Sherry's admission, the ground he'd once held sacred shifted.

But Luz Maria was still speaking, telling Sherry, "If you had seen their scars, their fear—"

"If *I* had seen them, I would have made them tell me

who paid them to lie," Sherry insisted as she moved toward Luz Maria. "You're a whore, too, just as bad as they are. Another whore who's ruined everything for me."

Grant grabbed Sherry's arms to keep her from surging past him. She jerked free of his grip with surprising strength.

"They were already calling Grant Daddy when you stole him," she shrieked at Luz Maria. "How does it feel to know you've taken *two* fathers from my kids?"

As Grant once again restrained Sherry, he saw Luz Maria's face as she looked past the struggling woman. And straight into his eyes. He saw the guilt and horror written in her expression, and he saw the death of his hopes for their future.

"I've been helping Sherry, that's all," he said desperately. "With the maintenance of the house and sometimes with the girls. After I was too late to save John, I felt so damned guilty, I . . ."

He felt eyes on him and spotted a middle-aged couple gazing out at them through the window of the neighboring condo. A man on his way to his car was staring up, too, from the parking lot.

Ignoring them, he said to Luz Maria, "I've never touched her, never even kissed her the way that you and I have—"

"Stop," said Sherry. "Stop. I'm tired of hearing how I'm nothing but John's pathetic widow. Tired of your pity and—"

"Why don't you drive her home?" Luz Maria asked him. "Take her home to her children before someone calls the police, and I'll talk to Jack when he gets here."

Grant felt Sherry trembling in his grasp, felt how much this confrontation must have cost her. Luz Maria was right; he couldn't simply turn her loose in this state. But at the same moment, he felt certain that if he left Luz Maria now, he would forever regret that decision.

At his hesitation, she said, "Go with her, Grant. We'll talk later."

So once again he let his concern for Sherry Zeman override his better judgment.

CHAPTER THIRTY-TWO

Unable to stand still, Luz Maria paced the confines of
the condo. Her muscles twitched and her hands shook
as if she'd downed a month's worth of espresso.

Sherry Zeman's pain had struck her like a closed fist.
Did the woman really have a claim on Grant, as she insisted? And even if Grant had helped her family only
out of a sense of loyalty to his late partner, how painful
must it be for her to learn he was spending time with
Luz Maria? Because true or not, Sherry—and Grant,
too, until recently—clearly blamed Luz Maria for Investigator Zeman's suicide.

And children were involved, too. The hearts of
children who had been so young when they had lost
their father, they probably had no memory of the
man.

Luz Maria shuddered, thinking of the shadow her
own father's murder at the hands of human smugglers
had cast across her childhood. Though she, too, had
been too young to remember the living man, in death
he had loomed so large, his fate had touched her with a

passion for helping the voiceless. No matter what it cost her personally.

Even the one man she'd let get through to her heart. Though she had been unable to trust her feelings enough to say the words aloud, she realized they were no less true. She did love Grant Holcomb—with a depth and fervor that made her feelings about Sergio stand out in contrast as no more than an unhealthy infatuation.

But in the end, her feelings didn't matter, not when following them would prove a selfish and possibly immoral act.

Tears burning in her eyes, Luz Maria walked to her open laptop and pressed the SEND button on the e-mail she had written.

The e-mail that would take her to South Florida, to start her life anew.

Reagan had nearly reached the causeway leading onto the island when she heard it—a rhythmic thumping unrelated to the beat of the Coldplay CD she had cranked up. She grimaced, already suspecting what the problem was as she turned off the music. The Jetta's right-side pull and the worsening thump had her gliding to the shoulder just before the Tiki Island exit.

She climbed out of the car, traffic whizzing past her, gusts that smelled of salt water and exhaust whipping her blond hair into her eyes. She made her way to the car's right side, then swore at the sight of the front tire, which had a strip of metal impaled through the sidewall.

Frowning, Reagan weighed her options. The sucker was flatter than a tortilla; there would be no driving on it without doing a lot more damage. She could change a tire; heaven knew she'd done it often enough in the heap she'd driven before this one.

But the deepening evening gloom and her location made her hesitate. The unusual sight of a slim blonde changing a tire on her own along the freeway would attract attention, and probably offers of assistance. Some would be kindly meant and others less so.

As independent as she was, Reagan had seen enough to make her a realist. Women had disappeared along this stretch of highway before, women whose nude bodies were sometimes later found floating in the bay— if they were found at all. Keeping that in mind, along with Jack's likely reaction to the news she had changed the tire herself instead of waiting for the roadside assistance he'd insisted that they purchase, she climbed back inside the Volkswagen and dug through her glove box for the phone number, then called for help.

She only hoped the service didn't keep her cooling her heels here half the night before sending a wrecker. *Friday nights bring out the crazies*, she thought as she relocked the doors and turned on the air-conditioning to wait.

Partially to kill time, she left a message for her husband to let him know what had happened and that she might be running late. Then she called Luz Maria at the condo.

But Luz Maria must have gone out, for her phone just rang and rang.

CHAPTER THIRTY-THREE

If Grant expected—with gut-clenching certainty—that Sherry Zeman would wail and plead all the way home, he was very much mistaken. Instead, she crossed her arms and stared out into the darkness through the Mercedes's passenger-side window, using the time-honored silent treatment to heap another helping of guilt onto his plate.

But this time, he wasn't having any of it.

"This bullshit stops tonight," he told her. "The only relationship we've ever had is friendship, and you damned well know it. Keep up this behavior, and I can't even offer that."

He sneaked a glance, saw her lip trembling, then ruthlessly refocused his attention on the glowing taillights ahead.

"No more stalking me, Sherry, and no more lying to department wives about my supposed *intentions*." He slowed with traffic near the exit for the dog track, then signaled to get out of that lane. He was taking her straight home with no detours. Let her and her sister figure out later what to do about her van. Sherry Zeman couldn't be his problem any longer.

She made quiet sniffling noises, and he fought back a pang of remorse. From this evening forward, he was living in the present, for the future. Not mired in a past they could do nothing to change. John never would have wanted them to endlessly punish themselves for his decisions. Funny, how Grant hadn't seen that for so long.

"And whatever you do," he told her, "no more whining to that steroid-popping Roy Reed."

Though Grant had gotten in his own licks, the big jerk had cracked one of his top teeth with the trash can lid attack. Damned root canal was going to set him back plenty.

"I wasn't," she said weakly, voice brimming with tears. "Please, Grant. Don't—"

"Was he the one who told you?" Grant asked.

"About . . . about you and *that woman?*" There was venom in the last two words—along with an ugliness he hadn't allowed himself to recognize in the days he'd seen her only as a helpless victim. "What does it matter who it was?"

Grant shook his head, then made an effort to soften his voice. "I mean about John, Sherry. About him and those women, the ones who accused—"

"I don't want to talk about that. It was a hard time—a terrible time."

"Was it Reed? Or was it someone from Internal Affairs, someone investigating the charges against—"

"No one had to tell me," she cried. "I . . . I figured it out early in our marriage, back when John was working in the Sex Crime Unit before our girls were born. I—I . . . oh, God, this sounds so horrible. I was having . . .

having female problems. And I tested positive for gonorrhea."

"That sorry son of a bitch." If John were here right now, Grant would belt him. It was bad enough his friend had screwed around on a faithful, loving wife, but having unprotected sex with hookers . . . "I'm really sorry, Sherry."

The clap was curable—unlike so many other STDs out there today—but still, he couldn't imagine how the breach of trust had damaged John and Sherry's marriage. Grant thought of the photo on his corkboard, the photo of what he'd believed had been the perfect family, a family so far removed from the parents who had raised him.

"I was so hurt and so angry. It could have made me sterile, and I wanted kids so badly. I gave John an ultimatum. Give up the women, transfer out of Sex Crimes—clearly, it was too much of a temptation for him, with so many of the victims being hookers—or I was gone forever. He begged me to stay, Grant. If you only could have heard him. He cried and swore he loved me, *only* me. Those other women, they were filth, he told me. Worse than animals. He promised he would never touch anyone but me from then on. And that he'd keep his distance from the prostitutes, never go near them again."

Grant swallowed hard, as Sherry's words resonated with Shanti Starr's reaction to John's photo. If Zeman thought of prostitutes as less than human, if he hated himself for his failure to keep his vows, would John feel a misguided need to blame and punish the women for his sins?

Would the same skill he used to carve decoys warp into something sick and hideous?

"He didn't keep that promise, did he?" Grant asked

Sherry. "That's why Internal Affairs linked him to those women, isn't it?"

"But he never cut them. My John couldn't do that."

This time, for the first time, Grant couldn't reassure her that he shared her faith. But neither did he have it in him to try to dissuade her, not when she had John's innocent young daughters to raise. If her belief kept Sherry going, he'd be damned if he would take it from her—or rob those girls of the faith that their daddy had been a righteous man.

They had nearly reached Sherry's house when the ringing of Grant's cell phone interrupted a long silence.

"I dug deeper on those background checks like you suggested," his partner Billy Devlin began without preamble. "Ran 'em on everybody associated with the Houston office of the Voice of Poverty. The whole staff and that low-rent freelance newshound, too."

"Yeah?" Grant asked. "Get anything good?"

"Turns out he's about to be charged with extortion, for the second time. Mr. O'Toole's got a nasty little habit of blackmailing people who turn up in some of his videos. Rich people, anyway."

"Like April Walsh?"

"Appears so."

"You know what he's got on her?"

"Not yet. But there's something else, too. Something more interesting still."

"Spit it out. What'd you find?"

"It's not what I found, partner," Billy answered. "What I *didn't* is the issue."

"What do you mean?" Grant asked.

Billy laid it out for him, from a series of huge bank account deposits to the surprising lack of records to a newly emptied apartment. Once he'd finished, Grant lost no time dropping Sherry off at her home, where her sister was staying with the girls. As soon as he had a word with Donna about Sherry's state of mind, he jumped into the Mercedes and sped back in the direction he had come. Back toward the Galveston condo where he'd left Luz Maria.

On the way there, he tried calling. As both the condo's line and then her cell phone rang, he repeated, "Answer it. Please answer."

But his mantra fell on deaf ears. Luz Maria either wasn't picking up or she wasn't there at all.

This time, the intruder chose a nondescript gray coverall rather than a business suit, which would stand out like a sore thumb among the vacationers along the seawall. Any passersby who spotted the short-sleeved jumpsuit, on the other hand, would immediately dismiss him as one of the anonymous workers who fixed broken disposals, painted flaking trim, or sent cockroaches off to meet their maker.

To augment his obscurity, he had ironed on transfer letters over the chest pocket. JERRY, the name read, because he'd liked the regular-guy sound of it. In lieu of the briefcase he'd brought for his last break-in, "Jerry" carried a small metal toolbox, which was of a perfect size to hold his tension tool set—something he knew he'd need since Luz Maria had neither answered his knock nor his phone call—his duct tape, and his favorite knife, since he'd ditched his gun after the shooting at the Ryland's grocery store.

He had thought of bringing condoms, too, for he'd regretted not using them with the neighbor woman. Then he'd figured, *What the hell? Might as well let Vallens take the rap for this job, too.*

Because once the money came in, the intruder would

have no more use for that moron. Once he'd earned what he deserved, he could ditch that poor, pathetic bastard, then live the life that he had finally found the balls to claim.

CHAPTER THIRTY-FOUR

By the time Reagan reached her mother and stepfather's condo, she was tired, hungry, and still furious about her run-in with the driver of the "courtesy truck" sent to change her tire. After making several pointed comments about how dangerous this stretch of freeway could be after dark, he had tried to extort a hundred-dollar "after-hours fee" to take care of her problem—though they both knew her plan would pay him for his time. She had whipped out her cell phone, then nonchalantly mentioned that her sister-in-law, the spokesperson for the Voice of Poverty, would *love* to hear about his little racket. He'd backed off quickly enough then. Still, as soon as the jerk drove off, Reagan had had to properly tighten all the lug nuts—or risk losing her wheel a few more miles down the road.

She was irritated, too, that instead of relaxing with her husband, she'd run down here on what she felt sure was a fool's errand. Her instincts told her Luz Maria was either having great sex—something Reagan had given up for the night—or out somewhere having a great time with Grant Holcomb. No matter what Jack said the investigator had written two years earlier, Reagan couldn't believe Holcomb had been faking concern for Luz Maria's safety when he had called the station. And if her sister-in-law had felt safe enough to shower with him in the condo . . .

He could have been lying, Reagan told herself. *Could have told Jack that because Luz Maria was no longer capable of coming to the phone.*

No way, she decided. What kind of stone-cold killer answered his victim's phone after doing her harm, an act that would clearly place him at the scene?

So by the time she let herself into the condo after her knock went unanswered, Reagan was fairly relaxed.

Until she was grabbed by the arm, jerked inside the dark foyer, and slammed down hard against the cool, tiled floor.

The bleakness of her thoughts had driven Luz Maria from the condo. Ignoring the phone that had just begun to ring—she was in no mood for conversation—she locked the door behind her, then headed down the sidewalk that topped the rock-lined seawall. She made her way in the direction of the beach, though that lively stretch of white sand would be closed for the evening.

But it was either move or give way to the tears that threatened. Outdoors, enough strollers, in-line skaters, and bicyclists were enjoying the warm evening breeze and the surf's music to make her feel safe. Better yet, their presence gave her reason to put on her bravest face.

Her legs were tired by the time she crossed the street and stepped inside a kitschy seafood restaurant. Real seashells and plastic crabs hung from nets festooning the walls, and the delicious scent of cooking seafood made her stomach rumble. There were people everywhere: couples at the dim bar, families on the patio—

unwitting enforcers of her hard-won composure. Using the credit card she had tucked inside her skirt pocket, Luz Maria ordered a salad of chopped greens topped with scallops, shrimp, and crabmeat to go with her water and the complimentary rolls. She probably shouldn't have spent the money—a take-out po'boy sandwich would have filled her just as well and better fit her budget, but she wasn't yet ready to go back to the condo— back to a bedroom still redolent with the scents of Grant and sex.

But no matter how long she dawdled over the flavorful distraction, the check arrived all too soon, and the crowd forming near the restaurant's entry made her feel guilty for taking up the table. She paid, tipping her patient waitress well, then decided to stop putting off the inevitable.

It was time to head back to her condo, where she would begin packing for the next phase of her life.

CHAPTER THIRTY-FIVE

Luz Maria was stronger than he remembered. *Longer and more muscular, too,* thought the intruder as he struggled to pin her down on the tiled floor.

She somehow hooked her leg around his, threw him off her as she shrieked, "Get the hell away from me, you bastard."

At the sound of the woman's voice, ice blasted through his arteries, and cold sweat made his skin slick. This was fucking crazy. How could he have the wrong one *again?*

"*It was an accident,*" he remembered himself saying. Mewling, pleading. Nothing but a quivering lump before those goddamned hard looks. "*I was only looking for the butterscotch candies she kept in her purse. I thought it was a toy gun, Grandpa, for my birthday. I was going to be five in two more days.*"

Incensed by the feeling of helplessness—the bitter taste of guilt—washing over him, he lunged back toward the woman, desperate to keep her from getting up, bursting out the door, and screaming her damned head off. But dark as it was, she landed a solid kick to his kneecap. *Jesus.* Agony shot straight up his femur, and for the first time in his life, he worried that some bitch was going to get the upper hand on him.

Take the power and leave him emasculated, weeping. Pour the howling, useless burden of a conscience back inside his skull.

The dim light from the parking lot lights outside the condo didn't touch the entry, but still he heard her rattling the doorknob. His adrenalin finally kicked in as he leaped toward the sound.

He plowed her to the floor and pounded until she wasn't fighting—wasn't even breathing anymore.

CHAPTER THIRTY-SIX

As Grant raced past the Gulf Freeway exit for the Mall of the Mainland, apprehension ballooned inside his chest until it hurt to draw breath. It was all coming together for him now: the complete absence of one player's history prior to three years earlier combined with the release of Kevin Vallens from the Texas Prison System only months before that.

They were the same person, damn it. The same bastard who had sexually assaulted, who had murdered, then found himself a goddamned brilliant place to hide. Who would have suspected . . .

Grant hit redial, calling Luz Maria's cell phone, then hung up when her voice mail kicked in once again. She wasn't just ignoring him because of the scene with Sherry, he was certain. Something there was wrong, dead wrong. His every atom vibrated with unshakable foreboding.

So the next call he made was to 911, where Grant asked to be connected to a Galveston police dispatcher.

If he was crying wolf, so be it. He couldn't take a chance on things turning out the way they had with Zeman.

The way they had when he'd ignored his instincts and arrived only minutes too late to save a man already far beyond redemption.

At the condo's door, Luz Maria stared down at her own hand on her key.

How could it be unlocked? With so many people, from her mother to her brother to Jason Whitfield, hassling her about security for so long, Luz Maria had gotten into the habit of securing every outside door she passed through. It was so ingrained, she didn't have to think about it.

Could this evening's events have distracted her enough to shatter that routine?

Luz Maria didn't think so, so she stepped back from the door. She caught the metallic gleam of something round—was that a key ring, tilted on edge against the condo's outer wall?

She snatched up the object, confirming at once it was a key chain—one whose helmet-shaped tab bore the name of the Houston Firefighters Federal Credit Union.

Her sister-in-law's car keys . . . But why would they be here?

Luz Maria leaned over the railing to look into the parking lot. Beneath a security light, she spotted what appeared to be Reagan's red Jetta.

Then Luz Maria remembered Grant telling her that her brother was on his way down. Her face heated with the realization that Grant and Sherry's departure had completely pushed all thoughts of Jack from her mind. He must have taken Reagan's car instead of his Explorer for some reason. Must have dropped the keys in his haste to get inside to lambaste her about Grant.

She braced herself, knowing how upset her brother always grew when she scared him. He'd scold her like a naughty child for not being here when he arrived.

In no mood for a lecture, Luz Maria was sorely tempted to turn around and sneak off. But no matter how often his overprotective instincts got under her skin, she loved her brother far too much to let him continue worrying for no reason.

She would go in and face the music, she decided. After taking a deep breath for strength, she opened the door. . . .

To a glimpse of utter hell.

CHAPTER THIRTY-SEVEN

Though Luz Maria saw it, she simply couldn't process what was happening. The figures on the entry floor, one kneeling and one facedown. The black streaks smeared across white tile—in this light, the substance looked like oil. The gleam from a strip of metal in a raised fist and the light tufts—was that some sort of fuzz, or human hair?

The shattered pieces of a picture that refused to come together. The ruins of a worldview she could not discard fast enough.

It was a sound that first smashed through the barrier of Luz Maria's shock. A moan that morphed into a human voice.

"Run. G-get help. Luz . . ."

The words were half coherent, ending on a gurgle as more black bubbled from the mouth of the face raised in her direction.

Reagan's face, her voice. Reagan, held down with a knife's blade plunging toward a spot between her shoulder blades.

There was never any question, never any choice involved in Luz Maria's reaction to his movement.

"*Noooo,*" she shrieked as instinct launched her at the man whose knee pinned Reagan to the floor.

Grant had flashing lights on his tail—he was speeding—as his car screeched to a stop in an open space along the street, some twenty yards behind a line of flashing red lights.

Not one, but two white Galveston patrol cars had pulled up in front of the building containing Luz Maria's borrowed condo, not including the one he had led here.

But it was the ambulance that paralyzed him.

Luz Maria—was she injured? Dead?

His head jerked toward a rap at the window glass to his left. A flashlight's beam shone in his face, blinding him.

"Open up," a woman ordered. Stern, unyielding: a cop's words.

He climbed out of the car, hands rising, and pleaded with the officer. "I have to know—is Luz Maria hurt?"

"Turn around and keep 'em up."

"I'm HPD," Grant told her. "An investigator in Major Assaults. My ID's in the left breast pocket of the jacket—gun's in a shoulder holster, left side, too."

She disarmed him first, then fished out his wallet. As her flashlight's beam swung to his department ID, Grant stared into the darkness, willing his eyes to adjust quickly.

"I called this in," he said. "I have to check on—" *The woman I love,* his mind screamed. But that wouldn't help him gain access to the scene. "—the victim in the case I'm working. She may be hurt. Or even dead. Please. It's urgent that I see her."

"This is related to an active Houston case?"

Now that Grant's vision had adjusted, he saw that the

officer looked a little like Mutton: dark curls tied back in a short ponytail, brown eyes, and a broad face to balance wide hips. The real Mutton, Grant figured, would have his badge for showing up and claiming to still be involved with this investigation. Not that he gave a rat's ass at the moment.

"HPD's and the FBI's. You're going to have a hell of a lot of law enforcement swarming this island in an hour's time. Let me fill your guys in on what's going down."

With a nod, she returned his badge, ID, and weapon, then led him toward the officer standing near his open car door and speaking into his radio.

But Grant's attention was wrenched toward the rescue personnel who carried a stretcher around from the back of the building, where the staircase was located. Breaking away from his escort, Grant raced over to meet the EMTs.

"Luz Mar—Reagan Hurley?" he asked as the blond hair triggered recognition. Though part of it was chopped haphazardly and her face was a swollen, bloody mess, he was certain it was Luz Maria's sister-in-law on the stretcher. Eyes closed and head tilted to one side, she appeared to be out cold.

What in God's name was she doing here? Had she come along with Luz Maria's brother?

He ran beside the emergency crew as they locked the stretcher's wheels and rolled her toward the waiting ambulance. "Reagan, can you tell me—where is Luz Maria? Is she up there? Did he hurt her, too?"

She coughed and sputtered, dribbling dark droplets. One of the EMTs helped rolled her to her side to let her spit out the blood choking her. Grant thought he heard her wheezing.

One of the two emergency workers, a younger black man whose badge identified him as a paramedic, told his partner, "Let's get her on albuterol. Med alert tag says she's an asthma patient."

Grant glanced toward the corner of the building. Would the cops stop him if he tried to run upstairs?

With her bloodied hand, the injured woman caught him by the wrist.

"Luz—" She struggled to catch her breath, yet pushed aside the paramedic's proffered mask so she could speak. "She's not there. Son of a—he took her."

"Where? He took her where?"

She coughed anew, shaking her head as if to indicate she didn't know. Her hand tightened on his wrist, her short nails digging ragged crescents in his flesh.

"Find Whit—Jason Whitfield," she rasped. "Whit . . . Whit's gonna . . . gonna kill her. You have to find that bastard *now*."

CHAPTER THIRTY-EIGHT

"You were as stupid as the rest of them. You thought I was just another goddamned faggot. Some fucking Step-and-Fetch-It for the Luz Maria Show."

As Whit pressed himself into her back, the hand wedged beneath her body ground into her breast painfully. And God help her, Luz Maria could feel the jut of his erection through the fabric of her skirt.

She fought to draw a breath to scream. But with her face mashed into the gritty sand, her ribs wedged between two of the huge chunks of granite lining the seawall's curved base and his weight pressed down on her, she could do no more than sob.

"You thought, 'Good old Whit, he's just the guy to keep me safe, right?'" Jason's breath came hot and fetid in her ear, along with that strange, strained voice—the same one she had first heard in the Ryland's parking lot. "Never knew I was the son of a bitch a pretty thing like you should be kept safe *from.*"

The sirens had been so close, Whit hadn't even had time to drag her to his car. With the cops coming, he'd half dragged, half pushed her down the concrete steps leading to the double row of boulders at sea level.

The police must be over them, in the safe world of the street and headlights, some sixteen feet above. If she could scream, they'd hear her. If she could only scream before Whit—*her own friend Jason Whitfield*—tore off her clothes and raped her.

Before he murdered her.

The Galveston officers radioed for backup to man a perimeter, with the intention of searching the area inside it. They also called for helicopter support and put out an all-points bulletin with the descriptions Grant had given them. They had summoned a crime scene team as well, to process the condo.

The patrol officers' attention had zeroed in on the one piece of evidence left at the scene: Trey-Don Peterson's blood-soaked rookie baseball card.

Grant had spotted it from outside the doorway, along with more dark splatters and some sawed-off clumps of Reagan's hair. Knowing what he did, he figured the card was a plant, something Whitfield meant to throw suspicion onto the friends of Tony Coleman.

"Stay out of there," a cop with an undershot jaw and brush-cut hair demanded. "We checked all the rooms, and the rescue crew had to go in, but we won't have you compromising the scene further."

It was obvious the Galveston cops were getting territorial, especially with the impending threat of FBI interference. It was equally clear that they were treating this case as a homicide.

But it can't be. It's only been, what, ten minutes, tops. Luz Maria has to be alive.

Unable to stand still, Grant separated from the others, then trotted up and down Seawall Boulevard in the hope of finding witnesses, of finding anything that might help.

That was when he saw it. The big, brown Buick. The car Grant had found parked two blocks from the condo was the same one Whit had driven the day he'd come to Luz Maria's mother's house, bringing with him his feigned outrage and an order that Grant leave.

But the beater's peeling hood was cool, and unfortunately, Whitfield had left no sign of his intentions. Unless he had another vehicle stashed somewhere, the bastard had to be close by—but where?

"Goddamn you," Grant bellowed as he kicked the Buick's hubcap, which flew off and clattered against the sidewalk at the top of the seawall.

Startled by the outburst, a strolling couple broke into a run to get clear of his temper.

He *couldn't* be too late to save her. Couldn't handle the riptide of guilt threatening to drag him under, the knowledge that just as he had failed the Zeman family, he was failing Luz Maria, too. That she would die without ever understanding how much she had touched him, how she'd pulled him from the blackness of the past into the light.

In his grief and fury, Grant almost missed the couple pausing half a block away, hesitating, their attention drawn by something over the seawall's edge.

Without consciously understanding why, Grant raced toward them, his feet thudding against first the pavement, then the wide, concrete sidewalk at its top. The young, blond woman heard him coming, then abandoned her partner to run screaming between two parked cars, out onto the boulevard. With a screech of brakes and the blare of horn, a cruising convertible narrowly avoided her.

While her companion went to her aid, Grant, still acting on raw instinct, drew his gun and rushed down a set of concrete stairs that led fisherman to a jumble of rocks that smelled of fish and rotting seaweed.

It was dark there, in the shadow of the massive concrete seawall, with little more than a scattering of stars to help him navigate.

He couldn't see, but he could tell something was down there. Something that drew him toward it.

A voice, a man's, behind those—was that a pile of sea-washed boulders, nestled close beside the wall's curved base?

As Grant edged toward it, words separated themselves from the splashing rumble of the light surf some ten yards away.

"Tex-Rid just wanted you shut up. They paid me well to scare you off before you could drum up interest in a hearing."

He thought he made out an indistinct murmur, higher pitched, and then a woman crying, "Ge-get off. Get off."

Luz Maria. Grant struggled to find a path around the rocks, to find the two people hidden in the darkness. He lost his purchase, slipping on one rock so his foot got wedged in a crevice between two of the jigsaw pieces of cut granite that shored up the seawall.

"But when the press reported you were going through with it," Whit continued, "when Grandma Wetback wouldn't be bought off, I upped the price, got myself enough to start a new life. In a country where I could live in style. Where I wouldn't have to hide as half a man. Let me show you what I really am, my little Looozie. Let me show you, little cu—"

"*Cabrón!*" The raw edge of fury overtook Luz Maria's terror.

The yelp that followed was clearly male.

"My goddamned face—you *bitch*," Whit shouted. "I'll fucking slit your throat for—"

Grant wrenched his foot free, then groped his way around the boulder, where he barely made out the dark shapes of two prone figures wrestling in a cleft ahead of him, heard the fierce sounds of their struggle.

The sound of thumping warned him moments before a whirlwind of gritty sand took to the air. Using his free arm in an attempt to shield his eyes, Grant waited for the helicopter's spotlight to show him what he needed.

Half-blinded, he caught little more than the glint of a long blade before he fired . . .

And prayed to God that his bullet had found the killer, and not the woman whose life had come to mean more than Grant's own.

EPILOGUE

As Grant headed toward the Heights neighborhood in Houston, it occurred to him he hadn't exactly been invited to the backyard barbecue to celebrate the unveiling of Reagan Hurley's "new" nose. Sure, it remained swollen and a little bruised, Reagan had told him on the telephone, but it looked one heck of a lot better than it had after Whitfield's fist realigned it on her face.

"I still can't believe it," Reagan had said, sounding surprisingly upbeat. "Here I was, an amateur boxer for eight years, and the first time I get my nose mashed is *after* I retire from the ring."

The blond paramedic, who had been on medical leave for the four weeks since her attack, had then dropped the hint that Luz Maria would be coming for the Saturday get-together. But Reagan ended the call abruptly when her husband walked into the room.

Grant might have shot Jason Whitfield dead and kept him from killing Luz Maria, but he had yet to completely win over Jack Montoya.

Or his younger sister. Though largely uninjured, Luz

Maria had been so traumatized by the events on Galveston Island, she had taken her cat and returned to stay with her mother these past weeks. When Grant had gone to see her, she wouldn't come to the door, and most of his calls to her had gone straight to her voice mail.

The one time he'd gotten through, she'd said little more than, "I'm sorry, Grant. It's just so hard to think straight, with everything that's happened. I need some time alone now. Time to consider whether it's still possible for me to stay in Houston. I appreciate your explaining to me about Sherry Zeman, and I'm glad for both your sakes that she's found the strength to move on. But for the moment . . . *Lo siento*, Grant. I'm sorry. I'm too confused to know if anything I feel is real. After trusting Sergio, and then Whit—I have to be certain. I hope you can understand that. And I pray you will be patient."

I do understand, Grant thought as he backed into a curbside space behind Luz Maria's box-shaped silver Honda. But he was damned well out of patience.

Since he had turned in his badge rather than face judgment by a department that had clearly given up on him, Grant needed to make some decisions quickly. In spite of the sarcasm he'd used to keep everyone at arm's length after Zeman's suicide, Grant had been surprised to learn he still had friends in law enforcement, including a former HPD investigator named Harry Burnett, who'd retired from the force after twenty years before going on to be elected sheriff of Bandera County, northwest of San Antonio.

"We could use a sharp mind like yours out here," Burnett told him. *"We may still be rural by your standards, but even country crime is growing these days."*

Starting anew as a Bandera deputy would mean a move, a lower salary, and the slower pace that existed a five-hour drive from Houston. But Grant wasn't going to kid himself. It would also mean the end to any possibility of a relationship with Luz Maria.

As he let himself into the backyard, there were six or eight people talking, drinking out of cans or longnecks, or hovering near the grill. Jack was flipping burgers while grinning over something with Reagan—who looked pretty in her stylish new haircut. But Grant's gaze latched onto Luz Maria. As she sat on the porch steps, her long, loose hair shone in a shaft of early autumn sunlight that highlighted its reddish undertones. She looked relaxed, wearing a pair of denim Capri pants with a green top and laughing at an adorable, darkhaired boy as he played tag with the white greyhound.

A surge of pure joy shafted through Grant, as well as a longing so deep and so painful, he felt powerless to put it into words.

But he was going to have to, or he might as well go home and start packing for big hat and cattle country.

He made a beeline for Luz Maria, only to be headed off by her older brother, steel spatula in hand.

"Excuse me, Investigator. But were you invited?"

"He certainly was," Reagan said as she hooked her husband's arm and tugged him back toward the grill. "Now how about taking off those burgers before I have to call a fire crew?"

Jack glanced at his smiling wife, whose face looked a far cry from the bloodied and swollen version Grant had seen outside the Galveston ambulance. Something passed between the married partners in their brief look, and Jack nodded, then said to Grant, "Beer's in the red cooler, Holcomb. Water and soda's in the blue one."

As Jack and Reagan turned away, Grant caught the blonde's attention long enough to mouth the words, *"Thank you."* Then his focus turned to Luz Maria, who was staring up at him, her big brown eyes sheened with some emotion.

He dared to hope it might be happiness to see him.

"You have something in your hair," she told him as she rose from her place on the back steps and touched his temple. "It looks like drops of yellow paint."

Grant shrugged, trying to look casual, though his heart was hammering. "Must've missed it when I was cleaning up. I've been doing a little painting around my place. Thought a yellow kitchen might be cheerful."

The house would fetch more money with a little TLC. And even if he ended up taking the second job offer he'd received and keeping the house instead, it was time to make it a place he could feel good about when he came home.

Luz Maria nodded. "Yellow's a good, chick-friendly color. And a lot prettier than green, in my opinion."

She followed up the statement with a smile that flooded the darkest corners of his soul with silver light.

"I've missed you," he said, and thought, *That's got to be the understatement of the year.*

But he was afraid to say too much to her too quickly, afraid to chase the happiness from her expression.

"I heard you quit the force," she said. "Investigator Devlin said so when he called to tell me the DA was pursuing indictments of Tex-Rid's CEO and lead attorney. So what now, Grant? What are you doing?"

He sensed that they were being watched discreetly, but his entire world had shrunk down to only Luz Maria.

"That depends," he said, "on you."

She shook her head. "Oh, Grant. I'm not even sure what *I'll* do. I mean, I know Voice of Poverty's back on solid financial footing, with all the donations that poured in after that big story ran on *20/20*. And I want to do the work again, I really do. But every time I think of walking back into that office—"

"What you need is someone there who makes you feel safe. Someone you can trust to watch your back."

"But . . ." Confusion crinkled her features. "But that was Whit's job, and he—"

"He's left a vacancy," Grant said, "a vacancy the director of VOP National called me about just last night. I've been offered the position of head of security for the Houston office, and the entire southwest region."

Luz Maria's eyes flared in astonishment. "*You?* You would be a part of the Voice of Poverty?"

"You know that video April made to try to lure you back? I've thought a lot about it since then, thought of all the good an organization like yours does. And I got to thinking, I'd be proud to be a part of something like that, and with my police experience, I think I have a lot to offer. But Houston VOP wouldn't be the same without you as its spokesperson. So many people here know you. Trust you. *Love* you."

He took both her hands in his and let the words sink in before he added, "Just like me."

She glanced up at him almost shyly through her lowered lashes. A light flush pinkened her cheeks. "I tried to back away from it, tried to keep myself from feeling," she said, "but it's no use, Grant. I love you, too. I love you very much. . . . Still, I'm afraid there's one big problem."

"What's that?"

"VOP has this stupid policy against coworkers dating. They had some problem in one of the other offices with an affair that turned into a stalking, so they—"

Without ever taking his eyes from her, Grant dropped down to one knee.

"What are you doing, Grant?" Luz Maria asked, the color deepening in her face. "Everyone is looking. Please get up."

"I don't care if the whole world's watching," Grant said. "And they can eavesdrop all they like. It won't stop me from telling you there's no rule against married coworkers. It won't stop me from saying you'd make me the happiest man in Houston if you'd agree to be my wife."

He heard a feminine gasp to his left, and out of the corner of his eye he saw Luz Maria's mother Candelaria clasp her hands, look skyward, and start murmuring a prayer in rapid-fire Spanish. Each time he'd stopped by her house, she had made it clear that she thought his dimples would look lovely on a fresh new set of *nietos*.

"Get *up*," Luz Maria hissed urgently. "Get up now. *Right this minute.*"

He stood, crushed that the sole romantic gesture of his lifetime had only succeeded in embarrassing the woman he loved.

But he might have misread her, because Luz Maria's eyes were shining with excitement. "You get your face right up here, Grant Holcomb. So I can kiss that gorgeous mouth of yours just as soon as I say yes. *Yes*, I'll marry you—and *yes*, I'll work at your side, and—"

Luz Maria didn't get the chance to finish before his lips came down to cover hers and his arms pulled her body to his. And as the onlookers' cheers turned to applause—and one or two wolf whistles—Grant could barely wait to begin their future . . .

And get working on the family that Candelaria's prayers had preordained.

Want more romance?
More suspense?
Turn the page for
a special preview.

COLLEEN THOMPSON

HEAD ON

Coming Summer 2007!

Ask anyone in emergency services—rescue crews and deputies, even the staff of a rural Texas hospital known to area residents as Jackrabbit General. They'll all swear it's true, what you hear about the full moon bringing out the crazies.

Friday the Thirteenth, too, draws out its share of bad luck, sometimes even among those who deny such superstitions. Accidents, assaults, attempted suicides: regardless of how the skeptics or the statisticians spin them, the unluckiest events take place on this unlucky day.

But every now and then, in a rare alignment of misfortunes, a Friday falling on the thirteenth coincides with the full moon. On this strangest of strange days, all bets are off and anything can happen.

Including the return of a small community's most hated prodigal, a shock too soon eclipsed by the sort of murder that shatters country-safe complacency and sends sales of alarm systems and handguns soaring. A murder rooted in a tragedy so painful it formed fault lines in the bedrock far beneath the timeworn prairie and the clear, unblinking sky.

"I love you like a sister, but don't be telling me which patients I can and cannot handle," Beth Ann Decker warned from the office doorway. She had already pulled on a jacket over her white scrubs and picked up her nursing bag. In ultraconservative Hatcher County, residents expected a medical professional to look the part—even if she was caring for them in their homes.

Flushing to the tinted roots of her strawberry blond hair, Cheryl Riker peered up from a cluttered desk in the center of an office crammed with file cabinets, two of which blocked sunlight from the only window. Beth Ann saw that she'd moved her computer—which must have crashed again—into a corner on the floor to make room for still more charts. These past few years, hospital district revenue had skidded downhill like bald tires on a patch of ice-slick asphalt. But even in the best of times, the hospice program was the redheaded stepchild of the system.

The chair creaked as the plump Cheryl struggled to her feet, probably in an attempt to look authoritative. Though she was technically the director of the program, she had never been much good at the bossing side of the equation. "Look, I'm sorry. I don't think it's a good idea for you to take this particular patient, that's all. Let me call in Vickie, cancel her vacation."

Beth Ann shook her head. "You can't do that. That poor woman's been carrying on about this anniversary cruise for months—and when was the last time she had two weeks off, anyway?"

Cheryl frowned, her face creasing into lines reminiscent of her mother's. Since her fortieth birthday earlier this autumn, Cheryl fretted about ending up looking like a Texas road map—a worry which only made her frown more. "If we had any other nurse available. . . ."

It wasn't a discussion worth repeating. With Emmaline Stutz out because of a bad back and the current hiring freeze, there was no one else available—and both women knew it.

Cheryl shook her head, concern in her brown eyes. "You can't go out there, Beth Ann. Hiram Jessup's daughter *died* in that wreck. And his son—well, you know what happened with Mark."

"Three years in hospitals and rehab centers, and you think it's possible I've forgotten any of the details?" How could she with people reminding her every time she turned around?

At her friend's stricken look, Beth Ann added, "Come on, Cheryl. It's been sixteen years. Mr. Jessup and I have long since made our peace."

Not that they'd ever come out and discussed it, but at least Hiram didn't storm out of the town's only grocery store during their infrequent chance encounters. He nodded almost amiably in church, too, when she showed up for Christmas services and Easter.

"What about that lawsuit?" Cheryl asked.

Beth Ann shrugged. "That's old business between him and my mama. It's nothing to do with me."

This wasn't exactly true, since her mother had filed suit on account of Beth Ann's injuries—or her medical bills, to be specific. But Cheryl, bless her heart, didn't argue the point.

"Maybe I should take care of this one . . . brush up with some field experience." Cheryl fingered the tiny gold cross pinned to the lapel of her wine-colored blazer. She had once confessed to Beth Ann that she had only taken the supervisory position, with its long hours and myriad headaches, so she could wear "grownup clothes." Scrubs, she complained, made her rear end look wider than a school bus.

Beth Ann crossed her arms, banging her cane against the door frame in the process. It was one more thing that kept her—and everyone else—from forgetting. "When was the last time you did patient care?"

"I handled Mr. Jessup's intake after Emmaline went home with that back. Did all the paperwork myself—"

"Paperwork." Beth Ann shook her head. "Just let me take care of this. Please."

"Why? Why would you do this to yourself?" Cheryl demanded. "Why's it so important to you?"

"Because for sixteen years, I've been fighting an up-hill battle trying to convince everyone in Hatcher County that my first name damned well isn't 'Poor.' I'm tired of it, Cheryl, tired of having everyone look at me with pity in their eyes and sick to death of my mother having a better social life than I do—and most people don't even *like* the woman. This is it for me. If I can't prove I'm a competent professional with a *future* and not just a past, I'm pulling up stakes and starting over somewhere new. Somewhere no one ever heard of the Hatcher Red Hawks or some old car crash."

After huffing out a sigh, Cheryl dropped back into her desk chair, which squealed in protest. "And you think that nursing Hiram Jessup's going to prove to anybody you've moved on?"

"It'll prove it to *me*," Beth Ann said quietly, a little embarrassed by her eruption. It had been coming for months, she realized. Since she'd moved into the new place with her mother—now known as "Lucky Lilly" in light of last year's miracle—Beth Ann had been thinking a lot about her life. Or almost total lack thereof. She hoped to God it wasn't yet too late to step up to the counter and claim her share. "Maybe that's all I need."

Cheryl glanced toward the Bible verse-a-day calendar on her desk, then tore off yesterday's page to expose the big, black *13* that lurked between the words *Friday* and

October. Looking up again, she asked, "You're sure about this?"

Beth Ann nodded. What did she care about some silly superstition? She attended deaths year round and had recently concluded that the failure to live fully was the greater misfortune.

Cheryl nodded. "All right. If that's the way you feel about it. But there's one thing you'd better know first. My sister Aimee knows about Hiram Jessup going on home hospice. And before you start lecturing me about patient confidentiality, I didn't say a word to her. She spotted my Tahoe over at his place when I did the intake, and she was talking to Norma Nederhoffer, that woman who does transcription for the doctors. Norma didn't tell her, either, but she has this sort of grave nod."

Beth Ann understood. In Kressville, a town of just over four thousand, the combination of Norma Nederhoffer's grave nods and the sighting of a hospice worker's vehicle at a person's house had the authority of gospel, or at least the *Wichita Falls Times Record.* Besides that, Cheryl's youngest sister Aimee—now Aimee Gustavsen—had been an infamous blabbermouth since Beth Ann first met her back in kindergarten. That girl could whip a rumor out of less substance than it took a prairie wind to spin up a dust devil.

"You know how Aimee's been lately," Cheryl continued. "Sort of disillusioned with this marriage business."

At thirty-three, the same age as still-single Beth Ann, Aimee was already on her second go-round, this time with a stiff-necked insurance agent who couldn't hold a candle to Aimee's nostalgia for the days she'd put out for pretty much every boy her Baptist parents bad-mouthed. Mark Jessup chief among them.

Beth Ann made the connection. "She called him, didn't she? Told him about his daddy?"

Cheryl nodded and twisted her plain gold wedding

band around her finger. "You know Aimee. Once she got it in her head it was Mark's duty to be here, wasn't anything going to stop her. A few days ago, she looked him up on her computer, found a number for that *company* of his in Pittsburgh." Her lip curled in a look of disapproval. "Then she calls him, bold as brass, and tells him it's his place to come and take care of his daddy."

Beth Ann snorted. "Mark Jessup won't be back. Not after his father turned on him like he did. Besides, people around here won't give two hoots about how rich he is now. All they'll think about is the boy they called Hell on Wheels and three dead cheerleaders, one for every year he served."

She squeezed her eyes together. "And then they'll think of *Poor* Beth Ann—oh, damn it. I'll bury him myself if he doesn't have the sense to stay away."

About an hour later that same chilly October morning, Beth Ann was stunned to realize her words were more than bluster. She really did harbor homicidal instincts.

Previously, she would have admitted she could pull the trigger of her late father's shotgun in the white heat of self-defense against some psycho rapist, or to protect her mama—though some of Kressville's population might fault her for the latter choice. But no matter how tough she talked, or how many people she had watched die these past few years as she'd worked in the hospice program, she couldn't imagine taking a life in cold blood.

Until she saw the big grill of the Ford pickup backed into the driveway of the lonely little house on Lost Buffalo Road. With pinpoints of light exploding across her vision, she gripped her steering wheel and dragged in deep breaths.

"No way is that the same truck," she told herself. "No damned way."

Like the Chevy Caprice she had been driving that Homecoming Friday, the pickup truck of memory had to be long gone now, crushed flat and pancake-stacked behind the fence surrounding Culpepper's Junkyard, a few minutes south of town. Beth Ann's job took her all over Hatcher County, but she'd drive ten miles out of her way to avoid that stretch of highway.

With all her flesh and blood reminders, she didn't need or want one as immutable as steel.

As her vision cleared, she realized that the pickup's paint job was a darker blue, that its bright chrome wheels and fancy mud flaps decked out a vehicle far newer and nicer than the one wrecked sixteen years before. Still, both intuition and the Pennsylvania plates assured her that the truck belonged to *him*.

That reckless son of a bitch, Mark Jessup. "Jess" to all his friends, back in the days when he'd still had some.

Why hadn't he just taken the easy way out—hiring a private health care aide or two to supplement the county's offering? That's what a lot of men did when their mama or daddy's final illness threatened to part them from their important, out-of-town jobs. Most of the women came back, then tied themselves into tight knots trying to juggle the needs of their kids back home against those of the ailing parent, but the men . . . Beth Ann wondered if in the high school shop classes she'd missed out on, the guys spent time soldering guilt-proof armor around each soft and naked conscience.

But evidently, Mark Jessup's shielding had a crack. Maybe on account of what had happened to his sister Jordan.

At the thought, Beth Ann considered putting her Subaru, a station wagon with peeling red paint, as homely as it was indestructible, back in gear and cruising past Hiram Jessup's place. Once she made it out of sight—a drawn-out process, considering the flatness of this stretch of prairie and the crisp brilliance of the cobalt sky—she could call the old man to say she'd had car trouble. Anyone who'd ever seen the war wagon would believe it.

Then she could phone Cheryl and tell her that maybe it was time to trot out those mothballed patient-care skills of hers after all.

But Beth Ann hesitated, convinced that sooner or later—probably sooner, considering her supervisor's penchant for easing her job stress by yakking with her little sister—Aimee would learn that Beth Ann had turned tail. And word would hit this county like hailstones bouncing off tin roofs.

She gritted her teeth as she pictured the dings and dents. *Did you hear what happened to Poor Beth Ann? Would've been kinder to whack the side of her head with a two-by-four than showin' up the way he did. Always the nervy one, that Jessup boy. Nervier than a rabid coyote.*

Facing Mark Jessup couldn't be half as painful as losing her toehold on what passed for respect here in Kressville. Damned hard-won respect, for a never-married female on the wrong side of thirty, a woman who had chosen to ease the passing of the dying instead of working with—or having—babies. A woman who had once been pulled alive from a smashed Chevy ringed with dead cheerleaders.

Maybe Beth Ann would have gone inside, or maybe she would have chickened out and driven north to Oklahoma and straight through to parts unknown. But she never knew the answer, because at that moment, the house's front storm door creaked open and a tall male trotted down the wooden steps from the front porch.

A man, not a boy. And still every bit as handsome as store-bought sin.

Beth Ann felt her stomach drop down through the floorboards, felt every molecule of air wrung from her lungs. All these years later, she still knew him, though time had filled out the gangly promise of once awkwardly long limbs, though the king-of-the-world grin that had won so many conquests had given way to an expression so grave and guarded it was hard to imagine he was the same person.

But she'd heard that prison would do that to a man.

There were other changes, too. His once tawny hair had darkened to a rich brown. He wore it thick and wavy and a little on the long side. Reluctantly, she admitted to herself it suited him, as did the faded jeans and denim jacket thrown over a navy sweatshirt. Heavy stubble darkened his cheeks, as if he'd missed a couple of appointments with his razor. Which made sense, for he must have moved fast to get here so quickly after Aimee's phone call.

But the suddenness of Mark Jessup's arrival meant nothing, Beth Ann figured as she pulled her car into the driveway. It was just a pretense of devotion, an act to show his hometown he wasn't some kind of monster after all.

Pretty ballsy, though, considering how people felt about him. If she didn't have so much cause to hate him, she might even admire it.

He didn't appear to notice her as he opened the truck's front door and pulled a suitcase from the narrow backseat. A big suitcase and a duffel, as if he planned on staying a while.

As if he had that right.

Of course he does, the nurse in her insisted. *He's the only family.* No one but his father was entitled to run Mark off at this point. As Hiram had before, on account of Jordan. As—dying or not—the old man might again.

Out of pure selfishness, Beth Ann hoped he'd do exactly that. But as she climbed out of her wagon and went for her supplies, she decided she had earned the right to peevish thoughts.

She hesitated, frowning down at the cane she'd left tucked behind her nursing bag. A glimmer of her mother's vanity flashed through her, and she thought of leaving the stick, so Mark's first impression of her would not be one of weakness.

Anger flared, and Beth Ann snatched the thing up. Other than the lackeys who worked for him in Pittsburgh, who cared what a murdering ex-con thought? She needed the cane for stability as she carried supplies in for her patient, so she would damned well use it.

Besides, that indignity beat the hell out of letting him see her fall on her rear while she struggled up the porch steps.

Leaving the hatch open—she'd need to make a second trip—she heard the crunch of footsteps on the gravel just behind her.

"Can I give you a hand with tha—?"

He stopped speaking as she turned, and Beth Ann felt perverse satisfaction as she watched the color seep from his face, heard the sharp catch of his breath.

"Beth Ann—you . . . ," he tried, but he could get no further. Though the duffel remained slung over one shoulder, his suitcase landed on the gravel with a thunk.

Once more, tiny lights burst across her field of vision, but she faked a smile anyway. Or at least she hoped that's what it looked like.

Professional, she ordered herself. *You're his father's nurse, that's all. Top of your class at Midwestern State.*

Leaning her cane against the bumper, she stuck out her right hand. "Yes, and the last name's still Decker. I'm the traveling RN assigned to Mr. Jessup."

Before taking it, Mark stared at her a beat too long. Looking for damage, she supposed, telltale remnants of the collision that had forever altered both their lives.

A chill wind rattled the dry leaves of the front yard's single, stunted scrub oak. The wind stirred the grasses of the lost Jessup acreage across the street, whistling through a trio of oil well pump jacks and peeling more white paint from the small house and its outbuildings.

Beth Ann stared right back at Mark, daring him to comment on the reconstructed nose and cheekbones. They looked good, everyone assured her, yet they weren't the same. She would never have the face she had been born with, or the healthy spine, left leg, or pelvis.

"And he's . . ." Mark hesitated, clearly searching for the right words. "My dad's okay with having you here?"

"It won't be a problem," she said simply. Hiram had never broached the subject with her, had never reminded her that she had been the one to tell his only daughter, *"Better hurry or we're going."* Jordan had a shy girl's terror of being bumped from the fragile fringe of popularity, so even after all these years, Beth Ann saw the blond girl hesitate, then turn and wave to her father instead of kissing him good-bye.

Beth Ann had replayed that moment endlessly, since it was the last intact memory she had B.C.—Before the Crash.

"Your father's a forgiving man," she added. "He's never once blamed me."

"Why should he," Mark asked sharply, "when he had me for that?"

She looked away, troubled by the glimpse of anger and raw pain. Her gaze sought out the solace of the nearest pump jack, the only one still rocking gently back and forth. The oil men called the things mosquitoes, for the way they sucked life—and cash—from this dry prairie.

But all around the county, the jacks were going still. Mama had been smart to insist on a monetary settlement instead of mineral rights. But unlike her recent stroke of fortune, that prize was long gone now, given over to the hospitals and the doctors: a long, long list of them.

"Let's go inside," Beth Ann suggested as she brushed a flutter of red bangs from her eyes. When loose, her hair's soft waves tumbled past her shoulders. Her best feature, people told her. She had clipped it back this morning, but the wind was making steady progress, pulling strand after strand free. Her nose was probably red, too, and she could use a tissue.

She must look a mess, she thought, then gave herself a mental kick. She wasn't some simpering fool—*like Mama*—she was a nurse, here with a job.

And she meant to prove that she could do it, even with a Jessup as a patient. For Larinda, Heidi, even Jordan . . . but mostly, for her own self-respect.

Rosario Gutierrez had the key to the columned white showplace known as The Lucky Pull, in honor of the day Lilly Decker walked into an Oklahoma Indian casino with the goal of meeting an oil-rich good time and walked out the winner of the largest progressive slot jackpot in that state's history. Though the wind blew cold beneath the hem of Rosario's black and white uniform, the fifty-three-year-old woman buzzed again and waited, half-leaning on her favorite broom, almost like the señora's daughter, Poor Beth Ann.

Rosario knocked, too, but no luck. Still, the maid hesitated instead of letting herself inside. The daughter didn't know it, but her *madre* had a lover. Maybe two of them, from the comings and goings that Rosario was too discreet to mention. But discreet or not, Rosario had been upset—*mortificado*—that day last June when she had taken her mop into the huge new kitchen.

It still astonished Rosario the thing she'd seen them doing on that hard countertop. And at Lilly Decker's age—*híjole!* Who would have believed it? So *this*, and not the fit of her silk blouses, explained the disgraceful woman's visit to the doctor for a pert new set of *chichis*.

Still no answer. Rubbing a chilled arm, Rosario thought of going home, where her daughter Carmelita had brought the baby for a visit. But Rosario took her obligations—and her paycheck—seriously, so instead she walked around to the attached garage and stood on tiptoe to peer into the window of the left bay. Señora's new silver Mercedes was still inside, and the right bay—where Poor Beth Ann parked every evening—remained empty.

Rosario nodded to herself, satisfied that this afternoon, no strange man's car was hidden in the daughter's spot. Maybe after a year's time, one of the neighbors had forgiven the señora for building a palace that dwarfed their fine homes. Rosario smiled as she pictured blond ladies together in a fussy parlor, eating tiny sandwiches with their pinkie fingers delicately crooked.

She drew the key out of her pocket, certain it would be safe to go inside now.

Not guessing that it wasn't. And that what Rosario saw would scar far more deeply than a summer afternoon's tryst on a custom granite slab.

The
DEADLIEST Denial
Colleen Thompson

The worst day of Claire's life begins with a 5:00 A.M. knock on her door, the summons every cop's wife dreads. But instead of telling her Spence has been killed in the line of duty, his sergeant has even worse news for Claire. Her husband is in jail. For murder. And there is irrefutable evidence that the person he really wants dead is *her*.

But betrayal turns to terror when Spence skips out on his bail and someone begins vandalizing her horse ranch. Her husband suddenly reappears with a story that sounds all too credible and a seductive magnetism Claire has never been able to resist. Is her refusal to turn him in, her need to believe in his innocence, nothing but… THE DEADLIEST DENIAL.

FADE *the* HEAT
COLLEEN THOMPSON

Someone is setting fires in the Houston *barrio,* and Dr. Jack Montoya is the first intended victim. Is there some connection between the torching of his apartment and the gorgeous blonde from his past who appears at his clinic on the same day? For sure, Reagan Hurley turns up the flames of his libido, but these days the beautiful firefighter is more interested in putting out conflagrations than fanning old sparks. Yet when a hotly contested mayoral race turns ugly, when Reagan's life is threatened and Jack's career almost destroyed, when desire sizzles uncontrollably between them, it seems that no one will be able to . . . *Fade the Heat.*

BLOOD
KIN
JUDITH E. FRENCH

Hidden behind the deceptive beauty of Tawes Island, secrets remain unspoken, waiting to be brought to light.

Bailey Elliot arrives on Tawes to look into her own past, but its wary residents don't take to outsiders digging up long-buried scandal. Her great uncle warns her she's not safe, and despite the sizzling attraction between her and Daniel Catlin, he tells her, "The sooner you leave, the better."

Now Bailey discovers a diary no one wants her to read, Daniel gives in to temptation, and a decades-old crime of passion is about to be reenacted....

CHARLOTTE MACLAY
MAKE NO PROMISES

Taylor Travini is used to roughing it. She and her brother are experienced travelers. But now Terry has vanished in Chile, and in searching for him Taylor has found a world of trouble. Offering to help is a stranger in a grungy Santiago bar.

Rafe Maguire has seen too much. His years with the Army Rangers hardened him, turned him mercenary. But though his hands are lethal weapons, Rafe can never snuff his instinct to protect.

An independent beauty and a war-weary veteran, both Taylor and Rafe have a lot to learn, including the discovery that life isn't worth living when you can...

MAKE NO PROMISES

ATTENTION
BOOK LOVERS!

Can't get enough of your favorite **ROMANCE**?

Call **1-800-481-9191** to:

✳ order books,

✳ receive a **FREE** catalog,

✳ join our book clubs to **SAVE 30%!**

Open Mon.-Fri. 10 AM-9 PM EST

Visit **www.dorchesterpub.com**
for special offers and inside
information on the authors you love.

We accept Visa, MasterCard or Discover®.
LEISURE BOOKS ♥ LOVE SPELL